SEASON OF KINGS

BOOK ONE OF THE RAVEN'S WAR TRILOGY

A.J. RETTGER

CONTENTS

Acknowledgements

This book would not be possible without so many people. Mom and Dad, I love you more than you can ever know and the fact that you support me on any wild, crazy, and cockamamie idea that springs into my head, I am eternally grateful. Ryan, Tyler, and Brayden, thank you for inviting me into the OG D&D group and for letting me try out my terrible ideas for books as campaigns on you. I hope this book reminds you of all the fun times we had sitting around a table and rolling dice. My amazing editor Stephen, thank you for fixing my plethora of grammatical errors and for taking the time to sit down with me and help me transform this story into the absolute best version it can be. To all my author friends, thank you for your kind words and encouragement over the last three years. Skye, I cannot thank you enough. You have been my champion, my biggest critic, and my rock through my writing career. I am so lucky to have met you and to be able to call you my mentor. I cannot think of anyone else I would rather learn from. Finally, thank you dear reader. I'm not sure if you picked up this book because it had a badass cover, or maybe you know me from my debut novel, or maybe it was recommended to you by a friend. Whatever the case is, thank you for giving this story a chance. I hope you enjoy it.

City of Bhotrin
Fortress of Tjarholm
KETEN
Caspula
DRUSSDELL
Drossberg
City of Mailleon
Valley of The Doom wood
City of Kartaga
ARTANZIA
Winterhelm
THE VALERI
N
EMPIRE
Kaspyia
Damash
THE SEA OF TRAGIC BEASTS
THE FORSAKEN LANDS
N

ACT I

CHAPTER ONE

GRIMM

Snow crunched beneath his boots as he continued to run through the waist-high powder. The bark of the war hounds slowly closed in.

The forest was only a hundred feet away; he knew if he could reach the treeline, he'd be able to lose his pursuers with ease. The cold air burned his lungs as he sprinted across the frozen ground, desperately trying to outrun the vicious men and dogs that were chasing him. Blood slowly seeped from the arrow wound on the top of his left shoulder, leaving a fresh, easy trail for his hunters to follow.

Suddenly, his footing gave way as he sunk deeper into the snow. He cursed under his breath as he looked behind him and saw that the war hounds were right on his heels.

He looked at the treeline and rose to his feet. He knew that the time for running was over.

The first hound lunged at him; teeth bared. The man stuck out his forearm to block the attack. The dog's teeth sank into his arm, and blood spurted out from the puncture wounds.

The man gritted his teeth in pain and began relentlessly punching the top of the dog's head with his meaty fist. Every blow forced the hound's bite to tighten around his arm, causing more blood to leave his body.

The second dog attacked his legs, as they were trained to do; the man quickly sidestepped and kicked as hard as he could at the war hound's jaw.

The sound of bones shattering pleased his ears. He turned his attention back to the dog that was hanging from his arm. He plunged two of his calloused, sausage-like fingers into the beast's eyes until the muscular jaws around his forearm slackened.

The third dog, unaffected by the brutality that it just witnessed, rushed the man, lunging at his midsection. The man caught the dog by the mouth with both his hands and began prying the two jaws apart until he ripped the bottom lip free of the war hound's head.

The man stood in the snow, his chest heaving, and looked at the three dogs lying motionless on the ground. A sickening smile spread across the man's lips as he started to walk back towards the forest. *Looks like we're having dog tonight.*

Suddenly, he heard the soft whimpering of an injured dog. He turned his head and realized that the second dog was not dead, but just badly injured. He sat in the snow and watched the beast try to comprehend what had just happened.

The dog pawed its face, as if trying to rub the broken bones in its face better. The man let out an exhausted sigh as he rose to his feet and approached the injured war hound. He ran a hand across the beast's body, feeling the creature's soft fur between his fingers.

Without uttering a word, the man picked up the dog by the throat and, with a quick flick of the wrists, snapped its neck.

The fire danced atop the thin pieces of wood he had gathered, a white plume of smoke rising in the air as a giant marker of his whereabouts. *Even they should be able to find that.*

The man laughed to himself as he tore another piece of meat free from the dog's corpse and tossed it onto the fire. He had never grown accustomed to eating dog meat. Even during the harsh winter months when food was scarce, he always found it too chewy and bland for his liking. But he knew that when his pursuers arrived and saw him eating their beloved war hounds, they would be shaking in their boots with fear.

The sun was just starting to set when he heard the distinct sound of snow crunching beneath footsteps. The man didn't raise his head to acknowledge his visitors, but instead popped another piece of chewy meat into his mouth.

He knew that they would want to talk to him first and try to convince him to surrender, so they wouldn't have to fight. He would indulge them in conversation, but they were fools if they truly believed he wouldn't fight to his last breath.

He pressed the heated tip of his knife blade against his shoulder where the arrow went in. He looked down at his arm and saw blood seeping through the wounds left behind by the dog's sharp fangs. He was about to tear a piece of sleeve off of his shirt when he heard the distinct crunch of snow under a man's weight.

"White-Eyes, is that you?" a familiar voice called from behind a snowdrift.

"Of course," the man answered plainly. "Is that Halfdan the Jackal I hear?"

The stranger rose from his hiding place and began chuckling maniacally. "You always did have a good ear for voices," he said, as he approached the campfire.

"Care for some meat?" White-Eyes taunted, extending a piece of cooked dog out to the laughing man.

"Tssk, tssk," Halfdan clicked. "Kjottun won't be very happy once he sees what you've done to his pets."

"They fought well, gave me a nasty bite on my arm."

Halfdan laughed again. "My, how you've fallen. The great Grimm White-Eyes, right-hand man to High King Uthredd, now on the run for something as simple as murder. Tell me, was she worth the fuck?"

Grimm didn't answer. Instead, he just popped another piece of the disgusting meat into his mouth, before changing the subject. "Where are the others?"

Halfdan sat down at the fire across from him; the flames illuminating his features. He had an aquiline nose, bent and disfigured ears, and menacing blue eyes. Tattoos covered his face, but the most prominent one was the image of a broken tooth below his left eye. "You know, I never liked your eyes," Halfdan chuckled. "They're white like a blind man's, and yet, you can still see."

"And I never liked your laugh. Does that mean you came alone?"

"No, the others are around," Halfdan answered, sweeping his long red hair out of his eyes. "But, they sent me here to try to talk you into surrendering."

"You waste your breath," Grimm responded.

"See!" Halfdan called out. "I told you he would not give up."

Three more men emerged from behind the snowdrift and approached the campfire. One, who was clearly the leader, Grimm recognized as the revered warrior Hafthør the Wise. He had a grey beard and a long, silvery-grey mane that went halfway down his back. Despite his age, Grimm still knew that he was in peak fighting condition.

The second man he recognized was Kjottun, Master of Hounds. His brown beard was braided into a single knot, and his head was completely shaven, save for a short strip down the middle. An expression of utter disgust was glued on his face as he approached the fire.

The third was a man Grimm did not know. It looked like he had barely seen seventeen winters and he was clearly intimidated in front of such a great warrior. *Probably trying to make a name for himself,* Grimm thought, shaking his head silently, as the men sat down beside Halfdan.

"What did you do to my dogs?" Kjottun growled.

"Don't worry. You'll be joining them soon," Grimm replied menacingly.

"White-Eyes, please listen to reason," Hafthør pleaded. "You are accused of rape and murder. The honourable thing to do is to come back to Skotheim and accept your judgement."

"I didn't rape her."

"That is for the lawmaker to decide," Hafthør retorted.

"Enough of this!" Halfdan exclaimed. "Let's just gut the bastard. He doesn't even have a weapon."

Halfthør waved a dismissive hand and looked deeply into Grimm's eyes. "Will you truly not concede, old friend? We've been on many raids to the mainland together, do not make me do this."

"I'm tired of killing, brother, but you give me no choice. Ready your axe," Grimm replied as he rose to his feet, trying to ignore the pain that was throbbing in his arm.

"Finally! Some action!" Halfdan laughed, as he pulled his sword free from its scabbard.

Grimm stood there patiently as he sized up the four men. He had been in worse situations, but never without a weapon. *This will be a challenge,* he thought to himself, as he cracked his knuckles in preparation.

The first one to attack was Kjottun, presumably consumed by rage over the loss of his beloved hounds. The Master of the Hounds let out a ferocious battle cry as he swung his greataxe in a high overhead arc, but Grimm caught the haft midair with his uninjured arm and broke it in two.

Kjottun stood there dumbfounded as he looked at the broken weapon in awe. Grimm quickly cleaved him between the eyes, splitting his head in two.

Hafthør and Halfdan rushed simultaneously. Grimm blocked every blow, although shockwaves of pain surged through his arm with each parry.

The two men attacked him from either side, desperately trying to tire him out. With his left hand, Grimm caught Halfdan's sword by the blade and quickly elbowed the Jackal in the face. Blood spurted on the ground as he staggered away from the fight.

Grimm then did a sharp pirouette and dodged Hafthør's lunging jab and sank the axe head into the veteran's throat. A mist of red covered his face as he ripped the weapon free from the old man's throat.

"What're you waiting for, boy? Kill him!" Halfdan shouted, as he stared at the young man frozen in fear.

While he was distracted, Grimm sauntered over and knocked the sword free from the Jackal's hand. He then dropped his axe and picked up Halfdan by the head and squeezed with all his might.

The Jackal let out a blood-curdling scream as his eyes began to protrude from his head. Grimm took a sharp inhale and smashed the Jackal's face against his own.

Then he did it again, and again, and again, until Halfdan was barely conscious. He then dropped the warrior on the snow-covered ground and grabbed the axe head.

He sliced Halfdan's belly open and began ripping out the man's innards and discarding them onto the snow. Halfdan howled in pain every time Grimm's hand reached into his body.

The young boy quickly dropped his sword and began to run away from all the carnage. Grimm shot to his feet and threw the axe blade at the coward, burying it directly in his head.

Once again, Grimm turned his attention to Halfdan, who was somehow still alive. He leaned down and stared the dying man in the eyes.

"I always hated your laugh," he whispered, as he plunged his fingers into the man's neck and began tearing away at his throat.

CHAPTER TWO

ANNA

The forest was peaceful that morning, as it always was. The birds' lovely songs echoed off the snow-capped mountains, the pine needles rustled gently against the wind, and snowflakes floated down from the heavens.

It was still early enough in the morning that most of the wildlife hadn't risen from their slumber yet. But there was still a hunt afoot. The sound of snow crunching beneath the footsteps filled the forest air. Rapid, frantic breathing could be heard reverberating off the tree trunks.

The orange rays of sunlight were just rising above the treetops; the time had come.

Anna stopped and knelt in the middle of the forest, her bow and knife at the ready. She wiped her ashen-white hair out of her eyes and tried to control her breathing. *In...* she thought as she inhaled, *and out.*

Suddenly, there was a crack of a branch directly to the right of her, but she didn't react. She knew her pursuer wouldn't be as clumsy, and as foolish, as to step on a tree branch. It was a distraction.

She waited, knees burning from the snow, for her attacker to make the first move. Her heart rate slowed as she felt him approach. Her fingers danced along the fletching of her arrow. Finally, she heard the snow behind her crunch under the weight of a man.

Anna spun around, ready to plunge her arrow deep into the hunter's chest, but she had miscalculated. The man had anticipated her impulsive attack and side-stepped out of the way.

The attacker swung his foot and hit Anna directly on the jawbone. She felt a tooth get knocked loose.

She sprang to her feet to attack, but the man had grabbed her by the scruff of her neck and threw her head-first into the trunk of a nearby pine. A piece of the bark broke off the tree and landed in her eye.

She winced in pain and held her hand out to try and stop the attacker, but the man did not seem to care. With his powerful legs, he kicked Anna's feet from under her. The fall left her gasping for air.

"You're too slow," the man said gruffly, as he picked Anna up out of the snow.

"I had a piece of wood in my eye," Anna replied sourly as she removed the splinter with ease.

"You think a werewolf or an ogre will take pity on you, if you have a piece of bark in your eye?" the man replied as he examined Anna's bloodshot pupil.

"No."

"Then why should I?"

"I'm only fourteen."

"Will a werewolf –"

Anna sighed and flailed her arms, "No, a werewolf won't care that I'm only fourteen. They'll kill me, and rip my still-beating heart out of my chest and eat it. Can we just go home now?"

"Okay little wolf, we can go home."

Anna cursed herself silently as she followed her father back to their hut. She honestly thought that this would be the day that she won, but once again her father proved too much for her. Every day since she was five, they had done these drills, and every day, Anna lost. But her father insisted that if he let her win, she would never be able to survive alone in the forest.

"You did well," her father said, interrupting her thoughts.

"I lost," Anna muttered, while she glared at her shoes.

"Winning isn't everything. You can learn more from failures than victories."

Anna rolled her eyes. She hated her dad's clichés; they never made any sense to her. *How can I learn from a failure? If I lose in the forest, I die. You taught me that.*

"You would've done better if you cut your hair... like I asked," her father continued, still not looking at her.

"I like it like this."

"It's easier for your opponent to grab in a fight. Plus, it hides your mother's eyes."

Anna looked up at her dad. She couldn't see his face, but she didn't have to. She knew that he had tears in his eyes. He always cried when he mentioned her mother. Anna couldn't even remember what she looked like, but her dad always told her that they had the same eyes.

"Do you miss her?" Anna asked, trying to take her mind off her humiliating defeat.

"Every day."

"What happened?"

"You know what happened," her father replied roughly.

Anna sneered behind his back. Every time she asked, her father gave a different answer. Sometimes, she got lost in a blizzard, other times, she was killed by the wildlife, but most times, she died from the supposed monsters that lived in the forest.

Despite her father's adamant belief that they dwelled in the forest, she had never seen any evidence of monsters, besides the bone-chilling howls that she heard in the middle of the night. Anna wasn't sure which version of her mother's death was true, but if she had to guess, it'd be the monsters.

Her father was obsessed with the ungodly creatures. Whenever he went into town to sell his pelts, he would always buy a book or tome about some beast that Anna had never heard of. Soon after, her father would make her read the book, so she could learn how to fight a beast she would never encounter.

After a silent two-hour walk, they finally returned home. Anna's legs were burning from exhaustion, and she just wanted to crawl back into bed. But she knew that would never happen. She had to finish her mind-numbing chores.

Sometimes, she wished she didn't have to live in the wilderness, but then she remembered how strange towns and cities were. The idea of living twenty feet away from a stranger always made her skin crawl.

"Go split some firewood," her father ordered.

"What are you going to do?" Anna replied sourly, already knowing the answer.

"I'm going to find us some food," her father replied. "After you're done with the wood, I want you to read the new book I got from town on my last visit."

Anna rolled her eyes; she despised the monotonous activities of reading dusty tomes and splitting firewood. She wished that just once, she would be able to go out into the forest and check the snares, or even go on a hunt. But her father insisted it was too dangerous for her to venture out alone.

She watched as her father started trekking through the thick snow towards the snares. She glared at him petulantly. She stewed in her anger for several minutes, before deciding to disobey her father, abandon her chores, and go on her own hunt.

Anna tossed the axe aside, picked up her bow and knife, and walked in the opposite direction to her father. The cold mountain air burned her lungs and her exhausted body pleaded for her to stop, but the prospect of proving her father wrong was a powerful motivator. Every time she considered taking a break, she pictured what his face would look like when she came back with a deer, instead of the rabbits and foxes he would always collect.

After about an hour of walking, she came across a large pool of blood on the ground. She paused and looked around, making sure no wolves were stalking her. She then noticed the long trail of smeared blood on the snow leading deeper into the forest. *No animals I know drag their prey elsewhere.* Anna crouched low to the ground and began following the trail of blood, an arrow already nocked in her bow.

There was a crack in the undergrowth, and Anna quickly dived behind the cover of a pine and tried to control her breathing. The sound of men walking echoed throughout the forest. *That's impossible,* Anna thought to herself. *Nobody lives in these woods other than me and father.*

"Where the hell are we going!?" one voice exclaimed.

"Shut yer trap, I heard something," the second voice commanded.

"You heard jack-shit!" the first exclaimed. "Bastard probably died in these woods years ago. Don't know why we're up here."

"He's up here. Just don't know where."

Anna peeked from behind the tree trunk to get a look at the two men. She knew it was a mistake, but her child-like curiosity got the better of her.

One man was sitting in a nearby snowbank, eating something from his pack. He had a grey, stubbly beard and a shaven head. Scars and bruises covered his face, evidence that the man loved to fight, but was seldom the winner.

The other man was tall and lean. He had a long mane of dark hair that was tied up into a fashionable bun. He had a patchy, black beard that complemented his jawline. Anna couldn't help but admire how handsome the man was, for a stranger.

"Let's just head back to camp," the scarred man interjected.

"No, we have to finish our patrol," the handsome man replied.

Anna leaned forward for a closer look and accidentally placed her foot on a branch that snapped under her weight. Both of the men's heads turned in her direction and made eye contact with her. Surprisingly, Anna didn't freeze, instead she turned and ran back towards home.

"Little girl!" the handsome man called out behind her. "We won't hurt you; we just want to talk!"

Anna could hear the lie reverberate off the tree trunks as she quickly weaved through the forest, trying to lose the two men who were undoubtedly pursuing her. Suddenly, she stopped, as an idea popped into her head. *This is the perfect chance to show father I'm a capable hunter.*

She turned her attention to the tree beside her and effortlessly began scaling it. She climbed high in the branches and waited for her pursuers to show themselves.

After about five minutes, the two men appeared, though she could hear their footsteps long before then. It seemed the handsome one was instructing the scarred man where to go, as he pointed to Anna's tracks in the snow. Both of them had their swords drawn.

Expecting the men to find her tracks, Anna had already readied her bow and nocked an arrow. She drew the bowstring back as quietly as she could and aimed it at the scarred man.

She loosed the bowstring, and the arrow flew noiselessly through the air and embedded itself directly in the man's eye. He dropped without uttering a sound.

The handsome man quickly dove behind cover. Anna cursed herself that she didn't get the second arrow ready soon enough.

"Little girl!" he called out. "There's no need to be frightened, we just want to talk."

"Liar!" she yelled, as she drew her bowstring back in anticipation of his next move. Suddenly, she heard the footsteps of a third man approaching from behind her. *Shit.*

"Anna?" her father called, as he began making his way towards the hidden handsome man.

"Harold, is that you?" the stranger shouted.

Anna turned her attention to her father and saw that he had his axe already in hand.

"You shouldn't have come here, Malakai," her father warned as he began stalking the man.

"You left us in such a hurry, I never got to say my farewells."

"Say them now, then, and be on your way."

Malakai let out a throaty laugh. "Seems a little heartless, don't you think?"

"Then it would suit you perfectly."

"What happened to us?" Malakai mocked.

"Tell me," her father responded, ignoring the man's question, "are the rest of the lads up here?"

"Aye. Planning on a reunion?"

"Nope, just planning on how many I have to kill before I live in peace again."

"With your daughter?"

Anna's father froze in place. His body tensed, and he glared at the tree that Malakai was hiding behind. "Mention her again and I'll make sure your death is slow and agonizing."

"She's very beautiful," the stranger mocked. "Reminds me of that whore you bedded in Winterhelm."

Anna's father charged at the tree, axe raised over his head. The stranger spun out from behind the tree and deflected her father's attack with his sword. But he failed to do the same to Anna's arrow, as it struck him in the throat.

Malakai collapsed, gurgling on his own blood as he writhed in the snow, clawing at his neck in a desperate attempt to stop the bleeding. Anna's father loomed over the dying man, sheathed his axe, and turned his attention to the tree his daughter was hiding in.

"Get down here, now."

Anna reluctantly shouldered her bow and began descending the tree. She knew she was going to get berated worse than she had ever been before. When she finally reached her father, he surprisingly didn't utter a word, but began silently walking back towards their hut.

The walk was excruciating, as neither said a word. Anna's hands started shaking as she thought about the two men she just killed. The horrific sound of Malakai choking on his own blood echoed in her thoughts. The eerily silent death of the scarred man also plagued her mind.

She wasn't sure what she thought killing a man would be like, but she didn't expect it to be so similar to killing a deer or a fox. Her conscience assaulted her as she looked up at her father, wishing that he would say something, anything, to get her mind off what she had done.

"Go to your bed," her father ordered as soon as they arrived at the hut.

"I killed those two men," Anna said in a barely audible whisper.

"Go."

Anna nodded her head and entered the hut. If there was one thing she hated most in the world, it was being confined inside that shack. It was cramped, musty, and reeked of mold.

The hut was no more than ten feet by ten feet, with a large wooden table taking up a majority of the floor space. Anna and her father slept in beds, one on top of the other. Anna was on the top bunk, while her father slept below. She angrily climbed up to her bed and stared at the decaying ceiling.

She had memorized every crack, every splinter, in every board. She remembered how she used to name them when she was little. She slid the knife out of her boot and pressed the tip of the blade to the wood when, suddenly, the door to the shack swung open.

Anna's father stood in the doorway with a panicked look on his face. He quickly locked the door and stared at Anna with eyes like saucers. "Cover yourself with the blankets, make sure nobody can see you," he instructed.

"What's happening?"

"Someone approaches."

CHAPTER THREE

ELBERT

The smell of rotting flesh filled the air as the guardsmen emptied the gibbets that hung from the city walls. The decomposed bodies often broke apart in their hands as they tossed the remains into the moat.

This would be the last time to dispose of the corpses before spring, as the moat would often freeze over in the winter months. Snow slowly started to descend as the last corpse fell into the murky water surrounding the city.

"Hurry up!" the prince yelled at the men he was supervising. "I'm freezing my balls off!"

"Yes, Your Highness," the sergeant responded, and quickly turned to echo the prince's orders to his men, albeit in a much harsher tone.

He always hated sentencing people to die in the gibbets; he always found it so tedious to clean up. He'd much rather behead them in a nearby field and let the buzzards feast on their treacherous flesh.

The prince rubbed his hands together and blew on them for warmth. His breath instantly turned to mist as it left his lips. His whole body shivered violently in a desperate attempt to keep warm. Winters in Artanzia were known to be cruel and unforgiving. He turned his head to the east and watched the sun peek over the frost-covered hills.

Suddenly, a page came running across the drawbridge. Judging from the state he was in, the news was urgent.

"Prince Elbert!" the page called out as he put his hands on his knees, trying to regain his breath.

"What is it?" the prince asked anxiously.

"Your father, he –"

Elbert waved a dismissive hand. "Must you bother me with news of my father this early? Surely he can wait till after sunrise to ruin his son's day."

"No, Your Highness, he –"

"He what?" Elbert asked angrily. "He's found some slave girl that he insists is my mother? Or has he slain another dragon? I swear the man loses touch with reality more and more with each passing day."

"He's dead!" the page blurted out, before clasping hands over his mouth.

The prince's heart skipped a beat. "What?"

"I'm sorry, Your Highness."

"Take me to him."

The page nodded, quickly turned on his heels, and led the prince back inside the city walls. He led him past the slums and up to the center of the city, to the square. From there, it was a long uphill walk to the palace, where the entire royal guard stood outside, waiting.

Their white enamelled armour glistened in the early sunlight. A guard stepped forward and removed his helmet. Elbert recognized the man as Sergeant Rupert Thames. He had wavy auburn hair and emerald green eyes. His nose was misshapen, and he was missing several teeth. Despite his gruff appearance, Rupert was the closest thing the prince had to a friend. He had been a royal guardsman ever since Elbert was a child, and was more of a father figure than King David ever was.

"Your Highness," Thames spoke, in a choked voice.

"Where is he?"

"In his chambers, Sire, we thought you would like to see him before we moved the body."

Elbert gestured for the guard to take the lead and followed him down the castle's winding corridor. He couldn't help but look at the tapestries and paintings that adorned the walls, great works of art that showcased the greatest kings ever to rule. Some led Artanzia on glorious campaigns against its unruly neighbours. Others established the kingdom as an economic powerhouse.

But now, Artanzia was a shadow of its former self. Years of plague and famine had decimated the population and crops, forcing the kingdom to lose its economic chokehold on the world. *It now falls to me to lead you back to greatness,* Elbert thought to himself.

His thoughts were quickly washed away by the creaking of the large oak door. The guardsman entered the room, followed by the prince. He stared at the bed where his father's withered corpse lay. He solemnly approached the bed and stared down at the body. He saw that the skin had turned a ghostly white and had begun to sag.

"Leave us."

Silently, Thames bowed and exited the bedchamber, leaving the prince alone with the king. The room was eerily quiet, and the only sound was the gentle crack of the fire in the room's hearth. Elbert walked over and stoked the flames with one of the iron pokers that adorned the side of the fireplace.

He placed the poker in the fire and waited for the tip to glow orange. He then walked over to his father's bedside and placed the red-hot poker in his father's dead hand. The skin instantly began to burn, and smoke rose from the king's palm, but his body remained completely still.

"It appears you really are dead," Elbert said aloud, as he pulled the poker away from his father's hand. "I was beginning to think this was a ruse." He walked over to the far side of the room, pulled one of the luxurious chairs to the bedside, and sat down. "Took you long enough," he said after a lengthy pause. "But then again, you always were a tenacious bastard. I wish that the plague would've taken you instead of mother. And I know Talbot would agree. Tell me, did you even care for my brother? Did you even notice that he wasted his life trying to win your love?"

Elbert paused to stifle the tears forming in his eyes and cleared his throat. He began to feel his neck tighten with anger. "The only thing you loved was wine and whores.

You watched your kingdom dissolve into practically nothing. You made concession after concession to foreign powers, and now I have inherited this kingdom of shit. Trust me when I say I will not make the same mistakes as you. I will restore our kingdom to its former glory, and my name will live on, and yours, dear father, yours will disappear in the annals of time. The only thing you will be remembered for is being a drunkard and a whoremonger. I hope the worms feast on your flesh."

He rose from his seat and spat on his father's corpse, then quickly exited the room. Outside, Thames stood at attention and awaited his orders. "Has the witan been assembled?" Elbert asked.

"Yes, Your Highness," the guard replied.

"Good, I wish to be king as soon as possible," Elbert said, before taking off to the throne room.

"What should we do about the king's remains?" Rupert asked.

"We'll hold a public service for him and then bury him next to my mother. I'm sure they'd want to be together," he called out over his shoulder, despite how much it pained him to do so.

"What do you mean, I'm not suited to be king?" Elbert shouted, as he threw a candelabra against one of the stone pillars of the throne room.

"We fear that..." the nobleman stammered, "your youthful energy may lead us astray."

"Lead us astray!" Elbert mocked. "And what, pray tell, do you think my father was doing all these years? Leading us towards the light?"

The nobles fell silent as Elbert paced angrily back and forth. His footsteps reverberated off the stone walls, filling the mighty throne room with their sound. He glared at the nobles as he paced back and forth, the hatred slowly consuming his body. *They want Talbot to be king. Do they think that pompous asshole has what it takes to lead a country? My brother doesn't know the first thing about statecraft, let alone having the mettle to make the difficult choices needed to run a kingdom.*

A noble stepped forth and cleared his throat. Elbert turned his head and scowled at the man, although he seemed unfazed by the prince's wrathful stare. "I think I speak for everyone when I say that Prince Talbot is much better suited to lead us," he said, confirming Elbert's suspicions. "Not only was he King David's eldest son, but he has a temperament more suited for governing."

Elbert snorted derisively. "And where is your saviour now? Probably out gallivanting with the townsfolk, pretending to be a knight."

"What you fail to realize, Prince Elbert, is that Talbot was trained to be king since his birth, whereas you were not. It would be idiotic for the witan to choose youthful vigour over years of experience and preparation."

Elbert ground his teeth together. He slowly clenched his hands into fists and squeezed until the knuckles popped. "Tell me, what is your name?"

"Lord Bellston, Sire."

"As Lord Bellston pointed out, my brother received all of the attention and training to become king, whereas I received none. I was like the last piece of meat you toss to the hounds. Discarded and forgotten. However, despite my father's lack of foresight, I have been preparing myself for this very role since the day I could read. Yet you insist on choosing my brother, a man who doesn't even bother to show up, as king?"

Suddenly, the giant oaken doors of the throne room swung open. Standing in the doorway was a man clad in a golden suit of armour that was stained with a fresh coat of blood. The man had a mane of wavy brown hair and a piercing set of green eyes. He had a strong jawline and a flawless face, save for the small scar on his chin. The man tossed his blood-spattered helmet aside and marched into the middle of the throne room with authority.

"My apologies for being late," he began. "But as my brother mentioned, I was preoccupied with pretending to be a knight."

The noblemen let out a small chorus of laughter, and Elbert saw that all of their bodies noticeably relaxed, while his tightened.

"Always the sourpuss, eh, brother?" Talbot mocked, as he placed a hand on Elbert's shoulder.

"I prefer the term realistic," Elbert retorted as he shrugged off his brother's arm. "But tell me, which damsel were you saving this time?"

"I believe you know her well," Talbot boisterously announced. "And why wouldn't you? You were obsessed with her for several years."

Elbert's blood immediately began to boil. Talbot always had a special talent for grinding his gears. He rushed his armour-clad brother and attempted to tackle him to the ground. But his older brother was quicker and pirouetted out of the way, while throwing a jab directed at Elbert's ribs.

The air rushed out of his lungs as he wheezed and gasped on the cold marble floor. His face began to turn red, and he could feel the tears start to form in the corner of his eyes. He slammed his fist into the marble floor and slowly lifted himself to his feet.

"Leave us. Elbert and I have much to discuss. We'll reconvene the witan at a later time," Talbot ordered.

The noblemen turned on their heels and quickly, yet silently, exited the doors of the throne room, the giant oak doors booming as they slammed shut behind them. Talbot let out a lengthy sigh and collapsed on the throne. He instantly started to slouch and relax his body.

"A man could get used to this," he taunted passively.

"You'll lead us into further ruin!" Elbert shouted. Veins were beginning to protrude from his forehead, and his knuckles had turned white in his clenched fists.

"How so?"

"You and father's idealistic bullshit is why Artanzia is in ruin. We need real leadership. We need someone who will make the difficult choices, no matter the consequences."

"And you believe that to be you?"

"I do."

"Do you remember when we were kids?" Talbot asked, seemingly avoiding the matter at hand.

"Care to be more specific?"

"When I rescued you from the frozen lake. I could've let you drown like the scared little pup you were, but instead, I risked my own life diving in to rescue you."

"What's your point?" Elbert grimaced. He hated how long-winded Talbot's answers were.

"The point being, does this sound like a leader who will lead his country to ruin?"

"You need more than bravery to rule."

"And you need more than a cold, vindictive heart. I daresay that if we were to rule together, we would make a half-decent regime."

"Are... are you asking me to join you?" Elbert asked, with a hint of hope staining his voice.

"Of course not," Talbot scoffed. "Why would I share power with someone who will oppose my every decision? Now leave me. I plan to get drunk tonight, as I am to be crowned tomorrow."

"The witan hasn't decided anything yet," Elbert growled.

"My crowning is a guarantee at this point. Nobody in their right mind would choose you after that display you put on."

Elbert turned his head and cursed silently to himself. He hated that he allowed his emotions to get the better of him in such a crucial moment. He sharply turned on his heels and began to exit the throne room.

"And brother," Talbot called out, "you'll never be king as long as I live."

"That arrogant, entitled bastard!" Elbert shouted as he threw an oil painting across his chamber.

The usually tidy room had been transformed into a collage of broken furniture, busted floorboards, and scattered linens. His chest heaved as he threw a chair at the wooden door before collapsing on the floor next to a half-empty wineskin.

"Fucker's probably out shaking hands with every shit-covered peasant," he growled, as he took a lengthy swig of wine.

Suddenly, he heard the loud drunken singing coming from outside his window. Elbert rose to his feet, pushed open the pane of glass, and saw that his brother was out for a moonlight stroll along the ramparts. Talbot turned his head abruptly and looked up at the window.

"Elbert!" he called out. "Come! Join me for a walk!"

Elbert slammed the window shut and took a few deep breaths before ultimately deciding that he would go and listen to his brother's drunken buffoonery.

The winter wind howled on top of the battlements. Elbert pulled his cloak tighter as goosebumps started to cover his body. He slowly began walking towards Talbot, who was spinning around in circles as he chugged from a near-empty wine bottle.

"What are you doing out here?" Elbert asked, hollering over the roar of the wind.

"Gettin' right drunk!" Talbot shouted, as he jabbed his younger brother in the chest with a muscular finger.

"It's freezing; we should go inside."

"Take a look, brother!" Talbot announced, pointing towards the torchlights of the city. "This city, and the kingdom it lies within, belong to me now. I know you think me an idealistic fool who cannot hope to undo our father's mistakes, but with the support of the populace, I know that anything is possible."

Elbert's heart sank. He knew his brother was right: the people of Artanzia adored him. It was almost as if he was worshipped as a god. Women swooned over him, and men moved out of his way when he walked the streets. His brother's words began to echo in his head. *You'll never be king as long as I live.*

Before he knew what was happening, Elbert drew his brother in close for an embrace and whispered in his ear, "You should've let me drown," then pushed Talbot from the ramparts.

CHAPTER FOUR

GRIMM

The icy wind howled as it blew the freshly fallen snow across the barren plains. His blood-soaked shirt had now frozen to his skin as he continued to push forward through the blizzard.

The torchlight from the town was a faint beacon of hope amidst the storm. There he could find food, shelter, and, with any luck, a change of clothes. His stomach instantly growled at the prospect of a hot meal. The last of the dog meat had run out three days prior, making him weak with hunger.

As he navigated through the storm, he could see that two guards stood watch at the gate, each of them equipped with a greataxe. *Shit,* Grimm thought to himself. He knew that there was no other way into the settlement. He palmed the dagger he stole from Halfdan the Jackal and approached the two guards. *If I have to kill them, at least their bodies won't be discovered till morning.*

"Whoa, traveller!" one of the guards called out as he shielded his eyes from the onslaught of swirling snow. "What's your business in Tølheim?"

"I'm just a weary man trying to rest his head for the night," Grimm called back, his fingers dancing around the hilt of the dagger in his hand.

The second guard stepped forward and held a torch up to Grimm's face. "Don't I know you?" he asked inquisitively.

"Afraid I don't know you," Grimm responded.

"Why are you covered in blood?" the first guard asked after seeing his crimson-stained clothes.

"I'm a hunter. I just gutted an elk three miles back. Had to abandon it to make it through this storm," Grimm lied.

"No, I'm pretty sure I know you," the second guard interjected. "Wait! You're Grimm White-Eyes!"

"By Heimer's beard, you're right!" the first guard exclaimed. "You'll have to come with us. High King Uthredd has offered a sizeable bounty for your capture."

"How much is it?" Grimm asked as he stealthily spun the dagger around in his hand, so the blade was pointing out.

"Your weight in silver, and I gotta say, you're a large fella," the second guard said fiendishly.

"I don't want to kill you," Grimm warned, "but you're standing in my way of getting off these damned isles."

"There's two of us and one of you. Surely you can't expect to win," the first guard retorted smugly.

"Bastard doesn't even have a–" the second guard added, but before he could finish, Grimm quickly plunged the dagger into the man's eye, puncturing the brain.

He then ripped the dagger out of the man's skull and tackled the first guard. Grimm drove the blade deep into the guard's neck several times until the spasming and gurgling stopped. Blood exploded from each of the stab wounds and covered Grimm's face in the warm, sticky liquid.

Grimm cursed silently to himself as he wiped the blood out of his eyes. He hurried into the town, trying to stick to the shadows as best he could, until he found a pail of frozen water resting on the porch of a nearby house. He ran to the pail, ripped it free from the landing, and stabbed his dagger into it, to break up the ice. Then he plunged his blood-stained face into the watery bucket until most of the blood had been washed away.

Suddenly, he heard the crunch of snow behind him. In an instant, he spun around and tackled the person with his blade held tight against their throat.

However, it wasn't another guard, as he expected, but a small dwarven girl. Her eyes were as big as saucers, and her matted, dark-brown hair was covered with snowflakes. He looked down at her wrists and noticed that they were bruised and chafed. Slowly, he brought his other hand up and turned her head. And there, on her left cheek, was the branding of a rune. *A slave,* Grimm thought, as he slowly pulled his dagger away from the young girl's neck.

"If you scream, I'll kill you, nod if you understand," Grimm instructed, his dagger still ready to strike. The dwarven girl nodded frantically. Grimm took a deep breath in and released the girl. To his surprise, the girl didn't immediately run away, nor did she scream, like he expected her to. Instead, she stood there with dumbstruck awe plastered on her face. After a few seconds of silence, the girl quickly ran off deeper into town.

Grimm sat down in the snow and let out an exasperated sigh. He knew he didn't have it in him to kill a child: it was the one line he couldn't cross. However, he didn't run away either; something deep inside his mind told him to stay and wait. Not sure what he was waiting for, he lay down and curled up into a ball, trying to conserve as much body heat as he could.

In a few moments, he heard the sounds of a small pair of feet sprinting back through the snow, but he heard no other sets of feet. He slowly rose to his feet and brushed the snow off his frozen body, and soon the dwarven girl returned, this time with a bearskin cloak clutched in her hands.

"For you," she squeaked, as she extended the cloak towards him.

"Why?"

"You're cold."

Grimm cautiously took the jacket, partially expecting the small child to have a weapon hidden underneath it, ready to deal the killing blow. But once again, he was surprised to find that the only thing underneath the cloak were her small, dwarven hands.

"Thanks..." he muttered as he threw the cloak over his shoulders and began walking away, only to hear small footsteps following behind him.

"What are you doing?" Grimm snarled.

"Following."

"Don't."

"Why?"

"Because I'm a wanted man."

"What does 'wanted' mean?"

"It means I'm dangerous."

"Why?"

Grimm rolled his eyes in frustration. He couldn't afford to have this little girl following him. She would surely lead to him getting caught, something that he couldn't allow to happen. He bent down so that they were at eye level and whispered, "I need you to find me a flower. It has blue petals and red thorns. Can you do that for me?" The small dwarf nodded excitedly and quickly ran off.

This time, Grimm didn't wait for the girl to return, and ran in the other direction as fast as he could, while still remaining stealthy. He expertly weaved his way through the town, avoiding the guards' patrols, until he came across the mead hall in the centre of town. He sleuthed his way to the side door and knocked four times, two in rapid succession, and after a three-second pause, two more.

The door opened and revealed a burly man covered in tattoos. He stood at least a foot taller than Grimm, and was a mountain of muscle. The man crossed his hairy arms as he glared down at him. Grimm stared up in utter defiance, his bloody dagger once again palmed in his hand.

"She's inside," the man grumbled, as he moved out of the doorway.

Grimm nodded his thanks and walked inside the kitchen of the mead hall. Without lingering, he walked towards the stairs leading to the wine cellar. The basement was musty, and was lit only by a handful of torches.

The sounds of mice scurrying across the dirt floor echoed off of the stone walls. Grimm looked around and saw a tall, slender woman standing in front of a table. She had her arms crossed as she glared at him.

"Grimm White-Eyes, as I live and breathe," she announced, while openly twirling a knife in her fingers.

"Evening, Thyra," Grimm responded, as he leaned against the cobblestone walls. "I'm assuming you heard the news?"

"Pretty hard not to hear," Thyra growled. "All of the isles will be looking for you, with the bounty High King Uthredd put on your head."

"That's why I'm here."

"Let's get a drink upstairs. I'm sick of being in this damned cellar."

"Plotting another shipment?" Grimm asked, as he glanced at the papers that littered the tabletop. He saw a map of the isles with names circled in red ink, but was too far away to make out the exact letters.

The woman scoffed and walked up the stairwell, gesturing for him to follow. With each ascending step, the cellar's miasma was replaced with the aroma of cooked venison and ale. Grimm breathed in the intoxicating smells and was tempted to allow them to whisk him away to simpler times. But he knew he couldn't afford such luxuries. Complacency as a wanted man meant death, or worse.

Thyra led him to the bar, sat down on one of the stools, and held up two fingers to the innkeeper. The man nodded and disappeared into the kitchen. Grimm looked around the tavern and saw that it was empty, save for a few hunters who were celebrating a boy's first hunt.

"I don't think I've ever seen this place so empty," Grimm stated, as he took a seat beside the woman.

The innkeeper came back with two horns of ale and handed them to Thyra and Grimm, before disappearing into the kitchen once again. Thyra quickly poured the drink down her throat, while Grimm left his untouched.

"You're hurt," she said, while gesturing to Grimm's injured arm.

"Courtesy of Kjottun's war hounds," Grimm replied stalely.

"I have a few bandages that I can give you that'll stop the bleeding."

"I'll be fine. Stupid mutt didn't manage to break any of the bones."

"Then why have you come here?" she said, a hint of frustration staining her voice.

"You know why," Grimm stated, as he surveyed his surroundings. "You owe a debt to me."

"The hell I do!" the woman snapped, before quickly recovering her composure. "I've paid my debt to you."

"If it wasn't for me, your head would be rotting on a pike atop Skotheim's walls," Grimm responded, before taking a sip of the ale. "I saved your life, and now you save mine."

"Even if I wanted to, I can't." Thyra sighed.

"Why's that?"

"Uthredd has ships patrolling the coasts. It'll be impossible to smuggle you to the mainland. We'd be caught for sure."

A smile crept on Grimm's face as he helped himself to another sip of ale. "And here I thought you were a fearless smuggler."

"Fearless, but not stupid."

They sat there, regarding each other in silence, for several minutes. Finally, Thyra cleared her throat. "Is it true what they say?"

Grimm shook his head with anger. "You know me far better than that."

"So, you didn't kill him?" Thyra asked, raising an eyebrow.

A small chuckle escaped Grimm's lips. "No, I gutted that fucker like a carp. But I didn't, you know..."

"I see," Thyra said, before turning back to her empty horn. "I wish I could help you, Grimm. I really do, but there's nothing I can do."

He let out an exasperated sigh as he finished the rest of his ale. The bitter taste filled his mouth and slid down the back of his throat. He licked his lips free of the froth and set his horn down. "Thanks for the drink." He slowly rose from his stool and made his way towards the door.

"Wait!" Thyra called out. She sprang from her seat and ran towards him. "Hold out your hand."

Grimm narrowed his eyes suspiciously, but ultimately did as she asked. Thyra then placed a small wooden medallion of a sword in his palm. He looked up at her in confusion.

"Aki's sword. If you somehow find a ship off the isles, may he bless your sailing with calm days."

Grimm nodded his head in a show of appreciation, even though Aki was not his god of choice. He instead dedicated his life to the creator god, Heimer. It was said that Heimer forged every soul on his giant anvil in the sky, and rewarded those who died with a weapon in their hand with eternal bliss in his mead hall. He pocketed the small wooden sword and reached for the door.

Suddenly, he heard the sharp, high-pitched scream of a little girl coming from outside the tavern. He ran to the window and saw three town guards harassing the small dwarven girl, who had inexplicably managed to find a bow and quiver.

"Shit," Grimm grumbled.

"What do you care?" Thyra asked. "It's just some slave girl."

Grimm didn't respond, but instead marched outside the mead hall, where a small crowd had gathered to see the spectacle. He effortlessly pushed his way through the crowd and yelled, "Let her go!"

The three guards all turned, looked at him, and began laughing. "What're you going to do about it, blind man?" the first cackled.

He shrugged the bearskin cloak off his shoulders and threw his dagger, striking one guard directly in the column of the throat. "My name is Grimm White-Eyes!" he bellowed. "And I demand that you let that girl go." The crowd immediately mumbled in awe as they all took one backward step in unison.

One of the two remaining guards quickly ripped the bow and quiver from the girl's hands, nocked an arrow, and shot it at him. Grimm nimbly sidestepped out of the way, and the arrow struck a bystander in the crowd.

He then charged the guard, tackled him to the ground, and began smashing his head against the frozen earth. The other guard reached for his sword, but it stuck in his scabbard.

Grimm ran over to him, knocked the guard's hand aside, and pulled the blade free of its sheath, before plunging it deep into the man's chest.

The crowd immediately dispersed in widespread panic. Their screams filled the night air as the sounds of doors slamming shut reverberated against the buildings. Grimm looked down, stared at the now-bloody dwarven girl, and extended a helping hand up.

The girl hesitated, but ultimately grasped his finger. With little effort, he lifted the girl to her feet and smiled at her. He then turned away, retrieved the sword, the bow, and the bearskin cloak, and began making his way towards the front gate.

"Good luck, Grimm!" Thyra shouted, as she watched the hulking warrior disappear in a cloud of swirling snow.

CHAPTER FIVE

ANNA

Anna's father quickly doused the fire in the hearth with a pail of water. The sound of the water sizzling on the coals filled her ears, and steam soon filled the cramped hut. Anna pulled the blankets over her head and clutched the handle of her knife tightly. Her father rushed over to her and planted a gentle kiss on her forehead.

"Stay put, little wolf, and everything will be alright."

"But who's –"

"There's no time. You must be quiet," her father hissed as he turned on his heels sharply and grabbed his bow, then exited the shack.

The sound of horses galloping could be heard in the distance. Anna closed her eyes and tried to count the different hoofbeats. *A dozen at least, maybe more.* She played with the knife in her hands underneath the covers, twirling it and letting it glide through her fingers.

She watched the shadows beyond the door intently. She saw her father's figure walk past several times before the sound of wood being split echoed beyond the hut.

It didn't take long for the unknown riders to reach the shack. Anna watched their shadows move past the front door as they encircled the hut.

The men lobbed various insults at her father, who, to her surprise, continued to chop wood methodically. The percussive cacophony overwhelmed her, and she was tempted to put her hands over her ears to block out the sound, when, suddenly, it came to a stop.

Outside the hut, she saw the shadow of a man dismount from his horse and approach her father, who refused to stop swinging his axe. A sharp hiss filled the air as the stranger unsheathed his blade. He then stabbed it deep in the ground and let out a hearty laugh.

"Harold! I've been searching all over for ya! Why don't ya invite me in for a drink, and we can catch up?"

"Piss off," her father grumbled as he swung his axe down once more.

"Now, now, there's no need for hostilities. In fact, I've come to offer ya a job," the man said as he began walking towards her father.

"Not interested."

"See, I think ya will be," the man retorted. "A few of my men were out here searching for food, and they never came back. Any idea what mighta happened to 'em?"

"Wolves, most likely," her father answered plainly.

"Hmm, I thought so meself, but then picture my amazement to find them both dead with arrows juttin' outta their bodies. Tell me, are the wolves different up here than up north? Have they really learnt to shoot arrows? Is that what you've been doing up here all this time, training wolves to use bows?"

Her father picked up another log and placed it atop the cutting block. Anna could see the shadow of the axe as he raised it high above his head. "No, that isn't what I've been doing."

"Then what have ya been doing? Still fuckin' that whore?"

Anna's father quickly brought the axe down and buried it in the cutting block. He then walked out of view towards the stranger and grumbled something. Anna couldn't make out the words, but knowing her father, it was a threat of some kind.

Not being able to see what was going on was unbearable. She slowly slid out from underneath the blankets and began crawling towards the front door. She knew that there was a sizeable gap at the bottom of the doorway that would give her a perfect vantage point to see what was happening outside.

From the crack, she saw that men on horses surrounded the hut. She also noticed that the man her father was talking to had long brown hair and a scraggly beard. His cheeks were full of old pox scars, and his nose was as red as a cherry. Anna noticed that the man's eyes were the same colour as his teeth, a rotten yellow.

"Where is that bitch, huh?" the pox-scarred man asked. "I want to meet the woman who stole me best man from me."

"She died a few years back," Anna's father answered, with a hint of rage in his voice.

"How tragic," the man replied. "But if that's the case, there's nothing stopping you from rejoining the ranks. Men, help Harold with his things!"

Her father quickly took the bow from his shoulder, nocked an arrow, and loosed it at one of the men who had dismounted, missing him by the slimmest of margins. *Intentional,* Anna thought to herself, although she couldn't understand why.

"Ya missed," the stranger stated plainly.

"On purpose," her father retorted.

"Please, Harold, you and I both know you're not one to give a warning shot. I'm surprised ya haven't tried to kill one of us already."

"I'm not the same man you knew, Iban, I've changed."

The stranger erupted in laughter. "Oh, that's rich! A bandit that's grown a conscience, a shame ya didn't meet that cunt from the Isles sooner, or the people of Elstow would still be alive."

"That wasn't my fault!" Anna's father shouted, as he readied another arrow.

"Wasn't yer fault? Harold, it was yer idea to burn 'em alive in the town hall!" Iban laughed. "You always were the most twisted fucker in our little family."

"We are not family."

"Of course we are!" Iban shouted. "We murdered, raped, and pillaged together. If that doesn't make us brothers, I don't know–" Iban's body came to a sudden stillness. His eyes locked with Anna's. A sadistic smile crept across his face. "Seems you've been hidin' someone from us. A child, perhaps?"

Anna quickly pulled herself away from the wall. In a panic, she crawled backwards to the other side of the hut, knocking over the wooden table as she did so. She twirled her knife around in her hands and held it by the blade, ready to throw it at whoever walked through the front door.

"Run, Anna!" her father shouted over the sounds of a struggle.

She quickly leapt to her feet and grabbed her bow and a quiver of arrows. She tossed another bucket of water onto the still-sizzling coals and drew her bowstring back until it kissed her cheek.

The door to the shack swung open, and without hesitating, she loosed her arrow. The figure in the doorway dropped instantly as the arrow embedded in his skull.

Anna nocked another arrow and sprinted atop the dead man and outside the hut. The light assaulted her eyes, and it took a few seconds for her vision to return.

She could hear the sounds of a man gurgling on his blood. She didn't dare look back, and prayed that it was Iban and not her father.

She continued to run until something caught her by her hair. Without thinking, she took the arrow that was nocked in her bow and stabbed it into the hand of the man that grabbed her.

There was a sudden yell of pain, and her feet hit the ground. She quickly readied another arrow and loosed it at the still-screaming bandit. She then spun on her heels and ran deep into the forest.

As she ran, she blocked out all sounds and focused on her breathing. She weaved through the underbrush with unbelievable speed. Anna and her father had practiced this exact scenario many times before.

She serpentined between the trees, making sure that her trail was difficult to follow. Every five steps, she would plant one of her feet and leap in the opposite direction, to ensure that her track wasn't connected.

Her legs soon began to tire, but she forced them to continue, making sure not to deviate from her father's lessons. After about fifteen minutes of hard running, she finally stopped and allowed herself a brief rest. She closed her eyes and listened to the forest. She heard the wind rustle the pine trees and the gentle lapping of a nearby stream.

"I've lost them, for now," she whispered to herself. She knew the bandits would still be pursuing her, but she also knew that she had put considerable distance between them.

Anna continued to walk deeper into the forest, as per her father's lessons, until she came to a tall pine tree. She looked up and saw her father's mark, a barely perceptible "X," carved into the bark.

Her eyes scanned the tree until she found it, a small bundle wrapped in elk hide hanging from one of the branches. She readied an arrow and loosed at the rope that tied the bundle to the tree. The small ball of hide tumbled from the treetop and landed with a mighty thud. Anna quickly ran up to it and unwrapped the bundle. She knew that inside were all the provisions that she would need to make it to Winterhelm.

"Salted meat, arrows, a canteen for water, and a knife. It's all here," she said aloud. "Now to get to Auntie Teale's."

Her father's words rang inside her head as she stood up and resumed walking. *Remember, if we ever get separated, and it's not safe to meet at the house, head north to Winterhelm. My sister Teale will take care of you until I arrive.* She never thought that one of her father's caches would come in handy, but for once, she was glad her father was right.

Anna continued to walk until nightfall, her feet aching from the uneven terrain. She found a hollowed-out log and curled up inside for the night.

Her frozen body pleaded for a fire, but she knew it would be a mistake. If the bandits were near, they would surely see the light of the flames. She soon forgot about her numb fingers and toes as her mind raced wildly over her father's fate. Once again, she clutched the handle of her knife tightly as sleep slowly consumed her.

It was just before daybreak when she awoke, the sun's light peeking above the treetops of the forest. Anna crawled out from the log and stretched her stiff, frozen limbs. She rubbed her hands together and blew on them for warmth, her breath turning into steam in the chilly morning air.

Thankfully, there appeared to be no signs of frostbite on her extremities. As she left the shelter of the log, her eyes widened when she saw the hoof prints in the snow. Anna immediately ducked down into a crouch and scanned the trees for any lurking bandits. She allowed herself to relax once again when she saw no signs of life.

"Must've ridden past in the night," she whispered, as she slowly stood upright.

Her stomach growled with hunger, and she took out a slab of salted meat and greedily wolfed it down. She knew it was a mistake to use her provisions so early. There was plenty of game in the woods, but she was too lazy and too tired for a hunt. All she could think about was her father.

Even though it was against all of her father's teachings, she knew she couldn't leave without knowing what happened to him. She quickly packed up her things and began walking back towards the shack. The forest was eerily quiet, and her footsteps seemed to echo for miles. Each crunch of snow sounded like a roar of thunder that never seemed to fade.

Suddenly, she heard another crunch of snow from something other than her own feet. She froze in place and effortlessly readied another arrow.

She took a deep breath in when she smelt the foul odour of decaying flesh. Against all instinct, she pinched her nose to block out the noxious smell. Then, she heard another crunch of snow from behind her.

She spun around, bowstring drawn back to her cheek, but nothing was there. Suddenly, there was a mighty thud from behind her. Anna leapt, turned, and fired an arrow mid-air at the motionless creature lying in the snow.

The creature didn't make a sound, nor did it move once the arrow was embedded in its side. She cautiously approached the body and realized that it belonged to a man and not a creature.

She turned the body over and nearly vomited at the sight. It was one of the bandits, whose face had been torn to shreds, and his entrails were ripped from his body.

Anna reluctantly stuck her hand inside the corpse and began examining the organs of the bandit. The body was ice cold, and she found that one organ was missing, the appendix.

Once again, the words of her father echoed in her head. "As far as I know, only one monster has a hankering for appendix, and that's the corvan."

She remembered the description vividly. A creature that looked like a man but had the head of a crow, with monstrously sharp claws. Tales spoke about a corvan's supernatural speed and how they like to play with their prey before killing it. Anna also remembered that the tome said that the creatures only came out of hibernation every fifteen years and would glutton themselves for a day, then go back into hibernation.

Goosebumps soon covered her skin as she heard the crunch of snow from behind her. Anna quickly ran through the snow, when she heard the pang of a crossbow.

She immediately froze in place as the bolt missed her nose by several inches. She whirled her head to the right and saw one of the bandits smiling at her, as he loaded another bolt.

Anna dropped to her knees and drew back her bowstring, but before she could shoot, a grey blur whisked away the bandit. She then heard the bone-chilling scream of a man having his insides ripped out. Anna turned, and began running towards the shack once again.

Suddenly, everything became real. The terrible monsters that she had heard thousands of stories about were now hunting her, and fear quickly gripped her heart. Her breath was shallow and rapid, and her heart felt like it was going to beat out of her chest.

The high-pitched caw of the corvan echoed throughout the forest as it undoubtedly pursued her. She continued to crash through the underbrush towards the shack as she heard the creature's footsteps drawing closer. Instinctively, she turned around and loosed an arrow, only to have it soar through empty air.

There was a loud thud from behind her. She spun around, readying an arrow as quickly as she could, but the corvan was quicker.

The monstrous beast tackled her to the ground and lifted its claw for the fatal blow. Anna grabbed the arrow with her right hand and thrust it upwards into the creature's chest.

The corvan reeled in pain while Anna rolled to her feet and lunged at the creature with her knife. She plunged the knife into the monster's throat and pulled it free in one fluid motion.

Blood exploded from the wound and bathed her in a thick coat of the sticky liquid. Anna let out a fierce scream as she stabbed her knife into the creature again and again. Each stab bathed her in less and less blood, as the monster's heart gradually came to a stop.

Anna fell backwards in the snow. Her chest heaved, and her heart raced wildly. She let out a scream of joy, and a smile broke on to her face.

She rolled to her feet and looked down at the corvan's corpse and couldn't help but laugh. *You weren't so tough. Father had me think you were invincible.* She pulled her arrow free from the monster's chest and continued on her way back to the hut.

She walked for another five minutes before she saw the plume of black smoke in the distance. Anna broke into a sprint, excited to tell her dad the unbelievable news. All the worries she had that morning about her father had completely evaporated, and she was sure he survived the encounter with the bandits.

As she came into the clearing where the shack was settled, she gasped in horror as she saw that their house was set aflame, and her father's corpse impaled on a large stake, almost splitting his body in two.

CHAPTER SIX

ELBERT

The seamstress' hands were a blur. She hemmed the fabric at blazing speed and with uncanny precision. The needle stabbed in and out of the cloth faster than Elbert's eye could follow. He often caught himself wondering if the old woman was a sorceress, but he thought it unlikely. *Why would she disguise herself as a seamstress, of all things?* He quickly shook the thought out of his head.

"Hold still!" the woman barked, through a mouthful of pins.

Elbert straightened his back and lifted his arms so that the seamstress could work on the sleeves of his robe. He turned his head and watched the elderly woman work, through the dust-covered mirror in the corner of the room. He was able to suppress an involuntary gag at the sight of his ceremonial robes. They were an awful cream-white with red stitching, and appeared to be made for a man twice his size.

"Hold still!" the woman ordered once again.

"Are you sure all of this is... necessary?" Elbert asked, turning his attention once again to the seamstress' nimble fingers.

"Of course it's necessary!" the woman hollered. "Can't go to your coronation looking like a beggar."

"This all just seems... a bit much," Elbert replied, hoping that he could get out of those awful-looking clothes.

"You need to look your very best today; not only are you receiving the crown, but you are to present yourself as king for the first time to the masses. Their first impression of you will be in these very robes."

That's what I was afraid of. "I'm just not sure that this is the right colour scheme," Elbert confessed.

The seamstress let out a long, exasperated sigh and pulled the pins out of her mouth. "Must I explain it to you again? You know, you really ought to listen to your subjects more attentively."

"And you ought to not have such a familiar tone with your king."

The woman's features went slack, and her wrinkled face quickly turned a shade of crimson. "Apologies, Your Highness," she responded ruefully. "The white represents your purity, both in body and spirit, while the red represents the royal blood that courses through your veins."

"So, there's no changing it?" Elbert asked, scared that he already knew the answer.

"Change it? I'd have to start over! The ceremony is in twenty minutes! I... I..."

"It'll have to do, then. My apologies for doubting you," Elbert mentioned plainly. *Let us hope the commoners have less fashion sense than I do.*

It was another ten agonizing minutes before the seamstress was satisfied with her ungodly creation, and allowed him to leave. He spent most of the time before the ceremony roaming the empty halls of the castle, and deciding what he was going to change and what he was going to keep the same.

He found himself to be nostalgic over very little, and decided to change almost all the décor in the palace. Occasionally, he would stop, and look out the frost-covered windows, and stare at the horizon. It filled his body with immeasurable joy that he was going to be crowned king of it all. Suddenly, he heard the clank of armoured footsteps behind him.

"The nobles have gathered in the courtyard, Sire. We're ready," Thames informed.

"The courtyard? But it's a blizzard outside!" Elbert exclaimed.

"Aye, but it's tradition. All crownings happen in the courtyard beneath the sacred tree, so the Gods themselves can witness it."

Elbert rolled his eyes before reluctantly following the guard towards the courtyard. "I never knew you to be a religious man, Thames."

"I used to be," he responded curtly.

"What happened?"

"I've been in too many battles, seen too many good folk die needlessly. Either the Gods don't exist, or they're right pricks who don't give a flying fuck about us."

Elbert smiled at the guard. Throughout most of his life, he had known Rupert to be a man that always stuck to protocol. But in rare moments like this, Elbert was able to get a glimpse at the man beneath the armour, and although he would never admit it openly, the guard was a man he cared about deeply.

"A shame, what happened to your brother," Thames replied, interrupting the prince's thoughts.

"What do you mean?"

"Well, to fall to your death just a day before you inherit a kingdom... is unheard of."

"The lesson to learn here is that one should never drunkenly walk along the battlements at night."

The guard nodded his head politely, but refused to utter a response.

"Please speak freely," Elbert added, hoping to provoke more honest truths from the man.

"It's just... many of the people, the nobles especially, are saying his death is quite suspicious; that you somehow had a hand in it."

"That's ludicrous!" Elbert shouted in faux surprise. "I was asleep in my chambers; the guards can confirm my whereabouts."

"Indeed," the guard replied. "But rumours like these spread like wildfire, when not dealt with immediately."

"So, what do you suggest?" Elbert asked, coming to a sudden halt.

"I dare not advise a king," Rupert retorted. "I am merely a humble guard, sworn to protect."

"Rupert, I've known you my entire life, I think we can dispense with the formal etiquette when we are alone. Now, please enlighten me," Elbert demanded.

"I would find out who is spreading these rumours, and prevent them from ever uttering another treasonous word."

"So, I should kill them?"

"Cutting out their tongues usually works, as well," the guard replied plainly.

"Then I task you with finding out what you can about these conspirators. Report back directly to me."

"As you wish, Your Highness," Thames said, bowing low as he did so.

Elbert rolled his eyes at the guardsman's return to proper protocol. "Now, let's get this damned ceremony over with."

The snow swirled beneath the ancient yew tree that stood in the middle of the courtyard. All of the surrounding shrubberies were covered in a thick blanket of snow. The nobles were already gathered in a large semi-circle at the tree's base, and wore equally ridiculous clothes.

Elbert shivered uncontrollably as he stepped onto the frozen grass. *Not designed for winter,* he thought to himself, as he adjusted his ceremonial robes. The snow crunched beneath his feet as he approached the noblemen. Lord Bellston stood in the middle of the assembly, with both the ceremonial crown and sceptre in hand.

"You're late." Bellston glowered.

"A king is never late; they arrive precisely when they mean to," Elbert retorted smugly.

"While the rest of us freeze our balls off," Bellston muttered under his breath.

"Pardon?"

"We are gathered here today," Bellston bellowed, ignoring the prince's question, "to celebrate the life of King David, and to pass his powers on to his only living son, Prince Elbert. It is a shame that we must conduct such a joyous ceremony on the heels of such tragedy. Last night, Prince Talbot was taken from us far too soon, as he fell from the battlements. But we must not fixate on the prince's demise, nor the peculiarities surrounding it."

One of the conspirators for sure, Elbert thought to himself, as he carefully scrutinized Bellston's face.

"Step forward, Prince Elbert, and receive the Crown of Artanzia, and the Blessed Sceptre," Bellston instructed, as he extended both of his hands.

Elbert approached the noble and dropped to one knee, smiling as he did so. The thumping of the prince's heart drowned out the noble's words. Childlike excitement consumed him as he felt the golden crown being gently placed on his head. The excitement grew as he held the gold-emblazoned sceptre in his trembling hand.

"Rise!" Bellston commanded. "And be henceforth known as King Elbert!"

The nobles let out an obligatory cheer as he rose to his feet. Elbert then cleared his throat. "As my first act –"

"Your first act will be to receive the gifts that your loyal subjects have prepared to bring you," Lord Bellston interrupted.

Elbert curled his lips into a frown and reluctantly nodded his head. *I would have very much liked to order your execution, but perhaps I should wait and see what evidence Thames can dig up first.* "Very well," he replied sourly, as he followed the retinue towards the throne room.

Receiving the gifts proved to be much more monotonous than Elbert had initially expected. Aside from the fact that most of the presents were things he had no desire to own, he was required to act as if each of the gifts were blessings from the Gods, and was expected to make a long-winded speech of thanks after receiving each one.

"Next!" Sergeant Thames hollered, as he gently pushed a dirt-covered man out of the way.

My brother would have received much more suitable gifts for a king. These people are openly mocking me. They think me a murderer.

An elderly woman hobbled forward and collapsed to her knees upon reaching the throne. "I have a gift for you, Sire, and it is my most prized possession that I humbly offer you." The woman extended her hand, and in the middle of her palm sat a talisman. It appeared to be forged out of silver, and was the effigy of a man clad in armour with a winged helmet.

"What is it?" Elbert asked in fascination.

"It is the medallion of Heimer, believed to be the creator of the world on the Mjältön Isles. We received it in exchange for saving a traveller's life," the woman responded.

"Thank you for this gift," Elbert replied, deciding to break protocol. He then turned his attention to the monstrous crowd of petitioners that had gathered before him. "These are all the gifts I have time for today. I humbly ask that you return to your homes and leave me to my affairs."

There was a groan of disappointment as the crowd of peasants exited through the giant oaken doors of the throne room. Elbert allowed his body to relax on the throne as he watched his subjects shuffle out of the room. *Talbot was right: a man could get used to this.*

Once the room had completely emptied, Elbert pulled out the medallion the old woman had given him, and flipped it over in his hand. The effigy was carved with such fine detail that he could make out the veins in the god's finely toned biceps. He picked up the chain that it was attached to and draped it over his head, letting the pendant clang off his chest.

"A king shouldn't be seen as a worshipper to that heathen god," a voice croaked from the other end of the throne room.

Elbert looked up and saw that there was an old, dishevelled man who had just entered the throne room, and was slowly limping his way towards the king. "I'm sorry, but I'm all out of time for gifts today."

"I have no gifts to offer, but instead have a deal," the cripple retorted.

"And just who are you to demand a deal from a king?" Elbert breathed angrily through his nose.

"You see, Sire, I'm a magus. I can achieve feats that others think impossible. You need only but tell me what you desire most in life."

"I desire for you to leave me be," Elbert snarled.

"Come now, Elbert," the magus clicked. "We both know you want to restore this country back to its former glory."

The king's body immediately stiffened. "How do you know that?"

"I can make your dream come true: I can transform you into the greatest ruler Artanzia has ever known! All in exchange for one simple thing."

Elbert let out an exhausted sigh. "How much gold?"

The magus spat on the floor and shook his withered head. "I have no need for gold. I only ask for the thing that you have, but do not value."

"Is this some sort of riddle?"

"I assure you it is not."

Elbert snorted derisively. "Very well, old man, I agree to your terms, only because you entertained me and, managed to lighten my mood over my brother's sudden passing."

The hunchback smiled as he extended a hand out to Elbert. His long yellow nails protruded out of his fingers like rusty, jagged knives. As soon as their hands touched, a searing pain filled Elbert's body, and he let out a bone-chilling scream.

It felt as if lightning had struck him, and that fire flowed through his veins. His legs suddenly grew numb, and he collapsed on the ground. He laid there, twitching uncontrollably, as the magus loomed over his paralyzed body.

"You're too kind, sire," the man mocked as he walked, completely unhindered, out of the throne room.

CHAPTER SEVEN

GRIMM

The blade pierced the skin and glided across the deer's stomach. Blood trickled from the wound slowly, and a small puddle of crimson formed in the snow beneath the corpse.

Grimm plunged his hands into the stag and began ripping out the creature's innards. His meaty fingers wrapped around the beast's heart as he tore it free of the veins and arteries. He tossed the organ aside, grabbed his dagger, and started to skin the deer with practiced precision.

He always enjoyed hunting. It seemed to fill his body with a certain calmness that he couldn't experience anywhere else, although he was never sure why. Perhaps it was the solitude of being alone in the woods that eased his mind, or maybe it was the lack of men screaming that allowed his thoughts to roam free. Whatever the reason, Grimm knew he had to treasure the moment while it lasted.

There's always another battle, he thought to himself as he pulled the arrow out of the stag's eye socket. *Pierced the brain at fifty yards. Not bad for a man who prefers the sword.* He grasped his blood-soaked dagger and marked a single line on the shaft of the arrow: a stupid tradition that he picked up back when he was nothing more than a common soldier in servitude to Uthredd. *Back when I wasn't wanted for treason, murder, and Gods know what else.* Grimm was never sure why he started counting his kills, but throughout his life, he learned that soldiers often had weird and unusual habits that were almost impossible to break once they set in.

He turned his head upwards and saw the crescent moon glowing high in the cloudless sky. *It's almost time.* He quickly skinned his prey with expert efficiency. The blade danced along the deer's corpse as it sliced the hide away from the meat.

Suddenly, there was the distinct snap of snow being crushed beneath the weight of a person. Grimm quickly rolled to one side, picked up his bow, and readied an arrow, all in one fluid motion.

He scanned the trees for any sign of movement, but was instead greeted by an eerie stillness. He pulled the bowstring back till it touched his cheek. The stave creaked under the pressure.

Then, he saw her. The small dwarven girl who had gifted him this very bow was staring back at him, eyes as wide as saucers.

Grimm cursed under his breath and rose to his feet. *Must've followed me. It seems I'm losing my touch if a child can get the drop on me.* "Come out," he ordered.

The dwarven girl shook her head and hid behind the trunk of a large pine.

"I see you," Grimm announced, as he dropped his bow to the ground. When the girl still did not emerge from her cover, he waved his hand dismissively and resumed skinning the deer.

After a few minutes of peace, he heard snow crunching beneath tiny footsteps. He then felt a soft, diminutive hand on his shoulder. "What're you doing?"

"Skinning."

"Why?"

"Because I need to eat."

"Why?"

"Because I have a long journey ahead of me."

"Why?"

"Because I have to leave this place."

"Why?"

A frustrated sigh escaped his lips as he stabbed the dagger deep into the snow. He turned his head and glared at the girl with the most fearsome look he could muster. To his surprise, the dwarf did not shirk from his glare, but instead started giggling. Grimm wasn't sure whether to be flattered or insulted. "Where are your parents?" he asked.

"Dead. Where are yours?"

"Also, dead."

"Why?"

Grimm rolled his eyes and pinched the bridge of his nose. "Is that all you know how to say?" he snarled, hoping to scare her away with the roughness of his voice.

"No," the dwarf responded.

He waited for another sentence, but it never came. The girl just stared at him with her brown eyes full of a sense of wonder that can only be found in a child. He picked up his dagger and resumed skinning the deer. "You should go back to the village... and don't you dare say 'why?'"

The word almost slipped from her lips before she quickly covered her mouth with both of her hands. For the briefest moment, a smile emerged on Grimm's lips before his glowering visage returned.

The dwarven girl let out another childlike giggle before running to hide behind another tree. Her tiny body disappeared behind the tree trunk for several seconds, before peeking her head out to make sure that Grimm was watching.

"Stay there," he ordered, as he carved out several slabs of meat, before wrapping them in a spare cloth. He once again turned his gaze to the sky and cursed silently. *I'm late.* He hated the idea of leaving the carcass behind, but he knew it would only slow him down. Grimm rose to his feet and began marching south towards the meeting place. He only hoped that Bearn would listen to him.

The rapid padding of tiny feet crushing snow echoed throughout the forest as the dwarven girl sprinted to catch up with the grizzled warrior. Grimm stopped in his tracks and growled, "What are you doing?"

"Following."

"Go home."

"Why?"

Grimm clenched his fist until his knuckles popped. He bit down a fiery retort that he knew the child was too young to understand. "Because it's where you belong," he said through gritted teeth.

"But they treat me mean there," the girl responded.

Grimm once again looked at the child's wrists, and saw they were badly bruised and scarred. His eyes narrowed as he began examining the dwarf with the greatest of scrutiny. *Only five years old. Too young to be a pleasure slave, probably just a servant. Girl doesn't know what "mean" is.* "Trust me. I'm a lot meaner than they are."

"Nope," the girl retorted. "You saved me."

Grimm swallowed another harsh rebuke. He knew that the girl had a point, and what was worse was that he couldn't think of a lie to tell her otherwise. Instead, he stormed off through the snow without uttering another word. The girl, on the other hand, bounded through the waist-high powder and began humming a song loudly.

"Quiet!" Grimm snarled.

"Why?"

"Because there are creatures that lurk in these woods, creatures that like to eat little girls."

The girl nodded her head and narrowed her eyes with fierce determination, then began mimicking Grimm's movement with uncanny skill. He was surprised to see that the girl instinctively started following in his footsteps. He turned his eyes towards the treeline, hoping that the smell of fresh blood wouldn't lure any monsters out of their lairs. He knew he could keep himself alive, but whether or not he could keep both of them alive was an entirely different matter.

It wasn't long into their march that the dwarven girl's silence faded. Once again, she started absentmindedly humming a tune and crunching through the snow. Grimm let out a frustrated groan and slung his bow over his shoulder. He then turned around and picked up the girl. She instinctively burrowed into his muscular chest and nuzzled her head into his broad shoulder.

Grimm was surprised by how familiar it felt. He had expected that another person's compassionate touch would feel alien after all this time. However, along with the familiarity came painful memories that he'd rather keep repressed. He shook the images of his deceased family out of his head and tried to focus on the southern horizon. But the nagging pain of the memories broke through his focus, and he was once again confronted by the ghosts of his past.

He saw his wife standing in a golden-brown field of wheat, draped in a near-transparent white dress. He then saw his son bound through the crop and leap into his mother's arms. Both of them erupted in laughter. His wife twirled the boy around in circles, their hands intertwined with one another. Upon seeing him, they stopped and beckoned for Grimm to come and join in on the fun. He reached his hand out to touch his wife's cheek, and then, in an instant, everything changed.

The field of wheat had disappeared, along with the smiling faces of his family. Instead, he was in a blood-stained bedroom, surrounded by the butchered remnants of his family. He saw his wife's mangled body lying on the bed. Her hands were bound, her legs spread apart, and her stomach sliced open, with her intestines shoved down her throat. He didn't dare look at the remains of his son; once was more than enough. But he couldn't help but manage to catch a glimpse of the splattered brain matter that decorated the walls.

This is the punishment I get for loving two different women. "I'm sorry," he whispered, as he wiped the tears out of his eyes.

"About what?" the dwarven girl murmured, as she rubbed her tired eyes together.

Grimm hadn't realized that he had spoken aloud. He cleared his throat and blinked away the tears before answering, "Nothing. Go back to sleep."

The dwarven girl voiced no protest, and instead burrowed in deeper for warmth. Grimm continued to walk in silent contemplation. He cursed the day that he left to fight in that stupid war. Not only had he lost a pivotal battle, but his pigheadedness cost him the only family he would ever know.

After ten minutes of hard walking, he arrived at the small cove where a boat was moored on the dock. The vessel bobbed and swayed as the tide gently washed over the stony beach. Grimm saw that the light inside the ancient fishery was on. *In a foul mood, no doubt.* He set the dwarven girl down, concealing her in the nearby shrubbery before walking towards the shack.

"Where are you going?" the dwarf girl asked, inexplicably rising from her slumber.

"To meet a friend," Grimm assured.

"Can I come?"

"No, you must stay here. Do not be seen." Grimm made sure his voice was hard and conveyed as much authority as he could. The girl crossed her arms and begrudgingly crawled back into the hiding place.

As Grimm ventured towards the hut, he scanned the surrounding trees for any hidden archers. To his surprise, he couldn't see any. *It seems Bearn kept his word or, at the very least, has found skilled men.* He palmed his dagger as he approached the creaky wooden door, but as he opened it, he was relieved to find the old warrior sitting alone in the fishery.

"You're late," the man grumbled.

"You look like shit." Grimm laughed as he eyed up his former friend. Bearn's body was a tapestry of finely honed muscle and was decorated with an abundance of tattoos. His head was now bald, and his beard was considerably greyer than the last time they saw each other. He wore the finest clothes Grimm had ever seen, but Grimm also noticed that his weathered battleaxe was still strapped across his back.

"Who's the kid?" Bearn growled.

"Just a stray I picked up, a former slave. You can have her if you want; I have no use for her."

Bearn waved a dismissive hand. "Pah! Have too many as it is. Surprising that, after all these years, this shack still reeks of fish guts."

Grimm hadn't realized the stench when he walked in, but now that it was mentioned, he found it hard to focus on anything else. "I'm surprised you came alone."

"That's what your letter said, dinnit?" Bearn snarled, as he lit another lantern.

"Does that mean you'll help me?"

"Dunno. Guess I just want to hear you out first."

"What do you need to hear? I'm sure Uthredd has told you the whole story already."

"I want your side. Remember what your father taught us as wee lads? Every sword has two sides: now let's hear yours."

Grimm let out an exhausted breath and pulled up a chair across from his friend. He stared into Bearn's blue eyes, and explained everything. "I killed High King Uthredd's brother. I don't deny that, but I didn't rape his wife. Stupid bitch probably lied to cover her own ass, once her husband found out about us."

"By the Gods, Grimm!" Bearn interrupted. "I ought to arrest you right now. You betrayed the bloody crown!"

"That fucker gutted my family!" Grimm screamed as he rose to his feet, Bearn doing likewise. "He killed them out of petty spite, all because I was ploughing his wife behind his back. If you could see what they did to my family, Bearn, your stomach would churn –"

"Grimm, you know I'll never betray the crown. I can't let you escape."

"I was The Shield of the Isles, and I did everything asked of me, without batting an eye! I butchered men, murdered women, and burned entire villages to the ground, and what're the thanks I get? A damned target on my back! Where's your loyalty to me? I saved your life more times than I can count. Gods, Bearn, I even gifted you your Jarldom, and you want to betray me as well?"

"You murdered Uthredd's brother, Grimm!" Bearn shouted. "A man you've known since childhood, and you butchered him like a common dog!"

"What about Freja? What about sweet Einar? Do they not deserve justice for how that madman ended their lives?"

"Don't forget you bedded his wife, Grimm. You tarnished their marriage and humiliated him. You had to know that there would be repercussions for your actions."

"That gives him no right to take my family from me. If he wanted retribution, he should've handled it like a man and crossed swords with me."

Bearn fell silent. He collapsed onto his stool and began stroking his braided beard. Grimm took a deep breath and did likewise.

Finally, after a lengthy pause, Bearn broke the silence. "I'm sorry about your family. I truly am. And what you say is true; Eirik's actions were far from honourable. But I can't help you escape the Isles, Grimm; I can't throw away my oaths to Uthredd as easily as you have."

"All I ask for is safe passage through your lands. I'll stick to the woods and avoid roads, except at night. I need to get on a ship that can smuggle me to the mainland. I'm dead if I stay here."

Bearn let out an exasperated sigh. "You're on your own, Grimm, but I'll give you a three-day head start before sending my men after you, as a show of my appreciation for all that you've done for me."

Grimm nodded his head politely. It was not the answer that he wanted, but it was better than having to fight Bearn. He knew that his old friend was probably the only person on the isles that had a chance of beating him in combat. Both men rose to their feet and pulled each other in for a brotherly embrace before they exited the abandoned fishery.

"Good luck, Grimm," Bearn said as, he stepped into his boat. "I truly hope we never meet again."

Grimm nodded his head before turning on his heels and walking back into the forest. The dwarven girl emerged from her hiding spot and tugged at his sleeve. "Where to now?" she asked excitedly.

"I don't know. I just don't know."

CHAPTER EIGHT

ANNA

The early morning frost covered her body. It was as if a sea of sparkling diamonds blanketed her. The small crystals of ice shimmered in the orange glow of the rising sun. The wind was surprisingly calm, which allowed the softest sounds to be heard over great distances.

Anna could hear the diminutive forest creatures scamper up and down the trees, their claws scraping against the hard bark. She reluctantly rose to her feet and stretched her tired, frozen body.

It had been a restless night. The idea of monsters waking from their hibernation filled her body with dread, along with the idea of what the bandits would do to her if she got herself caught. But perhaps the most unsettling thing was the image of her father's mutilated corpse, which plagued her mind throughout her slumber. She didn't want to believe it was true, that it was some kind of trick, but Anna knew in her heart that her father had suffered a horrific end.

She brushed the snow off her pants and stretched her aching legs. She had been running nonstop for days now, and was surprised that she still found herself still within the confines of the forest. Anna had never truly grasped how large this forest was, nor had she grasped the idea of how removed from civilization she and her father actually were.

"If all I see today is more trees, I'm going to lose it," she muttered to herself.

The idea that she was lost had never even occurred to her. Her father was adamant about training her to navigate through the forest blindfolded. It became so mundane that she had memorized every twig, root, and tree near their hut; but she had never ventured this far from home before, and these were new trees, twigs, and roots.

Anna's stomach suddenly gurgled. She reached down, brushed the snow off her father's cache, and retrieved the last piece of salted meat.

"Shit," she cursed, as she greedily devoured the strip of meat. She had been too reckless with her rations, and would now have to rely on the benevolence of the forest to provide for her. Anna knew that the forest was rarely kind to those in need.

She picked the gristle from her teeth and marched north, hoping to eventually find a main road that would lead towards Winterhelm. The cold winter air stung her cheeks as she walked; the slightest breeze made her teeth burn with pain. Her eyelashes soon stuck together with frost every time she blinked. The sensation of her eyelids ripping apart from one another always unnerved her, as she was scared that next time, she wouldn't be able to pull them apart.

Winters in the forest had always been cold, but this year was different. The temperature was the lowest it had been in recent memory. The wind seemed to have an inexplicably harsh bite to it this year, and the amount of snow was almost terrifying.

Anna's father had told tales of The Great Blizzard, a snowstorm so violent that it covered the tallest pines in the forest in a thick blanket of snow. She knew to approach these stories with a certain skepticism. She noticed that the more ancient the event, the more unbelievable the story would be. Undoubtedly, because of the storyteller's embellishment.

Suddenly, there was a crash and a hard thud to her right. In a single movement, Anna dropped to her knees and readied her bow with an arrow. After a few seconds of silence, she rose to her feet, bow still drawn, and approached the source of the sound. There was another loud crack, and, this time, she saw a treetop fall to the ground. Anna's heart leapt into her throat, but she knew she couldn't throw caution to the wind. She crouched low and approached the fallen trees.

In a matter of minutes, Anna was within eyesight of the toppled trees and saw that there was a company of men working. Some had saws, others had axes, some stripped the bark from the trees, while others split the trunks into logs.

Anna wasn't sure if these men belonged to the bandits that attacked her and her father, but her growling stomach pleaded for her to see if they had any scraps of food. She set her bow on her shoulder and approached the group of strangers, palming her knife in her hand, just in case.

"Whoa!" an older man shouted, as he waved his hands frantically. "Which one of ye brought yer daughter to work?"

Suddenly, all the men's eyes turned towards Anna, and she immediately felt vulnerable. *This must be how a deer feels when it's surrounded by wolves.* She slid the blade deeper up her sleeve. Her fingers played along the bone handle.

"She's covered in blood!" one man shouted.

"Why does she have a bow?" a young lumberjack asked. Anna turned her attention to him and was immediately flushed with a warmth in her stomach. He was around her age, but his body was toned with bulging muscle. He had a thin, patchy beard and a dark set of brown eyes.

"Are ye hurt, little girl?" the older man asked, bending down, so that he was at eye level with her.

"No," Anna replied.

"Where are yer parents?" he asked.

"Gone."

"So, you're out here all alone then, eh?" another lumberjack sneered. Anna glared at the man, but he seemed unfazed. He had a firm jaw and a short neck. Despite having an overhanging gut, she could tell that his arms and chest were quite strong.

"Keep it in yer pants, Lurtch," the bent down man ordered.

"I'm just saying she looks like she's been through a lot, could use the soothing company of a man." Lurtch smiled, as he grabbed his crotch aggressively.

Anna was tempted to send her knife spinning into the man's stubby little neck, but thought better of it. *These lumberjacks might be able to point me in the right direction.*

She turned her attention to the older logger talking to her. He had soft blue eyes and a thick grey beard. His face was riddled with wrinkles and scars, and it was hard to discern which were which. The man stroked his beard thoughtfully, and, with a painful grunt rose to his feet.

"Let's get her back to camp," the man ordered. "She's probably starving."

"Girls are only useful for three things," Lurtch interjected. "Cleaning, cooking, and fucking."

Anna once again turned her attention to the short-necked man, and her eyes narrowed with angered scrutiny. She fantasized about taking his life, but her growling stomach forced her to concede. The old man was right: she was hungry, and was in no position to turn down a free meal.

The group of men quickly began loading up their carts with the lumber they had collected. Anna was amazed by how fast they worked. Each man moved with the speed and strength of three. They tossed the heavy logs with unnatural ease into the back of the carts, and stacked them with expert efficiency.

In a manner of minutes, all of the trees had been chopped, loaded, and neatly piled into the wagons. Anna couldn't help but wonder what her father might have thought if he could have seen the strange men work.

"Hi, I'm Olaf," the young lumberjack said, interrupting Anna's thoughts.

The warmth in her stomach soon returned, and her fingers twitched uncontrollably. She had never felt this way before; the closest she had experienced was the excitement before a hunt.

"Do you have a name?" Olaf asked.

"Anna."

"That's a very lovely name," Olaf gushed, as he failed to meet her piercing gaze. "Would you like to ride back to camp with me?"

Anna nodded her head, followed the young woodsman to one of the ox-driven carts, and climbed into the back with him. It wasn't long before the rest of the lumberjacks climbed into the back of their respective wagons, and soon the convoy started noisily rolling through the forest.

"What happened to you?" Olaf asked, as he pointed at the frozen blood that covered Anna's clothes.

"A monster," Anna replied. "I killed it."

"Bullshit!" Lurtch called out from his wagon.

Before Anna could respond, Olaf reached out and grasped her hand. "Don't mind him. He's just hungry." The young man's smile sent a wave of comfort through her body, and she absentmindedly wrapped her fingers around the boy's calloused hand. "What kind of monster was it? A werewolf? Vampire?"

"A corvan."

"A what?"

"A corvan," Anna repeated louder, not sure if the boy was hard of hearing.

"No, I heard you, but what is that?" Olaf asked, his fingers loosening slightly.

Anna's fingers reactively tightened around the lumberjack's hand. She couldn't understand why, but the feeling of holding this boy's hand was something that seemed to ease her troubled mind. The images of her father's corpse faded away, and for the briefest of moments, she focused solely on the company of the young woodsman. Olaf smiled and tightened his grip around her hand.

Although they continued to hold each other's hands, the two failed to say another word to one another throughout the rest of the journey. Instead, Anna watched the activities of the other lumberjacks with fervent curiosity. The men sang songs she had not heard before, the lyrics often graphic and sexual, and they passed around a large metal container to one another, each taking small drinks from the canister.

"What is that?" Anna asked.

"Dwarven mead!" Lurtch called out, as he handed up a bottle of the drink to her. "Go on, take a sip. It'll put hair on your chest."

Anna unscrewed the lid and sniffed the bottle. Her nostrils immediately began to burn. She turned her head away and started coughing uncontrollably. She looked around the convoy and saw nothing but reassuring glances.

Reluctantly, she put the bottle to her lips and poured the liquid into her mouth. It was as if she was swallowing fire; despite the drink being cold, the liquor burned her tongue and throat as it flowed down into her belly. She quickly removed the bottle from her lips and once again began coughing.

Then, almost instantly, her vision became blurred, and the chill from the cold winter breeze soon faded. She looked around at the lumberjacks, but could no longer make out their faces. Her fingers felt numb, and her body involuntarily swayed from side to side. The loggers started to laugh, including Olaf. Anna clenched her numbed hands into fists.

"How'd that feel, girl?" Lurtch called out, as he cracked the reins.

"It tastes awful," Anna muttered as she passed the bottle to the blurred form of Olaf beside her.

"That's how you know it's the good stuff!" Lurtch laughed. "Dwarves only have two talents: forging weapons and making a strong brew."

Anna didn't like the feeling of being drunk. It made her feel even more vulnerable. It dulled all of her senses to the point that she felt utterly helpless. She wasn't even sure if she could throw a knife into Lurtch's neck from five feet away, even though she still really wanted to.

Anna flexed her hands together to abate the numbness, but it was no use. The effects of the mead were too strong for her fourteen-year-old body.

"When will it stop?" she asked, as she suddenly felt a gurgle in her stomach.

"In a few hours," one lumberjack reassured.

Anna quickly leaned over the side of the cart and began vomiting profusely. The bile stung her throat as it surged upward and out of her mouth. Her body heaved violently as it expelled the foul-tasting liquor from her body. Once again, the lumberjacks erupted in laughter.

"Get some rest, girl: it'll sober ye up," the elderly man instructed from the adjacent cart. "We'll wake you when we get to camp."

With a spinning head, Anna laid down on the pile of logs, which was surprisingly comfortable, and closed her eyes.

The sound of drunken merrymaking jarred Anna from her alcohol-induced slumber. She opened her aching eyes and saw that the world was still slightly spinning. She let out a groan of pain as she massaged her throbbing temples. Her stiff body cried in pain as she climbed out of the back of the cart. As soon as her feet hit the ground, she immediately staggered, somehow managing not to fall over. She felt like an utter fool.

The company of lumberjacks had gathered around a large bonfire and were already passing more drinks around. Anna's stomach churned at the thought of drinking more of the foul-tasting liquor. The loud, drunken shenanigans came to a sudden stop once they saw that Anna had awakened.

"Look who it is!" Lurtch called out, as he took a swig from a near-empty bottle of liquor.

"How're ye feeling, girl?" the old man asked.

"Ugh…" Anna grumbled, as she tried to shake the numbness out of her fingers.

"Knew we shouldn't've given you the mead. It'll knock a grown man on his arse. Can't imagine how yer feeling right now."

"Pah!" Lurtch spat. "She's just ready for a party. Come, girl, take a seat on my lap."

Anna scowled at the woodsman, walked to the opposite side of the fire, and sat beside Olaf. The young lumberjack smiled at her, and once again, the warm feeling in her gut returned. He then reached out and put a hand on Anna's thigh. The sensation took her aback, but yet it was oddly comfortable. She couldn't help but wonder what her father would have said if he were alive to see it.

"Look at these two lovebirds!" one lumberjack called out.

"They make a cute couple," another called out. "We should have a wedding."

"Shut up," Olaf retorted, crimson-faced.

"Listen, girl," Lurtch began. "If you want to experience a real man and not a boy, then come over here, and I'll show you a good time."

Anna could feel her face flush with colour. Partly out of anger, partly out of embarrassment. Being the centre of attention was not a welcome sensation. It made her feel like an object, rather than a person. "I'd like to turn in for the night," she announced loudly. Olaf quickly removed his hand.

"Ye can stay in my tent," the older man responded. "I always slept better under the stars, anyway."

Anna nodded her head in thanks and quickly shuffled towards the large tent on the edge of the camp, although calling it a tent was a bit of an exaggeration. The shelter was two large branches staked in the ground, with a large white canvas sheet draped over the top. Inside, the floor was loosely decorated with furs and two pillows. She reluctantly laid down on the hides and closed her eyes. The lumberjacks' voices cut through the evening air like knives slicing through a stick of butter.

"Gods, what a girl!" Olaf exclaimed.

"Today was a good day," another lumberjack agreed.

"Listen," the old man instructed. "I don't want any of ye to bother her while she sleeps. I'm the foreman here, and if I catch anyone disobeying my orders, I'll send ye home with no pay. Understood?" The group of men let out a collective groan but ultimately agreed to the supervisor's terms.

"You're a lucky lad, Olaf," Lurtch said.

"How so?"

"If that lil' thing were sweet on me, I would bend her over and take her right here in front of all of you!"

Anna cringed at the sound of the man's voice. She could see how his shadow moved against the canvas sheet, and it made her skin crawl. Her father had taught her about where babies had come from when she bled for the first time, and she assumed that Lurtch was alluding to having sex with her. She pulled her knife from her belt and placed it underneath her pillow. *If he tries anything tonight, I'll be ready.*

The lumberjacks continued to keep her awake with their buffoonery for several more hours. Most of the time, they talked about what they would do when they were back home with their pay. Many stated that their first stop would be an alehouse, even though Anna thought they had drunk enough ale in their lifetime already.

She found the conversations extremely curious. These men were obsessed with sex and drinking. *Are all men like this? Father wasn't. I rarely seen him even pick up a bottle.* She then remembered her father's obsession with monsters, how their house was teeming with obscure tomes about creatures that were so rare that they were only seen once in a generation. *Perhaps everyone needs an obsession.*

After another hour, the fire died down, and the men returned to their respective tents. Anna couldn't help but breathe a sigh of relief and closed her eyes. The effects of the dwarven mead were gradually fading. The world had stopped spinning, and feeling was beginning to return to her fingers. She caressed the handle of her knife underneath the pillow as she slowly drifted off to sleep.

Suddenly, there was the sound of crunching snow approaching her tent. Anna could tell that they belonged to a heavy man. She spun the knife around in her hand and gripped the blade carefully. She then rolled slightly on her side, to more easily throw it at the intruder when he undoubtedly entered her tent.

The footsteps stopped just outside the shelter. Anna could hear heavy breathing on the other side. She slowly pulled the knife out from underneath the pillow and prepared to throw it as soon as she heard the canvas sheet move.

After a few seconds, she heard it. The almost silent sound of flesh dragging across cloth. The knife leapt from her hands and tumbled through the air towards her attacker.

There was a hard thud, and then the sound of gurgling filled the night air. Anna smiled as she pictured Lurtch choking on his own blood outside the tent. She hoped that the last few minutes of his life were spent in a panic-filled fear as the blood squirted from his stump-like neck.

Anna arose from her covers and pulled back the canvas sheet. She let out an audible gasp when she saw that her intruder was not Lurtch, but Olaf. The young lumberjack spasmed wildly as he clutched the knife that was protruding from his throat.

Anna froze in place. All she could do was watch Olaf's fear-filled eyes as they came to the inevitable realization that she had killed him.

It took several minutes for the boy's body to stop writhing.

Anna quickly looked around the camp to see if anyone was still awake and might have witnessed the murder. Thankfully, they were all still in their tents.

She pulled the knife out of Olaf's neck and began running away from the encampment, unsure of where she would end up.

CHAPTER NINE

ELBERT

The healer's hut was unbearably warm. Smoke from the incense filled the cramped shack, as rays of light poured through the thatched ceiling. The sides of the hut were covered with shelves that teemed with jars of various plants and herbs. Elbert rolled his eyes as the healer grabbed another jar from the shelf and filled her syringe with the clear liquid.

"Smells awful," he said, as he plugged his nose.

"Rotflower extract," the healer replied. "Aptly named, as many hunters confuse the plant for a decaying corpse when smelled at a distance."

Elbert nodded politely, and breathed through his mouth to spare himself of the putrid aroma, which inexplicably cut through the pleasant smell of the incense.

"This may hurt, Your Majesty," the healer continued, as she readied her syringe.

"Trust me, I can handle–" Elbert started, before he yelped in pain as the elven healer stabbed the needle deep into his spine. It felt like he had been stuck on this table for eternity.

"Try to wiggle your toes," the elf instructed.

Elbert focused on his toes and tried to move them out of sheer will, but it was no use. His feet lay there motionless, as if they belonged to a corpse. He let out a frustrated sigh and slammed his fist on the table. "You're supposed to be the best healer in the kingdom! How is it that even you can't help me?"

"I'm sorry, sire, but it seems that the magic is too powerful to reverse. Perhaps if you consulted a mage—" the elf began.

"Don't you think I've tried that?" Elbert shouted. "My court sorcerer was utterly useless. He claimed it was black magic that stole my legs from me, and the only person who could reverse this curse is the bastard that cast it!"

"I'm... I'm truly sorry, I've–" the elf stammered.

Elbert looked up and saw that she was shaking uncontrollably as she fought off tears. His heart instantly sank. The poor woman was probably scared enough working on a human, let alone a king. He wanted to stand up and comfort her, but alas, he was stranded on the cold wooden table.

"I'm sorry, I shouldn't have yelled," Elbert started, but the elf refused to look at him. "Guards!"

As the two armoured men entered the hut, the elf froze in place. Every muscle in her body visibly tensed. She slowly placed the glass jar back on the shelf and turned around to face the two guardsmen.

"Yes, Your Majesty?" one of the men spoke, in a gravelly voice.

"Get me off this damned table," Elbert demanded plainly.

The crippled king swung his body around so that his lifeless legs dangled from the tabletop. He then reached out with one of his hands and gently grasped the elf's.

Her skin was surprisingly soft to the touch. He half-expected every peasant's hands to be tough and calloused, no matter their profession. He quickly gathered his composure and cleared his throat. "I thank you for your service, milady." He tried to hide the disappointment in his voice. For how much the elven healer charged, he was confident that the woman would have been able to cure his paralysis.

The two guardsmen picked him up, carried his feeble body outside the hut, and laid him down in the carriage, before marching back towards the palace.

On their journey back to the castle, a mob of peasants crowded the roads to look at the new king. Elbert was glad that he had ordered the windows of the carriage boarded up earlier that morning. *They'll have to find out about me, eventually* he thought to himself, as he untied the small wineskin that hung from his belt. He poured the bitter-tasting liquid into his mouth, and didn't stop until he had drunk every last drop.

He tossed the wineskin aside and chuckled to himself quietly. *Father would be proud.* Suddenly, the carriage came to a halt, and the door swung open. Waiting for him on the other side was Sergeant Thames. His helmet was held abreast, and judging by the expression on his misshapen face, he brought ill tidings.

"What is it now?" Elbert snarled.

"My apologies, Your Majesty. I just thought you'd like to know that the lords have gathered in the throne room. It seems they've called an emergency witan."

Elbert felt his neck tighten as he clenched his hands into fists. "Take me to them now!" he yelled.

The two guardsmen who had escorted him into town quickly picked him up and carried his useless body into the castle. Elbert watched the ceiling as the two guards expertly navigated the winding hallways and various stairwells that eventually led to the throne room. *It was designed so that peasants would get lost and we wouldn't have to hear their complaints. Well done, Grandfather.*

After several minutes of hurrying down the numerous corridors, the two guards pushed open the heavy oak doors that led to the throne room. The guardsmen's clanging footsteps echoed off the marble floor as they walked across the cavernous room. Elbert made sure to glare at as many nobles as he could as he was carried across the floor, before being set down on his throne.

"Will someone please explain to me the meaning behind all of this?" Elbert said, his voice filling the room.

"We are planning to elect a new king!" one noble courageously blurted out.

"My, my... I've only been king for a few days, and already I have a rebellion on my hands."

"Surely you will agree that by having a cripple as a king, we will be seen as weak," another noble called out.

Soon, there was a roar of voices filling the throne room, many of them supporting the idea of electing a new, able-bodied ruler. Elbert's body trembled, and he slammed his fist into the gilded armrest of the throne. "Silence!" he shouted. "I will not sit here and let you talk of treason so openly. My father would have had you hanged!"

"But you are not your father, Prince Elbert," Lord Bellston replied, stepping forward from the crowd of noblemen. "I think that I speak for everyone here,when I say that by having you as our king not only makes a mockery of the crown, but of Artanzia itself!" The rest of the nobles shouted in agreement.

Elbert massaged his temples as he tried to regain his resolve. *I can't execute all of them. A shame that they would rather have a drunken buffoon rule them than an ambitious cripple.* "I assure you that I am more than capable of governing this kingdom."

"Nobody doubts your capabilities, sire," Lord Bellston began. "But this is a symbolic matter. How will you lead our armies into battle when you cannot mount a horse? How will you fight for your country when you cannot stand on your own two feet? Or do you expect your guardsmen to carry you everywhere?" The noblemen erupted in a chorus of laughter.

"Get out," Elbert snarled.

"I beg your pardon?"

"Get! Out!" Elbert screamed, as he slammed his fist into the armrest once again.

The noblemen exchanged wary glances with one another before cautiously leaving the throne room. Elbert glared at them while they exited. He wished he could take their legs from them. He wished they could know the pain and humiliation of being a cripple.

As the giant oaken doors shut, Elbert allowed himself to relax, and tears flowed down his face. "How am I to lead this kingdom back to glory when nobody will give me a chance?"

Suddenly, there was a knock on the door. Elbert quickly wiped the tears from his eyes and cleared his throat. "What is it now?"

A servant entered the great throne room and was accompanied by a soot-covered dwarf. The stranger wheeled in a large chair that had a wheel attached to each of its legs. "Presenting Master Arlin, rumoured to be the best blacksmith in the city," the servant declared, before he closed the giant oak doors, leaving the king alone with the dwarf.

"Err... umm... apologies, Your Majesty," Arlin stammered. "I dinnae mean to disturb ye."

"Nonsense! What have you brought me?" Elbert inquired, even though he already knew the answer.

"Sergeant Thames commissioned me to craft something that would allow ye to get around better. I apologize for its crude appearance; I'll spiff up the next one to make sure it's fit for a king."

Elbert smiled. *Thames, the only man who supports me.* "I love it," he said, after a brief pause. "Tell me, how skilled a craftsman are you?"

"I don't mean tah tug my own beard, but there isn't a metal I can't work with," Arlin answered.

"Can you make a replica of my throne and attach wheels to the legs?"

"Absolutely! Shouldn't be a problem."

"How much did Sergeant Thames pay you for this little project?"

"Nothin', Your Majesty. I live to serve the crown."

Elbert let out a quick laugh and clapped his hands together. "Excellent answer. But come now, I can't have such magnificent work go unpaid. How does two hundred crowns sound?"

"I... I..." Arlin blubbered, as he began pinching himself.

"I take it that we are in agreement, then: two hundred crowns for a replica throne on wheels." Suddenly, an idea popped in Elbert's head as he peered down one of the winding corridors. "Tell me, dwarf, can you devise a way for me to climb stairs?"

Arlin cleared his throat. "Shouldn't be a problem, just give me a few days, and I'll have thought of somethin'."

"Very well, I hereby dub you the Royal Artificer and, as such, you are entitled to all the privileges that come with such a title."

Arlin's eyes widened. His mouth moved to form words, but the only sound to escape his lips was a raspy croak.

A smile spread across Elbert's face. "Congratulations; you're Artanzia's first dwarven noble."

The royal bath was a cavernous room tiled from floor to ceiling. Sculpted in the middle of the floor, surrounded by four tiled pillars, was a large, shallow soaking pool. Elbert always came here to think and escape the pressures of royalty, but ever since the royal healer suggested soaking his legs three times a day, he found it much less enjoyable. He knew that the court sorcerer was right. Only the hunchback's magic could undo the curse no matter how long he soaked his legs.

Steam rose relentlessly from the water until a thick fog filled the tiled chamber. Even though he could not see them, Elbert knew his guards were vigilantly standing watch in the corners of the room. He worried that this would be the closest to being alone that he would ever be.

He splashed the water out of frustration. The ripples travelled across the glass-like water to the other end of the pool before bouncing off the tiled wall.

Elbert felt utterly defeated. Without the nobles' support, he knew it was only a matter of time before a coup was organized against him. He briefly wondered who the witan would choose after his deposition. He pictured all the nobles in his mind and scoffed at the very idea of them sitting on the royal throne.

Save one: Lord Bellston. He was a respected man among the populace and would undoubtedly have the support of the other lords.

"I have to find some way to stall them," Elbert mentioned aloud.

"I beg your pardon, sire?" one guard responded.

"Nothing. Never mind," Elbert ordered.

He then stared down at his reflection, as if that version of himself had any of the answers he sought. The reflection greeted him with an unrelenting silence. He put his hands on the tiled floor behind him and raised himself out of the pool. "Guards!" he called out.

"Yes, Your Majesty?" they responded in unison.

"Fetch me Sergeant Thames. I have a matter to discuss with him."

The sound of armoured footsteps echoed throughout the royal bath as the guards exited the room. Elbert then slithered his way across the floor towards the wheeled chair that Arlin had crafted for him. He pushed it backwards until it hit a wall, then began to arduously climb into the seat. After a lengthy battle with the stationary chair, Elbert was able to turn around and sit in the dwarven contraption. He leaned back and rested his head against the wall, hoping to regain some of his breath.

"You summoned me, sire?" Thames' voice called out through the mist.

"Tell me everything you know about Lord Bellston," Elbert ordered.

"Well, he is an honourable man. He has always been kind to me and –"

"Flaws! Weaknesses! I need something I can use against him!"

"Hmm," Thames responded. "I believe he has a love for coin."

"Who doesn't?" Elbert snarled.

"My apologies, sire, he is also known to be quite ambitious and has a love for his children that puts most mothers to shame."

Suddenly, a scheme came into Elbert's head. "Thames, you're a brilliant bastard!"

"I am, sire?"

"Indeed. You just gave me an idea for how to ruin his little plot against me."

"But I have found nothing tangible that links Lord Bellston to a possible rebellion," Thames replied hesitantly.

"Oh, he's a part of it; I guarantee it," Elbert retorted. "Summon him to the throne room and have two guards come in and dress me; I have a proposition for him. One that he likely won't refuse."

"Mind telling me what I'm doing here, Your Majesty?" Lord Bellston said as he executed a perfect bow.

"You are my noble; you will come whenever you are summoned. Besides, we have business to discuss."

"We do?"

"Yes. I believe you have a daughter. Am I correct?"

"I do," Bellston said with narrowing eyes.

"Excellent news. I hereby offer my hand in marriage to your lovely daughter."

"You what?"

Elbert leaned forward in his throne. "I offer my hand in marriage to your daughter," he said, careful to enunciate each word clearly so he wouldn't have to repeat himself for a third time.

"Of course! That would be most agreeable!"

"Excellent! We will hold the ceremony tomorrow, in front of the entire kingdom. Let our two houses finally join and become stronger as one."

"I couldn't've said it better myself, Your Majesty." Bellston graciously bowed once more and exited the throne room.

Elbert leaned back in his throne and laughed as he watched the fooled man exit the palace. *That's right: slither away, you viper. Slink back to your cave filled with your brethren and tell them what happened. Tell them how you can't incite a revolution now that you have an invaluable informant by my side. "Father always said, keep your enemies close"... perhaps the old drunkard actually knew something.*

The cathedral was filled with people: both nobles and commoners alike. The creaking pews echoed throughout the marbled room as people shifted their weight from side to side, trying to get comfortable. Royal weddings were always tediously long, and the benches were notoriously hard on one's back. Light poured in through the stained glass windows, and illuminated the church to the point where Elbert had to shield his eyes from the reflections off the floor.

He silently shut the oaken doors to the chapel and wheeled his chair down the hallway back to his room. His nerves were eating away at him as a sea of doubt clouded his mind. He wasn't nervous about being wed. He honestly couldn't care less: Bellston's daughter was just a means to an end. His trepidation stemmed from the fact that this would be his first public appearance since he lost his legs. The possibility of the masses rejecting him as king pained him more than he cared to admit.

His room was at the end of the hallway on the left-hand side, the bride's room was on the right. He stopped between the doors and listened carefully to what was happening in the room opposite to his. He heard the faint sound of a bodice being tightened and the muffled tears of either the bride or her mother. *Nobody wants to be married to half a king.* He then turned his chair and opened the door to his chambers.

Standing inside was the seamstress, a few royal guards, and Sergeant Thames. All of them looked at the king with grave expressions.

"Are you feeling ill, sire?" Sergeant Thames asked.

"Not at all," Elbert lied. "Though the sooner I can get out of these clothes, the happier I'll be. No offence, milady."

The seamstress let out a contemptuous snort but failed to voice any grievances.

"Did you see the bride?" Elbert asked, once again turning his attention to Thames.

"I did, Your Majesty."

"Is she attractive?"

"Very."

"Good," Elbert said, as he breathed a sigh of relief. "I'd hate to take a sow to bed."

"Not like it matters, anyway," one guard whispered loudly.

Elbert quickly turned his head and glared at the man. But before he could discipline the man, Sergeant Thames cut in. "You're relieved of your duty, recruit. I want you to climb the north tower fifty times. Perhaps that will purge you of your treasonous thoughts, and teach you to mind your tongue."

The guard's face slackened, but he quickly gathered his resolve and exited the room with a sharp salute. A smile crept onto Elbert's face. *I would've taken his head, but perhaps ascending all two thousand steps in the north tower is a worse fate.* Suddenly, there was a knock at the door. "Come in!" Elbert shouted.

The priest silently entered the room. He was a stout man without a single hair on his head, save for his bushy grey eyebrows. He performed a flawless bow as he greeted the king, but failed to make eye contact with Elbert, as all good subjects should. "We are ready for you, sire," the priest announced.

Elbert let out a sigh. "Very well. Let's get this over with."

As he followed the priest to the chapel, he couldn't help but notice that his hands were sweating profusely. Every now and then, his hands would slip on the cold metal wheels of his chair. He was tempted to wipe his hands on his robes, but he knew that it would leave stains. *They'll already have enough reasons to reject me; best not to give them any more.*

As he entered the cathedral, everyone rose to their feet and turned to greet him. However, almost uniformly, everyone's face paled at the sight of Elbert. Hushed whispers filled the large room, and he could've sworn he heard a few sniggers.

Elbert's face began to redden as he tried to maintain his composure. As he wheeled himself down the aisle, he made a point of not looking anyone in the eye, and making sure that his nose was pointed towards the ceiling.

The sound of the metal wheels rolling on the marbled floor filled the entire room, and was the only thing to cut through the air of awkward silence. The roll down the centre aisle was only thirty feet, but it seemed to span a lifetime.

Sweat gathered on the back of Elbert's neck as he pushed his chair forward. His eyes darted from side to side, tempted to gaze at the gawking faces of those who lined the pews of the cathedral. He stopped at the steps in front of the altar and waited silently, until the guards lifted his chair and placed him beside the priest.

Suddenly, horns sounded from the back of the church, and everyone turned towards the oaken doors in unison. Accompanied by her father was Elbert's bride-to-be. When Sergeant Thames claimed she was attractive, he never would have pictured this. It was as if someone had brought an effigy of a goddess to life. She had long, golden blonde hair and a slender figure. Her face was perfectly symmetrical, and the only flaw in her appearance was her two different coloured eyes: one green and one blue.

Thankfully, she takes after her mother, Elbert thought to himself, as he wiped the sweat from his forehead with the back of his hand. *A shame that someone so beautiful has to marry a cripple.* The Lady Bellston quietly made her way towards the altar without taking her eyes off the king. Her stare was surprisingly warm and not full of disdain or disgust, as Elbert had predicted it would be. They linked hands with one another, and nodded at the priest to begin the ceremony.

"Greetings!" the priest bellowed. "We are gathered here today to see these two families joined in holy matrimony."

"What's your name?" Elbert whispered as the priest continued to ramble.

"Vivian," she replied meekly.

"I'm Elbert."

"I know," she replied kindly. She squeezed his hands tighter, and peered deeper into his eyes.

"Are you nervous?"

"Very. Never thought I'd marry a king."

"Or a cripple," Elbert added under his breath.

"The Gods ordained your family to rule, and nobody can take that away from you. Cripple or not."

A smile crept across Elbert's lips as he turned his attention back to the priest. He was rambling on about the Gods and their divine mission to lead Artanzia to glory, and how this union would strengthen the kingdom as a whole. Elbert struggled to contain his laughter. He knew that these were the same recycled lines that the clergy used for every royal wedding. *One man writes a speech, and it remains unchanged for generations.*

The ceremony itself passed by rather quickly. Something about holding Vivian's hand and staring into her mismatched eyes made the entire ordeal tolerable. At the end of the ceremony, the priest pronounced them king and queen, and ordered them to kiss. Her lips were soft, and the scent of her perfume lingered in his nose for several seconds afterwards.

The crowd erupted in obligatory applause as the new couple left the cathedral. Elbert wheeled his chair with one hand, and with the other hand, he maintained a firm grip on his wife's. The guards continued to escort them outside the church and along the road back to the palace. The commoners who couldn't get entrance into the cathedral lined the streets, and threw bouquets of flowers along the cobblestone path, as the couple ascended the road to the castle. The wheels of Elbert's chair clunked as they smacked against the hard stones of the road. A small bead of sweat trickled down the king's brow. The muscles in his arms cried in agony as they tried to fight the uneven surface of the cobbled street. *Perhaps I should have someone push me,* he thought to himself.

"Let me push you," Vivian said, as she looked down at her sweating husband.

"No need; I'm fine," he said, unwilling to appear weak to his new wife.

"A king should not be seen struggling so hard to move. The peasants will think you're weak."

"They'll see me as weak, regardless," Elbert retorted.

There was a slight twitch in the queen's face, but it disappeared and was quickly replaced by a flawless smile. "At least have one of your guards push you. I don't want you to be too tired for our wedding night nuptials."

Elbert begrudgingly nodded his head and waved Sergeant Thames over. "Sergeant, my arms tire. I want you to push me the rest of the way."

"Yes, Your Majesty," Thames replied dutifully.

Several times on the journey back to the palace, Elbert couldn't help but look into the crowd of strangers and read their expressions. Most hid their surprise well, but there were a few who had a look of shock plastered on their faces at the sight of their handicapped king. He made a mental note of their faces for the next petition day, making sure that he would deny their request, or rule against them, in whatever grievance they brought forward.

The halls of the castle were teeming with usually unseen servants, who had taken a brief pause in their duties to applaud the new couple as they were escorted towards the royal chambers. Many of the servants had a veiled look of surprise once their eyes landed on the king, who sat motionless in his chair. Elbert grimaced at the thought of so many eyes on his useless body. It seemed that everyone was judging him, even though they had no authority to do so.

The doors to the lavish royal chambers were held open for the king and queen, and once they entered, were closed and wouldn't open until morning, as per tradition. Elbert immediately poured himself a glass of wine and began massaging his temples.

"What's on your mind, husband?" Vivian asked.

"Nothing," Elbert lied.

"I am your wife now. Your problems are my problems," she retorted.

"How dare they? How dare they look at me with pity? How dare they judge me? I could see it in all of their eyes: how they were disgusted by me, their king!" Elbert's voice was soon echoing throughout the room, and was undoubtedly leaking through the large wooden doors, but he didn't care. He actually hoped that some of the servants and guards heard his anger. Maybe if they feared him, they would show him respect. "They openly mock me. They certainly ridicule me behind my back. They are treating me as if I'm not a king!"

"May I make a suggestion, husband?" Vivian responded after a lengthy silence. Elbert nodded his head. "It is like you said: the people will think you are weak simply because of your condition." She slowly walked over to Elbert and wrapped her smooth, silk-like hands around his. "But actions can always change their opinions. Peasants are no more intelligent than the deer who live in the forest. Both are mindless beasts that are easily tricked."

"Then what should I do?" Elbert inquired.

"Do something no other king has ever done. Launch a raid against the Mjältön Isles."

Elbert scrunched up his nose and tore his hands free of his wife's velvety touch, despite how much it pained him to do so. "That's rich!" he said with a faux laugh. "A cripple sailing across the sea to wage war against a bunch of barbarians leaves the kingdom in the hands of his wife, who just so happens to be the daughter of the man who mocks me openly. Did your father put you up to this? Do you expect me to fall for that?"

"But I am loyal to you, husband."

"How can I trust you?"

Vivian paused for a moment. The twitch in her face returned, but only for the briefest of seconds, before it disappeared again. She then walked towards the small maple table that held the pitcher of wine before pouring herself a glass. Once filled, she took a small sip, the red liquid staining her lips as she pulled the cup away from her face. "Let me tell you something, Elbert. My father is planning an insurrection, and has instructed me to be an informant. Unfortunately for him, I believe in the sanctity of our marriage, and I promise to be loyal to you till the day we die. In order to prove what I say is the truth, I can get you all the evidence you need to execute my father. Associates, meeting places, documents: everything."

Elbert felt his mouth begin to salivate as he fantasized about disposing of Lord Bellston. The sight of the executioner's axe severing the noble's head from his neck filled the king's body with glee. Suddenly, there was a nagging feeling at the back of Elbert's mind. *What if this is a ruse to gain my trust?* He quickly gathered his composure, swallowed his childlike giddiness, and wheeled his chair over to her. "Why tell me all of this? Why are you willing to betray your father?"

Vivian smiled. "For power. He wants to get rid of you so that the witan elects him as the new king. If that happens, I will lose my position as queen, and now that I am here, I have no intention of losing my crown."

Elbert couldn't help but smile. *Just as ambitious as her father. Perhaps she can be more than a pawn.* He reached out, caressed her cheek, and pulled her head down until they locked lips. A smile once again crept its way onto Elbert's lips, as he pictured the headsman decapitating Lord Bellston.

CHAPTER TEN

GRIMM

Travelling at night always proved to be a dangerous endeavour. Bandits and highwaymen patrolled the roads, while murderous monsters lurked in the forests, just out of eyesight.

And that was when the High King didn't have his men scouring the Isles trying to find him.

Grimm knew that his chances of making it to the coast were slim, but they grew even slimmer every day that he allowed the dwarven girl to remain with him. He had hoped that, by this point, she would have gotten bored with the monotonous walking and scarce eating, but somehow the child endured. He had thought about abandoning her. It wouldn't be hard, but he couldn't bring himself to do it. Something about leaving a child helpless and alone in a forest filled with ravenous creatures made him sick to his stomach.

"Where are we going?" she asked for the umpteenth time.

"The coast," Grimm responded gruffly.

"Why?"

"So we can hopefully flag down a ship to take us to the mainland."

The dwarven girl crossed her arms, sat down in the snow, and let out an exhausted sigh. "My feet hurt."

"I'm not carrying you," Grimm retorted. They had been travelling long enough together that he had begun to figure out the little girl's games. "Focus on something else. It'll take your mind away from the pain."

"Like what?"

Grimm ground his teeth together. He hated answering the juvenile's questions. He looked around the forest and saw nothing but the pine trees' dark silhouettes. "Count how many trees there are," he suggested after a lengthy pause.

"There are so many! There's got to be at least a hundred!" the girl shouted.

He winced at the loud noise, and his heart sank. *If any creatures weren't aware of us before, they sure as fuck know now.* He brought a single finger close to his lips, and listened to the forest for any disturbances in the snow. The little girl quickly covered her mouth with her hands and listened as well.

Grimm could hear the rustle of the pine needles as the wind blew through them. He also heard the faint hopping of a rabbit bounding through the snow. It was a frigid night, and he was surprised to find anything else stirring in the forest besides them.

He almost regretted choosing the woods over the roads. The roads would have been quicker and less dangerous, but he couldn't bear to think of what would happen to the girl if a band of highwaymen got their hands on her. As a result, against his better judgement, he chose the forest.

He waved his hand for the dwarf to follow and began walking through the snow, being careful where he placed his feet. *Better to err on the side of caution,* he told himself, as he continued to scan the trees for unseen threats.

The girl did not share his sense of caution as she jumped from footstep to footstep, humming loudly. It was becoming increasingly difficult for Grimm to keep his temper under control. He was tempted to scold and yell at the child several times, but once again, his heart failed him. Instead, he repressed his anger, and cracked his knuckles as a release.

"What's your name?" the girl suddenly asked.

"What?"

"Your name? What is it?"

"Grimm White-Eyes."

"That's a silly name."

"What's yours?"

"Sara."

"Around these parts, many would consider that a silly name."

"Why are your eyes white?" she asked.

Grimm let out a long sigh. He loathed having to retell this story. Not only was it painful for him, but he doubted that the child could comprehend it, which would lead to a plethora of more questions. "I was born with them," he said after a momentary pause. "My parents thought me blind when I was born, so they abandoned me in the woods for the wolves to feed on. But after three days, I somehow showed up on their doorstep, alive and covered in blood. From that day on, many people believed Heimer himself blessed me."

"Who's that?"

"Heimer is the god that forged the world. He shaped, designed, and created everything that we see around us. We are all his children, and as a result, we will all one day go up to see him and feast together in The Great Hall, provided you die a warrior's death with a weapon in your hand."

"I'm hungry," Sara said.

"We ate four hours ago."

"But my stomach hurts."

Grimm couldn't help but laugh. For someone who was once a slave, she certainly complained a lot. He stopped for a moment and scanned the trees once again. The landscape was starting to look familiar, and he thought he might know where they were. "Follow me. There's a lake nearby, and we can try our luck at fishing."

Sara's eyes lit up, and she began excitedly stepping in his footsteps towards the lake. He wasn't sure why he kept making concessions to the girl. Perhaps his paternal instincts were coming back, or perhaps he felt responsible for her being stranded out here with him. Perhaps it was a little bit of both.

His mind wandered back to the happy memories of his family. He remembered how he used to spar with his son, and how his wife would nag him for being too hard on the boy. He would give anything to hear his wife's nagging voice one last time.

The shore of the lake was covered in little black stones. The frozen water loomed beyond it like a sheet of frosted glass. Grimm had been to this lake only once before, and the sour memory came flooding back.

Many summers ago, on this very shore, was the first time he was forced to execute a man. Killing someone in battle was one thing, an honourable and noble way to take someone's life. But to kill a man who was already defeated, while they were bound and forced on to their knees: that was another thing entirely.

He had tried to make the death swift, but this was when he was still young and incapable of fully swinging a sword. The blade failed to sever the man's head in one swing. It took another two chops before the man's head was separated from his body.

Grimm stared at the rocks that covered the beach and was sure he could still see the bloodstains from the bound man. He didn't even know his name. All he knew was that the man supported the wrong king in the wrong war, and as a result, was denied entry to The Great Hall. He shook the thoughts out of his head and realized that Sara was already bounding onto the ice. The frozen water bobbed and shook with every step.

"Sara, don't!" he called out, but it was too late. With a sharp crack, she disappeared beneath the ice. He quickly shed his clothes and sprinted onto the ice. By some miracle, he reached the hole in the ice where the dwarf had fallen in, and dived in after her.

The icy chill of the water shocked his system as he swam deeper and deeper into the lake. The lake water burned his eyes as he forced them open in an attempt to find her.

After a few seconds of panicked searching, he found Sara's lifeless body sinking lower and lower into the lake. He kicked his legs harder and swam with vicious ferocity.

Reaching out, he grabbed her arm and began pulling her back up towards the surface. His body heat was rapidly escaping him as he swam upward. He knew he would not have long before he passed out.

Suddenly, he saw something big swim past, out of the corner of his eyes, and his heart sank. He knew they were not alone in the lake.

Upon breaking the water's surface, Grimm took a deep breath in and tossed Sara's limp body onto the ice. He then lifted himself out of the water, when something hard scraped his foot.

With a renewed sense of urgency, he kicked his legs feverishly, crawled out, and laid his body flat on the frozen lake, spreading his body weight evenly.

He wrapped Sara in his arms and began crawling towards the shore. The ice burned his naked back as he propelled himself forward with his numb legs.

It took only a few minutes to reach the beach, but it felt like a lifetime. He quickly rolled Sara off his chest, and began compressions to expel the water from her lungs.

His heart raced wildly as he pushed down on the child's body. *Don't you die on me, dwarf.* Part of his mind couldn't help but think this was a blessing. He'd no longer have to listen to annoying questions and could travel peacefully to the coast. But he shook the thoughts out of his head.

Another part of his mind began nagging him that it was his fault. How he failed to stop Sara in time, and how she would be another body on his conscience.

As the winter winds burned his wet and almost naked body, Sara suddenly coughed, and water spewed out of her mouth. Grimm breathed a sigh of relief and rolled her on to her side. He then stood up and began to put on his dry clothes, when there was a sudden crack from the lake.

Emerging from the waters was a colossal beast that was covered in a hard chitinous shell. It had a long spear-like tail, and mandibles that could easily sever a man in half.

Grimm watched in horror as the creature swam towards the shore, splitting the ice in two. He quickly grabbed his sword and charged forward to meet the beast at the edge of the lake.

The creature roared, as it attacked with its tail first. The sound of the barbed tip hissed through the air, but Grimm was able to dodge it easily enough.

However, the force of the impact shook the beach, and he quickly lost his footing. The crab-like creature swept its tail sideways across the beach and took Grimm's legs out from underneath him.

He lay on his back, winded, staring up at the night sky, when he saw the beast's huge mandibles slowly approaching him. He waited until they were a mere arm's length away before slashing his sword and severing one in half.

Black blood exploded from the wound, and the monster hissed and clicked in pain. Grimm quickly rolled to his feet and pierced his blade into the creature's mouth.

More black blood and another scream of pain erupted from the beast. This time, the creature countered with another stab of its tail. Grimm tried to parry the attack, but the monster was too strong.

The barbed tail punctured his shoulder. He felt the serrated edges of the tail cut muscles and tissue as it went into his body, then he felt the same edges rip the muscles and tissue on the way out.

Grimm collapsed in pain and reached out for his sword with his good hand. He crawled back towards Sara, thinking that fleeing might be his best bet.

He had never fought a creature of this size before; he didn't even know what it was. All he knew was that the monster had the upper hand.

The hissing of the tail signified that it was going to strike again. He quickly rolled out of the way and let the spear-like tip stab the stony shore of the beach. He then swung his sword with all his might, trying to sever the tip of the tail, but his blade bounced hard off the chitinous shell.

"Shit," he cursed to himself quietly.

He stood back, staring at the monstrous beast, wondering how in the world he was going to kill it. Then, after a moment's pause, an idea popped into his head.

He tossed his sword aside and charged toward the creature. He avoided the crushing mandibles with ease and grabbed on to one of the monster's legs.

The hard shell made it easy for Grimm to climb on top of the beast, despite his one shoulder burning in pain. Once on its back, he crawled toward the head of the creature and waited.

He saw the spear-like tip of the tail whirling in the air, preparing for a strike. His eyes widened with excitement as the tail surged towards him.

At the last possible second, he rolled out of the way and let the monster's tail puncture its own brain. The beast's blood spewed from the wound, and it painted the stones of the beach a darker shade of black.

The creature immediately collapsed on the frozen beach, and began writhing and spasming uncontrollably. Grimm fell to his knees with exhaustion.

The pain in his shoulder finally set in, and he touched the wound gingerly as he tried to assess the damage. He thought about cauterizing the wound, but knew no wood was dry enough to start a fire.

He would have to venture into a town tomorrow and find a healer. Grimm shook his head miserably, as he knew that going into town as a wanted man would undoubtedly mean more people would die at the end of his blade.

"Is it dead?" Sara asked, teeth chattering uncontrollably. He quickly realised that the child's condition was another problem he had to fix quickly.

Luckily, there was an easy solution. He grabbed his sword, sliced open the monster's soft underbelly, and began pulling out the innards onto the frozen beach.

"Ew."

"Get in."

"What?"

"Get in. It'll warm you up."

"But I don't want –"

Before she could finish her sentence, Grimm grabbed her by the collar of her shirt, tossed her into the beast's carcass, and crawled in after her. "We'll stay here tonight," he said, leaning back against the beast's shell.

"Thank you," Sara said, as she cuddled up against him.

"Try to get some sleep. We have a big day tomorrow," Grimm said, knowing that the child would see more death the following day.

CHAPTER ELEVEN

ANNA

The wind howled unforgivingly; it was much harsher on the open roads than in the forest. Anna never realized how much the trees protected her. Ever since fleeing the lumberjacks' camp, the country had been open, with scant protection from the elements. Barren plains and empty fields surrounded her, leaving her alone with her thoughts.

Olaf's blood-soaked visage plagued her mind. No matter where she looked, she couldn't shake the image out of her head. It was as if the young lumberjack's spirit haunted her, forcing her to relive the painful memory for eternity. She stared down at her blood-stained hands and noticed that they trembled uncontrollably; she wasn't sure if it was the result of the cold or the guilt.

"Stupid boy," she muttered to herself. "Why were you coming to my tent? Why didn't you just stay by the fire?"

No answer. Save for the wind that cut through her clothes, chilling her to the bone. She pulled out her knife and stared at the crusted blood that stained the blade. She was tempted to toss it away, be rid of the reminder, but her father's lessons once again nagged her. *Never throw away a tool. Even if it is broken, it can still prove valuable in survival.*

"What if I'm broken?" Anna asked aloud as she continued to walk along the road, mind swirling with thoughts of guilt and self-pity, when suddenly she heard galloping hooves.

She sprinted into the ditch and hid behind a large, concave snowdrift, then listened carefully. She counted three horses, and judging by the loud clanking, the men riding them were heavily armoured.

The riders stopped in the middle of the road in front of the snowdrift. Anna held her breath as she reached for her knife. She paused as soon as her fingers touched the bone handle, as she heard one man dismount from his horse.

"We've been riding for three fuckin' days!" one of them complained.

"I've got welts the size of coins on my arse!" another responded.

"Quit yer belly-achin'," the third replied. "We've got to get to Winterhelm by nightfall, so those welts on yer arse will only grow."

"What's the bloody hurry?" the second one asked. "I hear this new king doesn't even have legs!"

"He has legs, ye daft cunt; he's just a cripple!"

"Who the hell is he executin' even?"

"Some lord that apparently plotted against him. I want to be there to see the bastard's head roll," the first responded as he began walking towards Anna's hiding spot.

"And what do ye think yer doing?"

"I'm going to take a piss if that's alright, Your Majesty?"

The third man let out an exasperated sigh and leaned back in his saddle. "Hurry up, we ain't got all day!"

The snow crunched beneath the armoured man's feet as he approached the snowdrift. Anna held her breath. She didn't dare reveal herself to these strange men. Who knows how they'd react to a girl, let alone one that was covered in bloody clothes.

The man let out a groan as his piss hit the peak of the snowdrift. The smell assaulted Anna's nostrils, and she almost gagged, but somehow was able to stop herself.

The putrid scent burned her nostrils as she felt a few warm droplets drip onto her hair from the peak of the snowdrift. She stomached a scream of disgust as she placed a hand over her mouth.

The droplets of urine slowly transformed into a steady stream that poured onto her head from the top of the snowbank. Anna closed her eyes, praying that nothing would leak into them.

After a few painstaking seconds, the man began buckling his trousers and walked away from the snowdrift. The other two men resumed their riding position and took off down the road at a leisurely trot.

Anna peeked her head out from behind the snowdrift and watched until they rode from eyesight. Anna immediately began washing her face and hair with snow as her body squirmed in disgust. She spat from her piss-soaked lips and tried to rub her mouth clean with the snow.

Anna shuddered as the chill from the snow seeped into her body. What she wouldn't give to bathe herself in a river or a hot spring.

She turned to head in the direction the three men rode off in and let out a frustrated sigh. "Two days in the wrong direction." She waddled through the powder back towards the main road, and began following the three men's tracks, keeping an ample distance between them and her. The bandits and the lumberjacks had taught her a valuable lesson, that people viewed her as something rather than someone.

Her stomach growled as she continued down the road. She only wished that she would had had the chance to eat at the woodsmen's camp. The stark landscape offered little in terms of game, thus Anna was forced to starve.

She travelled into the wind, which bit at her cheeks like a ravenous dog. Her eyelids gathered frost and stuck together, as she continued to march forward to Winterhelm.

The sun soon began to set, and the evening chill descended upon her. She hugged herself tightly for warmth, but it was no use: the wind pierced every shred of clothing she had.

Anna was on the verge of collapsing when she saw the orange glow of a fire off in the distance. She also heard the unmistakable sound of a lute being tuned. Then, she smelled the distinct scent of roast pheasant over a fire. Anna's mouth watered as she approached the campsite with caution.

Her instincts told her to ignore the fire, to slip past unnoticed, but her starving stomach had other ideas. The smell was too inviting. She thought about asking the strangers for some of their food, but that was too risky. Who knows what they would want in return? She decided she would sneak into camp and steal whatever scraps they left behind.

Anna fell prone and began crawling towards the fire, making sure to hide behind every drift of snow along the way. As she scanned the campsite, she noticed that it was not the three armoured men from earlier, but a whole caravan.

She also noticed that none of the inhabitants were human. The encampment consisted entirely of elves, dwarves, and halflings, who all seemed to live together. Many were talking with one another, laughing, dancing, enjoying their meagre feast.

Anna couldn't help but watch with mild curiosity. She had heard her father's descriptions of the other races, but he failed to do any of them justice. The elves' ears were far less pointy than she expected, and the halflings looked surprisingly diminutive when compared to the relatively short dwarves. She had heard tales of non-humans being violent towards humans. Thus, remaining unseen seemed to be the safest option.

It wasn't long before the fire in the camp died down and the residents adjourned to their respective tents and wagons. Anna slowly rose to a crouch and stealthily crept into the campsite.

She could still hear the cinders of the fire sizzling as she snuck past a few sleeping elves. She went straight to the firepit and examined the spit for any scraps of food.

Luckily, there were a few morsels of food stuck to the iron rod that hadn't been claimed. She greedily devoured the scraps. She could not remember the last time she was so thankful to have food, even if it was somewhat bland.

Anna looked around the camp as she licked her fingers clean. So far, nobody had awakened. She knew she shouldn't push her luck, but she was still so hungry. She decided to investigate the wagons, to see if there was anything else to feast on. As she walked through the camp, she noticed that one of the sleeping elves had disappeared.

Suddenly a hand covered her mouth, and a blade kissed her throat. Anna froze in terror, but only for the slightest second, before she slowly reached for her own knife.

"Touch the knife and you die, *dahrenn*," the elf hissed.

Anna reluctantly raised her hands and cursed silently to herself. *Perhaps not all of father's tales were exaggerated. Elven hearing seems to be pretty keen.*

"What's going on?" another voice shouted from the other side of the camp.

"I caught this one stealing our food!" the elf answered.

Another elf emerged from the darkness. His head was wrapped in a red and blue cloth, and he wore tattered robes. Judging from the appearance, they used to be quite exquisite. The elf tossed his hands up into the air. "Can't you see she's a child? Let her go!"

"She's a thief!" the blade-wielding elf hissed once again.

"By the Gods, she's covered in blood. She could be hurt!"

"Let her go, Ethril!" a feminine voice called out.

Anna turned her head and noticed that a female elf was standing beside the one with tattered robes, and by now, the whole encampment was awake and staring at her. Once again, she was the centre of attention, and her skin began to crawl.

"Ethril!" the female elf shouted again. This time, the blade left her throat, and her captor backed away slowly.

"Are you okay, child?" the elf in tattered robes asked. "My name is Solin, and I'm the ringleader of this little troupe."

"I'm fine, just hungry is all."

"Master Seamus!" Solin called, "prepare some food for the young girl. Looks like she hasn't eaten in days."

"Thank you, I'm Anna."

"Nice to meet you, Anna. I'm Muril," the female elf greeted. "Can I ask: where are your parents?"

"Dead."

"So, you're travelling the world alone?"

"I'm trying to get to Winterhelm," Anna admitted as she tried to reveal as little information as possible.

"What luck!" Solin exclaimed. "We are travelling to Winterhelm as well: we've been contracted to perform in the city square after the executions."

"You're welcome to join us," Muril added with a friendly smile.

"Thank you, but I don't think I'd be very welcome," Anna said as she turned her head toward Ethril, who was glowering in the shadows.

"Don't worry about that sourpuss!" a female dwarf spat as she brought a bundle of clean clothes towards Anna. "Now, let's get ye outta those bloody rags."

"Thank you," Anna said as she took the bundle of clothes. She couldn't help but be awestruck at the non-humans' generosity. For the first time since the bandits' attack, she felt a sense of comfort and safety. "Is there a place I can change?"

"Follow me," Muril instructed. She escorted her through the camp, and Anna couldn't help but realize all the faces were smiling. Nobody seemed to have any objections to her using their supplies, save for the elf that held a knife to her throat.

"What does *dahrenn* mean?" Anna asked, not sure if she was pronouncing the word correctly.

"It means 'unworthy one' in Elvish," Muril answered quickly. "But a more important question is: whose blood are you covered in?"

Anna hesitated before answering. Despite all her time travelling alone, she had never come up with an excuse for why she was covered in blood. She quickly spat out the first lie that came to her head. "I was hunting. It's a deer's."

"Hmm," Muril said, her eyes scrutinizing Anna's blood-covered rags.

"Solin said you were hired to perform? What exactly do you do?" Anna asked, eager to change the subject.

Muril let out a soft laugh. "We're a travelling circus, my dear. Everyone here is a performer. Solin is the ringmaster, and he gathers people to see our shows. Ethril is a deadeye; in all his years performing, he's never missed a shot. We also have jugglers, fire-breathers, troubadours, and a company of mummers."

"What about you?"

"I tell fortunes."

"Can you tell me mine?"

Muril turned to her and smiled softly. "Perhaps another day. For now, you need to focus on gathering your strength again."

The elf led Anna to a small tent that was sparsely decorated with furs. The canvas walls billowed loudly as the vicious winter wind tore through the camp.

A pit of red-hot coals sat in the middle of the tent. It did little to combat the evening chill, but even the smallest amount of heat was greatly appreciated. Anna dropped to her knees and rubbed her numb hands over the coals. Her fingers began to painfully tingle as the feeling slowly returned to her hands. Suddenly, Muril closed the flap to the tent and knelt down beside her.

"This is my tent. You're welcome to stay here with me for the night." The elf's voice was oddly soothing and had an almost musical lilt to it. Suddenly, she put a soft hand on Anna's shoulder. "I promise nobody will bother you while you stay here with us."

Anna gulped. It was as if Muril could see right through her lies and seemingly knew about Olaf and the lumberjacks' camp. "What about Ethril?" she blurted out, trying to stave off her paranoid thoughts.

Muril let out an amused snort. "He has a hard time trusting humans, but once he warms up to you, he's loyal to the end."

Anna smiled. Her mind had already begun imagining what it would be like to join a travelling circus, although she wasn't sure what her talent would be. Surely her father had taught her numerous skills that the masses would deem exciting and dangerous? Perhaps she could be a deadeye like Ethril, or maybe Muril could teach her to read fortunes. Suddenly, there was a commotion coming from the centre of the camp. It sounded like a heated argument, but Anna couldn't understand the language.

"I'll be right back. Get dressed," Muril instructed.

Anna nodded her head, and disrobed once she was alone in the tent. The blood-soaked clothes peeled off her skin and cracked as she manipulated the frozen fabric. She looked at the clothes that the dwarf had given her and realized that they were of a strange design. The outside was covered in a thick, woolly hide, while the inside was smooth and cool to the touch. The clothes were obviously tailored for someone much larger than her, but she didn't mind. As long as they were warm and not stained with blood, she couldn't complain.

As she exited the tent, she immediately realized that the wind didn't pierce through her new clothes, although it still bit voraciously at her cheeks and hands. She made her way to the centre of the camp and saw that Ethril, Solin, and Muril were in a heated exchange as the other performers stood and watched. Anna couldn't help but feel guilty, as she watched the three elves yell at one another in the strange tongue.

"Don't worry about 'em," a gruff voice came from beside her.

Anna spun her head and noticed that a stout, bearded dwarf held out a bowl of stew towards her. "Thank you," she said as she grabbed the bowl from his calloused hands and began greedily devouring its contents.

"Ethril always finds something to bitch about," the dwarf continued. "Name's Seamus, pleasure to make your acquaintance."

"Anna. What is your talent?"

"Agh! I'm no performer. The only thing I'm good at is making a barely edible stew: me wife got all the artistic skill. She's a troubadour: loveliest voice in all the north if I do say so meself. How're the clothes?"

"A bit big, but they do wonders against the cold," Anna admitted.

"That's dwarven fashion for ya. Not much to look at, but will always be the most practical thing to wear."

"What are they arguing about?"

"Knowing Ethril, probably protesting your arrival, and allowing you to travel with us to Winterhelm."

"He really didn't like me stealing," Anna said ruefully, eyes downcast on the snowy ground.

"I think it has more to do with your race, rather than what you did. If you had been a dwarf, elf, or even a halfling, I doubt he'd make this much of a fuss."

"Why does he hate humans so much?"

"He was a slave to 'em," Seamus answered bluntly. "He escaped after five years of servitude."

"How?"

"His masters made the mistake of letting him get his hands on a knife. Killed the entire family in less than a minute." Seamus began scratching at his beard and spat on the ground hesitantly. "It's a shame, what a few years in chains can do to a person."

Before Anna could answer, Ethril threw his dagger across the camp and embedded the blade in the stump of a chopped tree. "She isn't one of us!" he blurted out. "Plus, she has no skills. We barely have enough food as it is. We can't afford to feed more, especially those who can't pull their own weight."

Without hesitating, Anna pulled her blood-crusted knife free from its sheath and threw it at the same tree as Ethril. The blade twirled through the air before sinking deep into the handle of the elven dagger. The entire camp turned and looked at her with expressions of utter amazement.

"Lucky throw," Ethril scoffed.

"Can you do it again?" Seamus whispered as he handed her a rusty steak knife.

Anna smiled as she snatched the knife from the dwarf's hands and sent it sailing across the encampment. Once again, the blade of the knife embedded into the handle of the previous one. The non-humans started murmuring to themselves, and they stared at her with wary glances.

"It appears that you have some competition, Ethril," Solin laughed.

The elven deadeye scoffed and stormed out of the camp without retrieving his blade. The rest of the performers instantly surrounded Anna and began bombarding her with questions about her past, and if she could show more remarkable feats of accuracy. For once, being the centre of attention didn't terrify her. She began smiling as she stared at the non-humans' faces, and her cheeks began to hurt as she tried to reply to their torrent of questions.

"Enough!" Muril shouted as she forced her way through the crowd. "The girl needs rest. You can continue to bother her tomorrow on the road."

Anna let out a disappointed sigh but ultimately agreed to go and rest. She was excited to sleep on plush furs instead of the hard, frozen ground for once. *Perhaps I'll have a good night's sleep,* she thought to herself, as she laid her head down on the makeshift bed. But as soon as she closed her eyes, the image of her father's flayed corpse, and the gurgling sounds Olaf made as he choked on his own blood, invaded her mind.

She squeezed her eyes tighter as she tried to block out the painful memories, but it was to no avail. This night would be as restless as the last.

The chill in the morning air ripped her from her nightmare-filled slumber. A thin layer of frost covered the canvas walls of the tent, and the coals in the firepit had lost their heat throughout the night. Anna covered her body in the furs, but it was no use. The chill of winter seeped through.

She reluctantly opened her eyes and saw that Muril was no longer in the tent, and that the camp was stirring with life outside. She took a few seconds to summon her willpower, rise to her feet, and leave the tent.

The camp seemed to be in as lethargic a state as she was. People shuffled mindlessly from one wagon to another, while others just sat close to the fire and shivered uncontrollably. Solin had a broad smile on his face and was talking to everyone in a cheerful demeanour.

Anna could tell that it was all an act. He was just as miserable as the rest of them. Winters in Artanzia were known to be extremely cruel, but this was out of the ordinary. The pairing of the relentless wind and the punishing temperatures made it almost unbearable to travel.

"This fuckin' cold!" Seamus shouted as he stirred the bubbling contents of his cauldron.

"Cheer up, Master Dwarf!" Solin exclaimed. "We will be in Winterhelm in a few hours, and then we can do what we do best: perform!" The camp let out a half-hearted cheer of excitement, which admittedly, brought a smile to Anna's face.

"We are nothing more than the *dahrenn's* dogs," Ethril muttered as he stared into the roaring fire.

"Not this again," Solin sighed.

"We go where they tell us to, we do what they tell us to, and they pay us whatever they want. Tell me how we aren't under their control?"

"At least we are getting paid," Muril stated sourly. "Some of our kin are still in chains."

"Exactly! We should band together and rise up against the humans, not invite them openly into our camp." Ethril shot a look of distaste towards Anna as he warmed his hands by the fire. Anna narrowed her eyes in response and sat down beside him in pure insolence.

"*Bloede dahrenn,*" Ethril cursed as he stood up and left the comfort of the fire.

"Scared I'll show you up again?" Anna called out without looking back.

Everyone went silent, and Ethril stopped in his tracks. The only sound was the howling wind, as it tore through the camp. The elf pivoted on his heels and pulled his dagger free from its sheath. Anna could see that his face was bright red, and his eyes were full of contempt. A devilish smile then crept across his lips as he tossed his dagger into the air before pulling out a second knife and throwing it, so the two blades collided in midair.

The camp of non-humans clapped politely as their gaze turned towards Anna. She could feel the weight of their eyes on her, and it made her heart race. She took out her knife and tossed it into the air. Then she quickly grabbed one of Seamus' steak knives and threw it at the twirling blade. The sound of the steel blades clanging off each other rang through the camp, and the performers erupted in applause once again.

"Incredible!" Solin exclaimed. "I think we've found our new act: the battle of the deadeyes! Elf versus human: if that doesn't draw in a crowd, I don't know what will!"

An enormous smile spread across Anna's lips as she stared at Ethril. All the mindlessly dull hours spent in the forest with her father had finally paid off. The idea of becoming a performer excited her. She could see the world, meet new and exciting people, and do something that she was good at. "When do we leave for Winterhelm?" she asked.

"We'll begin packing right now. I want to get this show on the road!" Solin exclaimed.

It took the non-humans about a half-hour of feverish work to pack up the encampment. The carts were loaded with expert precision and, if Anna had not known they had camped there, she would never have been able to pinpoint the campsite in the frozen tundra that surrounded them.

"Ride with me, *dahrenn,*" Ethril instructed in a flat tone from the top of one of the wagons. "I wish to speak with you."

Anna smiled and politely climbed up beside him. With a sharp crack of the reins, the convoy began heading north towards Winterhelm.

"Where did you learn to throw like that?" he asked with a hint of respect staining his voice.

"I've been throwing knives my entire life. There was nothing else to do in the forest."

"You grew up in a forest?"

"Yes, just me and my father. We lived in peace until bandits came knocking on our door."

"What happened?"

Anna then explained the events of the last few days. How some bandits tracked her and her father to their hut in the forest, and how she ran from them while her father fought them off. She told the tale of how the corvan had awoken from its hibernation and attacked her and the bandits hunting her. She also told, in graphic detail, how she killed the monster and returned home, only to find that her father had been flayed to the bone.

"I'm sorry," Ethril said after a lengthy pause. "All the humans I know live a life of luxury compared to us non-humans. I always assumed that they all lived pampered lives... it appears I was wrong."

"Seamus mentioned that you were a slave once?" Anna asked.

"A life better left forgotten," Ethril replied coldly.

Anna immediately winced at the elf's response. She silently cursed herself as she stared down at her boots. She had wished that the question wouldn't offend him, but was also too curious about his past not to ask. The rest of the journey passed in silence.

It was just past midday when the walls of Winterhelm came into view. The stone towers in the distance loomed above the frozen plains and looked vaguely threatening.

Anna had never seen so many stones stacked on top of one another. Her father told her stories about the architecture of Winterhelm, but she never believed them. Whenever she stacked rocks on top of one another, they always toppled over, so to imagine an entire city constructed from stone was almost unfathomable. However, this time, her father's tales proved to be no exaggeration.

"It's so big," Anna gasped as she stared up at the towering walls.

"Biggest city in all of Artanzia," Solin responded from another wagon. "They say you can find anything you're looking for inside those walls."

"Everyone be on their best behaviour when we arrive at the gates," Muril instructed. "That means you, Ethril."

The elven deadeye let out a defiant snort but otherwise remained silent. Anna noticed that his eyes hadn't left the horses and that his knuckles were white.

"Nervous?" she asked.

"Very."

"What does Muril mean by 'be on our best behaviour?'"

"She means don't do anything stupid. Guards will look for any reason to deny entry to a group of non-humans."

Anna stared at the elf with confused eyes. She couldn't comprehend why anyone would have animosity toward a troupe of circus performers, regardless of their race. "But you were hired to perform, weren't you?"

"Not exactly," Ethril admitted. "Solin heard a rumour that the king wanted these executions to be festive because they're cleansing the kingdom of traitors, so we decided we would travel there, hoping they'd let us perform."

Anna nodded her head and resumed staring at the enormous city walls. As they approached, she could begin to make out each stone in the wall. Some were large, others small, but almost all of them were perfect cubes. She then turned her attention to the main gate and noticed the large steel portcullis that blocked the road into the city. On the other side were two guards dressed in bland grey gambesons, each holding a halberd.

"Halt! Who goes there?"

"Greetings!" Solin exclaimed in an overly zealous voice. "We are but a company of humble circus performers, hoping to perform for His Majesty on such a joyous occasion!"

"You all non-humans?" the other guard asked.

"Why yes, we are known as –"

"Do you have a permit?"

"Well, no, but we heard that –"

"As per the late King David, all non-humans must pass a routine inspection and have the proper paperwork before entering the great city of Winterhelm."

Solin's face began to redden, and for once, it seemed that he was at a loss for words. His lips moved frantically, but no words were spoken.

"You've got to be joking," Ethril growled.

"Do I look like a jester, knife-ear?" the guard hissed back.

Anna saw that the elven deadeye reached for his dagger before stopping himself and returning his hand to the reins of the wagon.

"How do we get one of these permits?" Seamus blurted out from the back of the convoy.

"We have enough of your kind within these walls already," the other guard snarled. "Best you turn around and abandon any ideas you have about entering Winterhelm."

Just as Solin was about to turn the wagon around, Muril suddenly stood up and shouted at the guards. "We have a human with us! Does she need a permit to gain entry to the city?"

"No, all humans are welcome under the late King David's edict," the guard replied.

Muril then turned her gaze to Anna and waved her to come forward. Anna reluctantly dismounted from the wagon and approached the fortune teller. Before she could voice a protest, Muril quickly cut her off.

"Give me your hands."

"What?"

"Give me your hands, and I'll tell you your fortune."

Anna reluctantly extended her hands, but Muril quickly snatched them and gripped them tightly. Suddenly, the world went black, and it was just her and the elf standing in a void of darkness. Muril's eyes turned pitch black, and her voice became heavily distorted. "You have two paths ahead of you, child. One is forgettable, but full of peace: the other is a path of war, violence, and death. Beware the raven, for it will ultimately betray you."

Anna pulled her hands free of the elf's, and in an instant the black void vanished, and she was standing in front of the stone walls of Winterhelm. She looked around at her surroundings and noticed that not a second had passed since Muril took her hands. She also noticed a small stream of blood trickling out of the elf's nose. Muril discreetly wiped the blood away with the sleeve of her coat.

"Well? What's the hold-up?" one guard shouted.

"Go, child," Muril whispered as she pushed Anna toward the gate. "Your destiny lies in Winterhelm. Just remember what I told you."

Anna nodded her head politely, even though the fortune made very little sense to her. *"Beware the raven..." What does that even mean?* She looked back over her shoulder as the large steel portcullis rose, and the two guards waved her inside the city walls.

Her heart panged with sadness as she stared into the eyes of the performers, who had showed her nothing but kindness. She knew that if it wasn't for them, she would have starved or frozen to death. She waved goodbye, trying to stem the tears in her eyes, as she crossed the threshold into Winterhelm. As soon as she was past the two guards, the portcullis slammed shut once again, and the performers began the arduous task of turning their convoy around.

Anna was amazed by the structures in the city: it seemed that every building was taller than her house, and the fact that they were so close together amazed her even more. *How do they not fall into each other?*

She meandered through the wide cobblestone streets until she came to the city square. It was teeming with life and festivities. A smile spread across her face as she pushed through the crowd. She watched several performers and felt the sadness in her heart abate slightly. She saw a man spit fire, a woman juggle twelve torches at once, a man stick a nail in his eye without being harmed, and a woman command her many beasts to do tricks.

"Quick! It's about to start!" a boy shouted as he grabbed his mother's wrist and pulled her towards the centre of the square. Anna quickly began following them, as she did not want to miss another exciting performance.

As she approached the centre of the square, the crowd became more and more dense, and she had to shove people aside to get a look at the spectacle. She finally broke through the mass of bodies and saw a wooden platform, and a man on his knees with his head resting on a chopping block.

Anna's heart sank as she suddenly remembered the reason behind all the festivities. There was to be an execution. She had no desire to watch another man's life come to a gruesome end, but before she could turn away, the executioner's axe swung down and severed the man's head from his body.

CHAPTER TWELVE

ELBERT

A wicked smile spread across his lips as he watched Lord Bellston's severed head roll off the platform and into the crowd of peasants. He looked over to his queen, and noticed a barely perceptible twitch in her face as blood surged from her father's stump of a neck. *Perhaps she didn't imagine it would be this graphic,* he thought to himself, as he leaned back on his wheeled throne.

Master Arlin had only finished constructing it a few hours prior to the execution, but it was an exact replica of the one in the throne room, except for the fact that this one was portable. The dwarf's attention to detail was unmatched. He included every scuff, scar, and gouge in the old throne when creating the new one. Elbert let out a satisfied sigh as he let the comfort of his new throne consume him.

"May we leave, husband?" Vivian asked, avoiding eye contact with Elbert as she did so.

"Meet me at the castle, my queen," Elbert replied. "I have to make my speech to officially start the festivities."

Vivian nodded her head, and with a retinue of royal guards, adjourned to the castle. Elbert couldn't help but wonder if his new wife wasn't already secretly planning his demise, in an effort to seize power for herself, and as a way to avenge her father's gruesome end. "One can never be too careful," he whispered as he silently ordered the guards to lift him onto the wooden platform in the middle of the city square.

When constructing Elbert's wheeled throne, Arlin refused to use steel, as the king expected, but instead used a rare dwarvish metal that Elbert couldn't even begin to pronounce. As a result of being forged from this strange metal, the throne weighed about as much as a small wooden chest. The guards lifted the crippled king with ease and placed him on the small platform. Elbert rolled towards the edge before he stopped, a few feet away from his gawping subjects.

"Today is a glorious day!" he proclaimed, trying to project his voice as much as possible. "For we have cleansed our magnificent kingdom of the scourge of the treasonous Lord Bellston and his co-conspirators." He paused for dramatic effect; he had practiced this speech almost a hundred times. "I hereby declare the festivities to celebrate this momentous occasion open!"

As soon as the last words left his mouth, a cacophony of music filled the city square, just as he imagined. However, unlike he imagined, the crowd did not erupt in applause. Instead, they stood there, eyes fixed on their king, mumbling nervously amongst themselves.

Elbert felt the sweat form on his brow and drip slowly down his neck as he stared into their confused eyes. The music died down as the musicians realized that the crowd had not yet dispersed.

The king felt trapped. He wished he could just walk away from the awkwardness, but once again, his legs proved to be his downfall. Finally, after a long and unbearable silence, a man stepped forward from the crowd.

"Oi! An execution is all well and good, but who is gonna take his place?"

Before Elbert could answer, a woman stepped forward and added to the man's concerns. "It's only a couple of months till raiding season, and the Islanders will surely be back. Lord Bellston always sheltered us from the barbarians. Now what will we do?" The crowd nodded in agreement.

"People, please! I have a plan!" Elbert lied. "I know Lord Arlin has a new estate, and I'm sure he would –"

"I'll be damned if I'm staying under the same roof as a dwarf!" a burly man shouted. Most of the mob enthusiastically agreed with his sentiment.

Elbert sweated profusely. He knew moments like these were critical when garnering support from subjects. He cursed himself silently for overlooking Bellston's popularity. He thought that once Bellston was branded a traitor, everyone would be quick to forget all he did for the peasants; unfortunately, this was not the case.

His mind began racing as he tried to find the perfect sentence that would sate the mob's dissatisfaction and quell their worries. Suddenly, Vivian's voice rang inside his head. *"Do something no other king has ever done. Launch a raid against the Mjältön Isles."*

"I plan to do something that all predecessors failed to do," Elbert shouted, his voice cutting through the mob's noise. "I plan to launch a raid against the barbarian Islanders and give them a taste of their own medicine!" This time, after he finished speaking, the crowd erupted in adulation. Elbert breathed a small sigh of relief as he waved his guards to take him away.

"Sire..." Sergeant Thames said as he bent down to his king's ear. "Are you sure about this? Such an expedition is not only unorthodox, but could prove extremely hazardous."

"Gather the remaining lords and bring them to the throne room," Elbert instructed. "We have a war to plan."

"Have you lost your bloody mind!?" a terrified noble shouted, his fist trembling uncontrollably. "What makes you think this will be a fruitful endeavour?"

Elbert sat back on his throne and eyed the gathered lords with great scrutiny. He looked over to his side, and saw that a venomous smile was plastered on his queen's lips. Her heterochromatic eyes seemed to gleam with joy at the nobles' trepidation.

"According to my calculations, our army will be sufficient to capture several key strongholds in the Isles," Elbert lied.

"Do you not know that all the jarls have sworn fealty and allegiance to High King Uthredd?" the lord responded angrily. "That's got to be an army ten thousand strong!" The rest of the nobles murmured in agreement.

"And what would you estimate is the size of our army?"

"Some calculations you have done," the lord sniggered, but quickly swallowed his words as he caught Elbert's fiery glare. "Around three thousand, sire."

"May I make a suggestion, Your Majesty?" an elderly noble croaked as he stepped forward from the crowd of gathered lords. Elbert waved to give him the floor. "What, might I ask, is the aim of this campaign? Do you wish to conquer the Isles and have the barbarians as your subjects?"

The king gulped nervously. He hadn't thought about what he hoped to accomplish with this campaign, other than garnering more support from his subjects. His mind raced as he tried to conceive a lie that sounded like this wasn't a spontaneous plan.

"I say we set much more attainable goals," the old noble continued.

"So, what do you suggest?"

"We cannot hope to go to war with High King Uthredd. He has too many advantages. His army is superior, they know the land well, and they'd be able to fortify their defences after we landed." The old man paused to cough wildly into his sleeve. Elbert could see that a small splatter of blood appeared on the pristine purple fabric. "I say we take something that the barbarian king holds in high regard and ransom it."

"Why not just pillage towns and settlements?" another lord asked. "Surely we can do that without sending an entire army."

"The Islanders are born warriors, Lord Grelin," Sergeant Thames spoke up. "Every man, woman, and child would take up arms to fight against us. They value nothing but violence."

"Along the southern coast of the Isles, there is a fortress," the elderly noble interrupted. "They call it Tjørholm, and it is supposedly the site of a holy battle between their heathen gods."

Elbert scratched his chin and scrutinized the ancient lord. Wrinkles obscured most of his features, and his head was covered in a shaggy mop of grey hair. *Looks more like a beggar than a noble,* Elbert thought to himself. "Why there?" he asked. "What's the significance?"

"Rumour has it that Uthredd is a pious man. If we can capture a site so sacred to him, one that has walls and is well fortified no less, we could potentially sell it back to him in exchange for gold."

The room sat in the weight of the elderly noble's words. Elbert couldn't help but be amazed by the sound reasoning of the old man's plan. Before he could voice his approval, Vivian cut in, her voice cutting through the silence like a dagger slicing through a stick of butter. "What is your name, good sir?"

"Lord Frederick Gaunstad."

"And how have you come to know the Isles so well?"

"I have been in service to this royal family since I was a boy, my queen. During that time, I learned that it was wise to watch one's enemies and to document their every move."

"You have agents in the Isles?" Elbert gasped.

"They are at your command, my king," Frederick responded, while bowing clumsily.

"Can we take Tjørholm with our current forces?"

The old man hissed as he winced at the king's comment, as if it caused him physical pain. "That is the trouble, Your Majesty. Even if we levied some forces, we would still be hundreds of troops shy."

Elbert let out a frustrated sigh. "Very well: leave me. I have much to think about. We will reconvene tomorrow, once I have given this issue some more thought."

The nobles bowed, turned on their heels, and silently exited the throne room. Elbert stared up at the gilded ceiling and sighed once more. It felt like a horse was standing on his chest. If he didn't launch a campaign against the Isles, the possibility of revolt would grow with every passing day; but if he invaded the Isles and failed, his reputation would be forever tarnished. He felt his fingers go numb as he clenched the armrests of his throne, when suddenly, an idea came into his head.

"Sergeant Thames, how far away is Straven?"

"The prison camp?" Thames responded.

"Yes."

"About a week's ride, Your Majesty."

"And how many people are currently incarcerated, including the palace dungeons?"

"By the last count, around five hundred," Thames responded immediately, without a moment's hesitation.

"I want you to track down Lord Gaunstad and ask him: if we conscripted the prisoners, would we have sufficient forces to take Tjørholm?"

"You wish to use the prisoners as soldiers?"

"Fret not, dear Rupert," Elbert replied after seeing the worried expression on his guard's face. "I merely intend to use them as fodder."

"And who would be foolhardy enough to lead these men into such a battle?"

"I'm leaving that under your control," Elbert informed, as he gestured for a few of the other guardsmen to lift him into his mobile throne. "Find me a man that is desperate enough to take on such an assignment."

"As you wish, Your Majesty," Thames said, as he graciously bowed and went about his tasks.

"Husband, a word before you go?" Vivian asked, once Elbert was lifted into his chair. "Alone, if you please," she added.

The king smiled politely and waved his guardsmen away; then it was just him and the queen in the throne room. His stomach told him that something was awry, but when he looked into Vivian's eyes, his heart felt a sense of security. He wheeled his chair over to her and grasped her hands softly. "What is it, my queen?"

"What you are proposing is very dangerous, and could dictate how the people see you as a ruler. You need to ensure your success."

Elbert let out a laugh. "Don't worry, with the added forces from the prisoner camp, I'm sure we'll have enough to take the fortress. Besides, it's not like I'll be in any real danger."

"But you have to go!" Vivian blurted out, as she gripped her king's hands tighter. "Every time Artanzia has gone to war, the king has always led his troops into battle. If you don't go, they won't fight for you, and the other kingdoms will see you as a coward!"

His smile faded, and he let go of his wife's hands. "If you haven't noticed, my dear, I'm a cripple. How am I supposed to lead an army into battle when I can't even climb stairs on my own?"

"What about the dwarf? Surely he can craft something?"

"Arlin? I suppose he could: he's the greatest craftsman I've ever known. But even if I leave, who will rule the kingdom?"

"Well, me, of course."

Elbert's heart sank. Could it be that Vivian was just using him? That she planted the idea of going to war against the Isles in hopes that he'd die, and she'd be the ruler of the kingdom? *Who'd want to be married to a cripple?* He swallowed the lump in his throat and stared into his wife's eyes with all the hardness he could muster. "How do I know that you won't seize power from me while I'm gone?"

"Husband, I would never!" Vivian gasped, as her hand covered her chest. "I've already sacrificed my father for you. What more must I give to prove my loyalty and commitment to this marriage?"

Elbert rolled his eyes exhaustedly. He had just eliminated the last threat to his crown. And now, in the span of a few hours, he had an all-new one. To make matters worse, it was his own wife.

He gripped the wheels of his chair and wheeled his way towards the royal bath. *Perhaps this is what it means to be king,* he thought to himself. *Constantly looking over your shoulder until the people closest to you betray you.*

"Where are you going?" Vivian called out.

"To think," Elbert replied sourly as he pushed his way through the wooden door at the back of the throne room, slamming it behind him.

The steam from the bath slowly swirled to the ceiling, blanketing the tiled room in a thick mist. Elbert's crippled legs bobbed lifelessly in the water, toes breaking the glass-like surface of the pool.

Every now and then, he would smack the water and watch as the ripples scattered across the bath's surface. His eyes drifted to the middle of the bath, and a morbid thought entered his head. *Deep enough to drown a cripple.* A relaxed smile spread across his lips: this wasn't the first time that the idea had crossed his head since his encounter with the magus. All he would have to do would be to order the guards to leave the room, then helplessly paddle towards the middle of the bath, and sink.

Suddenly, the door to the bath swung open, and Sergeant Thames entered the steam-filled room. Elbert breathed a sigh of relief at the sight of the guard. He hated to admit it, but Thames was the closest thing he had to a friend. With a wave of his hand, the rest of the royal guard dispersed, leaving the two men alone in the cavernous bath.

"I've done as you've asked, Sire," Thames reported dutifully.

"And? Will the prisoners give us enough men to take the fortress?"

"Lord Gaunstad seems to think so, and I've already dispatched a messenger on our swiftest horse."

"Excellent," Elbert said as he splashed the pool once again with his hand. "And the other thing?"

"Lord Haustack is in the next room, changing," Thames replied. "I believe he has the man you're looking for."

"You've outdone yourself, Rupert," Elbert complimented, before wiping off the steam droplets forming on his brow. "Tell me something. Do you think I should lead my army in the assault?"

"Hmm," Thames replied hesitantly. "Tradition dictates that a king should courageously lead his forces into battle, but on the other hand –"

"We've never had a cripple for a king," Elbert interrupted sourly.

"How are you with a bow, sire?" Thames asked.

"I'm no marksman, but I can hit a stag at fifty paces."

A smile broke on to the sergeant's face as the door swung open, and a portly man wrapped in a towel entered the tiled room. "Presenting the honourable Lord Haustack, Your Majesty!" Thames exclaimed, as he bowed and retreated from the room.

Elbert examined the lord and realized that this man's best years were long behind him. He was old, scarred, and severely obese. *Clearly enjoyed a life of decadence and over-indulgence,* Elbert thought, as he watched the stout man waddle into the water.

"I hear ya have need of me," Lord Haustack began gruffly.

"Indeed I do, but I must admit, I've never heard a noble speak to a king in such a manner."

"Pah!" the hefty lord spat. "I've long outlived politeness and cordial responses. If you decide to take my head like Bellston's, you'd be doing me a favour."

"How so?"

"Got the black lung," the man wheezed. "Even the mages say they can't fix it: that I only have a few months of life left."

"My deepest condolences," Elbert replied.

"Fuck your condolences," Haustack barked. "Let's cut to the chase. Ya need a fool to lead a doomed regiment in yer army, is that right?"

"Indeed it is."

"I've a son. He's idealistic, brave, and not half bad with a sword. I suspect he'd be the perfect fit for yer little army."

"Your son?" Elbert said, confused. "You realize that this appointment will most likely cost him his life?"

"Of course I realize that!" Haustack raged, before succumbing to a coughing fit. "Ya see, he's from my second marriage. A child I have no love for, and one who will never inherit my estate. He'd rather be a hero than a lord anyway. Might as well give him the chance to die like a man."

Elbert smiled politely as he listened to the lord speak, but he couldn't help but draw parallels with his father. The disdain for his own children, the obvious gluttony, and the aura of pure selfishness that emanated from him. It was as if he was sitting across from King David himself. "I appreciate your candour, Lord Haustack, and I accept your son as commander of the prisoner regiment."

The portly lord slowly rose from the waters and wrapped himself in a towel before waddling towards the door. "Thank ya kindly, sire. I truly hope that yer campaign goes well and that I never see my son again."

"Your sacrifice is greatly appreciated," Elbert muttered through gritted teeth. Once the door shut behind the fat noble, he let out a long sigh and relaxed his body. "And may you choke on your own bile in your final days."

Sergeant Thames once again entered the chamber, walked towards his king, and lifted him out of the stagnant waters. "I trust that we found our man?"

"Indeed we did. However, I sincerely regret helping a man like that."

Thames let out a short laugh. "Yes, Lord Haustack can be a bit caustic at times, and his dislike for his second son is well known, but I fear the boy may be our only chance of finding someone to train and lead the prisoners' regiment. I've also given thought to what you said earlier."

"And what conclusion have you come to?"

"There is a local soothsayer in town: a clairvoyant, if you will. Before you roll your eyes, his predictions are incredibly precise. It would be an honour for me if I could take you to see him. Perhaps he can give you some guidance about what to do."

"Very well, take me to him," Elbert said reluctantly, as Sergeant Thames began dressing him in his fineries. He had never believed in clairvoyants in the past, but he figured he was desperate enough to try anything. *I've already condemned a man I don't know to death. What's the harm in seeing a charlatan?*

The soothsayer's shack was on the outskirts of the city. It appeared to be abandoned, save for the long line of people standing outside it. A small plume of white smoke rose from the dilapidated chimney. Elbert began to sweat nervously as he eyed the long line of peasants. The plan was to travel incognito, but surely a cripple with a portable chair was a dead giveaway to his identity, so he had Thames carry him on his shoulders towards the clairvoyant's hut. He feared that someone would recognize him as he pulled the cloak over his head.

"Fear not, sire," Thames began. "Nobody will recognize us here."

"I certainly hope not," Elbert responded. "If they do, my reputation will be forever tarnished, and I will become the laughing stock of the entire continent. A king who believes in soothsayers... it's like the start of a bad joke!"

"Shh," Thames warned. "Or the peasants will hear you."

The two of them stood in line for several hours. The winter wind cut through their rags as they shivered uncontrollably. Elbert watched the peasants as they left the hut. He was surprised to see a variety of reactions. Some left the shack joyful and full of hope, while others were sad and desolate. Many left the shack with confused looks on their faces, while some exited in a fit of rage. *Perhaps there is some accuracy to this clairvoyant. He is not just telling people what they want to hear.*

Finally, it was his turn. A diminutive young woman opened the shack and escorted them to the main room. Thames set Elbert down gently on a bed of furs. He looked around the room and saw that the shack was sparsely decorated, save for a few burning candles.

He sat across from a man whose face was covered in wrinkles and scars. The man had a bald head that was covered in tattoos, and in place of his eyes, he had empty sockets. The sight of the soothsayer made Elbert's stomach churn. Staring into the wrinkly black holes where the man's eyes used to be unnerved him greatly.

"A cripple," the old man croaked in a gravelly, ancient voice.

"I come seeking answers," Elbert responded in his most kingly voice.

"Everyone comes in search of answers, my child," the soothsayer replied. "But I am not omnipotent. I only see what the spirits allow me to see."

"The payment," the small woman interrupted.

Elbert glared at her, but to his surprise, she didn't flinch under his scrutiny. He tossed a bag of coins at her and replied sourly. "I trust this is enough?"

The woman nodded her head politely and backed into the shadow-filled recesses of the shack.

"Now," the old man began. "What is your question?"

"If I go with my army to the Mjältön Isles, will I have a kingdom to come back to?"

The soothsayer took a deep breath, lifted his head, and stared at the crooked ceiling. He began swaying from side to side, and then, suddenly, he started spasming wildly. His arms flailed from left to right, and his neck jerked violently. Foam oozed from the corners of his chapped lips, and his chest heaved with every breath. Then, the old man froze in place.

"I see..." he whispered. "I see a great battle between a sword and an axe. There's blood everywhere, and many will lose their lives. The sword cannot defeat the axe by itself. It must find the shield. At the end of the war, I see a wolf and a raven sitting atop a mountain of ash."

"What is that supposed to mean?" Thames exclaimed as he took a step forward toward the soothsayer.

The old man didn't flinch at the sound of the sergeant's armoured footsteps on the creaky floorboards. "I see only what the spirits desire to show me," he said, wiping the spittle from his lips.

"Our family sigil is a wolf holding a sword in his mouth, and my mother's family sigil was a raven. Perhaps it will mean that I am victorious?"

"You think the mountain of ash is Tjørholm?" Thames asked.

"I do," Elbert answered without a moment's hesitation. "What else could it possibly mean?"

"What's the bit about the sword finding a shield?"

"I'm not sure, but I feel that the spirits won't show him anything else," Elbert answered as he stared at the exhausted old man.

"Thank you for your time," Thames replied, as he hoisted Elbert back onto his shoulders.

The small woman opened the door to the shack and addressed the rest of the peasants waiting in line. "Those are all the visions my grandfather has strength for today. Please come again tomorrow!" Elbert's mind raced as he tried to decode the soothsayer's riddle. *The sword must find the shield. What is the shield?* The answers were undoubtedly on the Isles, and he smiled, as the coming weeks would be solely dedicated to preparing for the assault on Tjørholm. There, he would have his answers.

CHAPTER THIRTEEN

GRIMM

The crustacean's frozen body snapped and cracked as he pried its wound open in the early hours of the morning. Even though it was a new day, the unforgiving chill of the winter air had not abated.

Grimm hissed as his shoulder throbbed in pain. He pulled down the collar of his shirt to examine it, and he noticed that a cobweb of blackened veins expanded from the puncture wound. His eyes moved to his arms, where he saw that his skin had turned a sickly pale.

"Venom," Grimm whispered as he tried to control the fear that was slowly consuming him. It appeared that resting for the night was not the wisest decision. He quickly walked back to the corpse of the monster, reached inside, and pulled a still-sleeping Sara out with his good arm.

"Hey..." she murmured as she rubbed her tired eyes together.

"Quiet," Grimm ordered as he tried to remain as calm as possible. "We have to get to the road; then we can find a town."

The child shrugged her shoulders and began following the wounded warrior through the deep banks of snow. Colour had returned to the dwarf's skin, and she appeared to have recovered from her fall into the lake.

Grimm was torn on how to feel. On the one hand, he knew that if it hadn't been for Sara, he would likely be at the coast of the Isles and not desperately trying to find a town with a healer. On the other hand, the idea of being relieved by a child's death made his stomach churn. Even though she was slowing him down, a part of him was glad she didn't die during the night.

The pain in Grimm's shoulder flared up unexpectedly, and he collapsed to his knees. He clenched his teeth in agony, and he began sweating profusely. His vision blurred, and the sounds of the world seemed to fade away. All he could hear was the deafening pounding of his own heartbeat. Then, after a few minutes of anguish, the pain dulled to a barely perceptible ache.

He rose to his feet and continued to march on; not daring to look the dwarf in the eye. He hated appearing weak. All of his life, he had been taught to cover up weakness and to push through it. But doubts were creeping into his mind. This was not some berserker that he could cut down with a sword. This was a deadly venom that was gradually coursing through his veins. He could feel it slowly killing him.

He knew that if the first town they came across did not have a skilled healer, he would die. *Not like this,* he thought as he forced himself to push through the knee-deep snow. *Not like this.*

He collapsed several more times before they reached a snow-covered road. By this time, his breathing had become shallow, and he gasped for air with every breath. Sara walked up beside him and wrapped her tiny hands around his calloused, sausage-like fingers. Still, he avoided her gaze.

In the distance, he saw a plume of smoke, and his spirits lifted. He tore his hand free from hers and began walking down the road towards the sign of civilization. As he walked, he closed his eyes and whispered a small prayer. "Heimer, if you have indeed graced me, let this smoke be from a town with a capable healer. I only ask this so that I can die a warrior's death and be accepted into The Great Hall along with my forefathers."

"Who are you talking to?" Sara asked, looking up at the dying man with mild curiosity.

"No one, just uttering a prayer," Grimm stated as he marched down the road. *Probably the last one I'll ever speak.*

"What's a prayer?" she probed.

"It's when you ask the gods for a favour," Grimm replied flatly.

"What did you ask for?"

To not die. "For you to stop asking questions."

Sara wrinkled her nose and continued to walk beside him. It wasn't long before her strides were longer than his, and his feet dragged with every step. His hands became clammy as they trembled uncontrollably.

With every passing second, it seemed more and more likely that he would never see the lights of The Great Hall. Once more, he fell to his knees in agony. His body shook as he tenderly felt the wound in his shoulder. Sara's small hand touched his forearm, and he painfully shrugged her away. With all the energy he could muster, he lifted his head and stared at the billowing smoke in the distance. *So close, yet so far.*

"Get up!" the dwarf cried as she jabbed at his side. Her voice was riddled with concern and confusion.

Grimm slammed his fist into the frozen earth and pushed himself upright, his teeth bared, as he painfully extended his weary muscles. By the time he stood on his feet again, he was out of breath.

Every inch of his body throbbed in pain. Even his own heartbeat seemed to hurt him. With a giant intake of breath, he took a step forward and fell face first in the snow, losing consciousness.

The sharp whinny of a horse stirred him from his slumber. He groggily opened his eyes and saw that he was tied to the back of a horse. He tried to flex his muscles to break the bonds, but it was no use. He was too weak from the monster's venom.

Somehow, he lifted his head and saw an elderly man leading the horse down the snow-covered road, with Sara walking alongside him. From what he could see, they were only a few hundred yards from town.

"He's awake!" Sara exclaimed as she tugged on the stranger's sleeve.

"Blessed be! Heimer must be in a merciful mood today!"

"My sword..." Grimm croaked as he turned his head slowly. "Where is my sword?"

"Attached to my hip," the man replied. "Don't worry, you'll get it back after we get you to the healer."

"Who are you?"

"One of Heimer's children."

Grimm let out a short exhale through his nose. He had heard that response hundreds of times before. "A priest."

"You say that as if it were a bad thing."

"It is. Any man who refuses to use a sword is no man in my eyes."

"If it wasn't for me, you would've died miserably in the middle of that road. Far from a glorious death, wouldn't you say, brother?"

"So, I'm supposed to thank you?"

"No," the priest replied curtly. "Thank Heimer, for he is the one who destined for our paths to cross during your hour of need."

A dry, raspy laugh escaped Grimm's lips, before he began coughing wildly. As he watched the spittle escape his lips, he noticed that it had a red tinge to it. *That can't be good.*

"What's so funny?" the priest asked.

"People have been telling me Heimer has graced me my whole life. I just never truly believed it until now."

"Is he going to be okay?" Sara said, interrupting the two men's conversation.

"Oh, he'll live, love," the priest responded as he cupped her cheek gently. "Draygard is home to a famous healer. She used to be a shieldmaiden before a man severed her foot."

"Shit," Grimm groaned as he spat on the ground.

"You know her?"

"Aye, I'm the bastard that took her foot."

The priest let out a nasally laugh and wiped the tears streaming from his eyes. He walked around the horse and lifted Grimm's head until they made eye contact with one another. "Perhaps Heimer doesn't grace you after all," he said with a chuckle.

For the rest of the journey, Grimm refused to respond to the priest's remarks: Sara, however, did not feel the same. In fact, she encouraged the priest to talk more as she bombarded him with question after question.

He tried to block out the grating sound of their voices by focusing on the pain, but as if by some cruel trick of the gods, his pain had once again subsided, forcing him to listen to their conversation.

Suddenly, a thought entered the grizzled warrior's head. *Perhaps I can pass the child on to the priest. Surely a pious man will take better care of her than I. It's a win-win. She gets a companion who loves her nattering, and I can travel at my own pace again.* The thought put a smile on his face. He was surprised that his mouth could still curl into one, despite all that had happened. Between being the most wanted man on the Isles and being forced into a paternal role, he found that there was little to smile about.

In the span of several minutes, they arrived at the town of Draygard. It appeared like every other small settlement on the Isles, wooden houses with thatched roofs, and narrow snow-filled streets separating them.

The townsfolk gawped openly at the sight of a priest with a dying man tied to the back of his horse. Grimm immediately felt uneasy. *If one of these people recognizes me, I'm a dead man.* He tried to hide his face as best he could, and avoided the townsfolks' open stares. Suddenly, the horse came to an abrupt halt.

"Greetings, priest," a man's voice cut through the air. "What brings you through Draygard again so soon?"

"I stumbled upon a weary traveller who is in need of seeing Mjoll, your healer. As a holy man, it was my duty to help so that he may have a glorious death and enter Heimer's great hall." The priest's voice was charismatic and boisterous. It had an almost jovial quality to it as it filled the air of the town.

"Well, let's take a look at the feller," the man spoke as he stepped towards Grimm's bound body.

The priest quickly stepped in front of him, shielding Grimm's face from the stranger's lingering stare. "I'm afraid time is of the essence."

The stranger let out a loud snort and stepped aside. The horse immediately followed the priest as they continued down the snow-covered street. Grimm was able to look at the stranger's feet as he passed by. He noticed that he wore heavy plate boots and that the head of an axe was resting in the snow beside them. *Shit,* he thought to himself as he tried to hide his face with his mangy hair. *Just what I need, some town guard thinking that he's a hero.*

It wasn't long before the priest started cutting his bonds and helping him off the horse. He noticed that the healer's house was larger than the others.

He also noticed that a fragrant aroma seeped out of the window. The smell of burning callian always pleased him. The flower had a scent unlike any other when it was tossed onto a fire. During his days as a soldier, he learned that if one inhaled enough of the flower's smoke, it would numb any pain and bring on a state of euphoric bliss. His heart raced as he continued to think about breathing in the pleasant aroma.

He took a step towards the shack and immediately fell to his knees. He was too weak, and soon fear crept into his mind. *What if I waited too long? What if the effects of the venom are irreversible?*

"Mjoll!" the priest shouted as he struggled to raise Grimm to his feet. "Mjoll!"

The door to the house swung open, and standing in the doorway was a scarred, heavily tattooed woman with long blonde hair. Her arms were defined by finely honed muscle, and her hands were heavily calloused. At the bottom of her right leg was a crude wooden prosthesis which gave her a noticeable limp in her gait. Her lips curled into a frown as her eyes locked with Grimm's.

"What is that bastard doing here?"

"Please: he needs your help, Mjoll."

"After what he did!?" she screamed as she pointed down to her fake foot. "I'd sooner die than help that piece of shit!"

"You swore an oath!" the priest bellowed, the jovial tone in his voice now gone. "You promised Aki and all the gods that you would never turn a soul away when they were in need. And nobody needs you more now than him."

Mjoll let out a defeated sigh and limped towards the almost lifeless Grimm. "Come on, you fucker, let's see what I can do."

He tried to nod his head in thanks, but he was too weak. In fact, he was too weak for anything. Even the simple task of breathing was becoming a struggle.

His eyes felt suddenly heavy, and he knew he was about to lose consciousness once again. As they set him on top of a wooden table, he allowed himself to succumb to the darkness.

The sharp, sudden pain in his shoulder thrust him back into reality. He twisted his head and noticed that Mjoll had a pair of metal forceps buried in the wound. He writhed in pain, but the priest's hands quickly steadied him. He looked around the house until he saw Sara's concerned face staring at him from a darkened corner of the room. Fear filled her eyes, and tears were streaming down her face.

"Hold him still!" Mjoll yelled as she twisted the surgical tools deeper into the wound.

"I'm trying!" the priest snapped back.

Grimm took a deep breath and allowed himself to relax. He stilled his body and his mind and stared up at the roof. No matter how bad the pain became, he wouldn't allow himself to move.

Mjoll paused briefly, as she stared into Grimm's eyes with an expression of disbelief. She then nodded her head and began twisting the forceps once again. Grimm winced in pain, but somehow kept his body still.

After what seemed to be a lifetime of digging, Mjoll finally removed the tweezers and pulled out a dagger-like piece of chitin. "This is what was making you so sick," she sighed, as she collapsed on the floor, utterly exhausted.

"We almost lost you," the priest replied as he placed a comforting hand on Grimm's good shoulder. "Several times, in fact."

"Thankfully, I'm the best," Mjoll added, from the floor.

Grimm nodded his head and tried to get up from the table, but fell to his knees as soon as his feet touched the wooden floorboards. Sara let out a small whimper from the corner.

"Where do you think you're going?" Mjoll asked.

"The coast," Grimm snarled. "Now grab me my sword, or I'll take your other foot."

"Your mother didn't teach you much manners, did she?"

"My sword," Grimm repeated, as he slowly pushed himself to his feet.

"You never told me you were a wanted man," the priest began as he handed back Grimm's blade. "I'd've let you die and claimed the bounty myself."

A smile appeared on Grimm's tired lips. "How holy of you."

"I have a proposition for you that I think you'd be keen to hear."

"And what's that?"

Before the priest could answer, there was a commotion outside the hut. Grimm heard the unmistakable hiss of a sword leaving its scabbard. He cursed silently to himself as he realized that the priest wasn't the only one who had uncovered his identity.

"White-Eyes!" a familiar voice called out. "We know you're in there: come out with your hands up!"

Grimm let out a sigh, grabbed his unsheathed sword, and started marching towards the door. Mjoll quickly shot to her feet and grabbed his free hand. "What do you think you're doing? You're in no condition to fight. You can barely stand on your own two feet!"

"There won't be a fight," Grimm replied as he pulled his hand free from her grasp. "It'll be a slaughter."

Outside the house, he saw two men dressed in gambesons, with plate boots and gauntlets. One of them brandished a sword, while the other one wielded an axe. Grimm cracked his knuckles and took a deep breath. "Who here is going to become a legend?"

"Shut yer trap and drop yer sword!" the man on the right ordered. He had a patchy red beard with a young, scarless face. He had a barely perceptible shake in his hands, but a shake nonetheless.

A smug grin appeared on Grimm's face as he eyed up his opponents. Neither would be classified as battle-hardened men. He squeezed the handle of his sword, the cold leather wrap creaking under his grip. The anticipation was eating away at him. He waited with bated breath for one of the townsfolk to make the first move.

Suddenly, he heard the thrum of a bowstring. He instinctively fell to his knees, and the arrow sailed over his head by several inches. He shifted his gaze and noticed a fearful archer standing on the other side of the street.

Before he could insult his honour, the man with the trembling hands charged forward. Grimm tried to stand back up, but his legs were too weak.

The man collided with him, knocking him on to his back. Grimm let out a curse as he felt a small trickle of blood leak from his side. He quickly ran his hand over the wound and noticed that, thankfully, it was just a shallow cut.

The man with the axe charged forward and swung his weapon down at Grimm's head. Grimm rolled out of the way and stabbed his sword upward at the man's throat, but missed his mark. He rose to his feet, stumbled into the middle of the street, and waved his sword wildly before catching his breath.

The three men started laughing as they encircled him. Grimm noticed that the man's hands had lost their tremble. He gripped his sword tighter and bared his teeth before charging at the man with the axe.

Each swing of his blade was with lethal intent and with all the strength he could muster. The axeman desperately parried each blow, but it was clear that he didn't have the endurance needed to survive.

Grimm slashed his sword again, this time splitting the axe's haft in two. The man stared stupidly at his broken weapon before realizing that he was defenceless.

Grimm gripped his sword with both hands and swung downward, splitting the man's skull in two. Blood and brain matter splattered across the warrior's face as he fell to his knees in exhaustion.

He heard the crunch of snow beside him and felt the pommel of a sword smack the side of his face. He felt his jaw dislocate from the blow and reeled in pain.

Rising to his feet once again, he let out a ferocious, yet mumbled, battle cry, tackled the swordsman to the ground, and began choking him. The young man's face turned red, and spit stuck to his beard.

The man's eyes became bloodshot, and veins protruded from his skin as his complexion turned purple. Grimm squeezed his meaty hands harder, digging his thumbs into the youth's trachea.

He then heard the audible crack of a breaking windpipe, and the man's body went still. Grimm wiped the blood, sweat, and brains from his face and turned his attention towards the archer.

The man stood horrified at what he saw, then dropped to his knees and began to grovel. "Please have mercy! They made me do it! Said it was easy money. I didn't know it was you. I swear I didn't know!"

Grimm marched towards him, the tip of his bloody sword leaving a trail in the snow behind him. The archer immediately crawled away backwards, and let out feeble plea after feeble plea, as he stared up at Grimm's hate-filled eyes.

The blood-covered warrior placed a foot on the archer's chest and pressed the blade of his sword to the man's throat. His eyes darted down to see a dagger hanging from the archer's belt. "The dagger: put it in your hand."

"What?" the archer asked.

"Put the dagger in your hand," Grimm repeated.

The archer did as he was told, unsheathed the dagger from his belt, and gripped it tightly in his hand. Then Grimm smiled as he slowly leaned against his sword, applying just enough weight to puncture the man's neck. He pulled his blade free and left the man to drown in his own blood.

"By the Gods, Grimm..." the priest gasped, as he stared out at the carnage. "You could've let the poor sod live."

Grimm dropped his blade, and then stuck both hands into his mouth. With an audible pop, he pulled his jaw back into place. "That's the difference between you, priest, and me," Grimm snarled as he gingerly massaged his jawbone. "You'd rather appease your enemies, while I prefer to bury them."

"At least you had the decency to give him an honourable death," Mjoll commented as she exited her house with a tearful Sara hiding behind her.

"You were going to ask me something, priest?" Grimm snarled as he picked up his sword.

"I wanted to talk to you about the girl," the priest responded as he took a step forward.

"What about her?"

"I'd like to purchase her off you."

"What?"

"She's a slave. Name your price, and I'll pay it. Travelling alongside the most wanted man on the Isles is no place for a child. Leave her with me, and I'll see to it that she's safe and lives a comfortable life."

"Will she know the comfort of scrubbing your chamber pot? Or perhaps she'll know the comfort of your touch late at night in a few winters. No, the safest place for her is with me." Grimm instinctively gripped the hilt of his sword tighter. He wasn't sure why he was offended by the priest's offer. In fact, he had dreamt about it only a few hours prior. Perhaps it was because of how he asked it.

"I'm afraid I must insist or –"

"Or what?" Grimm snarled, his nose only a few inches away from the priest's. "You going to cut me down? Heimer favours me, remember?"

The holy man gulped and stepped aside. His head hung low. Grimm was about to step forward and grab Sara when Mjoll touched him gently on the shoulder and handed him a small bag of herbs. "Eat one of these, once a day. It should help with the pain until you recover."

"Thank you."

Mjoll then pulled him in close and whispered into his ear. "She won't bring your family back."

Grimm tore himself free from her grasp, grabbed Sara by the arm, and began walking towards the outskirts of town. Rage filled his body. He wanted to cut Mjoll's tongue out for even suggesting that he was trying to replace his family with Sara. But he knew that even with one foot, she'd be able to beat him in his current condition. He knew that he survived the encounter with the townsfolk solely because they were inexperienced at fighting.

He looked at the horizon beyond the gates of Draygard and knew that the coast was only a few days' walk away, although he had no plan for when he got there. He hoped he could flag down a nearby ship and bribe them into taking him to the mainland, but nothing was for certain. All he knew for sure was that the worst was behind him.

He couldn't have been more wrong.

CHAPTER FOURTEEN

ANNA

The mouldy bread crumbled in her hands as she picked it out of the gutter. She greedily gobbled it down, making sure to savor every bite.

Anna had no idea how vast Winterhelm was. It seemed like every day she discovered a new area of the city, making the task of finding her auntie's house almost impossible. To make matters worse, her survival skills proved useless within the confines of the city walls. There was no game to hunt, and it seemed everything was reliant on having coin. It had been four days since her last decent meal, and her mouth had salivated at the sight of the discarded bread.

She wiped the soggy crumbs from her lips and stared at her reflection in the filth-ridden gutter. She ran her hand through her matted ashen hair, and winced in pain as she tried to rip through the plethora of knots.

With even the slightest movement, her back ached. She had slept on the hard cobblestone streets every night, and it had taken a toll on her body. She then turned her attention to her clothes. Thankfully, the dwarven clothing had kept her warm through the coldest of nights, and she no longer feared freezing to death.

She reached into her frost-covered pockets and played with the silver coin that laid inside. It was all the shopkeeper could give her for her bow and arrows. *One measly coin,* Anna thought to herself as she rolled the coin through her fingers. *What the hell am I supposed to buy with this?* She regretted trading in her bow. She thought it would give her enough money to buy several meals, but she soon found out that crude-looking bows carved in the forest did not fetch a high price. Anna felt naked without it, but was thankful that she still had her knife, in case she ran into trouble.

It was still early in the morning, the sun barely cresting over Winterhelm's walls, but in a few hours, the streets would be packed with life. Anna was amazed at how so many people could live in such a place. She had been here for four days and never saw the same person twice. She slowly rose to her feet, making sure to keep her back as straight as possible, and began her daily search for her auntie.

"I don't even know what she looks like," Anna grumbled to herself, as she entered yet another unfamiliar district. The houses were taller than every tree in the forest, and they were constructed purely out of stone.

Unlike the other houses in Winterhelm, these appeared different. They had triangular windows and doorways and were topped with conical roofs adorned with clay shingles. Anna wasn't sure why, but she stared up at the peculiar-looking houses. They appeared to be replicas of one another, with the only difference being a change in the exterior colour or the rare additional window.

"Beautiful, aren't they?" an elderly voice asked.

Anna quickly spun around and was surprised to see an elderly man standing with a young woman. He had a wrinkled face, and his grey hair was neatly combed to the side. He was clean-shaven, and his soft eyes had a warm, welcoming quality to them. The man seemed ancient compared to the woman, who had a youthful, wrinkle-free face. She had long blonde hair and was decorated in a fine fur coat.

"These houses, each one is a masterpiece," the man continued, his eyesight never leaving the triangular houses. "They were constructed from a set of elven blueprints. Of course, only the wealthiest citizens were afforded the opportunity to live in such works of art." The man wiped a tear on the sleeve of his fine coat. "What I wouldn't give to live in an elven house."

Anna hated the idea of approaching strangers again, especially because it rarely worked in her favour. But she was desperate, and lost in a city where every street looked the same. "Perhaps you can help me," Anna asked, swallowing her pride. "I'm looking for my Auntie Teale's place, but I'm not sure where she lives."

The man stared up at the conical roofs for a second longer before shifting his gaze to Anna. "I'm sorry, I –"

"You should go and see Master Bran's archives," the woman interjected. "He has collected information on all of Winterhelm's inhabitants for centuries. But be careful: he is a dwarf."

Anna narrowed her eyes. "Where is it?"

The elderly man gave the woman a dirty look before eventually sighing and pointing down the street, back towards the city centre. "About a twenty-minute walk that way."

"Thanks," Anna replied as she hurried away from the couple.

As she walked down the winding street, she couldn't help but wonder what she would do once she found her aunt's. City life did not seem to agree with her, and she doubted that her last living relative would allow her to go back into the forest and fend for herself.

She then began imagining what her life would be like if she were forced to live the remainder of her days within Winterhelm's walls. She shook the nightmarish thought out of her head. *I can always leave, and go and meet up with Solin, Ethril, and Muril.* A smile crept onto her face, as she thought about her life as a deadeye in Solin's circus, but suddenly, the smile faded.

Muril's fortune began echoing in her mind, and the hairs on the back of her neck stood up. *Beware the raven, for it will ultimately betray you.* A chill ran down her spine, then she wrapped her arms around herself and focused on finding the city centre.

The so-called twenty-minute walk soon turned into an hour's trek before she finally made it to the heart of the city. It was heavily congested, and the deafening sound of people bartering pained her ears as she entered the square. She paused on the stone steps that descended into the city centre and watched as the sea of people sporadically moved around.

Everyone seemed to move in their own direction, with little regard to anyone else's path. They collided with one another without uttering an apology. Anna felt her hands sweat as she stared at the crowded square in horror. Suddenly, she felt a hand on her shoulder. She looked up and saw a man with yellow teeth wearing a small cap with a hole in it. His fingernails were jagged and discoloured. Anna recoiled back at the sight of him.

"Are you lost, dearie?" he said in a gravelly voice.

"I'm trying to find Master Bran's archive, but I don't know which building it is."

The man clicked his tongue mockingly and squeezed her shoulder tighter. "You must have a fortune if you're going to see the dwarf. Last time I checked, he charged fifteen crowns for any information."

Anna's heart sank as her hand instinctively went to the lone coin in her pocket. She cursed herself silently for being such a fool. *Everything in this city costs money, even information.* She started to walk away, defeated, when she felt the man's hand tighten once again.

"Are you looking for someone? Perhaps I can help; I've lived in this here city all my life! And the best part: I won't charge you a red fuckin' cent."

Anna paused and looked at the man suspiciously. Her gut told her not to trust the man, but she knew she had no other option. Perhaps it was just the man's dishevelled appearance that made her leery of him. Ultimately, she ignored her conscience and nodded her head. "I'm looking for my Auntie Teale, and I –"

"Teale! Why didn't you say so?" the man exclaimed as he grabbed Anna by the wrist. "I've known her for years. We even used to be sweethearts when we were younger. Come, I'll take you to her!"

Before Anna could reply, the man was dragging her down the streets, away from the city centre. She couldn't help but laugh at the man's youthful energy. He seemed to teem with excitement as he pulled her past crowds of staring people. Suddenly, he came to a halt.

"Hmm," he said as he scratched his chin. "I know a shortcut, but there's a stone fence in the way. We'll have to help each other over it. Sound like a deal?"

Anna nodded her head, and the man once again sprinted down a side alley, pulling her behind him. After about twenty paces into the alley, he came to a stop in front of a brick wall. The wall was about ten feet high and spanned the entire width of the alley.

"Here," the man coughed as he pulled Anna in front of him. "I'll hoist you by your waist, and then you pull me over."

Anna doubted the soundness of the man's plan, but once again, she agreed to go along with it, due to her lack of other prospects. She lifted her hands above her head and felt the man's grimy hands grasp her waist tightly.

Expecting to be lifted into the air, she was shocked to feel the man immediately begin pulling at her pants. Panic set in, and her brain raced frantically, trying to figure out what to do.

She reached down for her knife but found that the sheath was empty. She began kicking and screaming with all of her might, but the man's body weight was soon pinning her to the ground.

The man with the yellow teeth licked her cheek and smiled villainously. Anna squirmed as he began kissing his way down her body. She closed her eyes tight pretending that she was somewhere else, that none of this was happening, that it was all a bad dream. Suddenly, there was a shout at the end of the alley, and the man froze.

"What do you think you're doing?" the voice called out.

The man, while still pinning Anna to the ground, turned his head around and snarled, "Mind your own fuckin' business!"

"Don't you know that's one of Greaver's girls?" the voice replied.

Anna opened her eyes and saw that the man's complexion had visibly paled. He quickly climbed off her. Sweat was forming on his brow, and his eyes darted around wildly. "A thousand apologies, milady. I had no idea!" he exclaimed. "Please don't tell Mr. Greaver! I'll pay him double next month, just because of this misunderstanding."

Before Anna could reply, the dishevelled man sprinted out of the alley and past the shadowy figure, without looking back. She looked at the figure of her saviour as he approached her.

As he drew closer, she saw that he was only a few years older than her and was extremely handsome. He had a square jawline, wavy auburn hair, strong cheekbones, and comforting grey eyes. The handsome boy extended a hand toward her, holding her knife in his palm.

"I saw him take this off you back at the square. I followed you because I figured you'd need it." The boy smiled.

"How? I didn't even feel him take it."

"He's a pickpocket," the boy replied. "Lifts things off people without them noticing for a living. I'd hate to give that bastard any praise, but he's pretty damn good at it."

Anna swiftly snatched the knife out of the boy's hand and brushed her matted hair out of her eyes. "Well, thank you, but I should be –"

"Not from around here, are you?" the boy interrupted as he leaned against the stone wall of a building.

"No, I'm not."

"Name's Randall; welcome to Winterhelm. If you ever run into trouble again, just mention you're one of Greaver's girls, and everyone will leave you alone." Without uttering another word, the boy nodded his head and began to exit the alley.

Overwhelmed, Anna collapsed on the ground and began sobbing. She was sick of this. The pain of losing her father, and the realization that everyone outside the forest viewed her as a pawn, was too much. She was alone, scared, and had nowhere to go. Suddenly, she felt a hand on her shoulder. She looked up through her tear-filled eyes and saw the boy staring down at her.

"Are you okay?" he asked with sincerity.

"No!" Anna snapped. "My father's dead, and everyone sees me as a slab of meat! I don't know what to do! I'm just trying to find my auntie."

"You need to talk to Greaver," Randall said as he sat down beside her. "I was like you, once. That's when Greaver found me. He took me in and gave my life purpose again. I'm sure he can help you find your aunt."

Anna wiped the tears out of her eyes. "Who's this Greaver?" she asked.

"They call him the King of Crooks," Randall replied. "Every thief, pickpocket, and cutthroat in the city owes him fealty. Nothing happens in this city without him knowing about it."

"And he'll help me?" Anna asked bluntly.

Randall stood up and smiled brightly at her. "I'm sure of it."

"Take me to him."

Randall's smile widened, and he waved his hand for Anna to follow. If this Greaver was as powerful as Randall said he was, then perhaps he could point her in the right direction to her family and this nightmare would be over. Her fingers danced around the handle of her knife. She swore that she would never be taken advantage of again.

As the two of them walked through the streets of Winterhelm, a constant stream of words exited Randall's mouth. He would stop to point out some uninteresting landmark, or ask her a question that he would rarely wait to hear an answer to before speaking another torrent of words. Anna wasn't sure why, but she felt safe with him, to a degree. The boy was friendly and charismatic, and was seemingly willing to help her without asking for anything in return.

After about an hour of walking, Randall brought her into yet another cramped alley, and Anna instinctively reached for her knife, but let go once she saw the boy's reassuring smile.

"The password is 'putrid,'" he whispered, even though they were alone in the alley. Randall then pulled out a loose stone in the wall to reveal a set of menacing eyes staring back at them.

"Password," a voice croaked.

"Putrid," Anna replied.

Randall placed the stone back in its hole, and a segment of the wall opened up, revealing an entire hidden courtyard that was teeming with people. Anna was amazed that so much could fit in such a small place. She turned her head and saw Randall staring at her with yet another stupid smile plastered on his face.

"Welcome to the King of Crooks' domain. We call it The Garden."

Before she could reply, he quickly grabbed her hand and led her through the crowded courtyard. She stared into the shops' windows as she passed, but noticed that almost all of them had books in front of their windows. Randall stopped and pointed to one of the stores.

"They're all licensed as bookstores, but every one of them sells something that only criminals would need. That one there sells burglary supplies. Stuff like lockpicks, rappels, glass cutters, and everything else you'd need for a great heist." He then spun Anna around and pointed her at another shop that looked identical to the first. "That one is a fence, meaning if you happen to steal something of considerable value that's easily identifiable, you'd bring it here, and Torin will sell it outside the city walls and give you the profit."

"And the king lives here?" Anna asked, still trying to comprehend the vastness of the diminutive kingdom.

"He never leaves. Come on, let me introduce you to him."

On the opposite side of the courtyard from the hidden door was a series of stairs that descended down into the city's sewers. Anna instantly realized why the password was "putrid" as she plugged her nose in disgust, following a seemingly unfazed Randall down the stone steps. They came to a cavernous room at the bottom of the staircase which was surrounded by a moat of shit and piss. Small wooden bridges were placed on top of the moat and led to the room's center, where a hodgepodge throne sat.

"Greetings, Your Majesty, I bring you a guest," Randall greeted as he bowed low.

The man sitting on the throne rose to his feet. His head was completely bald, and he had soft brown eyes. There was a noticeable scar on his chin, and a hook in his nose that suggested it had been broken before. Anna stared into the man's eyes as he approached. The King of Crooks paused a few paces away from her and smiled.

"I don't believe I know you," he began, his voice filling the large room with ease. "My name is Greaver. They call me the King of Crooks."

"My name is Anna."

"A pleasure to make your acquaintance. I hear you had a run-in with a certain pickpocket already."

Anna's face turned bright red, and she stammered uncontrollably.

"Don't look so surprised, girl. I'm sure Randall told you that I know about everything that happens in this city, and let me tell you: he won't be hurting any more little girls."

"Why's that?" Randall asked.

"It'll be hard to do anything with a slit throat," the king replied. "Now tell me, what brings you to my venerable kingdom?"

Anna couldn't help but smile at the gruesome news. "I'm looking for my Auntie Teale. I'm afraid that all I have to go on is her name and –"

"No need, child. I know of whom you speak," the king replied as he sat back down on his throne. Suddenly, his smile faded. "I'm afraid to be the bearer of bad news, but your aunt died three years past. I'm afraid a sickness swept the city, and many people perished."

Anna's heart sank. She felt a lump in her throat, and her hands began to shake. It felt as if someone had punched her in the gut and taken all the wind out of her lungs. Her legs became wobbly, and she would have fallen to the ground if not for Randall's quick reflexes, catching her as her knees gave out.

"Are you sure?" she asked, still in disbelief.

"Afraid so," Greaver replied. "There's only been one lady to dwell within these walls with that name for as long as I've been king. I'm sorry to say that it was a shame to hear of her passing. But tell you what, you're welcome to join our little family, and stay as long as you like."

"Really?" Anna asked, while she cleared her throat.

"Yes, but beware that no-one lives here for free. Everyone must pull their own weight: I'm not running a charity." Anna nodded her head appreciatively. "Randall, go get some food in her. She looks absolutely famished."

Randall bowed once again, grabbed Anna by the hand, and led her back up the stairs into the courtyard. Once they were out of earshot of the king, he smiled and looked at Anna. "I think he likes you."

"Why's that?"

"He wouldn't offer a place in his family to just anyone. The king has a real gift for spotting potential, and I think he saw some in you."

Anna smiled at the boy's compliment, but quickly tried to mask it by turning it into a scowl. "Let's go get some food," she said stalely, as she tried to hide the happiness in her voice.

The tavern in The Garden was as cramped as the hidden courtyard itself. Every table was at total capacity, and there were even a few people sitting in the rafters. Anna couldn't help but look around curiously as Randall led her through the ocean of bodies.

It seemed that everyone was smiling at her. However, these smiles had no malicious intent behind them. Instead, they were the warm, welcoming kind that you might greet a loveable relative with. Soon, they came to a table that was filled with children all around her age.

"Maggots, let me introduce you to our newest addition: Anna!" Randall announced charismatically.

A short, stocky boy stood up and aggressively brought her in for a hug. Anna was sure that she felt a few ribs crack under the enormous pressure. "Name's Tig!" the boy announced in a deep, slurred voice. "I'm the muscle," he added as he flexed his biceps flamboyantly.

"I'm Maeve," a petite girl interrupted. She was a few years younger than Anna, and had she not known better, she would have thought that they were long-lost twins. "Pleased to have you join our little group."

"They call me Chuckles!" a wild-haired boy added hysterically. "Probably because I can't stop laughing when we're pulling a job."

"That dark-skinned fella is A'Chula," Randall said, pointing to the silent adolescent at the table. "He doesn't talk much, but he can pick any lock in the city!"

"Why doesn't he talk?" Anna asked.

"Probably cause he was a slave," Tig replied. "He's from the Forsaken Lands and escaped his mistress while she was visiting the city."

"Welcome to the Maggots, Anna!" Randall boisterously hollered as he grabbed a mug off the table and raised it high in the air.

"The Maggots?"

"Randall's idea," Maeve said as she rolled her eyes.

"It makes sense!" Randall replied defensively. "Maggots clean wounds so that they can heal, and believe me, this city is a festering wound that needs our help to restore it back to its glory."

"Yup," Tig responded mockingly. "We're civil fuckin' servants!"

"I like it," Anna replied.

Randall smiled devilishly once more and placed a hand on her shoulder. "To the Maggots!" he barked as the six adolescents smashed their mugs together and began the first of many debauchery-filled nights.

ACT II

CHAPTER FIFTEEN

ELBERT

Wind blew snow across the stony shore, covering the black rocks in a thin layer of white. The rigging of the ships creaked ominously as the westerly gale assaulted the sails.

The shoreline of the Isles was barren and devoid of any life. In fact, judging solely by the beach, it seemed that these landmasses were utterly uninhabitable. Snow covered everything, and there was scant protection from the wind. Beyond the rocky shoreline, a desolate white field extended far into the horizon.

Elbert didn't care how destitute the landscape looked; he was just glad to be off that damned boat. It had been several hard weeks at sea, and after the third day, he had lost control of his stomach. Vomiting over the ship's side became a daily ritual that he hated, but could not stop. Many of the men stared at their king with smirks of amusement on their faces, until they caught a stern glare from the sure-footed Sergeant Thames.

When Elbert wasn't puking, which was seldom, he found himself thinking more and more about the campaign and he began strategizing about the assault on Tjørholm. First, he would have to get the lie of the land and scout the defences of the Islanders' stronghold. Next, he would have to devise a plan that wouldn't result in total annihilation on the first day.

Elbert knew he was far from a military mastermind, but before departing on his voyage, he had taken every book about warfare from the royal library. He combed through the pages of the books, writing in the margins with his notes, as he formulated ideas and stratagems of his own.

He also spent a lot of his time thinking about the people at his disposal.

There was the young Abram Haustack, who was doomed to lead a company of degenerates into battle.

Unlike the other lords, who had pledged their sons to lead their conscripted forces, Lord Grelin had decided to lead his troops himself, while leaving his estate under the control of his daughter. Elbert couldn't help but find the noble's willingness to march into battle admirable.

Then there was his loyal servant, Sergeant Thames. No one in the entire kingdom had shown as much devotion to the crippled king as him. As a result, Elbert called him into his chambers during the voyage.

"You summoned me, Your Majesty?" Thames spoke as he poked his head through the doorway after a brief customary knock.

"I did. Please take a seat," Elbert stated as he poured two glasses of wine from a golden pitcher.

Thames did as he was told and sat down in a small wooden chair. It creaked under the weight of his armour, and the king could see that beads of sweat had formed on the guard's head.

"Fear not, Rupert," Elbert began. "This is not a solemn occasion. In fact, it is quite the opposite. We are celebrating." He handed one of the glass cups to Thames and greedily began slurping his down.

"What are we celebrating?" Thames asked politely as he sipped his drink.

"I'm appointing you captain of the royal guard during this expedition," Elbert replied as he wiped his wine-stained lips. "You are one of the few people who has shown me respect, and it has not gone unnoticed. You will be my right-hand man. Assuming that you agree, that is."

"Of course!" Thames shouted as he placed his glass aside. "I will not disappoint you, sire, I promise."

"I know you won't. Now go and inform the men that you're their superior."

"As you wish, Your Majesty."

The sound of a ship's hull crashing into the shoreline snapped Elbert back into the present. He watched as his mighty fleet began to moor on the barbarians' beaches.

A smile crept its way along his lips. Pride filled his body as he began fantasizing about what the historians would say about this momentous occasion. *Elbert, the mad cripple who dared to challenge an entire nation of savages... and won.*

"Sire," Lord Grelin shouted as he approached his king.

Elbert let out a sigh. He had learned during the voyage that if Lord Grelin wished to speak to him; it was never with pleasant news. In fact, the noble brought nothing but problems to the king's attention.

"Sorry for disturbing you, Your Majesty," Grelin began. "But the men are sea-weary. We need to make camp soon, but there's no protection on this beach."

"So, we march until we find cover," Elbert snarled in retort.

"The men are exhausted, sire, and I'm afraid of how the order will impact morale."

"Their bodies should teem with pride," Captain Thames cut in. "There is no higher honour than to serve your king. A little march will do them some good. It'll help them stretch their legs and get the blood flowing."

"And if they refuse to march?" Grelin snapped back.

"They'll be flogged."

"Enough!" Elbert commanded as he slammed his fist into the arm of his mobile throne. "I will not beat the men so early in the campaign. We must show restraint. Make no mistake, gentlemen, this will be a long and tiring endeavour." As his eyes scanned the beach, his gaze came to a stop on the company of former prisoners. "Lord Grelin."

"Yes, Your Majesty?"

"Order a few of your scouts to survey the area. We want to make sure we won't get ambushed in the middle of the night."

"What about our shelter? It's too damn cold for the men to stay out on this beach unprotected."

"Leave that to me."

"As you wish, Your Majesty."

"Lord Haustack!" Elbert cried out.

The young noble quickly abandoned his men and ran across the beach towards the king. Elbert could see the company of prisoners snigger as they watched their "leader" sprint across the stony shore.

"Yes, Your Majesty?"

"Make some of your men useful and have them unload the clay pots and candles I had ordered to be brought with us. They are to give every soldier his own pot and five candles."

"Pots and candles, sire?" Lord Haustack asked, his voice wavering slightly.

Elbert pinched the bridge of his nose in frustration. Before the voyage, he had had a difficult time convincing the lords that a terracotta pot hanging above five candles would provide adequate protection from the harsh climate of the Isles. It seemed that Lord Haustack still failed to grasp the concept. "Do you doubt my calculations?" Elbert sneered.

"Of course not, sire, it's just, wouldn't fires make more sense?"

"And have the entire Isles see the smoke and flames?" Thames snarled, while giving the young lord a fiery glare.

The young noble nodded his head, but his eyes looked back towards the moored ships. "Can't we spend another night on the boats?"

Elbert's stomach churned at the idea of spending another night in that wooden prison. "We brought the pots and candles for a reason; plus, it won't hurt for the men to become acclimatized to the storms of the Isles."

"As you wish, Your Majesty," Haustack responded.

"And try not to forget your position, Lord Haustack," Elbert continued. "You lead a company of murderers and rapists, degenerates who have no place in a civilized society. They belong here with the barbarians."

"I'm not sure I catch your meaning," the young noble replied.

"They're expendable," Elbert hissed.

Lord Haustack's eyes widened, and colour immediately faded from his cheeks. His lips moved frantically, but no words came out. His body trembled uncontrollably, until he finally gathered his composure and gulped. "Sire, you can't be serious. They're still people. Men who have strayed from the path of good, but can still be redeemed. They're —"

"Lord Haustack, let us take a walk," Captain Thames suggested, although he voiced it more like an order.

The young noble reluctantly nodded his head and followed Thames out of earshot. Elbert looked over his shoulder and saw that the guard shot him a reassuring glance.

Relief flooded Elbert's body. He then wheeled his chair across the beach toward the company of criminals and cleared his throat. "Men, your first assignment is to unload the pots and the candles that we brought with us, and distribute them amongst the men. Each soldier should receive a pot and five candles."

"Or what?" one man sneered.

"Or the freedom that I have promised you will be revoked, and you'll soon find yourself at the bottom of the ocean," Elbert replied in a cold voice. Although the criminal tried to hide it, the king could tell that his response made the man uneasy. A smile crept along his lips. "Now get to work, or your entire company will forgo their rations." The would-be soldiers slowly rose to their feet, walked towards the ship, and went to work without uttering another grievance.

Elbert heard heavy footsteps coming from behind him. He slowly turned his chair around and saw a smiling Captain Thames approach him. "Did you quell the young lord's worries?"

"I did," Thames replied. "I told him that he has a unique opportunity."

"And what opportunity is that?"

"Because he leads a company of expendable men, he will be at the forefront of our assault, where all the glory is to be had. He is the only lord who is poised to walk away from this campaign as a hero."

"Provided he lives," Elbert muttered.

"You intend for him to die?" Thames gasped.

"I'm just being realistic. This is war. We are attempting something that has never been done before. To think that we will escape this without suffering a single casualty is idiotic."

"But you do have faith in our mission?"

"Of course, but make no mistake, Rupert, this will not be an easy fight; the deck is stacked against us." Elbert mentioned absentmindedly, as he turned his head towards the horizon.

"How so?" Thames replied.

"They are the ones fortified, they know the terrain, they can call for reinforcements, and they have most likely stockpiled provisions. The only advantage we hold is the element of surprise, and if we lose that, we may be fucked."

"Then let us pray our ships were not spotted," Thames added gravely.

Elbert nodded his head and wheeled himself across the beach, to where his tent had been erected by the rest of the royal guard. The red canvas walls flapped wildly and provided little cover from the cold, but did save him from the unforgiving wind. He rubbed his hands together for warmth, and waited for Lord Haustack's company to finish their task.

In just under two hours, every soldier had his own pot and was rubbing his hands together for warmth. The glow of the candles decorated the beach in a faint orange light. From inside his tent, Elbert could hear the spirits of the men rise as the soldiers' voices drowned out the howling wind. He smiled as he unfurled his map of the Isles.

He had barely begun examining the map when there was a sudden commotion in the camp. He quickly spun his chair and sped out of his tent. "What's going on?" he shouted, hoping someone would answer him.

"The scouting party found someone!" Captain Thames said as he suddenly emerged from the crowd.

"Who?"

"An Islander and some girl, apparently. He supposedly cut down ten of our men before being captured."

Shit, Elbert thought to himself. *If we have been spotted, this raid will be over as quickly as it began.* On the northern edge of the beach, three scouts entered the camp with their swords pointed at a tied-up man's neck.

Elbert's eyes widened as he watched the man approach. He was a mountain of muscle. Both his hair and his beard were matted and tangled, giving the man a wild, dishevelled appearance. The man held his head high as he entered the camp, making sure his face was visible for all to see. His eyes were white, as if he were blind; but judging by the way he walked, the man could clearly see. Elbert wheeled his chair towards him.

"Greetings," he began. "I am King Elbert of Artanzia, and who might you be?"

"Just a traveller," the man responded.

"I find that hard to believe. A mere traveller cannot kill ten of my men before being captured. Who are you, really?" The man said nothing, but continued to glare menacingly at the king. Elbert turned his head and noticed the frightened dwarven girl who was cowering behind the hulking Islander. "Is this your daughter?"

"What happened to your legs?" the Islander replied.

Elbert clenched his fists and swallowed his rage. He knew he had to be calm. He had to know if this man was alone or not, then he could kill him.

He waved his hand, and one of the scouts held a blade to the Islander's throat. To his surprise, the man didn't flinch.

"Kill the girl," he ordered. The child screamed as the guards grabbed her, but once again, the man did not flinch. In fact, all he did was stare menacingly at the king. "Wait!" Elbert ordered. The entire camp looked at him. "You truly don't care for this girl, Islander? Then perhaps you won't mind if I take her under my wing as my ward." Elbert locked eyes with the child and extended a hand out to her. "What's your name, child?"

"Sara," she replied meekly.

"Would you like some food? You look starving." The girl nodded her head cautiously and took a step towards the king, but the white-eyed man quickly stepped in front of her, blocking her path. Elbert smiled and sat back on his throne. "So, you do care for this girl. I must say, you put on quite a convincing display. Have you ever played cards? I've got a feeling you'd be good at it."

The Islander remained silent, glaring at the king as the fresh blood dripped from his clothes and onto the black stones of the beach. Elbert was amazed at how the man showed no weakness. There was no fear in his eyes, nor did he show any sign of discomfort from the cold. The king smiled as he locked eyes with the girl once again. *Perhaps one weakness.*

"What shall we do with him?" Captain Thames asked.

"Tie him to a pole and let him starve. I'll deal with him once the storm passes. As for the girl–" The man let out a throaty chuckle as he stared up at the sky. "What's so funny?" Elbert demanded.

He laughed. "This isn't a storm: this is just the weather!"

"Surely he's joking?" Captain Thames replied, as he looked at his king with eyes full of worry.

"You mainlanders are soft. Want to know why none of your ancestors dared to come to the Isles? Because they knew it was suicide. If we didn't kill you, the elements surely would."

A wave of uneasiness spread throughout the gathered soldiers. Many began murmuring to each other; their voices kept low in a hushed whisper. Elbert curled his lips as he listened to his soldiers' doubts. "Enough!" he shouted, his voice cutting through the air. "Tie this man up and put a gag in his mouth. I'm sick of hearing his shit. As for the girl, have her brought to my tent."

The barbarian failed to struggle, to the king's surprise, when the soldiers began escorting him across the camp. In fact, it appeared that he walked willingly.

The girl, however, kicked and screamed once she realized that the two of them were being separated. Captain Thames hugged the child tightly and tried to avoid her flailing limbs as he carried her back to Elbert's tent. The screams of the dwarf echoed throughout the evening air, and for the briefest moment, Elbert regretted his actions.

"We should just kill him, Sire," Lord Grelin spoke up, interrupting Elbert's thoughts. "Put the bastard out of his misery."

"And what about the girl?" Elbert replied, his eyes not moving off the wailing child.

"As much as it pains me to say so, a quick and painless death would be the kindest course of action. We either abandon her where she'll freeze or starve to death, or we keep her with us. And let me assure you that an army has no place for a child as young as her."

"Unlike you, Lord Grelin," Elbert snarled, "I will not put a child to death simply because of the company they keep. Plus, I feel she will be useful in getting that man to talk."

"You intend to keep him alive?"

"Call it a hunch, but I think we can still learn something from him."

"Like what?"

"I intend to find out," Elbert said as he turned his chair and began rolling back towards his tent, where the screams of the child could still be heard.

As he pushed the canvas flap open, he saw a crying Sara sitting on a bed of plush furs and a wincing Captain Thames covering his ears on the opposite side of the tent.

"Leave us," Elbert ordered.

"Your Majesty, are you sure?"

"She's a child, Rupert. I'm confident I'll be able to handle myself."

Captain Thames nodded his head and exited the king's tent. He paused beside Elbert and bent down to whisper in his ear. "I'll be right outside, ire."

Elbert waved him away dismissively, rolled his chair into the centre of the room, and pushed himself off his wheeled throne, falling onto the plush bed of furs beside the still sobbing child.

Suddenly, Sara's crying abated slightly, and she wiped the tears out of her eyes and stammered. "Wh... wha... what happened to your legs?"

Elbert looked down at his useless legs and felt a pang of remorse in his heart. He noticed that they were getting skinnier; that the muscles were starting to atrophy. The possibility of him never being able to walk again was becoming more and more likely.

He turned his head and looked at Sara, who had an expression of pure curiosity plastered on her face. "A wizard took them."

"Why?"

"I don't know; perhaps I'll have the chance to ask him one day."

Sara's face suddenly slackened, and her voice trembled once more. "What are you going to do to Grimm?"

So that's his name. "Nothing," Elbert lied. "I just want to have a few words with him."

"He doesn't talk much."

Elbert let out a short, nasal laugh. "Yes, I've noticed that. How did my men capture you two?"

"Grimm told me to hide, so I did. I'm very good at it, too. Then there was lots of yelling and swords banging. Then a man grabbed me by my hair and held... he held..."

"A blade to your throat?" Sara nodded as tears streamed down her face again. "And let me guess, Grimm threw down his sword when he saw you." Sara nodded once more. "I'm sorry that happened to you, but nobody in my camp will ever hurt you again. You are my guest, and a king's guest can have anything she desires!"

Sara looked up and smiled tearfully. "Really?"

"Really. All you have to do is ask."

"Can I have some food?"

"Of course!" Elbert exclaimed. "Rupert! Come in here." In an instant, the canvas flaps blew open and Captain Thames appeared in the entryway. "This here is Captain Thames, Sara. If you need anything, just ask him. Rupert, be a dear and bring some food for our distinguished guest."

"As you wish, Your Majesty." Captain Thames replied, while bowing low.

"So, you're really a king?"

"Indeed I am."

"I've never met a king before."

"There's a first time for everything, I suppose."

"Does this mean you'll let Grimm go?"

Elbert shook his head sadly. "I'm afraid I'll have to keep him for a few days until he feels like chatting."

Sara rolled her eyes and let out an exasperated sigh. "That'll be never."

"I can be quite persuasive." Elbert winked as he adruously began to climb back into his throne. "But I bid you farewell, milady. Feel free to roam about the camp as you see fit, and treat this tent as your own personal quarters."

Sara smiled before letting out a long yawn, and she laid down on top of the furs and closed her eyes.

The sight of the sleepy child warmed Elbert's heart, and he instantly regretted all that had happened to her. *Having a blade held to a person's throat was stressful enough, but twice in one day? I cannot imagine...* As he rolled out of the tent, he noticed that Lord Grelin was standing outside, waiting for him.

"What is it now?"

"My scouts are positive that the man was alone, except for the child. They even found their camp where the two had spent several weeks together."

"What were they doing out here?" Elbert wondered as he looked over his shoulder and peered at the sleeping child through a hole in the canvas doorway.

"Perhaps you ought to ask her," Lord Grelin suggested.

"In the morning: let her rest. She's had an eventful day. Have your men scour the area once more. I need to be sure that he was alone, and that there weren't more of them. We cannot be discovered yet. Otherwise, High King Uthredd's army will be on us at dawn."

"As you wish, Your Majesty."

Elbert spent the rest of the night rolling around the camp to talk with the lords who would lead their respective companies into battle. Many immediately made lofty promises of bringing Uthredd's severed head to his feet, while others pledged to single-handedly capture Tjørholm for him.

Each of the nobles tried to stand out but ultimately failed, as Elbert forgot their names the second he wheeled away from their illuminated pots. He was surprised by how all the men blended together. They all seemed to be cut from the same pompous, generic, bootlicking cloth.

As he was having his ear talked off by one noble, he felt the firm grasp of Captain Thames on his shoulder. "Pardon the interruption, Your Majesty."

"Please, Rupert; you're not interrupting at all," Elbert said, as he waved his hand dismissively at the young lord standing in front of him.

"I noticed that you gave your tent to the girl, and I just wanted to inform you that the royal guard has erected another tent for you to sleep in tonight, although it is more modest."

"Modesty is an important quality for a king to have." Elbert smiled, even though he was afraid of finding out what "modest" actually meant.

While Thames escorted him across the camp, the king stared at Grimm, who was chained to an old mast that had been staked into the ground. His hands lay in his lap, and he stared directly into the wind, paying no mind to the nearby soldiers or the gawking king.

"What are your plans for him, sire?" Thames asked, his voice breaking the silence that had arisen.

"I'll talk to him in the morning. My gut tells me that he will be useful, although I'm not sure how."

"Permission to speak plainly, Your Majesty?"

"Granted."

"I don't like the look of him. He's a killer through and through. I say we cut his throat and let the crabs feast on his corpse."

"A harsh judgement."

"My gut is telling me he is dangerous; the way he is so calm... it unnerves me."

"He's chained up. What harm could he possibly do?"

"I knew some of the men he killed. They were damn fine with a sword. I'm confident that this Islander is more dangerous than he appears."

"Thank you for your advice. I'll take it into consideration, but I'm afraid I'm too tired to make a decision right now. I need rest."

"Of course, Your Majesty."

On the opposite side of the camp sat a small tent that made Elbert's lips curl into a sneer. The shelter was only big enough for the king to sleep in and did not provide sufficient room for carrying out his morning ablutions. As the grizzled face of Captain Thames turned to present the tent to him, Elbert managed to contort his mouth into a thankful smile.

"It looks... quaint," he said, as pleasantly as possible.

Thames nodded his head politely. "If Your Majesty wishes, I can always move the girl to this tent and –"

"No!" Elbert exclaimed as he held up his hands. "This will do. Besides, it's not like I need the room to stretch my legs."

Thames let out an amused snort and once again nodded his head. "Then I bid you a good evening, Your Majesty."

"Goodnight, Rupert," the king replied as he wheeled into his tent, crawled onto the bed made of furs, closed his eyes, and let sleep consume him.

A blood-curdling scream for help jolted him from his slumber. His eyes darted around the small tent, and he heard the thumping of heavy footsteps outside.

He hurriedly crawled into his chair, wheeled past the canvas flap, and saw that most of his men were running to the other side of camp. Elbert quickly followed.

His heart raced wildly as he fantasized about what had happened. Had they been discovered? Were they currently amid an ambush launched by one of Uthredd's scouting parties? He urged his arms to push the wheels of his throne faster and faster until he got to a large crowd of soldiers on the other side of the camp.

"Move!" Elbert ordered, as he pushed his way through the mass of bodies, not caring who he ran over while doing so.

Once he was at the front of the crowd, Elbert's stomach sank. He saw the limp, dead body of one of his soldiers lying at the feet of the barbarian prisoner. Captain Thames held a blade to the man's throat. Grimm's face was beaten and bruised, and yet, he still had a sickening smile on his lips.

"What happened?" Elbert yelled, his anger flooding his voice.

"A soldier got too close to the prisoner, Your Majesty," Thames responded flatly. "Two men had to beat him to free their comrade, but by then, it was too late."

"How did this happen? He was chained up!"

"I used my legs," Grimm laughed. "Although you'd know nothing about that, I'm sure."

Elbert rolled his chair forward until he was mere inches from the prisoner's face. He scanned the man's bloodied face, rage slowly consuming his body, then reached out and grabbed Grimm by his hair. "Make peace with whatever gods you believe in, because you'll be seeing them soon," he growled through gritted teeth.

"I don't think so," the barbarian replied.

Elbert's grip loosened slightly as he was taken aback by the man's arrogance. He squeezed the man's hair tighter, trying to make him wince from the pain, but it was no use. "What do you mean?"

"Before I killed that pig-fucker, he mentioned you intend to take Tjørholm. I must admit, I've never heard of a ballsier plan. But you'll never be able to capture it without me. I know every stone in that fortress."

"He's lying!" Thames exclaimed. "Speaking out his arse to save his own hide."

"Don't you know who I am, mainlander?" the man shouted back in response to the captain. "I'm Grimm White-Eyes, Shield of the Isles, High King Uthredd's right-hand man!"

The camp stood in stunned silence, most undoubtedly in disbelief of the Islander's words. Elbert blinked sporadically as he tried to comprehend what he had just heard. *Could this savage truly be who he says he is?* he thought to himself, before shaking his head and clearing his throat. "Leave us," he ordered the men. The soldiers froze in place: none dared to move a muscle.

"You heard your king, back to your posts!" Captain Thames hollered. This time, the men lazily went back to the pots in the middle of the camp and began murmuring amongst themselves as they walked.

"I believe this is the part where we come to a deal," Grimm announced smugly.

"Do you have any proof that you are who you say you are? All you've given us thus far is the word of a murderer and a savage."

"Do you know of any other bastards with white eyes? Besides, if that's not enough for you, you can capture any other Islander and ask them who I am. They'll tell you that not only am I the man I claim to be, but I'm also the best swordsman on the Isles."

Elbert waved his hand at Captain Thames, and immediately the guard removed his sword from the prisoner's throat and placed it back in its scabbard. "Why would you willingly betray your king for us foreigners?"

Grimm let out a short laugh and shook his head. "Let's just say the king and I don't see eye to eye right now."

"What do you want in return?"

The barbarian's face slackened suddenly. "The girl is not to be harmed. If any of your men so much as look at her, I'll gut them right where they stand."

"Very well, is that it?" Elbert drawled out.

"After you've taken Tjørholm, I want a ship to take me to the mainland."

"You intend to live amongst us civilized folks?" Thames scoffed.

"I intend to live as a free man," Grimm responded menacingly.

"Very well, I agree to your terms," Elbert began. "However, I don't think you are who you say you are, and you will therefore remain tied to this post. Captain, bind his legs so that we don't have any more incidents, and dispose of the body."

"Yes, Your Majesty."

"You're making a mistake!" Grimm called out, as the king wheeled his way back towards his tent. "You'll never take Tjørholm without me!"

Elbert paid him no mind. He was tired, and needed his rest. *Tomorrow, we will take Tjørholm.*

CHAPTER SIXTEEN

ANNA

It was an uncharacteristically warm day, and as a result, the marketplace was full of people. The sun hung high in the air, and threatened to melt all the snow that had accumulated throughout the winter thus far.

Adding to the warm weather was the lack of wind. At this time of year, the wind was usually unforgiving and pierced the thickest of coats, but today it was nonexistent. This allowed the people of Winterhelm to wear looser clothing, making it easier for Anna and her friends to lift things off them.

She had only been with the Maggots for weeks, but she had learned so much during that time. Randall and his friends had taught her the many ways to pick someone's pocket successfully; and they showed her all the best hiding spots, on the off chance that the city guard ever pursued her. She also learned that whatever they stole, Greaver took a sizeable cut.

Randall had become more and more vocal about his displeasure with the King of Crooks, making sure only to voice his grievances when he was alone with the Maggots. Greaver had apparently ruled over Winterhelm for several decades, and Randall was adamant that it was time for a change. When he wasn't complaining about the King of Crooks' unfairness, he usually talked about the city's nobles and how he despised them.

Anna couldn't help but admire the young thief's beliefs. It truly seemed that Randall wanted to make the world a better place. They had often spent their nights walking around the city, as Randall rambled about the injustices he saw in the world while Anna listened attentively. The passion he spoke with always warmed her heart. She could listen to his ambitious fantasies for hours and never tire.

"You ready?" Randall whispered, his voice cutting through Anna's thoughts.

"Yup," Anna replied as she nimbly stretched her fingers, ready to snatch the coin purse out of a wealthy noble's pocket.

Whenever they decided to lift coins off people, they always targeted the wealthy. Rich people often had a cavalier attitude towards money, and were less likely to miss a few coins. Today's target was a portly man dressed in fine clothes, who waddled from merchant to merchant, spending heaps of coins at each stall. The man's frivolous spending made him a prime target.

"Remember the plan?" Randall asked.

"Mhmm," Anna nodded. "Chuckles will distract the noble while Maeve distracts the guards." It always amazed Anna how Maeve could summon tears on command, and how effectively she could pretend that she lost her mother. *If her life had turned out differently, perhaps she'd be a world-class mummer,* Anna thought. "I'll lift the coin purse from the noble, and Tig will block his path towards me," Anna continued, pushing her thoughts aside. "Then I'll slip the purse into your pocket, so that if I get caught, I won't have it on me."

"Exactly." Randall smiled.

They had executed this exact scheme several times in the past, and it always went off without a hitch. Randall's plans were flawless. He seemingly had all the answers, had thought of everything that could possibly go wrong, and had accounted for it in his stratagem.

With a silent nod of her head, Anna weaved her way through the crowd as the plan went into motion. As she neared the noble, she started to lower herself into a deep crouch so that she was out of the guards' view and hidden by the mass of bodies. Her eyes darted between the man's pocket and her feet. If she stepped on someone, she would surely draw attention to herself, which would put the whole endeavour in jeopardy.

The man stopped at another stall, and Anna paused. She couldn't steal the purse when he was at a stall. The risk of being seen by the merchant or another patron was too great. She remained crouched and watched the man peruse the merchant's wares. *Come on... come on,* Anna silently commanded, her fingers fidgeting anxiously. She had learned to love the thrill of stealing. It filled her body with such a high that she doubted anything else could compare to it.

Finally, the fat noble nodded his head, paid the merchant, and moved towards the next cart. Anna quickly, yet stealthily, closed the distance.

She turned her head and saw that Tig was standing right behind her. He gave a reassuring nod. Anna turned back around and reached into the man's pocket. She felt the fat purse between her fingers. As soon as she had a firm grip on the leathery pouch, she pulled it out of the pocket and turned around.

Suddenly, her arm jerked tight, and she was forced to spin back around and face the portly man, who in turn was staring at her. Both of them stared at one another with awestruck expressions, until they both looked at the coin purse that was tethered to the man's pocket.

The noble opened his mouth, undoubtedly to scream for help, when Tig slammed his fist into the man's teeth. The portly lord fell to the ground with an audible thud, and people quickly turned to see what had happened.

"Cut it!" Tig hissed from over his shoulder, as he had already begun fleeing through the crowd.

Anna pulled out her knife, and a couple of bystanders screamed in shock. She cut the tether attached to the man's coin purse, and quickly fled the marketplace as well.

She cursed herself as she shoved people aside. *How could I be so stupid?* She serpentined between the people, hoping to lose any pursuers that may have been chasing her.

As she reached the edge of the crowd, she saw A'Chula standing near a side alley with his hand extended. Anna tossed the coin purse through the air, and it landed directly in the dark-skinned boy's hand. He then turned around and darted into the darkness of the alley.

"That's her! Thief!" a voice called out from the crowd.

Anna sprinted away from the marketplace, and her mind raced as she tried to remember the nearest hiding place. The adrenaline must have clouded her recollection, because the only safe haven she could think of was The Garden.

She looked behind her and saw that three city guards were chasing after her. Quickly, she changed her direction and ran down another street before changing it again.

She hopped over fences, barrelled through houses, and climbed over walls, all to lose the guards. The cool air burned her lungs as she continued to run towards the hidden doorway.

Several times, she had made a wrong turn. She cursed that all the streets looked the same.

She turned down yet another alley, relieved to find that it was the correct one. In a panic, she pulled out the loose stone from the wall and was greeted with the menacing eyes that she had grown accustomed to.

"Password?" the voice croaked.

"Putrid!" Anna shouted, not sure how far behind the guards were.

The door slowly opened, and she squeezed herself through the gap, not willing to waste any time waiting for the gatekeeper to open it fully.

She breathed a sigh of relief once she saw the courtyard of The Garden. She was safe at last.

Anna patiently waited in the courtyard for several hours before her friends finally came through the stone door. The first was Chuckles, who was laughing uncontrollably. Anna just then realized that he wasn't there to distract the noble, and she scowled at him as he approached.

"What's so damn funny?" Anna snapped as Chuckles sat beside her.

He didn't respond. In fact, it seemed like he was unable to speak through the laughter, and Anna found it amazing that he could even breathe through all the hysterics.

"If you would've done your job, I wouldn't've gotten caught," Anna frowned.

"I'm... I..." Chuckles started, but she waved a dismissive hand towards him. She was in no mood for apologies.

Next to come through the doors were Tig and Maeve. Both seemed to share Chuckles' amusement as they laughed, until they caught Anna's glowering stare. Maeve looked away sheepishly, while Tig scratched his neck, no doubt forcing his brain to think of the words for a proper apology.

Anna couldn't stay mad at them. They had both done what they were supposed to. She reluctantly smiled, hugged both of them, and then listened to Tig's extravagant and exaggerated tale about the entire event.

"You should've seen that noble's ploughing face!" he bellowed, as he erupted into laughter once again.

The door to The Garden swung open again, and A'Chula walked through, tossing the hefty coin purse up in the air and catching it in his hand. A devious smile appeared on his lips. Although Anna had yet to hear more than five words from the former slave, she had learned his body language. Just by reading his posture, she could tell what kind of mood he was in, and whether he thought a job was a good idea or not.

After about an hour of reminiscing in the courtyard, Randall came through the doorway, and he did not share in the rest of the group's mirth. He scowled, and stormed right up to Chuckles before slamming his fist into the bridge of his nose. The laughter immediately stopped.

"You fucking idiot!" he yelled. "You could've got Anna captured, or worse!"

"Sorry, Randall," Chuckles replied, as he tried to stem the stream of blood that was pouring out of his nose.

"It's okay," Anna chimed in. "Nothing happened, and we all made it out safely."

"No thanks to this simpleton," Randall muttered under his breath, as he spat in Chuckles' direction. "If you'd stuck to the plan, everything would have gone swimmingly!"

Anna had never seen this side of Randall, and she was unsure how she felt about it. They had never had a job go awry before, and she wasn't sure exactly what he was mad at. Was he mad that she almost got caught, or was he upset because Chuckles screwed up his perfect plan? Perhaps it was a bit of both.

"What were you even doing?" Randall snarled.

Chuckles did not reply. His head stared at the frost-covered cobblestones of the courtyard as blood slowly dripped from the tip of his nose.

"Well?" Randall prodded.

"There was a girl," Chuckles muttered under his breath, barely audible.

"I beg your pardon?" Randall hissed through gritted teeth.

"There was a girl!" Chuckles shouted. "I thought I had more time before Anna made her move, so I went to see if I could get her name and -"

Randall marched forward, grabbed Chuckles by the collar of his coat, and pulled him in close. "You risked all of this for some fucking trollop? Thank fuck A'Chula was there, or –"

"Enough!" Anna shouted. "I don't need you to defend me, and Chuckles made a mistake. It happens. Now let it go."

Randall instantly let go of the boy's coat and shook his head, but he refused to speak another word. Tig and Maeve consoled Chuckles as they began walking towards the tavern. Anna turned her head to A'Chula, who was still holding the purse in his hands.

"How much is in there?" A'Chula looked down and opened up the leather pouch. He dumped a handful of coins into his palm and shook the bag to indicate there was still more in the purse.

Anna smiled and nodded her head. "Good. Perhaps we can afford a private room tonight."

The tavern was once again brimming with patrons. Every table had at least five people crowded around it, and all of them were drinking profusely. Anna could never understand how this tavern always seemed so busy. No matter the time of day, it always seemed like the small inn exceeded maximum occupancy.

The Maggots walked up to the barkeep. With Randall leading the way, he dumped a handful of coins onto the counter and smiled at the man behind the bar.

"One room, please, for all of us." Randall's voice was commanding, but the slight waver showed a hint of child-like giddiness in it.

The tavern keeper looked at the mound of coins curiously. His eyes scanned each of the children before he finally grunted in approval. "Good haul today, eh?" he croaked, as he scooped the gold coins into his pocket.

"We did alright," Randall replied coyly.

"Follow me," the bartender instructed.

He led the Maggots to the second level of the tavern and escorted them down a long hallway to two large oak doors at the end. The man turned the key and unlocked the room. Pushing the two oaken doors aside, he revealed a large suite with a bath basin, a gigantic bed adorned with the finest sheets, and a balcony view of The Garden.

"Hope this is to your liking," the barkeep muttered. "It's our finest room."

"It'll do," Randall replied, before dumping a large number of coins in the man's hand. "We would like round-the-clock drinks, and one of everything on the menu. I intend for us to live like gods tonight."

The innkeeper nodded his head and made his way back down the hallway, leaving the adolescents to their devices.

"Whoa," Chuckles gasped as he staggered into the cavernous room. "This place is massive."

"How much is left?" Tig asked, as he tried to grab the coin purse from Randall, who promptly swatted away the giant's meaty fist.

"We have a small fortune here, and I intend for us to eat and drink it all away. What's the point of having this much gold if we can't treat ourselves for all our hard work?"

The rest of the Maggots nodded their heads in agreement. Maeve grabbed Anna by the hand and pulled her toward the luxurious bed, flopping onto the soft satin sheets. Tig and Chuckles admired the room and all of its elegant artwork. Randall waited impatiently by the door for his food and drink, while A'Chula stood out on the balcony and stared out into the crowded courtyard of The Garden.

Anna smiled as she let the lavish bedspread engulf her. She felt her body sink into the mattress, and the tension in her muscles disappeared in an instant. Never before had she experienced such comfort.

The bed that she had slept on for most of her life was barely a bed at all. It was more like a pile of animal pelts on top of a stiff wooden board. She exhaled as she allowed her body to collapse further into the soft mattress. If this was a sign of things to come, she was going to enjoy life as a Maggot.

There was a knock at the door, and Randall swung the doors open, but he did not say a word. In fact, the entire room went eerily silent. Anna sat up and saw that Greaver was standing in the doorway, smiling at the six thieves.

"I heard you lot had a successful day today," he began, his voice trailing off as he casually sauntered into the room. "Upon hearing this, I awaited atop my throne for you to share the good news with the man who so graciously took you all in and gave you purpose. Imagine my surprise when I hear that you six bugger off to the inn instead, and spend more coin than most have seen in their lifetime."

The air was sucked out of the room. All six youths recoiled from the king's words and refused to make eye contact with him. Greaver paused and wiped a finger along the tub, as if inspecting it for dust, before continuing. "I'm sure that this was all a misunderstanding, though. The excitement went to your young brains, and you forgot to pay your dues to your king."

Anna gulped as the King of Crooks' eyes locked on to her. Even though his eyes were not hard, she felt incredibly uncomfortable under his gaze. It was similar to her father's when he used to scold her for wandering off into the forest alone.

"Sorry, Greaver," Randall replied meekly. "Here's your cut. We should've brought it straight to you."

The King of Crooks clapped his hands and smiled as he snatched the coin purse from the boy's hands, before patting him on the cheek. "No apology necessary, as long as forgetfulness does not become a habit of yours." Greaver turned and stared at Anna once again. "Let's take a walk."

Everyone's eyes focused on her, and she felt an uneasy warmth consume her body. She timidly hopped off the bed and followed the man out of the room and outside the tavern. As they walked through the courtyard, Greaver didn't say a word. In fact, he didn't even acknowledge her existence; he continued about his day as if she wasn't even there.

"It appears you're adjusting well to your new life," he said, after a lengthy silence.

The sudden sound of his voice startled Anna, and her brain froze, not sure how to respond to such a statement. After a few seconds of staring into the King of Crooks' soft brown eyes, she regained her composure. "Yes, I'm very fortunate that you have taken me in."

Greaver laughed. He patted her on the back before wiping a tear out of his eye. "No need to grovel, my dear," he explained. "I merely wish to check in on you." He came to a sudden stop and crouched so that they were at eye-level. "Your journey has been long and hard thus far, the exact details I cannot imagine. I invited you for this walk to see how you're doing."

Anna was taken aback by the sincerity in the man's voice. She had never expected a man like him to care about her. She was unnerved, however, at how easily this man could guess her past. *Perhaps all children who come to him have had a hard life, and he is just making an assumption,* she thought to herself, not truly believing her words. The way the man talked, it was as if he knew of all the burdens she carried, all the painful memories, and truly wished to help her.

"I like it here," Anna replied truthfully, after a momentary pause. "I'm lucky to have found such great friends."

"Indeed, you seem especially close to Randall."

"He is really nice and –"

"Do you like him?" Greaver asked, raising an eyebrow.

Anna's face flushed red. She had enjoyed Randall's company, but never imagined him as anything more than a friend. After her encounter with the pickpocket, love was the furthest thing from her mind. Since then, she had recoiled from every man's touch, albeit ever so slightly, so as not to show any weakness.

"I think we are just friends," she replied.

"Hmph," the King of Crooks snorted, before continuing on his walk, gesturing for Anna to follow. "Did he ever tell you about how he came to me?"

"No."

"Oh, it's a magnificent story. Would you like to hear it?" Anna nodded her head politely. "Young Randall used to be in service to a certain family. Now, this wasn't just any old family; these people were nobles. One day, I stopped by to visit this particular family." Anna shot him a confused glance. "It pays to have some high-born connections in my line of work," he explained, before turning his head forward once again. "As I was visiting, one of the maids dragged Randall in by the ear. She pulled a pearl necklace out of his pocket and accused him of stealing. Well, the man of the house instantly whipped into a frenzy. He threatened to flay the boy alive and dump his bones in the gutter. I immediately interjected, and offered to pay them the boy's weight in gold and silver if I could take him under my tutelage."

"Why?" Anna asked, in utter disbelief.

"Even though the maid had found the pearl necklace, she did not see the large collection of rings he had hidden in his pockets. The way he had pocketed those rings told me that this was not the first time he had stolen from his master's home. It was just the first time he got caught."

"And you wanted to teach him."

"Exactly!" Greaver exclaimed. "I know talent when I see it, and let me tell you: nobody has more talent at thieving than Randall. Except maybe you."

"Me?" Anna blushed.

"Oh my, yes. People are still talking about the silver-haired girl who darted through homes and leapt over walls in order to escape the city guards. You can't teach instincts like that."

"Thank you," Anna replied, feeling energized by the compliment.

"When you're done celebrating with your friends," Greaver began, "I'd like to have you and Randall for dinner. There's nothing I love more than a good heist story."

"I'll ask," Anna responded. The King of Crooks smiled and waved his hand dismissively, prompting her to return to the tavern and tell her friends everything that had just transpired.

"A dinner?" Randall asked in disbelief, as he took another healthy swig from his mug of ale.

"Mhmm," Anna responded. "So don't drink too much."

"That ship's sailed," Randall slurred under his breath.

"How come we aren't invited?" Chuckles belched, as he helped himself to another drumstick from the roast chicken sitting on the table in the middle of the suite.

"Probably doesn't want to see your ugly mugs," Maeve mused, as she poured more ale into the silver goblet she had found.

Tig slammed his empty mug onto the table and wiped the froth from his lips. "I'm surprised that he didn't invite A'Chula, being the chatterbox that he is." Everyone laughed at the big man's joke, except for the former slave, whose expression remained as stoic as ever.

Randall reached for a slice of freshly baked bread, when Anna smacked his hand away and scowled at him. "Save some of your appetite for Greaver's," she ordered.

"Yes, Mother," Randall mocked as he lunged towards the bread plate once again.

Despite his drunkenness, he moved with surprising speed, but Anna was faster. She pulled the plate out of his grasp and threw it out of the window and into the courtyard. The rest of the Maggots erupted in raucous laughter. Even A'Chula cracked a smile on his usually emotionless face. Randall stood up from the table and shot a fiery glare towards Anna. However, it was only for the briefest of moments, before he too joined in on the laughter.

Anna reminded herself how dangerous alcohol was. She remembered when she tried it for the first time back at the lumberjack's camp, how it dulled her senses and made her queasy. However, the Maggots did not share her apprehension about the foul-tasting drink, and greedily helped themselves to a mug whenever they could.

This made Anna feel compelled to do the same, and as a result, she often helped herself to the obligatory one or two drinks when at the tavern. Relief flooded her body when she saw that the ale had not diminished Randall's jovial nature. In fact, he seemed more charismatic while under the influence, and more confident in himself, as impossible as that seemed.

"When do we leave?" Randall asked as he poured himself another mug.

"We should leave now. The sun's already setting," Anna informed him, as she began walking towards the door.

"Good, I'm dying to know what our loving father has to say to us," Randall added sarcastically. Anna always cringed when he referred to Greaver as their father. Although she was thankful for all that the man had done for her, she only had one father. And he was gone, and she was the last of her family.

The cold winter air bit at their faces as they exited the warmth of the tavern. Anna instinctively pulled her coat tighter, while Randall shivered uncontrollably. They walked hurriedly across the courtyard towards the "throne room," counting the seconds until they were once again shielded from the winter wind's harsh bite.

"I never asked you," Randall said, his voice shaking from the cold. "What happened to your mom and dad?"

Anna flinched at the question. She had no desire to bring up those painful memories. The image of her father's skinless corpse still haunted her dreams and threatened to appear in her mind once again. "They're dead," she responded coldly.

"Never knew my parents," Randall replied, as if it would bring her some comfort. "My mother was a popular courtesan, so my father could be anyone."

"And your mom?"

"She had no love in her heart unless it came with the promise of coin. As soon as I could walk and talk, she kicked me out. I've been on my own ever since."

Despite the retelling of his sad upbringing, Randall was smiling from ear to ear. It amazed Anna at how the boy's cheerful demeanour never diminished. There had only been a handful of times when the boy's usual upbeat attitude was replaced by another emotion. Unfortunately, it was often anger.

The sewers had lost their once-pungent aroma during the several weeks since Anna had joined the Maggots. Now she could enter the King of Crooks' domain without plugging her nose, but it was still noticeable. Greaver was already waiting for them at the bottom of the staircase.

Without uttering a word, he motioned for them to follow to a side room that Anna had never noticed on any of her prior visits. Inside the adjacent room was a table large enough to seat twelve people. However, there were only three chairs available.

Randall and Anna sat on opposite sides, while the King of Crooks took his spot in an ornate chair at the head of the table. As soon as they were seated, three servants seemingly appeared out of thin air and placed their dishes in front of them. Anna looked down at her meal and licked her lips.

"Roasted salmon, garlic potatoes, and a side of corn," one servant announced, before exiting the room silently.

"Dig in!" Greaver announced as he picked up his utensils and began daintily skewering his potatoes.

Anna started with the corn. She had never enjoyed it and always found the vegetable to be bland and lacking flavour, so she wanted to get it out of the way.

She couldn't take her eyes off the salmon. The slab of meat seemingly called out to her, begging her to devour it. She was able to break her stare at the fish for long enough to realize that Randall wasn't touching his food. Instead, he played with a single potato on his plate, rolling it from side to side.

"Did the drink spoil your appetite?" Greaver said, without looking up.

"No," Randall responded, but Anna could tell it was a poor lie. The boy was swaying in his seat and could hardly keep his eyes open.

"Do you know who you robbed today, Randall?" the king asked, this time staring at the drunken boy until he made eye contact with him. Randall didn't respond. Instead, he stared nervously at Greaver. After a long and excruciating silence, the king continued. "That was the honourable Clifton Saltworth, a wealthy man who just happens to be the head of the merchants' guild."

Anna could sense the tension in the air, and she did not like it. Her muscles tensed, and she soon realized that this dinner was an excuse for the king to berate them privately. But why was she here? Why did he not scorn her while they walked through the courtyard? Perhaps she did something wrong that the king had not yet alluded to.

"Mr. Saltworth and I have a certain understanding," the King of Crooks continued. "My people do not target him, and in exchange, he agrees to smuggle the occasional exotic item for me into the city's walls."

The room fell silent, and suddenly nobody was eating their food. Anna's back was as stiff as a board, while Randall's head hung loosely from his shoulders, staring at his lap.

"Look at me, boy!" Greaver shouted, while slamming his fist on the table. Randall did as he commanded. "Do you see the predicament that you put me in? Saltworth is calling for your head, and I have a difficult choice to make."

Randall's body suddenly came to life. It was as if the drunken stupor he was in had worn off in an instant. The boy stared at his king with fear, and a hint of contempt, in his eyes.

"I can either turn you two in to the merchant, who will undoubtedly enact his vengeance upon you. Or I can repay the merchant for his losses out of my own pocket. Neither of which is very appealing to me."

"How was I supposed –"

"Shut your fucking trap!" the king hollered as he shot to his feet. "You've caused me enough trouble as it is. I don't need to hear your pathetic excuses. How many years have I treated you like a son? Has all my time teaching you been for nothing?"

Suddenly, there was a knock at the door. Greaver grunted for the interrupter to enter. Anna was surprised to see it was a woman. She was maybe ten years her senior and had dark brown hair. She had a thin frame and was dressed in rags; rags that were soaked in blood.

"What happened?" the King of Crooks shouted.

"The damned dwarves," the girl hissed. "They ambushed us as we were trying to secure the goods from the docks. Little bastards are sneaky."

"Go see a healer. We'll talk there," Greaver ordered, before turning his attention back to the two children seated at his table. "This just might be your lucky day."

"How so?" Randall boldly asked.

"Because if those damned dwarves stole my cargo, the cargo that Saltworth was supposed to secure, me and the merchant would be even."

"What dwarves?" Anna asked sheepishly, not sure if she was allowed to talk. Greaver had calmed down since the blood-soaked woman's interruption, so she figured it was safe.

"Oh, just some young upstarts that wish to dethrone me," the king explained casually. "Every few years or so, someone tries to cut out a piece of my kingdom, a kingdom that I built." Without uttering another word, the King of Crooks left the room, slamming the door behind him.

Anna looked at Randall's face and saw an expression of pure hatred plastered all over it. It was clear that he resented being scolded, and it was also clear that the boy was willing to do anything to wreak vengeance for the disrespect he had suffered.

She also knew that she and the rest of the Maggots would surely follow their leader in whatever he had planned, and it unnerved her. She greedily devoured her food once again, knowing that her strength would be needed in the coming days.

CHAPTER SEVENTEEN

GRIMM

The cold iron burned his skin as the frozen metal greedily stole the heat from his body. His wrists and ankles were chafed from the shackles. Gusts of wind would blow little shards of snow and ice across the beach, stinging the cuts in his face from last night's beating.

Yet, despite all these unpleasantries, Grimm was oddly comfortable. He sat there, watching the mainlanders struggle to survive in the Isles' harsh conditions. All the soldiers shivered uncontrollably. Most huddled around their pathetic earthenware candles, desperately absorbing the warmth they exuded, while others disobeyed orders and tried to start actual fires, only to be caught in the act and reprimanded by their superior. A smile broke out on Grimm's face. Something about watching the foreigners suffer seemed to ease his own suffering.

A sharp shrill sound from the sky turned his eyes upward. He saw two winterhawks circling above him. His smile widened. Winterhawks were solitary creatures, so seeing two of them at once was often considered an omen: one that preluded a bloody battle.

Grimm was eager to see how the mainlander's army would fare against his fellow countrymen. He had no illusions about who would win. This army lacked discipline, and judging by the looks of the men, very few had seen actual combat. *Give me twenty good men, and I could fight this army myself,* Grimm thought.

He turned his attention to the far side of the beach, where a company of men were stationed. This group caught his eye because of their blatant disrespect towards their leader. The superior, who was more of a boy than a man, failed to discipline his men, even when they openly mocked him. He had heard several soldiers refer to this group of men as "a company of bastards" throughout the night, although he wasn't sure why, nor did he have any desire to ask.

Sara approached him, carrying a steaming bowl of what appeared to be stew. She smiled as she looked at him, and he scowled in return. He would not let these mainlanders use her as leverage over him. She sat down in front of him, legs crossed, and placed the small wooden bowl in his calloused hands.

"Here," she said, her smile failing to waver.

"Thank you," Grimm replied coldly, as he continued to stare at the company of bastards. The young superior was trying to organize them in a line, but they openly defied him. Men would switch places with one another as soon as he turned his back on them, and others spat at their leader's feet when he issued a command: an action that always went unpunished.

"What are you looking at?" Sara asked.

"Them."

"Why?"

"So I can learn."

"Learn what?"

"Learn their strengths, their weaknesses, and how I can use them to get out of here."

"The man in the chair said if you just talk to him, he'll –"

Grimm spat on the ground and glared at the child. "These mainlanders cannot be trusted, Sara. All they do is lie and deceive. If we aren't careful, they'll make us their slaves, or worse."

The dwarf's eyes widened, and she looked around the camp cautiously, as if the soldiers were about to slam a pair of shackles on her at any minute. Grimm nodded his head and turned his attention to the bowl of stew the girl had brought him. He lifted it to his lips, and was slurping it down when he heard a group of men approach from the side.

"Stay away, girl, that there's a monster," one of the approaching soldiers advised.

Sara looked at the soldier in confusion and then turned her head towards Grimm, as if she expected him to explain what the man meant.

"He killed one of our lads last night," the soldier continued. "Snapped his spine like a twig."

"Leave, Sara," Grimm commanded as he stared back at the soldier.

The girl nodded her head and turned around, but was quickly grabbed by one man. "Where are you going, little one?" he cackled as she began struggling in his arms.

Without hesitating, Grimm lunged forward, but the chains went taut before he could reach the laughing soldier.

"Well, well, well," the first man mused. "Appears the savage has a heart. I wonder why you're so fond of that girl? She's clearly not yours."

"Perhaps he likes them young," a third man added, breaking his silence.

"Is that it? You backwards heathens like to fuck children?" The man quickly unsheathed his blade and held it to Grimm's throat. "I should gut you for what you did to Colin. He deserved better."

Grimm relaxed his body and smiled. "Want me to tell you how he squirmed before I killed him? How he cried for his mom before I snapped his spine with my legs? Poor bastard couldn't even win a fight against a chained man. I think he met a better end than he deserved."

The soldier's face contorted into a rage-filled grimace, and he pulled his sword back, ready to swing it at Grimm's head, when there was a sharp whistle from across the camp. Grimm and the soldier turned their heads, and saw that the scarred guard was marching over with incredible speed.

"What do you think you're doing with that sword?" the man snarled as he approached the men.

"Nothing, Captain Thames," the man replied meekly.

The scarred man swiftly shifted his gaze to the man who was holding Sara in his arms. The soldier had terror on his face, and Grimm could see that his legs wobbled uncontrollably.

"I suggest you unhand that girl and never lay one of your dirty paws upon her again." The man immediately released Sara and backed away quickly. "Now then," the scarred soldier continued, "I suggest you three report back to Lord Grelin and never come near the prisoner again, or else I'll be tempted to set him free."

The three soldiers meekly nodded before shuffling back towards the main camp. Sara and Grimm both turned towards the scarred man, but the man's attention was focused entirely on the girl. "Did they hurt you?"

"No."

"I think King Elbert wants to see you. I think he mentioned a gift of some kind."

Sara's eyes lit up, and she started sprinting across the camp towards the large and luxurious tents. The scarred man then turned his attention to Grimm, and the two men glowered at each other in silence.

Both men refused to speak. It was as if whoever started the conversation first would be seen as the weaker of the two. Grimm backed up so that there was slack in his chains, and leaned his back against the pole staked into the ground. The scarred captain's eyes scanned his body with extreme scrutiny. Unlike the other soldiers in the camp, Grimm could tell that this man had seen combat before, and not only that, but he had also taken another's life.

"I'll remind the men that you are not to be disturbed until you feel like talking to King Elbert," the man stated plainly.

"Tell that cripple that I'll talk to him once he stands on his own two feet."

The scarred man's eyes glinted with rage. However, to Grimm's surprise, he did not approach, nor did he unsheathe his sword. He continued to stare at Grimm, just beyond his reach. *Well disciplined,* Grimm thought. *Let's see if we can break him.*

"I can't imagine what your life is like," he began. "To let half a man rule over you, it must be –"

"Utter another word about my king, and I'll gladly cut out your tongue," Thames growled.

Grimm slowly leaned forward. "Tell me, what does that legless fucker's arse taste like?"

The man reached for his sword, but stopped mid-motion. He froze there for a few seconds, before returning his hand to his side and marching away in a huff, not allowing Grimm to sink another barb.

There was shouting on the far side of the beach. Grimm turned his head to see that the company of bastards were lazily grabbing their weapons as their commander barked out orders. It was hard to make out what the boy was shouting over the howling wind, but Grimm was confident he heard the words "scouting party."

He looked over at the soldiers and quickly realized that very few knew how to carry a weapon. It was evident that many were still getting used to the weight of their sword, while others visibly struggled to put their blade back in its scabbard. He shook his head in disappointment. *Axes and spears,* he told himself. *Even the simplest of men can fight using an axe or a spear. A sword takes training: training these men don't have.*

Suddenly, the sound of stones being crunched beneath metal wheels forced him to turn his head back toward the main camp. He saw that King Elbert was slowly rolling his chair towards him, and surprisingly, he had a smile on his face.

"Good morning," the king greeted. "Did you have a comfortable sleep?" Elbert's voice was full of sarcasm and condescension.

"I suspect I found it more comfortable than your men did," Grimm replied.

Elbert let out a short, nasal laugh. "I suppose you're right. We civilized people aren't used to surviving out in the wilds like you primitive savages."

"Nothing says civilized like having someone that wipes your arse for you."

The king's smile vanished. "Enough niceties. I came to ask you a few questions. First, what can you tell me about Tjørholm?"

Grimm's face slackened, and he refused to speak another word. Negotiations were never his strong suit, but he knew that when facing a cunning opponent, it was better to stay silent, rather than say anything that may be used against him in later discussions; and he had no doubt that this king was cunning. He could see it in his eyes. It was the same look Uthredd had when he was younger. *Wonder who would win the battle of wits between those two?* He thought to himself.

"Why protect the girl?" Elbert probed further.

The king's question caught Grimm off guard. He had not expected a change of subject so soon. "She's just a stray I picked up during my travels."

"I don't think that's quite true," Elbert replied, his smile returning. "It's obvious that you care for her, and I ask why? She's clearly not of your blood, so why does she matter to you?"

Grimm tried to think of a believable lie, but he couldn't quite manage. He wasn't sure why he cared for the child. She was a slave; to most people, she was regarded a little higher than dirt. In the past, he had had no love for slaves. Admittedly, he had been downright cruel to some. But there was something in Sara's eyes, something that awoke a piece of him: a piece of him that he had long thought dead. After giving the question some thought, he decided not to answer.

"If you don't give me something to prove your value by this evening, I'm afraid there'll be no point in keeping you."

Grimm swallowed in sour acknowledgement. Elbert had said it so matter-of-factly that he knew it was no idle threat. This was a king's promise.

As he watched the crippled king roll back towards camp, his mind formulated a plan. He knew he had no chance of escape, that much was clear; but he figured he could take a few of the mainlanders with him if he broke free of the shackles.

He inspected the cold iron manacles around his wrist and looked for any defects in the metal that he could exploit. Much to his chagrin, they were flawlessly crafted. They differed from the shackles used on the Isles. In fact, they seemed much more sophisticated. Instead of having a single lock keeping the arms of the shackle in place, there appeared to be three, each with a differently designed keyhole.

"Marvellous, aren't they?" a gruff voice spoke suddenly.

Grimm quickly lifted his head and saw that a bearded dwarf was standing in front of him, well out of reach. His skin was stained black with soot, his arms were finely muscled, and his hands were covered in blotchy scars. "These your designs?" he asked politely.

"Aye, King Elbert asked me tah come up with a more secure shackle. Each of yer cuffs has to be opened with three separate keys in a particular order."

"Quite imaginative," Grimm replied as he returned his gaze to the iron manacles clamped around his wrists and ankles. "I suppose it is safe to assume that you have the only three keys?"

"Indeed I do."

"I don't imagine there is any way I can persuade you into setting me free?"

The dwarf took an involuntary step backwards and shook his head nervously. "I cannae do that."

Grimm nodded his head in understanding, then tilted it skyward, hoping to see the two winterhawks once again. "Is there something you need, or did you just come to look at the bloodthirsty Islander?"

The dwarf began pulling at his beard. Little black clouds of soot escaped the tangled mess with every pull. Finally, after a moment's pause, the smith cleared his throat and spoke. "I see ye've adopted one of my kin as yer own. I dunno why ye did it, but I just wanted to thank ye. Not everyone welcomes us non-humans so openly."

"She was a slave."

A shocked expression took over the dwarf's face, but he quickly regained his composure. "Still, ye coulda' left her in servitude, but ye brought her with ye. On behalf of all dwarves, I thank ye."

He was about to make a snide remark about wishing that he had left the girl behind, when the realization of his impending doom suddenly hit him. The idea of asking this foreigner for help disgusted him, but he wanted to know that Sara would be looked after if the king followed through with his threat.

"The king has promised to kill me come sunset: if that happens, I want you to swear to me that you'll look after the girl." Grimm's voice was hard and unwavering. He stared at the nervous dwarf with the most menacing stare he could muster. After a moment's hesitation, the dwarf nodded in agreement. "Good, now leave me to my thoughts."

The dwarf nodded and left Grimm alone on the beach. He spent the rest of the day mentally preparing for his inevitable death. He would be damned if he would give up the secret to storming Tjørholm without some guarantees. He tilted his head downward, clasped his hands together, and closed his eyes.

"Heimer, I've come to ask another favour from you," he whispered. "If I should die tied to this post like a rabid dog, I pray that you find it in your heart to still let me into The Great Hall. I've lived a warrior's life, and I've never strayed from your guidance. I humbly ask that you give me this one mercy."

Grimm lifted his head and listened for a response. All he heard was the grumbling of soldiers and the howling of the winter wind. As the day dragged on, he continued to wait for any sign that Heimer was listening to him. A ray of sunlight to break through the clouds, a brief pause in the unrelenting wind, or some other subtle change in the weather that could be interpreted as a divine answer to his prayer. Before he knew it, the sun was setting on the western horizon, and the crippled king and the scarred man approached him.

"So, have you decided to share what you know about Tjørholm?" King Elbert asked, his hands folded comfortably in his lap.

Grimm eyed the two men with great scrutiny. To his surprise, he saw that neither man had malice in their eyes, nor did he see any sign that they were going to enjoy the execution. Although the soldier stood there with his sword half-drawn, his expression was one of pure apathy. On the other hand, the king looked as if he regretted what he was about to do. His brow was furrowed, and he stared through the Islander as if he was looking at a distant object. Grimm shook his head and met the scarred man's emotionless stare. "Do what you must."

The soldier turned towards the king for reassurance, and Elbert nodded his approval. The man drew his sword with a flourish and held the tip to Grimm's throat. A single drop of blood flowed down his neck as he stared at the clouds overhead. The scarred man drew back his sword for a mighty swing when there was a sudden commotion. All three men turned their attention to the camp, where a mature man in fine clothes came running over towards them.

"What is it, Lord Grelin?" the king asked, a hint of panic lingering in his voice.

"Lord Haustack's scouting party was ambushed by a patrol of Islanders, Your Majesty."

A smile crept along Grimm's face. *Bearn's men, no doubt. Let us hope these mainlanders killed all of them, or else their expedition will be over before it began.*

"That's not all, sire," the middle-aged man continued. "It's Lord Haustack. He's been gravely wounded, and most of the prisoner company did not survive the attack."

Elbert cursed under his breath, and the scarred man sheathed his sword and cleared his throat. "How many of the company remain?"

"Less than half."

Grimm erupted into laughter at the news. His throaty cackle echoed throughout the mostly silent camp. It was the sign that he had been waiting for. He laughed at the absurdity of Heimer's timing.

"What's so damned funny?" Lord Grelin growled.

"It appears your king will have to accept my bargain now," Grimm replied, wiping the tears from his eyes.

"And why is that?" Elbert hissed.

"Unless you killed everyone on that patrol, I guarantee Uthredd will know about you by morning. If that's the case, he'll march an entire army against you. So, the way I see it, you have two choices. Kill me now and sail back to the mainland with your tails 'tween your legs. Or, agree to my demands, and I'll get you inside Tjørholm by morning."

The mainlanders were stunned into silence by Grimm's logic. Both the scarred soldier and Lord Grelin stared at Elbert anxiously. The king's skin visibly paled, and his calm disposition was noticeably shaken. *Clearly, he doesn't like being backed into a corner.* Grimm chuckled at his thought as he awaited the cripple's response, already knowing what he was going to say.

"Lord Grelin, bring me the most senior soldier left in the prisoner company, so that he can answer my questions. Captain Thames, I need you to make sure the wounded are tended to. Make sure the healers start with Lord Haustack and any other senior officers first."

"Your healers should focus on the ones who will live to fight another battle, regardless of their status," Grimm advised snidely.

Elbert shook his head angrily and rolled back towards the camp with the other two men in tow. Grimm chuckled as he watched the three men leave, pleased that the gods had once again saved him.

The sun had long since set, and the wind had died down; when Elbert, the scarred captain, and the smith returned. Grimm slowly rose to his feet and stretched his arms as he awaited his release. He noticed that the entire camp of soldiers was watching in horror, as their king was about to release a man who had killed eleven of their comrades in less than a day. Their awestruck stares put a smile on the old warrior's lips.

Elbert held out his hand, signalling for the other two men to stop just out of arm's reach of the prisoner. "You're positive that you can get us inside of Tjørholm?" Doubt lingered in the king's voice, but it was clear that the man had no other choice.

"I swear it," Grimm promised as he shook his wrists for the dwarf to come forward.

The smith cast a side-eyed glance towards Elbert, who then waved his approval. With three distinct clicks, the shackles fell from his wrists and ankles. Grimm massaged his tender and chafed skin gingerly, before turning his attention back towards the three men. "Someone get me my sword."

The walls of the king's tent rustled in the wind, and the edges of the map on the table fluttered uncontrollably. It was a crude drawing of the landscape, and Grimm was unsure how the mainlanders had acquired such a map, but he knew that it would do for tonight's purposes. He pointed to the southwestern corner of the castle with a meaty finger. "There. That's how I'll get in."

"There's nothing there but a wall. Sire, I implore you, don't listen to this heathen!" Lord Grelin exclaimed, but he was quickly waved into silence by his king.

"There's a sewer grate there," Grimm explained. "Time has eaten away at the mortar surrounding the grate. By now, it'll be big enough for a man to squeeze through."

"That's your plan?" Grelin cried out, but was once again silenced by Elbert.

"How do you know it'll still be there?" Thames asked. "Perhaps they've patched it."

Grimm snorted in amusement. "The man who watches over the stronghold is as lazy as they come. He asks only the bare minimum of his men, and I would bet my life that he hasn't ordered any of his men to do repairs."

"Need I remind you that you are not only betting your life, but ours as well?" Elbert chimed in, who up until that point, had been listening intently.

"What you fail to understand, Legless, is that the Isles have never been invaded before, and it's been many years since the clans warred against one another. There hasn't been a need to repair it."

"Very well."

"If I'm not back by morning, consider the endeavour a failure, and sail back home while you still can," Grimm instructed coldly.

"You seriously don't intend to capture an entire fortress yourself, do you?" Thames gasped. "Your Majesty, allow me and a few hand-picked men to join him. We have no reason to believe he won't alert his brethren to our presence."

"Handing over an entire foreign army would land you back in the good graces of your king," Elbert surmised.

You don't know Uthredd at all, Grimm silently concluded. "Your men are welcome to join me, Legless. More hands make for less work. But they'll have to lose the shining white armour. We mustn't be seen."

"Lords," Elbert began. "Organize your troops to march and make sure they dim all of their armour and weapons. We don't want the enemy spotting us."

"What do you have in mind, Your Majesty?" Lord Grelin inquired.

Elbert tapped on the map. "Our men will wait here, just out of range of their archers. Once Thames and the Islander storm the castle, they open the gates. In the confusion, our army will storm the stronghold and provide support."

"And if they see the army?" Thames asked.

"Then I presume they will line the walls with their men and wait until we come into range, giving you a much-needed distraction."

"A decent plan," Grimm agreed.

"Anything else you need to tell us about Tjørholm before we mobilize?"

Grimm thought about it for several moments. He debated whether or not he should tell the mainlanders about the nature of the stronghold. Tjørholm was a cross between a city and a military outpost. Although very few people lived there, most of the civilians were pilgrims, who came to see the site of the legendary battle between the gods Varg and Orka.

He didn't want to condemn harmless commoners to death, but he also knew that such things are uncontrollable in war. Plus, he had to capture the stronghold, unless he wanted to live out the rest of his days as a wanted man. After much consideration, he shook his head and decided not to share his thoughts. "Nope."

"Very well. Rupert, prep your men, and I'll mobilize the army after you've departed."

Thames nodded his head and exited the tent in a hurry. Grimm followed suit. Outside the tent, the captain moved with urgency, so much so that Grimm struggled to keep up with the man's fast-paced strides. Upon reaching the quarters of the white-armoured guards, the soldiers rose and stood to attention. Once they caught a glimpse of Grimm following their captain, they exchanged wary glances with one another.

"Gentlemen," Thames began. "We have a job to do. We are to assist the Islander in breaching the walls of Tjørholm, and opening the gates so the rest of our army can storm in. Questions?"

Nobody uttered a word. The expression of stern determination was plastered across all the soldiers' faces.

"Good. Warrick, Isaac, Greebold, and Hastings, you four will join the Islander and me. The rest of you will assist the main army in their assault."

The company of men nodded their heads and prepared for the night's task.

"And men," Grimm interjected, "lose the armour."

"What's he on about?" a youthful-faced man replied, casting a confused look towards Thames.

The captain let out a sigh and glared at the Islander before turning his attention back towards his men. "Stealth is of the utmost importance. We cannot risk the glint of the moonlight reflecting off our armour and alerting the enemy."

The men once again nodded their heads in understanding, and Thames and Grimm walked out of earshot. "Listen, heathen," the captain started. "If you're thinking of betraying us, just know I'll cut you down before you ever get the chance."

Grimm let out an amused laugh. "I knew you were just like me. We're both killers."

"We are nothing alike."

"No? Tell me, have you ever killed a man and regretted it?"

"I only ever killed out of duty; you kill for the pure enjoyment of it."

"I do what I must in order to survive, and no matter how much you lie to yourself, you do the same."

Thames huffed in what could only be described as annoyance and marched back to the tent sheltering his men. "Meet us at the edge of camp, when you're ready," he called back over his shoulder.

A smile appeared on Grimm's lips. *Tonight is going to be an exciting night.*

Tjørholm's gargantuan walls towered in the night sky. Grimm fondly remembered walking along the battlements. He had spent countless hours patrolling the grounds of the religious stronghold when he was a mere soldier. During that time, he committed every street, every alley, and every inch of the fortress to memory.

He turned his attention to Thames and the four other guards that accompanied him. Without their white enamelled armour, they looked like common cutthroats. Grimm was about to say as much, but he decided to swallow the snide remark. Now was not the time for talking.

He led them through the snow-covered fields, keeping in a low crouch until they were along the south wall of the stronghold. The five mainlanders quickly joined him. Grimm lifted his head and watched the shadow of a sentry walk along the battlements directly above them. Fortunately, years of complacency had seemingly dulled their senses.

"What now?" Thames whispered.

Grimm craned his neck, motioning for them to follow as he crept along the southern wall. The skill to walk through snow without it crunching underfoot was one that Grimm had mastered early in his military career. He was thankful that the mainlanders had seemingly mastered the same skill. He knew that a single slip of the foot was all it would take to alert the fortress of their presence and cost them their lives.

After a few minutes of sleuthing through the snow, they arrived at the sewer grate. Grimm let out a sigh of relief, as he saw that not only was the hole in the wall still there, but it had grown in size since his last visit.

Silently, he unbuckled his belt from his waist and entered the hole, taking great care that his sword didn't clang against the metal grating. Upon entering the sewer, a miasma of foul odours assaulted his nostrils. Tears involuntarily swelled in his eyes, but beyond that, it did not bother him.

"By the gods, what is that smell?" one guard asked quietly.

"What do you think it is?" another snarled in retort.

It is the smell of battle, Grimm thought to himself. In his experience, battlefields smelled a lot like sewers. Before they died, many men soiled themselves, allowing the stench of urine and shit to waft through the air as the battle raged on.

Despite the large opening in the wall, Tjørholm's sewer was quite cramped, especially for a man of Grimm's size. He crawled on all fours through the muck, until he finally reached the metal grate at the other end of the tunnel.

"Now what?" Thames hissed.

Grimm just shook his head and lifted the iron bars, to find that they were still unattached to the walls. He smiled as he hefted the metal grate to one side and quietly set it down. *It's as if I never left.*

The six men quickly exited the shaft and began rubbing snow on themselves as a way to get the stench off their bodies. Grimm was the only one who seemed to be fine with the filth that covered him. The kick of a loose stone from the ramparts alerted them that another sentry was approaching. They quickly darted behind one of the nearby buildings and waited until the Islander passed.

"Let's split up," Thames ordered.

Grimm nodded his head in approval. "Agreed. You and you head to the barracks. It is in the northeastern corner of the stronghold. Prop something heavy against the door."

"We don't take orders from you," one guard hissed.

"It's a good idea, Isaac," Thames interjected. "The last thing we need is more Islanders to deal with."

Grimm nodded his head in thanks, but all he received in response was an icy glare. He brushed off the captain's brusqueness quickly. "You two clear the battlements, the arse-licker and I will open the gate for the rest of the army."

"Greebold, you will join the Islander. Warrick and I will take to the ramparts."

White-Eyes nodded his head. It did not matter to him which of the foreigners came with him. He had picked the captain simply because he wanted to see how the man killed.

With each of the men receiving their instructions, they split up. Grimm watched the man named Greebold sneak through the moonlight with admiration. He was a relatively portly man, but was deceptively light on his feet. He had short dark brown hair, and rounded free-lobed ears that protruded from the side of his head.

As an Islander guard approached the side alley he was hiding in, Greebold leapt from the cover of darkness and pulled the unsuspecting guard into the shadows. Grimm heard the unmistakable sound of a dagger piercing flesh from across the street.

There was another guard about fifteen feet away from Grimm, and he decided to quickly, yet quietly, close the distance. It only took a few seconds before he was mere inches from the man.

"What smells like shi-" the man muttered, before Grimm stabbed his sword through the Islander's neck. The guard let out a barely audible gurgle as his body writhed uncontrollably on the ground.

Grimm turned his head to the ramparts, and caught the last few seconds of a guard's life as Thames slit his throat from ear to ear with a dagger. The two men exchanged looks for a brief moment before returning to the task at hand.

The team of six men made quick and efficient work of the oblivious guards patrolling around Tjørholm. Grimm hated to admit it, but he was impressed by how easily the mainlanders killed their targets. In less than ten minutes, they had cut down close to thirty guards without raising a single alarm. Each sentry died as silently and as pathetically as the last.

Grimm thought he would have more reservations about killing his own kin without allowing them to face him in battle, but he knew that if he wanted to escape the Isles, the foreigners would have to occupy the fort. He only hoped Heimer would judge mercifully on the souls of the men he killed tonight.

As he surreptitiously approached the main gate, he saw that three guards stood watch. Grimm scanned his surroundings and saw no trace of Greebold anywhere. He quickly gauged the space between them, and calculated how long it would take him to reach the first guard. He inhaled sharply and leapt from the cover of darkness.

By the time the first guard had noticed his presence, his head had already been severed from his body. The other two guards stared with awestruck looks on their faces.

Grimm swiftly swung his sword again, spilling the guts of the second man. By this time, the third man had pulled his sword free of his scabbard, but it was too late. Grimm had already shoved his own blade through the man's gaping mouth.

"Well done, savage," Greebold complimented as he emerged from the shadows.

"Help me with the doors," Grimm growled as he moved over to the winches which were connected to the heavy oaken doors.

Greebold and Grimm took a winch each, and began turning the wooden spindles counterclockwise. The heavy iron chains rattled and clanged as the doors of the fortress slowly creaked open. The sound of mass confusion flooded Grimm's ears as he heard the bewildered Islanders watching him turn the wooden winch.

"Intruders!" one guard bellowed as he charged towards the two men, with more of his comrades following close behind.

"I'll hold them off!" Greebold shouted as he sprinted towards the charging guardsmen.

Grimm let out a snort of derision, but continued to arduously turn the wooden wheel. From across the frozen field, the thunderous cry of a thousand warriors echoed throughout the plains. He watched as the shadowy figures sprinted towards Tjørholm's walls.

Suddenly, there was a loud cry from behind him. He turned around and saw that Greebold was lying on the ground with an axe in his gut. The three Islanders that had attacked him now turned their attention to Grimm.

Two of the guards rushed him simultaneously. Grimm smiled as he locked the winch in place. He reached for his sword, and realized that he had foolishly left it embedded in the mouth of the man who was guarding the doors. Cracking his knuckles with anticipation, he waited for the two men to come within reach.

Both islanders swung their blades in unison, one chopping at Grimm's head, while the other attacked his knees. Grimm quickly pirouetted out of the way, missing both swords by a hair's breadth.

He then drove his right fist into the nose of one of the men. The man staggered backwards as blood poured from his nose.

The whistle of sharp metal soaring through the air pricked his ears. Grimm ducked the attack aimed at his head and spun around to land a series of punches in at the second man's groin.

The guard keeled over in pain. Grimm grabbed him by the scruff of his neck and slammed his face repeatedly into the frozen earth, until the Islander's brains began to leak out of his broken skull.

The man with the broken nose let out a ferocious battle cry and charged to avenge his fallen comrade, while the third guard cautiously flanked the white-eyed killer.

Grimm turned his body to miss a clumsy thrust from the second man and countered it with a quick jab to the throat. The man immediately wheezed for air.

Grimm wrapped his meaty, muscular arms around the guard's, neck and, with a sudden jerk, snapped his spine in two.

The third Islander suddenly paused. He started to slowly back away. Grimm smiled as he picked up one of the dead men's swords, when a blade pierced the guard's stomach from behind.

The Islander spat blood as the sword was ripped free from his body. Grimm saw Thames standing behind the corpse when the guard's lifeless body collapsed to the ground.

"He was mine!" Grimm seethed.

"Ought to be quicker," Thames retorted, before running back up the stairs towards the ramparts.

Grimm turned his attention back to the gate, and saw that Elbert's army was only a hundred paces away. "Fuck this," he growled as he ran deeper into the fortress, looking for more guards he could fight.

The more the night dragged on, the happier Grimm became. He missed war. Ever since Uthredd had unified the Isles, the closest thing to an actual battle that he had experienced was raiding the mainland, and farmers rarely put up a fight.

The smell of burning buildings, the sound of men dying, and the taste of blood in his mouth made him feel twenty years younger. His blade never stopped swinging, and it never failed to draw the enemy's blood.

These men have gotten soft, he thought to himself as he hacked apart another Islander's body. *Years of only raiding have dulled their skills. Where are the real men who will challenge me?*

There was a high-pitched scream. Grimm turned his head to see a pair of soldiers pulling a woman from a burning building. The woman was clutching a silver medallion around her neck as the mainlanders pulled her out of the blazing inferno.

"Let her go," Grimm snarled as he marched over.

"Fuck off, heathen," one soldier replied.

"Yeah, fuck off, or I'll fuck you as well!" the other retorted.

Grimm looked at both men, and then looked at the tearful woman. He could have easily killed both men, but Elbert had already overlooked one murder, and Grimm doubted that he would overlook two more.

He walked up to the first soldier and glared at him. Surprisingly, the man held his stare. After several seconds of silence, Grimm plunged his sword through the head of the woman, killing her instantly.

"What'd you do that for!?" the two men shouted in unison.

Without uttering a response, Grimm walked away. He did not wish to explain that the woman deserved better than to be raped and killed. She was a devout follower of Orka, as all pilgrims who came to Tjørholm were. At least now, she had died with dignity and could be allowed admittance into The Great Hall, if the gods were merciful.

"Who cares?" he heard one soldier shout from behind him. "I haven't seen a cunt in months; I'll still fuck her!"

Grimm shook his head in disgust as he continued to search for more Islanders to kill.

It took less than an hour for Elbert's forces to capture the stronghold. With the barracks barricaded, and most of the patrolling guards already cut down, there was little resistance left to oppose the invaders.

A sizeable crowd stood in front of the barracks to watch the building being engulfed by flames. The screams of men being burned alive filled the evening air. Most of the mainlanders were laughing or hurling insults at the men inside. Grimm watched silently as he whispered a prayer for the men's souls.

Suddenly, there was a heavy hand on his shoulder. "Not bad, Islander," Thames complimented.

"Looks like you made it out in one piece," Grimm replied, without looking up.

"Indeed I did, but I lost a few good men today."

"It's war. People die."

"I must say, you kill your own people quite voraciously. Are all Islanders as violent as you?"

Grimm spat on the ground. "They aren't my people, not any more." The lie tasted sour on his tongue, because deep down he knew there was some truth to it. His own people had outlawed him and, as a result, he had allied himself with their sworn enemy. He did not consider himself a mainlander, but also knew that he could not call himself an Islander any more.

"Enjoy the night while you can. We have a lot more of your people to kill," Thames teased as he walked closer to the burning barracks.

Grimm resumed whispering his prayer and turned his eyes skyward. "Heimer, please have mercy on me."

CHAPTER EIGHTEEN

ANNA

Winterhelm's southwestern corner was a peculiar neighbourhood. Unlike the rest of the city, the houses were almost entirely built out of aged wood rather than stone, and they had thatched roofs instead of wooden ones.

The streets here also differed from the rest of the city. As soon as you entered the southwestern part of the city, the cobblestones disappeared, and in their place were roads made of dirt.

"What is this place?" Anna asked, as she cautiously eyed the crooked wooden houses.

"This neighbourhood is called The Splints," Randall replied.

"And why are we coming here?" Anna asked for the umpteenth time. But, just like all the other times she had asked him, Randall decided not to answer.

She continued to follow Randall through the cramped streets of The Splints, and couldn't help but realize that it was mainly non-humans who dwelt here. Rarely did she see another human, and if she did, they were usually horrifically disfigured. She wasn't sure why Randall was leading her into a neighbourhood where the residents clearly had nothing to steal. But he had dismissed her questions and insisted that she trusted him.

It wasn't long before the residents of The Splints noticed the two youths walking through their neighbourhood. Many mothers ushered their children inside, while others slammed their doors shut. Anna's stomach became uneasy as she watched the people cast sideways glances in her direction. She didn't belong here. She desperately wanted to turn back and return to The Garden and see her friends, but Randall had assured her that it was a mission of utmost importance.

"You still haven't told me why we are here," Anna stated, hoping that this time she would get a straight answer from the boy.

"Just trust me, Anna," Randall responded as he walked with a certain swagger through the slums.

"Why did you bring me?" she inquired. "Wouldn't you rather have brought one of the others?"

Randall let out an amused snort. "Tig is too hot-headed. Chuckles would probably abandon me the moment a girl caught his eye. Maeve is useless in a fight, and A'Chula isn't exactly great with other people."

"So I'm what's left," Anna muttered under her breath.

Randall quickly came to a stop and placed both hands on her shoulders. When she did not meet his gaze, he gently put a hand under her chin and lifted her head, until they were staring into each other's eyes. "You're perfect," he explained. "You have all of their strengths and none of their weaknesses. You are the only person I can trust with this."

Anna suddenly felt very warm. She could feel her cheeks flush with colour, and a wave of anxiety soon consumed her. She nervously broke eye contact with Randall so she could regain her composure. After several seconds, she turned back to him. "Will you at least tell me what we are doing here?"

Randall sighed. "We are meeting the leader of the dwarves who are trying to overthrow Greaver."

"What!?"

"Keep your voice down!" Randall whispered harshly.

"If Greaver finds out, he'll –"

"He won't find out, not unless you tell him."

"But Randall, I –"

"Anna, you have to trust me. This will all work out in the end, but the less you know, the better. It's for your own protection."

Anna scowled in disapproval. An obscene retort was on the tip of her tongue, but she stopped herself after noticing a few shadowy figures watching from the back alleys.

"We're being watched."

"I know," Randall responded before letting go of Anna. "Greetings, gentleman. We are here to see your boss!"

Silence followed. Anna slowly started moving towards her knife when a gruff voice called out from the darkness. "Keep yer hands where we can see 'em!"

Randall and Anna lifted their hands in unison, and watched as a small troupe of dwarven rogues emerged from the shadows. Each dwarf wore a dark leather tunic and had a belt of throwing knives around his waist. Their faces were darkened with what appeared to be coal, allowing them to hide more easily in the shadows of the buildings.

"Yer Greaver's kids," one dwarf stated, after eyeing both of them up, his eyes lingering on Anna longer than Randall. "Ye've got a lot o' balls comin' here."

Randall spat on the ground. "I'd sooner die than kneel to that cocksucker for one more day!"

The dwarf let out a chuckle and pulled a knife from his belt. "It might just be yer lucky day, then!"

The group of rogues chuckled menacingly. Anna counted the dwarves as she thought about reaching for her dagger. Would she have enough time to send it spiralling into one of their skulls? Or would the group of dwarves descend on her like a pack of wolves taking down a deer?

She looked over at Randall and noticed that his body was loose. She was surprised to see that his face was devoid of any worry or fear. Just as she was about to reach for her dagger, she saw the dwarf's body relax.

"Hammerfist will like ya, kid," he said, as he returned his knife to his belt.

The dwarf motioned for them to follow, although they were presented with little choice. The remaining rogues had blocked off the only exit out of The Splints. Randall, paying the others no mind, followed the dwarf. Anna reluctantly joined him.

For over an hour, the dwarves led them through the winding streets of The Splints. While Randall followed obediently, Anna made mental notes of buildings that caught her eye. During the escort, she noticed that they had passed the same house for the third time.

"You're leading us in circles," Anna growled, her hand slowly inching towards her dagger.

The dwarf escorting them let out a throaty laugh, but his brethren seemed to grumble in disgust. "Pay up, gents!" he hollered at the others. "We wondered who would be the first to notice. Those dunderheads all chose the lad, but I could tell ye had a keen eye, lass."

The rest of the dwarves unenthusiastically handed over their coin purses as Randall crossed his arms. "So, you've just been leading us around in bloody circles for an hour? What's the point of all this?"

The dwarf paid him no mind as he began counting his winnings.

"Are you listening to me, you fucking stone shitter?" Randall reached out and gripped the dwarf's arm. Suddenly, the hiss of a dozen knives leaving their sheaths filled the otherwise empty street.

Anna cursed, and was about to reach for her own dagger, when she saw a dwarven woman appear seemingly out of thin air. Like most of the people in The Splints, she was dressed in rags, but she had a fox-skin shawl draped around her neck. She had braided dark brown hair, and eyes as green as emeralds. As she approached, Anna noticed that she had an unseemly sneer on her lips.

"Unhand my man, child. Unless you want me to send you back to Greaver piece by piece?"

Randall let go of the dwarf's arm and turned towards the woman. "Who the blazes are you?"

"Regina Hammerfist. From what my spies tell me, you wanted to meet with me."

Anna saw Randall's face turn bright red as he mindlessly stammered nonsense. The dwarven woman laughed maniacally.

"What? Were you expecting a man? Don't think I can lead 'cause I ain't got a cock 'tween me legs?"

Randall's charming smile returned, and he dropped to one knee. "I've come to swear fealty to you."

Once again, the dwarven woman erupted in laughter. This time, her men joined her. "You've got to be kidding, love! Why would I ever accept your pathetic offering? You're clearly a spy for Greaver."

"Let me prove it to you!" Randall shouted, suddenly rising to one knee. "Let me show you that my friends and I have value!"

Regina scratched her chin as if deep in thought. After a moment's deliberation, she smiled. "I'm sure that's exactly what that blowhard Greaver told you to say."

"Greaver is past his prime. He's been at the helm for too long, and we need a new leader: someone who isn't scared to get their hands dirty, and isn't afraid to take the fight to our true enemies."

"And who, pray tell, would that be?"

"The nobles."

The rogues started laughing, but their queen quickly silenced them with a wave of her hand. "You've got spunk, kid; I'll give you that. Tell you what, if you manage to pull a job for me, I'll accept your fealty. How does that sound?"

"Name the job."

"There's a certain man in this city, a wealthy man by the name of Odion Rawley. Not quite a noble, but the bastard rubs shoulders with 'em. He has a large collection of valuables and antiquities in the basement of his estate. I want you to rob him blind."

"You want us to steal his entire fortune?" Anna gasped in disbelief.

"Is that too hard for you, love?" Regina mocked.

"Not in the slightest," Randall interjected, before Anna could get another word in.

"Very well, now leave my neighbourhood and don't come back until the job's done."

Randall bowed once again and began dragging Anna out of The Splints by the arm. Once they were out of earshot, he turned to her and seethed. "Why did you open your mouth!?"

Anna recoiled from the verbal jab before contorting her face into a sneer and jabbing a finger into the boy's muscular chest. "Don't talk to me like I'm an idiot! If it weren't for me, those dwarves would probably still be walking us around The Splints!"

"Do you realize what you've done?" Randall hissed. "Now she wants us to steal an entire bloody fortune because you opened your big mouth. I was planning on talking her down slowly, but you had to intervene. All I said you had to do was trust me, and you couldn't even do that! Perhaps I should've brought A'Chula. At least he knows when to shut the fuck up."

Tears swelled in Anna's eyes, and she quickly slapped Randall across the face. The sound of the slap reverberated off the dilapidated houses, followed by a deafening silence. Anna glared at Randall with utter contempt, her nostrils flaring with every breath. Just as he opened his mouth, she spat in his face and stormed off back towards The Garden.

Anna's hand throbbed as she walked through the city. She hadn't meant to slap Randall that hard, but she had to admit it felt good. When she thought about how much her hand hurt, she smiled, because she knew that Randall's face would definitely hurt more. Her smile widened considerably.

Upon reaching The Garden, Anna walked directly into the tavern, ordered a bottle of vodka, and left. She had no desire to talk about the day's events with anyone. In fact, she had no desire to talk at all. Even ordering the liquor seemed a chore to her.

She walked around the city and occasionally took a few swigs from the bottle. Usually, when she was this upset, she would go for a hunt or practice throwing knives, but that was simply impossible in the city. So, she figured that dulling her senses with the repugnant liquor would be the next best thing.

After several minutes of walking, she saw an old stone building covered in vines. She could see that there were gaps between the stones, the perfect size for a hand. Anna drunkenly grinned as she sized up the building. She had yet to watch a sunset since arriving in Winterhelm. She remembered how she used to climb the mountainous pines in the forest and watch the sunset, whenever she was done with her chores. *A simpler time,* Anna thought to herself.

Holding the bottle of vodka between her teeth, she scaled the stone building. Her movement was fluid, and she didn't have to think about where she would place her next step. It all came back naturally.

It took her less than two minutes to reach the tiled roof of the building, where she sat, drank her bottle of liquor, and watched the sun dip below the city's walls. She was amazed at how the sun's rays glistened off the snow. It looked like every building had a little sea of diamonds resting upon its roofs. She watched as the sky turned from dark blue to red, and finally to black.

By the time the city was bathed in moonlight, Anna was thoroughly drunk and barely able to keep her eyes open. To her surprise, she didn't feel cold; in fact, she felt incredibly warm. She threw the empty bottle of booze from the rooftop and listened to it smash against the cobblestone streets. A girlish giggle escaped her lips.

"Hey, who threw that?" a voice shouted in the night air.

Anna laughed in response. Tears of pure mirth streamed down her face. Her stomach ached as it convulsed with every throaty guffaw. However, her laughter was cut short when she heard someone climb onto the roof behind her.

"There you are! I've been looking everywhere for you!" a familiar voice said.

"Why, so you could yell at me some more?" Anna snarled, not bothering to turn round.

Randall sat down beside her and let out a defeated sigh. "I'm sorry. I lost my temper. I don't tell you things only because I'm trying to protect you."

"Protect me?" Anna gasped in disgust. "From who? From Greaver, the man who took me in and gave me a home when nobody else would? What exactly are you protecting me from?"

To her surprise, Randall didn't get angry. Instead, his expression looked more mournful than anything. "Follow me," he ordered, before rising to his feet and climbing down the side of the stone building.

Anna reluctantly followed, not sure where he would lead her, but her gut told her it was important. After a few minutes of walking, the warmth of the vodka began to fade, and she felt the chill of the winter air bite at her exposed flesh. "Where are we going?" she asked, her head suddenly starting to ache.

"We're almost there," Randall replied.

After what seemed like a lifetime, he finally stopped outside a tavern. Judging from the crowd outside and the silhouettes through the windows, it appeared to be a popular one.

"I'm not in the mood to drink." Anna slurred.

"I want you to look through the window and tell me who you see playing cards."

Anna furrowed her brow in confusion. She shook her head, making sure that she had heard him correctly. "You want me to do what?"

"Tell me who you see at the card table."

She shrugged her shoulders and let out an annoyed snort. She didn't have time for Randall's cryptic answers. As she approached the window, a pang of worry entered her head. She was a drunk girl in a neighbourhood that she did not know. Perhaps this was

Randall's plan, to abandon her and serve her up as a piece of meat to whoever lurked inside this tavern. *All because of a slap.*

Anna turned her head and was stunned to see that Randall was still standing where she left him, ushering for her to continue. She shook her head but reluctantly pressed on.

Upon reaching the tavern's steps, she pressed her face against the window, but could not see through the thin layer of frost. She closed her hand into a fist and rubbed away the ice with the side of her hand. Anna pressed her face against the glass once more and peered inside. She recoiled from the glass and reached for her dagger, once she saw who was sitting at the card table. A firm hand caught her by the wrist.

"Not yet," Randall instructed, his voice unnaturally monotone.

"You knew he was alive?" Anna squealed, as she tried to wrestle free from his grip.

"I just found out today when I was walking back to The Garden. I saw him in the city square, pickpocketing."

"So Greaver, he... he...."

"He lied," Randall said sinisterly. "That's what he does: manipulates people into doing what he wants. His entire kingdom is built on lies. He says he is going to fix this city, to make it better for everyday people, but all he ever does is sit on his fucking throne." Randall gripped Anna's hands tightly and stared into her eyes. "I need you to trust me. Trust that I'll make the city a better place; and that we'll cleanse this place of filth like Greaver, and the piece of shit in there."

Perhaps it was a result of the liquor, or perhaps it was that her rage was placed elsewhere now, but she found that, at that moment, she forgave Randall. She nodded her head and squeezed his hands tightly. "When do we strike?"

A smile appeared on Randall's lips. "He's always the last to leave. And I don't think you'll need my help."

"You're letting me do this alone?"

"I'll be close by, in case you need me, but I trust that you can handle it. Just like I hope that you trust me."

Anna smiled and pulled Randall in close for a hug. She squeezed as hard as she could, as glee and relief filled her body. She was beyond thankful for the opportunity to enact her revenge by herself. Joy filled her body as she pictured how she would make the man pay for laying a hand on her.

The moon hung high in the air, blanketing the entire city in a pale white light. The streets were silent as the last of the tavern's patrons began funnelling out of the doors and started to stumble back to their homes. As Randall had predicted, the pickpocket was the last to leave. He shouted something inaudible to the innkeeper before making a rude gesture and began walking down the alley.

Anna emerged from the shadows, dagger in hand. It felt good to hunt once again. However, this time was different. In the past, she had only hunted for survival, while now she hunted for pure pleasure.

Years of practice came back to her in an instant: walking silently behind her prey, being able to keep out of sight, and with the patience needed to wait for the opportune moment to strike. She twirled the dagger in her numb fingers as she stalked the pickpocket. She was going to make sure that he never hurt anyone ever again.

After ten minutes of stalking, the man finally turned to go down a side alley. Anna smiled as she gripped the dagger's handle tightly. *This will be the last alley you ever see.*

She cautiously entered the alleyway and saw that the pickpocket was leaning against a stone wall, relieving himself. The sound of piss melting snow, and the man's drunken humming, reverberated off the buildings.

Anna stayed in a low crouch, slowly creeping into the shadows of the building. Once she was behind him, she lunged.

The blade pierced the soft flesh of his back, and the man let out a surprised gasp. She ripped the dagger free and plunged it in again, this time just under his floating rib.

The drunken pickpocket spun around and tried to strike her, but she was too fast and he was too drunk. She nimbly ducked his clumsy, flailing punch and quickly swept his feet from under him. The man landed with a hard thud.

Anna climbed on top of him and plunged her dagger into his stomach. Blood and bile leaked out of the corners of the man's mouth, as his breathing became laboured. She twisted the blade, forcing the man to let out a garbled scream.

Anna leaned down until she could feel the warmth of his breath on her cheeks. His breath stank of stale ale and rotten cabbage.

"Do you remember me?" she hissed.

"G..G....Greaver," the man stammered, through a mouthful of blood.

She ripped the dagger out once again and pressed the blade to the man's throat. The pickpocket's eyes bulged at the sudden realization that his life would end at the hands of this little girl.

Anna's lips contorted in a sickening smile. The fact that this man felt as helpless as she did when he attacked her filled her body with joy.

She stared into the man's fearful eyes and made a mental note to remember this moment. She savoured the power that she had. The ability to end or spare this wretch's life was in the palms of her hands.

But she knew that this would only end one way. She'd be damned if she let the man walk free, after what he tried to do to her, and what he undoubtedly did to countless others.

She moved the dagger from his throat and stabbed it in his chest. After a quick twist, she pulled the dagger out and stabbed him again.

And again, and again.

She stabbed him until there were more holes than man left. Tears leaked from her eyes, and her face contorted into a nasty grimace.

She bared her teeth as she plunged the blade into the pickpocket's lifeless body. Her clothes were stained black with blood, but still she continued to stab. She let out a scream as she plunged the blade into the man's eye socket.

By the time she was done stabbing, her arms were exhausted. Her chest heaved uncontrollably as she rolled off of the corpse and laid down in the snow beside it.

She watched as the mist of her breath rose into the night sky. She turned her head, and looked at the corpse, and saw that the pickpocket was no longer recognizable. A sense of pride washed over her.

After several minutes of lying in the blood and snow, she rose to her feet and made her way back to The Garden, sticking to the shadows as best she could. As she walked, she scanned the rooftops for any sign of Randall, but she saw none.

However, she wasn't worried. In fact, it made her feel better about herself. To kill the pickpocket without the help of anyone else filled her with rising confidence.

When she arrived at the door to The Garden, she was surprised to see that it was open. She peeked her head inside and saw a large crowd of people in the middle of the courtyard.

Anna's gut twisted with anxiety. She quickly sprinted into the courtyard, and pushed her way through the crowd, and saw that lying in the middle of the courtyard was a bloody, lifeless Maeve.

CHAPTER NINETEEN

ELBERT

Ash, blood, and snow blanketed Tjørholm's streets. The stench of burnt timber and scorched flesh polluted the early morning air. Corpses were being dragged outside the city walls when Elbert rolled through the city gates.

The aftermath of the battle made the king's stomach churn in disgust. Severed limbs, disembodied innards, and copious amounts of blood littered the ground. He swallowed the bile rising in his throat before continuing towards the main keep.

The initial reports suggested that the battle had been a complete success. They had suffered minimal casualties, and they had captured the stronghold without resorting to a prolonged siege. Many Islanders, including the women, fought until their dying breath, making it impossible to capture them as prisoners.

Upon hearing this, Elbert shook his head in disappointment. He had hoped that if he had fifty hostages, it would give him leverage when it came to ransoming the fortress back to the barbarian king.

On his way to the keep, he came across a blood-soaked Captain Thames. The captain erupted in laughter upon seeing the king's face.

"Fret not, Your Majesty, for none of this blood is mine," he declared boisterously.

A relieved smile appeared on the king's lips. "I'm glad to hear it, Rupert. Care to accompany me to the keep?"

"I'd be honoured, Your Majesty."

As they made their way through the blood-stained fortress, Elbert was forced to order a stop so that he could regain his composure.

The carnage unnerved him. He had seen countless depictions of famous battles during his youth, but none of them were as bloody as this. His skin paled as he caught sight of a butchered boy. It was difficult to guess his age, as his head had been completely bashed in, and chunks of brain were scattered across the snow-covered ground. The child's corpse loosely gripped a pitchfork. *Likely tried to stab it into a soldier's gut.*

Elbert felt a firm hand on his shoulder. He turned his head and saw Thames' scarred, blood-stained face staring down at him. The guard had a warm, comforting smile. A smile that, until now, Elbert thought was beyond him.

"Do you wish for me to escort you to the keep alone?" he whispered.

"No," Elbert started, as his eyes drifted to another corpse. This one was a woman whose throat had been slit. The clothes she wore were torn, and her pants were around her ankles. Elbert suddenly felt the colour return to his face, and pointed at the befouled corpse. "What is the meaning behind this?" he shouted, his voice shaking uncontrollably.

Thames' smile disappeared in an instant, and a disgusted grimace stained his lips. "It appears some of the soldiers got carried away last night."

Elbert sneered at the response. "Carried away? This is not acceptable! I want the men who did this found, and brought directly to me."

"That is a near-impossible task–" one of the guards from the escort chimed in.

Thames shot the man a fiery glance before returning his attention towards the king. "As you wish, Your Majesty: we will begin our investigation right away."

Elbert dismissed the entourage of guards with a wave of his hand, and was left alone in the bloody streets. He slowly rolled up to the woman's corpse and stared down at her face.

Despite the grey tinge to her skin, he could tell that she was quite beautiful; it was a shame that her life had ended the way it did, and he felt genuine pity for her. Tears swelled in his eyes as he averted his gaze and continued towards the keep.

There would be a time to mourn, but first: business had to be conducted.

Tjørholm's keep was surprisingly ornate. Behind the massive wooden doors was a large foyer with two ascending spiral staircases. The floor was made from polished stone, and had a large painting in the centre of it.

It would have been awe-inspiring, had it not been stained crimson from the recent assault. In the middle of the foyer knelt three men, all badly beaten, and all with their hands bound together. Two of the men were lowly guards, who were of no importance to the king. The third, however, was the man who supposedly ruled over Tjørholm; the man sworn to protect it from invaders.

"Fuck off, you pig fuckers!" the man screamed as he spat at Elbert's feet.

The king nodded his head, and Thames delivered a swift kick to the man's gut, which resulted in the Islander vomiting onto the blood-stained floor. "I will not ask again," Elbert began. "Tell us what you know about Uthredd's forces, and you may yet live through this."

"And forsake my soul?" the Islander asked in disbelief. "It may surprise you, but not all Islanders are as corruptible as him." The man pointed with his lips at Grimm, who was brooding silently in a corner.

"You're lucky you're still alive, Soren. Judging by the size of your belly, you've clearly enjoyed your time as Warden of Tjørholm," the barbarian replied from the corner of the room.

"Go fuck yourself, White-Eyes! Not only did you betray our king, the man who was like a brother to you: but now you've sided yourself with the goat fuckers from the south! You'll never see The Great Hall. I'll make sure of that."

"You forget, brother, you need to die with a weapon in your hand in order to see The Great Hall, and I doubt these so-called 'goat fuckers' will be inclined to give you one."

The Islander went silent. His eyes shifted to the pile of puke in front of him. Elbert silently commanded Thames to lift Soren's head so that he was forced to make eye contact with the king. The Islander's eyes avoided Elbert's, but it was clear he was listening.

"If dying with a sword in your hand is what you wish, then I'll gladly send you off as a warrior," Elbert said. The Islander's face twitched but then quickly relaxed. The king continued, "but you need to tell me about Uthredd's army. What can we expect from him?"

The Islander bit his bottom lip, and after a lengthy pause, shook his head in defiance. Suddenly, one of the guards looked up and made eye contact with Elbert, his eyes glistening with tears.

"Will you truly let us go, if we tell you all we know?" he asked sheepishly.

"You fucking coward! Don't you dare sell out your kin for these–" Soren screamed, before receiving another swift kick in the gut from Thames' armoured boot.

"I promise," Elbert said, a warm smile appearing on his lips.

"Tjørholm is sacred to him. There is nothing he loves more than the gods," the guard explained. "He will levy warriors from all the clans and lay siege. He will stop at nothing to get this fortress back."

A silence fell over the room, but Elbert was unfazed. From what he had heard about the northern king, this was exactly what he had expected. *A mindless barbarian attacking wildly. Like a dog backed into a corner,* he told himself. "Thank you for your honesty. Guards, escort these men to the dungeons."

Elbert's guards quickly saluted and dragged the three men down the corridor and out of sight, with Soren thrashing and cursing the entire way.

"I could've told you the same thing. Why not ask me?" Grimm asked plainly.

The king turned his head and saw that the white-eyed warrior's expression remained unperturbed. It was as if he was bored by the ordeal of interrogating prisoners for information. "Leave us, Islander. We have private matters to discuss," Elbert commanded. Grimm shrugged his shoulders and exited the keep without another word.

"Where are the rest of my lords?" Elbert asked.

"They await you in what appears to be the dining hall, Your Majesty."

"Show me," Elbert commanded.

Thames led him down the same corridor where the three Islanders had been dragged. It amazed Elbert that blood was seemingly everywhere. The walls, the floor, and the ceiling had all been stained a dark shade of red. He looked down at the wheels of his chair and noticed that once-shining grey metal had adopted the red colouring of its surroundings. The blood had also found its way on to his hands. Elbert sneered at the sight.

"Rupert, I wish to be pushed the rest of the way."

"As you wish, Your Majesty."

They came to the junction at the end of the corridor. On the right was a descending staircase which presumably led to the dungeons, and on the left was an open archway that led to a large dining hall.

The room was lit with sconces, and a large wooden table in the centre extended for the entire length of the room. *Could comfortably seat fifty,* Elbert thought to himself.

He noticed that his handful of lords had already seated themselves, and were quietly waiting for his arrival. Thames rolled Elbert to the head of the table and then silently stood to attention at his side.

"Gentlemen," Elbert began. "Today marks a new day in Artanzia's history. We have done the impossible!"

The lords erupted in cheers, and a few banged on the table with enthusiasm.

Elbert smiled as he held up a quieting hand. "However, a lot of work still needs to be done. Uthredd has undoubtedly heard about our arrival, and he will soon hear about Tjørholm's capture. We need to prepare."

"I say we fortify the weak spots, especially those that we exploited," suggested Lord Grelin.

"Agreed: anything else?"

"I've been working on some schematics, Your Majesty," Arlin spoke up, as he unfurled a couple of papers in front of him. "If I have access to a decent forge, I can create a few ballistas that will send those Islanders runnin', tails 'tween their legs."

"How long will it take you to craft one?" Elbert inquired.

"With a few helping hands, I'd say about two days per ballistae."

"Uthredd will already be mobilizing his forces. I suspect him to be at our gates in under a week," one of the other lords chimed in.

Elbert stared at the man for some time, examining his features. He was middle-aged, with a receding mane of brown hair and a thick goatee. *Must be the eldest son of one of the elderly nobles,* Elbert thought to himself, before suddenly remembering the man's name.

"And what do you suggest, Lord Penerack?"

"I've seen few battles, but from what I've read, digging is the best defence."

"Digging?"

"Trenches, Your Majesty," Penerack explained. "It renders both cavalry and siege engines useless. Allows us to establish a perimeter."

"Only one fucking problem," another lord interjected. "The ground is frozen solid. If we move forward with that plan, Uthredd will be upon us before we even get a six-foot hole in the ground."

"Agreed," Elbert said, after some deliberation. "I say our best strategy going forward is to construct Lord Arlin's ballistas and to fortify the fortress' weaknesses."

"Aye." the lords said in unison, except for Lord Penerack, whose face had turned bright red.

"On to another matter. Lord Haustack is still in critical condition, and thus his men are leaderless. We need someone to volunteer to lead the prisoner company."

"I have a few excellent captains under my banner," Lord Grelin stated. "I'm sure they would relish leading their own company."

"I was thinking someone more... disposable," Elbert replied.

A hush fell over the table. The lords looked at one another in confusion before turning back to their king. "Who, Your Majesty?" one of them bravely asked.

"The Islander. Grimm White-Eyes."

Several of the lords gasped in shock, and a few spat on the floor. Elbert even heard Thames' sharp intake of breath to voice a retort, but the captain stopped himself.

"With all due respect, Your Majesty," Lord Penerack said, speaking over the loud murmur of the other lords, "Wouldn't you be more comfortable with one of your fellow countrymen leading the company? Someone who could be trusted?"

Elbert grinned and leaned back in his chair. "I would not. You see, Grimm, like the prisoner company, is expendable. They are a group of men we intend to use as fodder. Uthredd will not assemble his army as one big force and then march on Tjørholm. From what I've gathered, he is an impatient and reckless man who will stop at nothing until this stronghold is back under his control. His army is scattered across the Isles, and he will order his men to meet in front of our gates."

"How can you be so sure?" one lord asked.

"Because that's what I would do if I needed to expel a foreign invader from my kingdom in a hurry. What you fail to see, gentlemen, is that Uthredd's reign is built on fear and the portrayal of strength. Every day that we occupy this fortress, he loses support. Doubt seeps into his subjects' minds, and that is something we can exploit. I intend to send the Islander and the rest of the prisoner company on a few raiding missions to attack the Islander troops while they camp at night. If we are successful, we will cut down some of Uthredd's forces before they get here: if not, then we didn't waste any good men."

"What if the Islander refuses, Your Majesty?" Lord Grelin enquired.

"He won't. He is a desperate man who wants nothing more than to leave these Isles. He will do what we ask, as long as we dangle that carrot in front of him. Are there any objections?"

The lords remained silent, and after a lengthy pause, they rose from their seats.

"One more thing," Elbert said, causing all the lords to freeze where they stood. "It has come to my attention that some of your men have been defiling the womenfolk that we found here. This behaviour is unacceptable. I will not tolerate my army acting like these heathens: we will not stoop to their level. Am I understood?"

"But Your Majesty," Lord Grelin replied meekly. "Looting and pillaging are some of the few benefits to being a soldier. The men might –"

"They might what?" Elbert shouted. "Do I not pay them handsomely for their service? Do I not supply them with all they need to live while they are away from their homes? Are you accusing me of being a selfish king, Lord Grelin?" The lord uttered no response. "If any of your men are caught raping the locals, not only will I take their cock and balls, but I will also take yours. Am I understood?"

The lords nodded fearfully in agreement.

"Good. Rupert, take me to see the Islander."

As he made his way through the newly conquered stronghold, Elbert noticed that many of the men's demeanours had changed. Before the assault, they would look at their king with expressions of either disdain or pity. But now, the soldiers greeted him with smiles and low, formal bows. It was as if they had started seeing him as a man rather than a cripple. It was as if they had started to see him as their king. Elbert's head lifted slightly as he continued to roll through the corpse-littered streets.

Captain Thames led him to a secluded corner of the fortress, where they found Grimm bathing himself with a bucket of icy water. A puddle of shit, piss, and blood had pooled at his feet as he scrubbed the filth from his unkempt mane. His bare chest was exposed to the elements as he washed it with the chilled water. His torso was a tapestry of scars and old battle wounds. Each cut told the tale of some poor bastard that didn't manage to slice deep enough.

Sara sat on the stone steps of a pillaged house and watched, with a bored look glued on her face. Her expression changed, however, once she saw the king roll down the street.

"Elbert!" she squeaked.

Elbert smiled as the child sprinted down the street and wrapped his lifeless legs in a vice-like embrace. He smiled when he looked down at the child. Although Thames had suggested that even Sara should follow proper protocol when addressing the king, Elbert had quickly dismissed him. She was too young to remember all the arbitrary rules of addressing nobility, let alone understanding all of them. He also found the child's familiarity to be surprisingly refreshing.

"Legless," Grimm greeted, as water dripped from his soaked beard.

Elbert felt his lips contort into a scowl. The Islander's candour was not as appreciated as the dwarf's. He gently shooed Sara to the side and rolled his chair until he was directly in front of the hulking warrior. Water dripped from Grimm's muscular body onto Elbert's knees, although he didn't notice. He was too busy staring at the void-like eyes of the Islander. After a lengthy pause, Elbert cleared his throat.

"I've come –"

"Which boat is taking me to the mainland?" Grimm interrupted.

"I beg your pardon?"

"I gave you Tjørholm. Now you will give me a ship that'll take the girl and me to the mainland. That was our deal."

"Unfortunately, there has been a change of plan," Elbert said snidely. "I am still in need of your services."

"And what are you willing to give me for these services?" Grimm asked, in an equally obnoxious tone. "You already owe me a ship."

"You'll get your ship once our business in the Isles has been concluded." Elbert's voice was firm and unwavering. He made sure to enunciate every syllable to drive his point through the undoubtedly thick skull of the Islander. "If you don't like it, you're free to leave and continue living off the land like the backwards savage you are."

Grimm cursed under his breath and shook his head in frustration. Several seconds passed before the shirtless warrior made eye contact with the crippled king once again, but when he did, it was a fiery glare filled with contempt and rage.

"What would you have me do?"

"One of our nobles, Lord Haustack, was indisposed by one of your king's patrols, and –"

"Uthredd is not my king," Grimm interjected angrily.

"Very well, former king," Elbert corrected. "Lord Haustack is gravely wounded, and cannot lead his company of men. They require a leader, and we want to you act as their commander until Lord Haustack recovers."

The Islander let out a hearty laugh. His voice boomed off the ravaged houses and empty streets. "You want me to lead the company of bastards?"

Elbert frowned at the mention of the prisoner company's nickname. He was made aware of it shortly after landing, and was not fond of it, no matter how fitting it was. "That is not their official name, but in short: yes, I do."

"So you want the biggest bastard to lead all the other bastards?" Grimm asked with a smile on his face. It seemed that the Islander found the whole situation to be quite humorous.

"Is that going to be a problem?" Thames interjected.

"I figured your ugly mug would've been the leader, since you're as much of a bastard as me."

Thames reached for his sword, but stopped himself once he caught his king's glare. After exchanging a few silent looks with each other, Elbert turned his attention back towards the Islander. "Why must you antagonize me and my men? Were you not taught a modicum of respect?"

"On the Isles, respect is earned, not given," Grimm replied plainly, all of his mirth disappearing quickly.

"We want you to take the men out on raiding missions. We believe Uthredd will have his forces meeting somewhere nearby. Your job is to take your men and ambush them as they travel."

"By men, you mean the bastards that can't swing a sword? Those poor sods need training before they can even think about taking on a group of Islanders."

"Training is under your jurisdiction, but you will march out when I order you to, whether your men are ready or not," Elbert said, with a note of finality in his voice. Before Grimm could reply, Elbert spun his chair around and rolled back towards the keep, Thames quietly falling in behind him.

The thought of Grimm meeting a bloody end surrounded only by criminals put a smile on the king's face as he wheeled through the cobblestone streets. He couldn't help but fantasize about the thoughts that would run through the Islander's head as he slowly bled to death at the hands of his former brethren.

However, his smile soon faded as he remembered the scars that covered the man's body. *A man like that does not die easily.*

CHAPTER TWENTY

ANNA

Stitch's house stank of rotting teeth, dying flesh, and dried blood. He was the only healer in The Garden, and everyone went to him, whether it was to stitch a cut or pull out a broken crossbow bolt. He was the best of the best.

Or so Anna was told.

From what she saw, the man was so drunk that he could barely walk in a straight line; and even in his current state of inebriation, his hands still shook violently. The man's skin paled as he dabbed Maeve's bruised face with a wet cloth, her blood staining the rag a deep tinge of crimson.

"Will she be all right?" Randall asked, being the first of the Maggots to speak since they had arrived at the healer's house.

Stitch grabbed a nearly empty bottle of vodka from a nearby table and took three healthy swigs, then pulled out a small vial from his apron pocket and tipped the contents into his hand. It was a white crystalline powder. He quickly brought his hand up to his nose and snorted the substance through both nostrils. His eyes immediately widened, and Anna noticed that the trembling in Stitch's hands dissipated slightly.

"She got one hell of a shit-kicking," the healer responded in a gruff, calloused voice. "Lass is lucky to be alive."

In the back of the room, Greaver cleared his throat. He had been surprisingly quiet until now. The Maggots and the healer turned toward the King of Crooks, all except Maeve, who showed no signs of life other than her shallow breathing.

"The Blackguard doesn't take kindly to thieves," the king said in a disinterested tone.

"Who?" Anna asked.

"Ever since that cripple's departure, Queen Vivian has been making moves to seize control from her newlywed husband. The first was hiring the Blackguard as her personal bodyguards."

"Why are they called the Blackguard?" Tig asked stupidly.

"Because their leader is a vile man named Mortimer Black. A former mercenary, who only values coin and violence."

"So, what are you going to do about this?" Randall asked angrily.

"Me?" Greaver gasped. "What would you have me do? Schedule a meeting with Queen Vivian herself and lecture her about what her new bodyguards are doing to my children? Despite my title, boy, I am not, in fact, nobility. There isn't a damn thing we can do, other than staying out of the Blackguard's way."

"Lazy prick," Randall mumbled under his breath.

"And where were you?" the king asked, his voice suddenly turning cold.

"Planning a job."

"Without your gaggle of miscreants? I find that very unlikely."

Randall said nothing.

"Last time I checked, you were in charge of this ragtag outfit. As their leader, it is your responsibility to make sure nobody gets hurt." Greaver paused dramatically as he approached the seething youth. The king stooped down until they were at eye level. "You'd better pray to the old gods and the new that Maeve makes it through this. Or else."

They continued to stare at each other, but neither offered any more words. After what felt like an uncomfortable eternity, Greaver stood upright and walked out of the healer's house, leaving an awkward silence behind him.

Anna turned her attention back towards Stitch, who was struggling to thread a needle. Either the healer wasn't bothered by the king's threats, or he was so focused on the simple task at hand that he had not noticed them, because he showed no inkling of the uneasiness that the rest of the house felt.

"Fix her up, Stitch," Randall ordered. "The rest of you with me. We are going to take a walk around the city."

"I'll do my best, kid," Stitch replied, as he snorted another line of powder up his nose.

The Maggots followed Randall outside and into The Garden, and realized that the courtyard was largely abandoned. Only a handful of criminals walked across the grounds, and all of them avoided eye contact with the group of youths.

"What's everyone's problem?" Tig asked, as he scratched the top of his head.

"I don't know, but let's get out of here," Randall replied.

As they made their way towards the hidden door of The Garden, Anna paused and looked back towards the throne room. She wanted to confront the king about his lie. *How could he protect someone like that?* Anna thought to herself. *He just wanted to use me, to manipulate me into doing his bidding.* Her hand slowly reached for the handle of her dagger. *He'll learn his lesson, the same way the pickpocket did.*

"Let's go," Randall instructed.

"Go ahead: I'll catch up," Anna replied as she started marching towards the throne room.

"No."

"Excuse me?"

"We need to stick together. We can't afford to have Greaver crawling any further up our ass than he already has."

"He's right, Anna," Chuckles replied. "Greaver's really upset with us after Maeve's accident. It's best if we don't leave each other's side."

Anna glared at the King of Crooks' throne room once more and let out a defeated sigh. "Fine. Where are we going?"

"Odion Rawley's." Randall smiled.

"Are you fucking mad!" Tig shouted.

"Shhh!" Randall hissed. "Want to alert the entire garrison to our plan?"

"I'm sorry, Randall, but what you're talking about is crazy."

"Crazy? You're the crazy one if you can't see that Greaver is a shell of the man he used to be. He won't even try to get revenge for Maeve's attack. The man I knew when he took me in would've stormed the castle and demanded to see that cunt Vivian that very second!"

"But you're talking about overthrowing him; the man that taught us everything!" Chuckles added.

"He took you in for what: so he could line his pockets with more coin? He steals from the rest of us and never gets off his fat fucking ass. It's time for a change."

"And you think these dwarves are the answer?" Tig asked.

"I never said that," Randall replied coyly.

"And you're okay with all of this?" Tig asked, turning his attention towards Anna.

She hesitated briefly. She remembered how Greaver took her in when she had nothing and no one. The man saved her life and gave her purpose. She turned her head and glanced at Randall. His eyes were staring back at her expectantly, but he gave her a reassuring smile.

"Fuck Greaver," she replied sourly. "He's a liar and a snake and I, for one, refuse to give that prick another copper."

Randall wrapped his arm around Anna and pulled her in tight. "I'm beginning to think that Anna has more balls than all of you combined."

"Okay, but like... you want to rob this guy? I mean, look at his house!" Chuckles replied.

Anna turned her attention to Rawley's estate and realized that Chuckles had a point. The yard was surrounded by a seven foot high brick wall, topped with iron spikes. Behind the walls was a plethora of guards roaming around the grounds of the manor. The house itself was a monstrosity of architecture. It had four levels, and towered above its neighbours. There were two large bay windows on every floor that were great vantage points of the entire yard.

"How are we even supposed to get in there?" Tig asked.

"That's how." Randall pointed as he saw a group of dark silhouettes passing through the manor's front gate. "Rawley hires kids to clean his house. All we have to do is pose as the cleaners, and we're in."

"That's your plan?" Tig gasped. "Do I look like a fucking cleaner to you? Plus, there's no way Chuckles can pull this off without laughing his arse off."

"I haven't worked out all the details. I'll need a day or two to come up with a foolproof plan."

"So, what are we doing here?" Chuckles asked.

"Learning," Randall replied rudely. "Watching the comings and goings of the guards, when their shift changes are, how often they take breaks, and if there are any blind spots that we can take advantage of."

"So, we're going to spend all damn day out here, then?" Tig complained.

"Yes, so get comfortable."

As the sun began to set, the snow that lined Winterhelm's streets glistened like a sea of diamonds. Anna and A'Chula watched Rawley's estate from the safety of rooftops across the street. Randall, Tig, and Chuckles had all elected to take a nap while Anna and A'Chula kept watching the guards.

So far, they had noticed two shift changes: one at midday and one around dinner time. The changing of the guards was the most exciting thing to happen to them during their watch. Time seemed to drag on. Seconds became minutes, minutes became hours, and hours seemed like days. Anna caught herself drifting off to sleep several times, but the harsh winter wind stirred her from her drowsiness.

"Think Maeve will be all right?" she asked, knowing full well that she wouldn't get a response. The sight of the girl's battered face lingered in her mind.

She couldn't remember the last time she had seen someone that badly bruised. It took her back to the days of training to fight monsters with her father in the forest. Her dad was as relentless as the beasts he was pretending to be. Many times, she would limp home and crawl into bed with bruised or broken ribs. Yet despite this, she still remembered her time with her father fondly. In a way, she missed the boring nightly lectures, the rigorous training, and being forced to read obscure tomes about even more obscure monsters. She wondered what her father would think of her now.

"Hmph," A'Chula grunted, interrupting her thoughts.

"I'm worried about her," Anna confessed. "But I promise I'll find the bastard that did that to her and gut him like a carp."

A'Chula nodded his head in understanding.

Suddenly, a gilded carriage pulled up in front of Rawley's gates. Anna scuttled across the snow-covered rooftop to get a better view. She saw the shadowy outline of a well-dressed woman exit the house and approach the wagon.

The guards on duty fell into deep bows as the woman walked past them, before resuming their regular duties. The woman elegantly climbed into the carriage and shut the door. With a crack of the reins, they began rolling away from Rawley's estate.

"Stay here. I'm going to follow her," Anna ordered as she began nimbly climbing down the roof. She didn't wait for A'Chula's response; she knew there wouldn't be one, or, at best, there'd be an audible grunt that could be interpreted a thousand different ways.

She followed the carriage's tracks in the snow and was surprised that it led her to one of the poorer parts of Winterhelm. It wasn't The Splints, but it wasn't far off. Anna watched as the woman exited the carriage and began walking down the street with an escort of armed guards. She made sure to stay in the shadows and began stalking the woman. The same way she had stalked the pickpocket.

After about ten minutes of tracking, it became clear that the woman was looking for something, or someone. She stopped at several houses, knocking on the door, and after a brief discussion with the inhabitants, continuing to another house that was seemingly selected at random.

The woman intrigued Anna. Despite the armed escort of guards, she always approached the houses alone. Her head was held high, and her body language didn't suggest a hint of fear or agitation. She wondered what kind of person the woman might be and what her connection to Rawley was.

If she was his wife, why would she come to one of the poorest neighbourhoods in the city and start banging on doors? If she was a servant or concubine, why was she so well-dressed, and why did she have an escort of guards? These questions swirled in Anna's head, when she noticed that the woman and her entourage had come to a sudden stop.

"Come on out. I know you've been following me," the woman called out.

Anna cursed under her breath. She thought about fleeing or reaching for her dagger, but her gut told her not to. She couldn't risk arousing any suspicion, not before the big heist. Plus, she wanted the answers to her questions about the woman. Anna straightened her back, and cautiously approached the retinue of guards and the woman.

The woman turned around and smiled. "Leave us," she ordered. Without hesitation, the guards crossed to the other side of the street: far enough away to be out of earshot, but not so far away as to leave the woman completely helpless. "What can I do for you?"

Anna was taken aback by the warmth of the woman's voice. She stared into the woman's eyes and saw that there was no malice or even annoyance in them. Instead, she saw that they were full of compassion and understanding.

"Would you like some food?" the woman asked.

Anna nodded her head excitedly. Although she was far from starving, she had spent the entire day watching Rawley's estate, and had failed to bring any food along. The woman reached into the pocket of her coat and pulled out a sweet wrapped in a thin cloth.

Anna unwrapped the candy and popped it into her mouth. Her pupils dilated as soon as the sweet taste hit her tongue. It was like nothing she had ever tasted before. It was minty, then fruity, then savoury; and then it repeated the cycle. Anna looked up into the woman's matronly eyes in astonishment.

"Sorry, I have nothing more nutritious. Do you have a name?"

"Makayla," Anna lied, although she wasn't sure why.

"Well, Makayla, mind telling me why you were following me?" Still, no coldness or anger in the woman's voice, just plain curiosity.

Anna's mind raced as she tried to think of a lie. After a pause that seemed to span hours, she spat out the first thing that came into her head. "A couple of girls I know told me that you hire people like us for cleaning."

The woman's face lit up. "Indeed I do! Are you looking for work?"

Anna nodded her head. "My friends and I are."

The woman's eyes narrowed slightly. "You're a bit older than I usually hire, but if it keeps you kids out of trouble, I'll gladly pay you for your time."

"You'll pay us?" Anna asked, astounded.

"Of course! Didn't the other girls mention that?"

"What if we aren't good cleaners?" Anna asked, trying to put on the most innocent face she could muster.

The woman smiled. "All I ask is that you and your friends try your best."

Anna smiled. "What's your name?"

"Alcina Rawley."

"When can we start?"

"How about tomorrow; around midday? I'll pay each of you a gold coin."

Anna nodded her head excitedly. "Great, we'll be there!"

"Now run along home," Alcina advised. "It's getting late for a young thing like yourself to be out here alone."

Anna nodded her head once more, then sprinted back towards the richer part of town, so that she could tell the other Magoots the good news.

"You did what?" Randall exclaimed, his voice shaking from what appeared to be excitement.

"She wants to hire us, to clean her place tomorrow!" Anna replied, equally excited.

Randall pulled her into a deep embrace and wrapped his arms around her tightly. Her stomach immediately fluttered with nervous energy, and she felt her cheeks flush with colour, as her face buried into the boy's muscular chest. She wanted to push him away so that she could regain her composure, but a part of her wanted to stay in Randall's embrace forever.

The boy's grip loosened, and he pulled back and kissed her on the forehead. "I fucking love you!" he laughed, as he turned around to the rest of the Maggots, who were all smiling.

"Holy shit, Anna, you're a mastermind!" Chuckles gushed. "How did you even come up with a lie like that on the spot?"

"I don't know," she confessed as she brushed the silver-blonde hair out of her eyes. "I kinda just panicked and blurted out the first thing I thought of."

"Tonight, I'm buying you drinks till you pass out!" Tig boisterously exclaimed.

"No," Randall cut in. "We can't be hung over tomorrow. Need our wits about us while we are in there."

"Can't even drink a little?" Tig pleaded.

Randall smiled and let out a sigh. "Alright, maybe a few."

Their walk back to The Garden was full of youthful energy. Chuckles couldn't stop laughing long enough to get a word in. Tig had begun fantasizing about what he was going to purchase after the big heist, and even A'Chula spoke a few monosyllabic words. When they were about to reach The Garden, Randall grasped Anna's hand and pulled her aside.

"Follow me." He smiled as he led her down an alley, away from the others.

"Where are we going?" Anna asked, the giddiness evident in her voice.

"You'll see," Randall replied coyly.

The moonlight sparkled off the snow and illuminated the city in a soft white glow. Anna's mind raced as Randall led her through the snow-covered city. She wasn't sure where the boy was taking her, but she could tell from his demeanour that he was excited and nervous at the same time. She thought about collapsing into the boy's arms once again, but shook the notion out of her head. *Best not to get my hopes up,* she told herself.

After about fifteen minutes of running, Randall finally stopped at one of Winterhelm's graveyards. An eerie silence that hung in the air, and suddenly the city didn't look so magical.

"Come on," he said, tugging at her arm to follow.

Anna obliged, but the giddiness inside her had noticeably subsided. Her body was filling with a different nervous energy. Energy that suggested something bad was about to happen.

They weaved through the graveyard before finally stopping at a grave that was unmarked, apart from a small twig staked into the frozen earth.

"What is this place?" Anna asked.

"I wanted to thank you for all you've done for us," Randall started. "Ever since I found you, you've changed all of our lives for the better. You've changed my life for the better."

"Randall –"

He held up his hand to stop her. "I just want to show you how special you are to me, so I'm showing you something that I've never shown anyone. This is my sister's grave."

"I didn't know you had a sister."

"Nobody does, not even Greaver." Randall paused; tears were swelling in his eyes. "Before he found me, my sister and I worked for a noble family. Everything was going fine until I broke some stupid glass vase. My sister immediately suggested that she take the blame, and being the coward that I was, I let her."

"What happened?"

"The nobles became unhinged. They said it was 'inexcusable' and that my sister had to reimburse them. Unfortunately, that damned vase was worth more than both our lives combined. So the nobles punished her. They... they..." Randall's voice cracked.

Anna stayed silent, but reached out and touched his hand.

"They fed her to their fucking dogs!" he shouted. "They murdered her, and nobody gave a fuck. The city guard didn't even come by to ask questions. As far as they were concerned, it was one less child living out on the streets."

"I'm sorry, Randall," Anna said as she squeezed the boy's hand tighter.

"There wasn't even enough of her left to bury. All I have left to remember my sister by is this marker and my tattoo."

Before Anna could ask, Randall unbuttoned his shirt and showed a tattoo of a raven on his chest.

"She always called me her raven. Said I was just as cunning as those damned birds."

"Randall, I had no idea –"

"Why would you? Like I said, I haven't told anyone this, not even Greaver. I just thought you should know because you're special to me."

Anna squeezed his hand tighter. "Thank you for sharing this with me. I won't tell anyone."

Randall turned his head towards Anna's and smiled. She felt his warm breath on her lips. The tears made his eyes sparkle majestically. Anna leaned her body closer, and Randall did likewise. After a brief pause of uncertainty, they kissed.

His lips were soft and warm to the touch. Anna's mind swirled with panic and excitement. She tried to block out her memories of the pickpocket and the young lumberjack. Randall's tongue danced in her mouth, and she desperately tried to imitate the motions with her own tongue.

Randall's body pulled back slightly. "Is this your first time?" he asked.

Anna felt her skin redden with embarrassment. Was it that glaringly obvious? She averted her eyes and nodded her head. She wanted to spit out a fiery retort, but quickly found out that the words died in her throat.

Randall cupped her cheek and pulled her in closer. "Don't worry. We'll take it slow."

His tongue once again penetrated her mouth, but this time she was prepared for it. She grabbed him by his broad shoulders and pulled him in tighter, thinking that he might like it. It surprised Anna, how good kissing felt. If she had known this, she would have had her first kiss much sooner.

The boy's hands slowly slid down her body. Anna's body quivered. As Randall unlaced her trousers, a surge of trepidation flooded her body. She placed both hands on Randall's chest and forcefully pushed him away.

She had expected the boy to be mad, but instead, he just smiled—that damned charismatic smile.

"Sorry, I'm just not ready for that," Anna confessed, as she retied her trousers.

"It's okay; plus this probably isn't the proper spot for it either," Randall said, a hint of mirth staining his voice. "Let's get back to The Garden. The others will be waiting for us. We have a big day tomorrow."

CHAPTER TWENTY-ONE

GRIMM

S parks flew across the courtyard as Grimm easily parried one of the attacks. The other two soldiers lunged at him simultaneously from opposite directions.

He quickly pirouetted out of the way and smacked one man in the nose with the blunt part of his blade. Blood poured out of the man's nose as he fell to the ground, which had already been stained red with the blood of the other men.

The two remaining soldiers were panting aggressively. Their sweat seeped through their clothes, and their limbs had a slight tremble to them. Grimm stretched his back until he heard an audible pop. He let out a long, relaxed sigh. He couldn't be more comfortable.

"Are you giving up, bastards?" he called out, his voice echoing off the fortress' stone walls.

"No, sir!" they replied in unison.

"Then attack!"

Both soldiers exchanged wary glances with each other before they charged at their commander. Grimm smiled as his opponents closed the distance.

He tossed his blade to the ground and ran towards them, equipped with only his fists. One of the men paused, while the other let out a frustrated battle cry as he raised his axe over his head.

Grimm easily sidestepped the clumsy swing and countered with a jab to the jaw. The man retaliated with a side swing that the old warrior had expected.

The Islander spun out of the way and delivered a flurry of blows to the man's midsection before delivering a swift kick to his knee, making the soldier's legs buckle. He then grabbed the man's head and smashed it against his own, until he heard the deafening crunch of a nose breaking.

Grimm tossed the man's unconscious body to the ground and stared at his last opponent. The man looked as if he was about to shit himself. And after a week of knowing the soldier, Grimm wouldn't put it past him.

"I yield!" the man yelled, as he tossed his weapon to the ground. There was a chuckle of amusement from the crowd of onlookers.

Grimm smiled and opened his arms wide for an embrace. The soldier stupidly fell for the obvious trap and approached for a hug. The Islander quickly closed his arms and slapped the man on both ears.

As the soldier reeled back from the pain, Grimm punched him square in the teeth, making sure to knock at least three of them loose.

With all three opponents on the ground, Grimm turned his attention to the rest of his company. "If I hear another man beg for mercy in training, I'll chop off his head. Am I understood?"

"Yes, sir!" the soldiers replied in unison.

"Uthredd's men will show no mercy, and neither will I. Islanders don't take prisoners unless they are women or children. And although you fight like children, I doubt they'll think of you as suitable slaves."

Silence.

"You're dismissed," he continued, his voice booming throughout the courtyard.

The company of bastards saluted sharply and began walking back to their quarters for some much-needed rest. Ever since Grimm had assumed command a week ago, he had worked them to the point of exhaustion; and on some days, even further. He hated to admit it, but the men had made great strides in such a short time.

He credited it to how hard he was training them. The men sparred at least three times a day, which was often three times more than the other companies. Grimm also ordered every man to hand in his swords. Instead, they trained with axes and spears, weapons much more suitable for untrained hands.

Finally, unlike the other companies, they did not train with blunted weapons. Grimm thought it defeated the purpose. *In order to learn, one must have the scars to remember the lesson,* Grimm told himself, as he stared down at his own scarred arms and remembered all the lessons he had learned in his life.

"You push them too hard," Thames said, disturbing Grimm from his thoughts.

"Hmph," Grimm snorted. It had become a daily ritual. Thames would watch Grimm train his men, then come over and ridicule his leadership style. Grimm had grown tired of it.

"Your men need rest, and you cannot send them into battle with broken bones," the captain continued.

"Why not?" Grimm replied. "It's how I was trained. I fought my first raid with three broken ribs and a dislocated shoulder. I'm building warriors, something you would know nothing about."

"It amazes me that your people haven't murdered each other into extinction yet," Thames snarled as he sharply turned on his heel.

Grimm laughed quietly to himself. He had wondered about that very question himself. He walked back to his tent, and found Sara anxiously waiting for him.

"Did you win?" she asked excitedly.

"What do you think?"

Sara's face frowned slightly. "It's not fun when only one person wins."

Grimm suppressed a smile, and bent down and looked into her eyes. "Would you like to win when you know the other person let you? Or would you rather earn it?"

Sara harrumphed and shifted her gaze to her toes. "I'd like to earn it," she confessed under her breath.

"That's what I thought," Grimm stated as he slowly stood upright.

"Can you teach me how to play?"

"Ha! You want to be a shieldmaiden?"

"More than anything!" Sara squealed.

He thought about dismissing her childish notions before he remembered that he had started training when he was about her age. Nothing intense, just learning how to swing a sword and how to hold a shield. Against his better judgement, Grimm conceded.

"Here," he said, as he handed her one of the wooden swords he had confiscated from his men. "Swing from your hips."

"Hiyah!" Sara shrieked as she swung the wooden blade with all her might.

"No, like this," Grimm instructed, as he placed his calloused hands on her diminutive hips. Then, he turned her body with his hands, to show her the motion she should be making.

"Like this?" she said, as she executed a perfect swing.

"I've seen better," Grimm lied. It appeared that this former slave girl had a talent for killing.

"Training a future knight, I see," said a voice from the front of the tent.

Grimm didn't have to lift his head to know that it was Elbert. The king always managed to find him after training, no matter how hard he tried to hide.

"May I speak with you outside?" Elbert enquired.

"If you must," Grimm retorted as he stepped out of the tent. Outside, the cold air was as refreshing as a frothing mug of ale. He would have found it peaceful, had he been alone. "What do you want, Legless?"

Elbert sighed. "Would it kill you to address me by my proper title?"

"It might."

The king shook his head angrily. "I am looking for a status report. How long until your men are ready to go out on raids? Our scouts have reported seeing several armies approaching from the north."

"A few months," Grimm replied plainly.

"A few months!? We don't have that kind of time: we need to attack Uthredd's forces now!"

"You're the one who handed me a company of men who can't fight. Warriors are not made overnight."

"Be that as it may," Elbert hissed. "You will take your men out on a raid tonight. There is an Islander camp only a few hours' ride from here, according to Lord Grelin's men."

"Fine," Grimm replied, knowing it would be of no use to argue. The fact that he had managed to stall the king for this long was nothing short of a miracle. At least now his men had some combat experience, and several could swing an axe competently.

"You'll leave at dusk," the king informed.

"I'll leave now," Grimm retorted. "Want to get the lie of the land before the sun sets."

Elbert nodded his head. "Very well. I'll inform the stables to get the horses ready."

"Tell them to prepare five."

Elbert's face contorted into one of utter bafflement. "Five? Are you out of your bloody mind?"

"If I had competent warriors, I'd only need three."

Elbert shook his head in disbelief. "As you wish, but I'll be sending Rupert with you to make sure things don't get out of hand."

"That ugly fucker will only get in the way," Grimm snarled.

"As your king, my word is final."

"You're not my king," Grimm seethed. He watched Elbert arrogantly roll away before he felt a sudden smack against his calf.

"Like that?" Sara beamed.

Grimm glared at the child, tore the wooden blade from her grasp, and tossed it across the camp. He grabbed the girl by the collar of her shirt and lifted her into the air. "Swords are not toys! Do you understand me!" he screamed. Sara nodded her head vigorously as she began bawling. Finally, he dropped her to the ground and walked to tell his men the news.

Sara's sobs echoed in his mind as he marched through the camp. He did not regret yelling at the girl; it was a necessary lesson if she was going to take swordsmanship seriously. He did, however, regret not praising her for the power she put behind the blow. There was a dull throbbing sensation in his calf that put a slight limp in his gait. A smile crept along his lips. *She's already better than all the bastards.*

As he entered the bastards' quarters, the exhausted men were already standing to attention. Grimm scanned his men, trying to find the most competent soldiers in his company of thieves, murderers, and rapists.

However, he knew it wouldn't matter who he chose. None of his men had the skills necessary to survive a fight with an Islander. Their only hope would be to sneak into the enemy's camp at night and slit their throats while they slept.

"At ease," Grimm grumbled, as his eyes continued to look for the most promising recruits. "King Elbert has ordered us to go out and hunt us some Islanders tonight. Any volunteers?" Silence. Which was expected. The men had only been soldiers for a week, and after the thrashings they received in training, he doubted that any of them relished the idea of going into an actual battle.

Suddenly, a man stepped forward. He was tall, and looked as if he was a skeleton with skin. He had deep bags under his eyes and hollow, sunken cheeks. His brown wispy hair covered his eyes, and his hands trembled noticeably.

"I... I volunteer," the soldier said meekly, with a shaking voice.

Grimm nodded his head in approval. *He'll be the first to die,* he thought, as his eyes returned to the company of men. "Anyone else?"

Unsurprisingly, the first man's courage did not inspire any others to step forward. The Islander let out a sigh and picked out three soldiers at random. "You, you, and you. Gather your things and meet me at the stables. We'll leave as soon as you're ready." Without waiting for a response, he walked away from the bastards' tents.

Thames was already waiting for him at the stables, a smug smile plastered on his face. "Ready to kill more of your countrymen?" he asked snidely.

"You know, mainlander, battle is often a hectic and confusing time. It'd be a shame if I confused you for an enemy," Grimm replied.

"I'll be sure to watch my back," Thames replied, as he turned his attention back towards his mount.

Grimm eyed the horses with carefully. They were all larger and more muscular than the horses that roamed theIsles. The captain had already chosen a dapple grey mare, leaving three chestnut geldings and a fiery black stallion for Grimm and his men.

The stallion locked eyes with the warrior and immediately began rearing and stamping its feet angrily. Grimm took an involuntary step backwards.

"I don't believe my eyes!" Thames exclaimed. "The savage is scared of a horse!"

"I'm not scared of them," Grimm snapped back. "I just don't like the cunts when they're antsy."

"That is a warhorse," Thames replied smugly. "A mount bred to carry a soldier into battle and fight alongside him."

"Unruly beast," Grimm muttered under his breath. He had half a mind to choose one of the chestnut geldings, but knew that he would be leaving himself open to ridicule. Reluctantly, he ran a hand along the neck of the stallion. The horse reared once again and let out a high-pitched whinny. Grimm quickly stepped back so that his feet weren't crushed beneath the beast's hooves.

"Hurry up and mount that thing!" Thames called out from his saddle. "We don't have all day."

"And you'd know all about mounting things, wouldn't you, captain?" Grimm jeered as he approached the horse cautiously once again.

It took three more attempts before the horse finally calmed down and allowed the Islander to climb on its back. By then, the four soldiers from Grimm's company had arrived and had mounted their steeds.

"Are we ready to depart?" Thames asked impatiently.

"Let's ride," Grimm said as confidently as he could, praying that the stallion wouldn't buck him off as soon as they started moving.

The first hour of the ride proved to be the most challenging. He spent the entire time fighting with the stallion for every inch. Whenever he got the beast to take one step forward, it would immediately take two steps to the side. On several occasions, he thought about chopping off the animal's head and walking the rest of the way, but he refused to let a horse get the better of him.

Finally, he decided to let go of the reins and let the stallion gallop unchecked across the frozen plains. Immediately noticing the slack in the reins, the horse took off like an arrow across the snow-covered fields. The wind bit at Grimm's cheeks as he gripped the horn of his saddle with all his might, afraid that he might be thrown.

As if sensing his fear, the stallion kicked up its back end and tossed Grimm from the saddle with ease. He landed hard against the snow and felt the air leave his lungs as he watched his mount gallop off into the distance. The four soldiers erupted in laughter, but Thames did not.

"Why are you laughing?" he barked, ending the laughter immediately. "That is the king's property that is galloping through the snow. If that horse is not brought back here immediately, I'll personally take one of your heads to the king as recompense."

The four soldiers gulped in unison before one of them kicked his mount into a gallop to go after the stallion. Thames slowly trotted up to Grimm, who was still wheezing on the ground, and offered him a hand up.

"Are you alright, Islander?"

Grimm pushed the helping hand aside. "Fucking horse," he muttered under his breath.

A smile broke across the captain's lips. "I hope you don't mind me disciplining your men. You seemed to be at a loss for words."

Grimm met the scarred man's gaze with a cantankerous smile of his own.

The men waited for about ten minutes until the soldier returned with the stallion, which had seemingly had a change in temperament since dismounting its rider. Grimm scowled at the beast as he ripped the reins from the soldier's hands. He cautiously climbed back into the saddle and noticed that the sun was beginning to set.

"We're losing light," he said.

"Then let us ride hard; but try and stay on the horse this time, won't you?" Thames teased, as he kicked his horse into a gallop.

Grimm gripped the reins tightly and kicked the stallion into a gallop, but this time the horse lazily went into a canter and refused to go any faster. "Fucking horse," he muttered.

They came across the Islander's camp just as the edges of the sun were kissing the western horizon. The camp was in a small valley, giving Grimm and his men the high ground. They slowly dismounted, and crawled on their stomachs through the snow until they could both see the encampment and remain hidden.

"How many do you think there are?" one soldier asked.

"Fifty or so," Thames replied. "Must be a lesser lord, if that is all the men he could muster."

"You don't know the half of it," Grimm replied, as he rose to his feet.

"What are you doing?" Thames hissed.

"I know those banners: they belong to Jarl Sven Gormsson. He hates Uthredd as much as I do. We might've just found an ally."

"Right, you four stay here. The Islander and I will approach the camp."

"No," Grimm snapped. "Sven may hate Uthredd, but he hates mainlanders more. It's best if I go alone."

"So you can betray us? I don't think so."

"It's either I go alone, or we fight all fifty of his men at night. The choice is yours."

"I say we let Commander Grimm go and talk to them," the tall volunteer said.

"That's 'cause you're a coward," another soldier snapped. "I say we cut these Islander dogs down like the scum that they are!"

"Agreed! My axe is hungry for some Islander blood!" a different soldier agreed.

Spoken like men who have never seen men die before, Grimm thought to himself. "Tell me, what were your crimes? What did you do to end up here in the bastard company?"

"Thievin', sir," one replied.

"Thievin', sir," replied another.

"Raped some tease of a trollop," the third grumbled.

"Poaching, sir," the skinny man said.

"Poaching?" Thames asked in disbelief.

"Aye, I was tracking a deer when it wandered on to the king's land. Didn't realize where I was when I shot it. Thankfully, King David was feeling merciful that day and sentenced me to a life of hard labour instead of ending my life."

"So, none of you have ever killed a man?" Grimm asked, already knowing the answer. The men responded with silence.

"If that's the case, then keep your mouths shut and let the real men talk." He turned his attention to Thames. "What do you think?"

"Hmm," the captain said as he scratched his chin vigorously. "If this lord hates your king as much as you say he does, perhaps it is best if we talk to him. We could use more men. But be warned, if this is some sort of ruse –"

"Your ships are my only way off the Isles, so trust me when I say, if I was going to betray you, I would've done it by now."

Thames nodded his head, and Grimm began walking down the slope towards the camp. He could feel his heartbeat quicken as he heard the scouts' shouts of alarm. His hand instinctively went to his sword, but he forced himself to move his hand away. *Not looking for a fight, just a talk,* he reminded himself. *Heimer's beard. This was always Uthredd's sort of thing.* It wasn't long before a small group of men surrounded him, bows and spears pointed at him from a cautious distance.

"By the gods," one Islander stammered. "It's Grimm White-Eyes!"

A sudden murmur of excitement and fear passed through the group of men.

"I'm not here to fight," Grimm announced. "I'm just here to see Jarl Sven Gormsson."

The men exchanged wary glances for the briefest of moments before turning their attention back towards the white-eyed warrior. "Very well, but leave your sword here."

Grimm swallowed his frustration, but ultimately obeyed by the men's orders. He was not in a position to make demands. He stabbed his blade deep into the frozen earth and followed the group of guardsmen deep into Jarl Gormsson's camp.

A large bonfire had been constructed, and the smell of cooked venison filled the evening air. Grimm could also smell the mead, as he watched several men crack open a few kegs. His stomach immediately growled and his throat went dry. It had been so long since he tasted the winterberry mead of the Northern Isles. He was tempted to say it was the best he had ever had.

"Heimer's beard, is that who I think it is?" a loud voice boomed from across the small encampment.

Grimm turned his head and saw a large potbellied man exit a tent. The man's head was completely shaven and covered in tattoos. His grey beard went down to his belt, and his arms were the size of tree trunks. He was exactly how Grimm remembered him, save for the leather glove on his left hand.

"Sven Gormsson!" Grimm beamed. "The only unnamed jarl in the entire isles."

"It's Sven Blackhand now," the jarl corrected as he removed the glove, revealing a hand covered in dead black skin.

"How'd that happen?"

"Fought an ice wraith a couple of winters back," the jarl replied. "Fucking bitch touched this hand. Killed it completely."

"Can you move it?"

"Nah, it's completely useless to me. I thought about cutting it off but just couldn't bring myself to it, ya know?" Grimm nodded his head in understanding. "But let's talk about you. How do you go from licking Uthredd's arse every morning to killing his brother?"

"You get sick of the taste."

Sven erupted in laughter and waved his limp, dead hand for Grimm to follow him into his tent. Inside was little decoration; the jarl had always been a practical man. He had a bed of furs laying on the ground, and his armour displayed on a stand in the corner of the tent. Other than that, the tent was empty.

"Is it true what they say? Have you allied yourself with the invading mainlanders?" Sven began, as he poured himself a mug of mead.

"They're my only way off the Isles," Grimm replied plainly.

"Ah, I don't blame ya," the jarl responded. "I would do the same thing if I were in your boots."

"Then help us fight Uthredd. Join me, and together we can be free."

"You always were an idealist."

"What does that mean?"

"You would think Heimer would've given you a brain in that thick head of yours!" Sven laughed, as he took a healthy gulp from his mug. "Can't you see you are just replacing one king for another? You'll never truly be free, Grimm. You'll always live to lick someone's arse."

"You're wrong."

"Am I? Tell me, do you think this mainlander king will let you set up a nice homestead in his kingdom and never ask you for anything ever again? Do you truly believe that?"

"What other choice do I have?"

"None, but as long as you've made peace with becoming another man's dog, then —"

"Are you going to help me or not?" Grimm interrupted.

"No," Sven replied. "Unlike you, I refuse to be ordered by mainlanders. They are sheep, and we are wolves. It is the natural order of things."

"Then we are done here," Grimm growled as he turned on his heel.

"You cannot leave," Sven informed.

"You plan to hand me over to Uthredd?"

"Fuck Uthredd!" Sven announced. "I've always wondered who would win in a duel between the two of us. Grimm White-Eyes, Shield of the Isles, and Sven Gormsson."

Grimm let out a defeated breath as he saw where this was going. "You want to duel me?"

"Who wouldn't want a chance for eternal glory? You can't be the best swordsman on the Isles forever, you know."

"First blood? Or to the death?"

"To the death, of course."

"I'll need a sword."

Sven let out a drunken laugh. "I knew you couldn't refuse a challenge!"

As he left the tent, Grimm couldn't help but shake his head in disgust. *Are you truly going to duel a one-handed drunk and pretend that it'll be an honourable fight? But if he is eager to enter to The Great Hall, who am I to refuse him entry?* He shrugged his shoulders as he picked out his sword.

The entire camp had gathered around the bonfire to witness the fight between their jarl and the legendary white-eyed warrior. Sven bounced energetically from side to side. He goaded the audience as he twirled his sword in his one good hand.

Grimm stood opposite him and casually stretched his back. He couldn't believe how the muscles in his back stiffened with age. It seemed like every day, there was a new ache or pain in it. A couple of the jarl's men spat insults at him, but he tuned them out. Insults were the least of his worries.

Every Islander army had a bard to chronicle their deeds, and Sven's bard acted as herald for the fight. He was a short and stout man with a shamefully beardless face. His trumpet blared a dissonant note, and a hush fell over the crowd.

"Brothers and sisters!" his voice charismatically boomed. "Tonight is a blessed night, for our mighty jarl, Sven Blackhand will fight the legendary warrior, Grimm White-Eyes!" The crowd erupted into a cacophony of applause. The bard waited until they finally settled down before continuing. "This is no ordinary fight, either," the bard explained. "This is a fight to the death!"

The army of islanders started shouting and cheering with uncontrollable bloodlust. Their shouts reached a fever pitch when Sven raised his sword in the air, as if he was already declaring himself the victor. The bard held out his hand to silence the soldiers, and after several minutes, the anxious silence returned.

"Care to make this interesting?" Grimm said, cutting off the bard before he could continue to build anticipation.

"What do you have in mind, White-Eyes?" Sven replied, smiling.

"If I win, your men march back to their homes and ignore Uthredd's call to arms."

"And if I win?"

"Not only will you have the glory of being the man who finally killed Grimm White-Eyes, but you'll also be the bastard who brought High King Uthredd the head of his brother's murderer."

Sven scratched his chin in thought. Grimm knew it wasn't much of a wager. Sven could easily still have all those things if he declined the offer; but Grimm had to secure himself some reassurances that he'd make it out alive. Fighting a one-handed drunk man was one thing, but fighting an entire camp of bloodthirsty Islanders was another.

"Very well," Sven conceded. "Men, if this is to be my last edict, then so be it. If I shall fall, march back to your homes, hug your wives, and ignore all of High King Uthredd's calls to arms. Am I understood?"

"Aye!" the soldiers shouted in unison.

"Now, can we get this under way?"

The bard nodded his head and chopped the air with his hand. "Begin!"

Sven quickly closed the distance and took a haphazard swing at Grimm's head. The old warrior nimbly dodged the jarl's reckless attack.

Grimm parried a blow with ease before delivering a swift punch to Blackhand's face. The jarl stumbled backwards, before lunging forward once again. Grimm nimbly sidestepped out of the way and pushed Sven into the burning bonfire.

Sparks danced up into the air as the drunken jarl tumbled into the burning logs. He began screaming as his beard caught fire, then started flailing wildly as he pushed himself out of the flames.

Grimm dodged a flailing swing of Sven's sword and brought his own blade down in a single swift chop, severing the jarl's good hand from his body.

The crowd of islanders let out an audible gasp as they watched their leader fall to his knees. Blood spurted from the end of his arm.

Grimm quickly grabbed a handful of snow and pressed it against the jarl's burning beard. The smell of burnt hair flooded his nostrils, and Grimm immediately recoiled from the stench.

Sven looked down at the fresh stump at the end of his arm with a baffled expression. Then, after several seconds, he turned his head so that his gaze met Grimm's.

"How will I enter The Great Hall now?" he asked, trying to stem the tears that were streaming from his eyes.

"Rope!" Grimm called out. "Give me some fucking rope!"

It only took a moment, but it felt like days before a young Islander returned with a bundle of rope. Grimm quickly cut off a length of rope, and began tying the jarl's sword to his useless hand.

He looked at Sven's dumbfounded face and saw that the jarl's skin was already beginning to pale. He doubted that Sven would have the strength to keep fighting.

"You fought well, brother," Grimm whispered as he pressed his forehead against Blackhand's. "When you see Heimer, give him my regards."

Sven nodded silently as his eyes stared down at the sword crudely tied to his hand.

Grimm then stood up solemnly, raised his sword above his head, and split the jarl's head open, killing him instantly.

He tossed his bloody sword into the snow, turned towards Sven's men, gave a reverent nod, and left the camp.

By the time he reached his own sword, he saw Thames and his four soldiers charging towards the camp, weapons raised above their heads. The men slowed down to a walk as they saw a blood-soaked Grimm approach.

"What happened?" the skinny poacher asked.

"What had to be done," Grimm replied as he walked past them.

"Will this Jarl Gormsson be joining us?" Thames inquired.

"No, he's dead," Grimm responded as he continued to walk back to his horse, not wishing to answer any more questions.

CHAPTER TWENTY-TWO

ELBERT

The painting on the floor of Tjørholm's keep had beguiled the crippled king for hours. The painting was a large circle trisected by thick black lines. Each segment of the circle had a different, smaller painting inside it.

The one on the right-hand side of the circle had an almost black backdrop, with the only colour appearing to be the thin orange lines that bounced off a charcoal-coloured anvil.

The painting in the bottom third of the circle depicted an Islander raid. Houses burning, men killing, and women being taken away against their will were painted for all to see.

The illustration in the leftmost third of the circle appeared to be of a great feast. Blood-soaked warriors sat at a table, with mugs of what appeared to be ale in their hands. All the Islanders had smiles on their faces, despite several depictions of fights breaking out in the background.

Finally, in the centre of the circle, surrounded by archaic Islander runes, was the painting of a fractured and broken skull.

Elbert's eyes strained as he continued to stare at the painting, trying to decipher its meaning, when he heard armoured footsteps approach from behind him. He spun his chair around and greeted his guardsman, along with the former Warden of Tjørholm.

The king clapped his hands, and a servant quickly brought two cups filled with wine. The boy gave one glass to the king and the other to the clearly enraged Islander.

"Glad you accepted my invitation," Elbert said pleasantly, as he swirled the wine in his cup playfully.

"Not like I had much of a choice," the Islander replied.

"I don't believe I ever caught your name."

"Bælor the Mighty."

The king failed to suppress a laugh. The very idea of someone being "mighty" and allowing themselves to be captured seemed almost laughable. "Tell me, Bælor, what does this painting on the ground mean?"

"Listen, goat-fucker," the Islander began, "you didn't call me up from that shit-stinkin' dungeon so we could talk about some bloody painting. Now, what is it you want?"

Always straight to the point with these Islanders, Elbert mused to himself. "I want you to give me information on High King Uthredd's army. But I'm sure a smart man like you already knew that."

Bælor laughed. "Aye. And I'm sure a smart man like yourself already knows that my information will be outdated, and of no use to you."

"You'd be surprised," Elbert retorted, as he wheeled closer to the stinking barbarian. "Tell me, how do Islanders storm walls such as Tjørholm's?"

"They don't," the Islander replied. "Tjørholm has never been invaded before. It was dubbed as impregnable."

A smile crept along the king's lips as a dirty joke sprang to mind, but he managed to still his tongue. "So, there is no strategy to breach our walls?"

"I didn't say that. Uthredd is a clever man. I'm sure he'll have something very special in the works for you."

Just as Elbert was about to ask another probing question, a boy ran into the keep with a letter in his hand. "Excuse me, Your Majesty," the messenger gasped. "Captain Thames and the bastard company have returned from their raid, as well as news from the mainland."

"Guards, return Bælor to the dungeons," the king commanded as he rolled towards the wheezing boy. He took the scroll of paper from the messenger's hand and unfurled it. His eyes widened as he read every line, and his brow furrowed with anger. Once he was finished, he crumpled the piece of paper and turned his fiery glare to the boy, who was still struggling to breathe. "Summon my lords, tell them to meet me in the mead hall, and bring Captain Thames as well."

"At once, Your Majesty," the boy said, before taking a sharp inhale of breath, then starting to run back out of the keep.

Elbert turned his attention back towards the mural and floor and curled his lips into a nasty frown. "I knew marrying that bitch was a mistake."

Silence engulfed the hall. Artanzia's lords looked around with confused and baffled expressions plastered over their faces. Elbert set the scroll of parchment down on the large wooden table and waited for someone to speak. After several minutes, Captain Thames cleared his throat.

"What are your orders, Your Majesty?"

The king slammed his fist against the table hard enough to knock over several of the lords' wine glasses. "I order you to give me some bloody counsel! I'm an entire ocean away from my kingdom, and my wife is plotting to steal my throne out from under me!"

The nobles looked around sheepishly at one another, until Lord Grelin finally rose from his seat. "With all due respect, Your Majesty, the letter never said that she is plotting to steal your throne."

Elbert glared at the man. "Tell me, Lord Grelin, why else would my wife hire a group of mercenaries that answer only to her when she already has half of my royal guard?"

"Perhaps she doesn't feel safe while you are away?" another lord chimed in.

Elbert's head snapped to the lord who spoke, and he immediately stared down at the table, avoiding the king's glare. "Yes, I'm sure that's it. Because who doesn't feel safer when they are standing beside a cripple?" A couple of the nobles sniggered at the king's comment. "I fail to find what is so fucking amusing about this situation," Elbert snapped. It was at this moment that he tried to rise to his feet so that he could stare down at his lords. But when he commanded his legs to stand, they unsurprisingly failed to move an inch.

"Perhaps the mercenaries were hired as extra protection for the baby," Arlin suggested, breaking his habitual silence. There was a murmur of agreement from the other lords.

"That in itself is another problem," Elbert began. "You see, I have yet to consummate the marriage." There was an audible gasp from several of the lords.

"So you're telling us that the queen–" Lord Penerack began.

"Indeed," the king interrupted. "Queen Vivian has committed adultery and is claiming that the bastard that is currently festering in her womb is mine."

"Why would she do such a thing?" Thames asked.

"As I tried to explain earlier," Elbert growled, "this is Vivian's way of trying to seize Artanzia's throne for herself. By claiming that she is with my child and poising herself to be regent, once the child is born."

"But wouldn't her plan fall apart upon our arrival?" Lord Grelin asked.

"That's the thing, Lord Grelin. She doesn't expect us to return. Vivian is assuming that if Uthredd's forces don't kill us, then the voyage back to the continent surely will."

Another unbearable silence filled the room. The only sounds were the deep, angry breaths of the king as he awaited a response. Finally, Captain Thames cleared his throat.

"I suggest you write a letter to the people, Your Majesty, exposing Vivian's action and denouncing her as queen."

"That'll never work!" Lord Grelin snorted. "It'll take near a month for word to return to the mainland, and if what Your Majesty says is true, she will undoubtedly have the support of some of the commoners. Civil war will ensue."

"So, what is your suggestion?" Elbert snarled as he gripped the edge of the wooden table tightly.

Grelin's face went pale, and he started sweating profusely. "I... uh... I..." he stammered.

"Spit it out, man!"

"I suggest we abandon Tjørholm and sail back to Winterhelm."

Elbert's knuckles audibly popped. "You what?"

"If you allow me to explain, Your Majesty, I –"

"We are on the cusp of greatness, and you want all of our sacrifices to be for nothing? What about Lord Haustack? What do I tell him when he finally recovers? 'Thank you for your sacrifice, but we decided that it wasn't ever really needed.'?"

"Lord Haustack's condition is regrettable, Your Majesty," Lord Penerack interjected. "But I agree with Lord Grelin. We already have plenty of plunder. You've sent the Islanders a powerful message. You've accomplished what no other monarch from the continent has ever done, and we have lost only a handful of real soldiers. The only company to sustain considerable losses was the bastard company. I –"

"Do not refer to them by that dreadful moniker in my presence," Elbert ordered as he relaxed his grip on the table. He silently mulled over Lord Penerack's words in his head before casting a searching glance at Captain Thames, who was watching his king intently.

Elbert took a deep, defeated breath when the doors to the mead hall swung open. The king lifted his head and saw an angry Grimm sauntering into the room, with a joyous Sara following behind him.

"Will someone please explain to me why in the everlasting fuck I'm not invited to this? Whatever this is!" the Islander shouted as he helped himself to an empty chair at the table.

"Because these matters do not concern you, savage," Thames spat.

Sara gleefully ran around the table, hopped into the king's lap, and hugged him tightly. Elbert forced a smile and patted the child's back, then returned his gaze to Grimm, who was now reclined with his feet up on the table.

"Your Majesty, this is not the place for a child, nor is it the place for –"

The king lifted a silencing hand, his eyes refusing to leave the Islander's. "Tell me, Grimm," he began. "My wife is trying to steal my kingdom from me, and my lords suggest that I abandon my occupation of Tjørholm and sail back to the continent. What do you advise?"

The Islander snorted a laugh before he sat upright. "Of course your men told you to run. They're cowards. They don't even lead their own men into battle."

"The last time a lord led his men into a fight with you savages, he barely escaped with his life," Lord Penerack snapped back.

"At least he'll die a warrior's death. One worth remembering. Who will remember a lord who grew fat and old, and died in his bed covered in shit and piss?" Grimm replied smilingly.

"Captain Thames suggested I send a letter back to the mainland, publicly denouncing the queen," Elbert added.

Grimm let out a sigh. "As much as I hate to say it, that scarred bastard is right. Keep Tjørholm and send a letter back to the mainland."

"You would openly advocate that I stay, even though it would delay your freedom?"

The Islander shrugged his shoulders. "What does it matter? The siege will only last a month at most."

"You're that confident in our victory?"

"Tjørholm has enough rations stored to feed your army for several months, and before us, the walls had never been breached. So unless Uthredd has a dragon up his sleeves, I doubt his men will get inside. After a month, he'll have to broker a peace, tail 'tween his legs, and I wouldn't trade that sight for all the gold in the world."

"Very well," Elbert concluded. "We'll dispatch a letter at once. That'll be all, gentlemen."

"Your Majesty, you can't be serious!" Lord Grelin interjected.

"Need I remind you that my word is final, Lord Grelin?" Elbert threatened.

"No, Your Majesty," he replied sheepishly.

"Then you're dismissed."

As the lords exited the room, clearly disgruntled, Grimm rose to his feet and approached the king. Elbert noticed that Rupert's hand shifted to the pommel of his sword.

The Islander silently lifted the small dwarven girl from the king's lap and escorted her out of the room. Elbert had entirely forgotten that the girl was sitting in his lap. Perhaps it was because she was so small. Or perhaps it was because he couldn't feel anything in his legs.

Sara let out a disgruntled groan as she followed Grimm outside the mead hall. "Why can't I stay and play with Elbert?"

"Because you have to train," the Islander replied stalely.

"The girl can stay with me as I write my letter to the continent: it really isn't a bother."

"The girl stays with me: she needs to train."

"I'm sure her training can wait an hour or two. Let me take her off your hands."

The Islander stepped forward, his hand inching towards his sword. Out of the corner of his eye, Elbert noticed Thames did the same.

"Leave us, Sara," Grimm ordered. "And close the door behind you."

The dwarf let out a disappointed sigh but did as she was told. Once they were alone, Grimm slowly walked to the opposite end of the table, and leaned against it. The Islander's gaze did not leave the king's eyes. Elbert felt a shiver run down his spine as he stared into the white, milky eyes of the warrior.

"Tread carefully, Legless," Grimm growled. "Or else I might lose my temper."

"Are you threatening your king?" Thames shouted as he pulled his sword halfway out of its scabbard.

"Just a friendly reminder to keep his royal nose in his own business."

"Why, you –"

Elbert raised a silencing hand and turned his attention to the seething guard. "No offence taken, Rupert. I'm sure the Islander means well, but he lacks the social skills to word it more tactfully."

A sneering smile cracked the Islander's lips. "Glad we're at an understanding." He slowly stood upright and left the hall without uttering another word.

"Your Majesty," Thames began, once they were alone. "You cannot allow such open defiance. It will show weakness and the lords will –"

"Pox on the lords!" Elbert snapped, as he rolled his chair away from the table. "Do you remember what I did to the last lord who openly defied me?" Thames stood silent. "I took his damned head. Do not worry, Rupert, the Islander will answer for his actions: but for now, we need him."

"And what about the girl?"

"That I'm not sure of," the king confessed. "But I do know that the war is far from over, and everyone, even the girl, will have their role to play."

CHAPTER TWENTY-THREE

ANNA

"**O**n the left, dear!" one of the senior servants shouted as she smacked Anna's hands with a wooden spoon.

The girl glared up at the elderly lady as she spoke through gritted teeth. "Of course, how silly of me."

It had been a week since her first encounter with Alcina Rawley, and she had spent every day working in the house, preparing for the heist. Unfortunately, she proved too talented at cleaning, and her mistress convinced her to join her servants full-time.

The rest of the Maggots weren't so lucky. Tig broke a rather expensive vase within the first half hour, and was forced to leave the property and never return. Chuckles was caught flirting with one of the girl servants in the kitchen and was scolded by the head chef, which resulted in both him and the girl being barred from the grounds for life. A'Chula managed to survive a few days until his constant silence rubbed the butler the wrong way, and he was asked to leave.

The only one who kept their head above water was Randall. It appeared that his skills as a servant had not diminished with time, as he proved to be an expert at etiquette and understood how the hierarchy of the house worked.

Anna couldn't be bothered with remembering all the archaic rules of the house. "Serve to the left," "address people by their title, not their name," "stand up straight," "tuck in your blouse," and worst of all was curtsying to each of Madam Rawley's guests. If this was what her life would have been like living with her Auntie Teale, she was glad she had found the Maggots. She had thought about quitting several times, but Randall had always persuaded her to stay.

The two adolescents spent most evenings together, after their long days at the manor. He would mock the butler's commands in a near-perfect impersonation, and she would complain about the other maids.

After telling each other about their days, they would tear at each other's clothes and lock lips. Their intimacy had grown since that first night in the graveyard, and Anna had become bolder during the last week. She still wasn't ready for full intercourse, but she did feel comfortable fondling him.

On one occasion, she had allowed Randall's lips to wander from her neck to below her waist. The sensation was enthralling. Her muscles tightened, her heart felt as though it would burst out of her chest, and she moaned uncontrollably. After several ecstasy-filled minutes, it felt like lightning had struck her. It was one of the best feelings of her life.

As she massaged her reddened hand, she stared into the other room at Randall. Ever since that night, she had wanted to spend every waking second with him, and experience that feeling again. Could this be love? When she closed her eyes, she saw him. When they were apart, she thought about him. And when they were together, she savoured him. Their eyes locked from across the rooms, and he smiled playfully at her. Her knees went weak, and her stomach felt squeamish, until another hard rap of the wooden spoon brought her back to reality.

"You can flirt on your own time!" the senior maid barked.

Anna finished setting the table, while secretly wishing that she could snatch the spoon out of the maid's hand and beat her with it. It wasn't long before Alcina Rawley walked into the dining room with an entourage of fancily dressed women and gushed at how the room looked.

"Oh my, doesn't this look wonderful!" she exclaimed.

"Breathtaking," one woman responded.

"Absolutely marvellous!" another stated.

"Come, take a seat!" Alcina squealed, as she clinked a silver fork against a clear crystal wine glass. Anna stepped forward. "Makayla, please be a dear: run to the cellar and bring us a nice vintage."

Anna nodded her head and silently exited the room. She hated fetching wine. Not because the job was hard, but because the sommelier always eyed her suspiciously.

The first time she met him, she thought he could see through her guise as a servant; but if he did, he never let on. As she walked down the hallway, a hand reached out and gently touched her fingers. She turned her head to see a smiling Randall.

Her heart fluttered, and she seriously considered pushing him into the closet and having some quality time with the boy, but she knew it was too risky. Randall had reminded her on several occasions that when they were at the manor, they were working, and had to keep their minds on work, which meant no fooling around.

She painfully tore her eyes away from his, and continued down the hallway until she reached a descending hardwood staircase. The stairs creaked with every step until she reached a small, stuffy room filled with wine. Standing in the middle of the room was a man with a shaved head wearing a white doublet.

"Good afternoon," he said customarily.

"The mistress would like a vintage," Anna responded. She had learned to repeat Alcina's words to the sommelier, and the man would give her the proper bottle of wine. She hated to admit it, but she needed the man's help. Without him, she would undoubtedly bring the wrong bottle to the table. All the wines looked the same, and the words on the labels meant little or nothing to her.

"At once." The sommelier smiled with hard eyes. He turned his back and quickly scanned his shelves before pulling out a bottle of vaguely red liquid. He dusted off the label and presented it to Anna as if he were handing her a small child. "A lovely vintage from the year ten-seventy-four. Aged to perfection in oaken barrels. This wine has an exquisite full-bodied taste that I'm sure Madam Rawley and her guests will thoroughly enjoy."

Although the man had a smile on his face, Anna was unnerved by his harsh and sinister stare. She wanted to glare back at him, but feared that it would expose her as the thief she was. As a result, she pretended to be scared by the man and took the bottle from his hands without making eye contact, before returning upstairs.

The laughter in the dining room was audible from the wine cellar. It wasn't until she reached the main floor that the laughter suddenly stopped. Anna's body tensed as she knew that could only mean one thing.

Odion Rawley.

The master of the house was not a pleasant man. He was tall and muscular, but that was where his attractive features ended. He had a crooked nose and a balding head of hair. He was always in a foul mood, and he seemingly hated to see others happy. If he was nasty when he was sober, then he was downright cruel when he was drunk. He would never hit his wife, but the servants were another story. Anna had seen several of the maids leave the house with black eyes or broken noses. They also left with more coins than the others.

As Anna entered the dining room, bottle of wine in hand, she saw a glowering Odion standing in the entryway, glaring at his frivolously dressed wife.

"Another fucking dinner party?" he slurred.

"How else am I supposed to occupy my time?" Alcina replied politely.

"By not inviting every harlot in this city to break bread at our fucking table!" he shouted as he slammed his fist against the wall. "It's bad enough you hire these urchins for our help; most of them don't know how to clean their own arse, let alone clean my house!" His glare shifted towards Anna, who felt the anger slowly rising in her body as she gripped the neck of the wine bottle tighter. "You, girl: what's your name?"

"Makayla."

"A whore's name," he muttered under his breath. "Tell me, where did my wife dig you up from?"

"We met near the Splints, sir," she replied as meekly as she could.

"The Splints!" Odion exclaimed. "Might as well bring known pickpockets into our home! I'd be surprised if the little tart hasn't lifted something already."

"Enough!" Alcina shouted before regaining her composure. She donned an innocent smile and turned her head towards her guests. "I'm terribly sorry, but I fear that we will have to reschedule our dinner for another date." Alcina's guests nodded politely and quietly shuffled past a fuming Odion and out of the door.

"Bedroom. Now," Alcina said firmly.

"Why? Afraid to yell in front of the help?"

"Now!"

There was a stunned look on Odion's face before his usual frown reappeared. Then, with an audible huff, he turned and ascended the staircase towards the master bedroom.

Alcina turned her attention to Anna, and her friendly smile reappeared on her face. "Take that bottle back to the sommelier; I fear there won't be any need for wine today."

Anna nodded her head and left the room to return the wine bottle. As she was about to descend the staircase to the cellar, she noticed that Randall was waving her over from across the hallway. She waited until she heard Odion's muffled shouting from behind the closed bedroom door before she crossed the hallway.

"What?"

"What do you mean, 'what?' I wanted to talk to you."

"Randall, we aren't supposed to be seen talking, you know –"

"Alright, I'll keep it short then. Have you found the safe?" Randall's eyes gleamed with desperation.

"No, but I don't see how –"

"Listen," Randall interrupted. "Tomorrow is the day of the heist; it has to be."

"What, why?" Anna asked.

"I heard that Rawley will attend the annual horse racing tournament at the Mallax Estate outside of Winterhelm. He'll be gone the whole day."

"What about Alcina?"

Randall's face contorted into an ugly sneer. "Alcina? Are you on a first-name basis with that pretentious woman?"

Anna felt her cheeks flush with anger. "And what if I am?" she snapped. "She treats me with respect and genuinely wants to help –"

"Please," Randall snorted. "You think because she hires a couple of urchins to clean her house, she's a saint? She's as vile and toxic as the rest of them."

"If you interrupt me once more, I'm going to hit you," Anna warned.

"Look, you need to find the safe. It's happening tomorrow; it'll be our best chance."

"What about the guards? There are only five of us without Maeve."

"Let me worry about the guards. You just find the safe."

Anna cast him a wayward glance, but ultimately did as she was asked. He had never led her astray thus far, and he was the only one who told her the truth about the pickpocket. She had no reason not to trust him. "Fine," Anna huffed, refusing to let Randall think she had let him off the hook easily.

She turned and began down the staircase towards the cellar once again. Her heart pounded as she thought about handing a full bottle of wine back to the sommelier. She wasn't sure why she was so anxious around the man. For most of her life, she did not have a lot of experience dealing with people, other than her father. Yet, she knew that something was off about the man, but she couldn't figure out what.

As she entered the sommelier's room, the man greeted her with a warm smile but a vicious glare. "Curious," the man began. "Rarely do I have bottles returned to me *full*."

"Alcina—umm—Madam Rawley was interrupted," Anna stammered, silently cursing herself for forgetting one of the archaic rules of etiquette.

"Yes, he is a boorish man," the sommelier cooed. "But you know what they say. Opposites attract."

Anna scrunched up her nose at the phrase. She had never heard it before, and from her experience, it had no truth to it. Her father had never talked about her mother being the opposite of himself, and she didn't see Randall as the opposite of her. If anything, they were cut from the same cloth.

"You're a bit of an odd one," the man continued. His voice was warm and inviting, but his eyes were cold and scrutinizing. "You told Madam Rawley that you had lived here your whole life, yet, you have an accent I've never heard before."

"Ever been to The Splints?" Anna retorted, hoping that his answer would be "no."

"Indeed I have," he replied coyly.

Shit, thought Anna, her mind racing to think of a believable lie. "My family recently moved here," she floundered. "But my parents died soon after their arrival, and I was left on my own." *Keep the lie vague,* she thought.

"And how did your parents die?" the man asked quickly.

"I don't want to talk about it," Anna lied some more, before turning sharply on her heel to leave the cellar.

"I hope you rob him blind," the sommelier called out playfully.

Anna froze. *How could he know?* she asked herself. She wanted to reach for her dagger and silence the man before he could expose her and Randall's plan, but then remembered that she did not have it on her. Daggers did not suit servants.

"Don't be surprised. You're a terrible liar," the man said as he slowly approached Anna. "I knew you were a thief the moment you walked in."

"How?" Anna asked, despite her instincts telling her not to do so.

"Your eyes," he explained. "They say the eyes are the pathway to one's soul, and yours were dotting around the house for things to steal the moment you walked in."

Shit.

The sommelier grabbed her by the shoulder and gently spun her around so that they were face to face. "It is easy to lie to ignorant people like the Rawleys, but to lie to one who's been on the streets: that is another thing entirely."

"Teach me," Anna asked pleadingly.

"Oh, I wish I could, little one; but what would be in it for me?"

"We'll give you a piece of the loot."

The sommelier's eyebrow raised. "We?"

Shit. Anna quickly changed the subject. "What's your name?"

A venomous smile crept along the man's lips. "I'm afraid I have many names. I've served many wealthy and powerful people, many of whom decided that my name was not proper or exotic enough, so they changed it."

"What does Alcina call you?"

"Cassius. But what do I call you?"

"Makayla."

"Oh, come now: I just told you that you couldn't lie to a liar. Now, what's your *real* name?"

"Anna."

"A boring name for an extraordinary girl."

Cassius leaned forward so that she could feel his hot breath. Anna immediately recoiled. A smile crept along the sommelier's lips.

"Don't be afraid, dear. I won't hurt you. You see, I'm a eunuch."

"What's a eunuch?"

"A man who'a had his balls cut off," Cassius stated crudely. "Now, what is it you want to steal from Odion Rawley?"

He stared deep into her eyes, and she felt every hair on her neck stand on end as his glare lingered. Every now and then, he would squint or tilt his head, as if he were examining a fine painting. Anna bit her lip anxiously, as the man's eyes refused to move. She thought about just turning around and leaving, but he knew too much. She couldn't risk him telling the Rawleys, or worse, the guards.

Finally, Cassius' eyes lit up. "You're looking for the safe."

"How did you know that!" Anna exclaimed, astonished.

"A little secret: never talk about the job at the job." Cassius winked.

Blood rushed to her cheeks, and she felt the back of her neck clam up with sweat. Her eyes darted around nervously. She wanted nothing more than to run away, but her legs refused to move.

"Don't fret, child. I won't rat you out. Greaver's money is safe."

"How did you know we are with Greaver?"

"Please, every young thief and cutthroat in this city is enamoured by the so-called 'King of Crooks.' Well, he isn't the only nobility in the game."

"You mean Regina Hammerfist?" Anna blurted out. As soon as the words left her mouth, she knew it was a mistake. She was usually a very guarded person, but Cassius had a way of making her feel so uncomfortable that she felt like talking to fill the awkward silence in the air.

The sommelier's eyes narrowed. "How do you know about Regina Hammerfist?"

"We met her, accidentally, in the Splints."

"And she's the one who set you up to rob the Rawleys. Very clever, working for two lords at once. Not bad for a child."

"I'm fourteen."

"Of course you are," Cassius mused. "Tell you what, when you and your little friends come here tomorrow, I'll point you towards the safe, as long as I get a cut."

"Deal," Anna agreed, glad to be done with the conversation. She spun on her heel and started up the staircase, two steps at a time.

"See you tomorrow!" Cassius called out cheerfully from the cellar.

"You promised a cut!" Randall shouted. "We have to give everything to Hammerfist!"

"I'm sure she won't miss a few gold coins," Anna defended herself.

"By the gods, Anna, sometimes I think you don't think things through!"

"Without me, you'd still be watching Rawley's house from across the street. Without me, you wouldn't know where the safe is. Without me, you'd never be able to pay Hammerfist!"

"Without you, I wouldn't have to pay Hammerfist an entire fucking fortune," Randall snapped back.

Anna's fist was like lightning. There was an audible pop as she connected with Randall's nose. She watched with joy as her blow took the boy off his feet and into the muck of the street. A laugh escaped her lips.

"Oh, you find that funny, do you?" Randall seethed as he wiped his bloody nose.

Anna shrugged her shoulders.

He quickly launched himself out of the filth and tried to grapple her. But he was much slower than her father, and she spun out of the way. Unfortunately, Randall's arms were longer than her father's, and he grabbed her by the collar of her shirt. He pulled her in tight and pinned her against one of the walls of the alley.

She tried to punch him again, but this time he caught her fist and pinned it against the wall as well. Her stomach fluttered anxiously. She felt her cheeks flush with warmth, and a smile broke on her lips.

She punched with her other hand, only this time much slower than before. Randall caught her hand with ease and pinned it against the wall, as he did with the other one. A smile appeared on his lips as well.

Anna lunged her lips forward until she met Randall's. Immediately, their tongues danced in each other's mouths, and their arms wrapped around each other in an embrace. Her hands reached down and began untying his trousers.

Randall pulled away and lifted Anna's chin. "Are you sure?" he asked, the anger in his voice completely gone.

"Yes," she whispered, as she plunged her hands into his trousers.

CHAPTER TWENTY-FOUR

GRIMM

The audible crack of the horsehair string reverberated off Tjørholm's stone walls. The eight-foot-long bolt soared in the air, turning in a perfect spiral until it stuck deep into the frozen earth. There was a momentary silence, followed by overzealous applause. Many of the lords patted Arlin on his back, and even the king clapped his hands gleefully like a child.

Grimm stood in silent amazement as he stared at the monstrous bolt that protruded out of the snow beyond the fortress walls. When Elbert had invited him to watch the demonstration of the dwarf's ballista, he wasn't sure what to expect. He had never seen siege weapons before, as Islanders were not ones to hide like cowards behind walls, and the farmers and townsfolk of the mainland had few siege weapons lying around when raiding season arrived. He did not think any weapon could propel a bolt that far, let alone with perfect aim.

"How many giants are needed to run this weapon?" Grimm asked honestly.

The lords erupted in laughter.

"Just three regular men. That's all she needs," Arlin replied.

"How does it go so far?" Elbert asked, his eyes gleaming with curiosity.

The dwarf pointed at the metal coil on the end of the shaft. "This here spindle tightens as you draw the string back. When the trigger is pulled, the spring surges forward, transfers its energy into the bolt, and propels it further."

"You're a bloody genius, Arlin!" the king exclaimed as he patted the dwarf on the back. "And you can make four more of these before Uthredd's army arrives?"

Arlin scratched his beard nervously. "Eh, I may have tugged my beard a tad too hard, Your Majesty. Making these coils is long and hard work, and my helpers aren't as adept as they initially claimed."

Elbert's brow furrowed, and his lips sunk into an angry frown. "How many can you make?"

"One more."

"How fast can you reload?" Grimm asked, hoping to draw the king's ire away from the dwarf.

The dwarf's face turned red, and he was pulling on his beard so hard that Grimm thought he was going to pull the hair right out of his face. "Well, with the extra distance and power, we had to sacrifice something –"

"Master Arlin, you told me that I would have five of your machines, and now you're telling me that not only will I not have that number, but they will be slower than normal ballista?"

Arlin avoided eye contact with his king. "Yes, Your Majesty."

"Get back to work then," the king commanded. "We need to put every second to use by the sound of things."

As the king and his lords left the ramparts, Grimm lingered on the walls for a few moments longer. Every day, Uthredd's army was getting closer, and it seemed like every day he was asked to raid more Islander camps.

He was tired, his body ached, and his eyes were heavy. His men, to their credit, had yet to voice a complaint, but he could see it in their eyes. They were exhausted, and silently hoped for a good night's rest. Grimm leaned forward, rested his hands on the stone wall, and let out a long sigh. Elbert was running him ragged, and although he had an entire army at his disposal, he always chose the company of bastards to carry out raids.

"I did my best," a voice muttered softly.

The Islander turned his head and saw that Arlin was still standing beside him, his gaze fixed on the bolt beyond the walls. "I did my best, and it still wasn't enough."

Grimm shook his head. He had never been good at comforting people; he had always viewed that as women's work. Unsure of what to do or what was expected, he placed a hand on the dwarf's shoulder and squeezed gently. Arlin turned his head, looked up with tearful eyes, and nodded his head in acknowledgement.

"You did good," Grimm mumbled awkwardly.

"King Elbert said –"

"Fuck him," the Islander grunted. "Why do you care what he thinks?"

"He made me a lord."

"So?"

"I was nobody before King Elbert. I was just a humble blacksmith, nothing more."

Grimm shook his head once again. "You mainlanders do everything ass backwards."

"What do you mean?"

"Titles are given to you; they are unearned, and can be bestowed as easily as they can be taken away. Here on the Isles, things are different. You have to earn your name and earn your title. Uthredd was not born High King of the Isles. He earned it. I was not named Shield of the Isles simply because I was his friend. I had to kill ten other men, who all wanted to be the king's right-hand man. Unless you did something to earn that lordship, then you are still that humble blacksmith."

Before Arlin could voice a response, Grimm descended the rampart steps and walked into the streets. He had said more than he cared to, and wanted to get out of the awkward duty of consoling a crying man as quickly as possible. As he walked back to his company's quarters, he noticed the banners that the other soldiers had erected since their occupation of Tjørholm. They depicted a black raven holding a cluster of arrows in its talons, flying across a field of powder blue.

"Grimm!" a voice called out.

He turned his head and saw Sara sprinting towards him.

"What?"

"Two men are fighting!"

"With swords?"

Sara nodded her head vigorously.

"Ugh." Grimm pinched the bridge of his nose and let out a sigh. "Fine, take me to them."

The courtyard was small and covered in snow. Men crowded together, no doubt trying to get the best view of the fight. Grimm could hear steel clanging against steel from across the street. He cleared his throat and shouted as loud as he could. "Bastards!"

The soldiers snapped to attention without turning around, and an eerie silence hung in the air for several seconds. The Islander weaved his way through his men until he got into the middle of the courtyard, where two bloodied men were standing at attention, waiting for him.

He was surprised to see that one of the fighters had been the skinny poacher that had joined him on the night he killed Sven Blackhand. Judging by the look of the man, he had clearly been losing the fight. The other man was short and stout, and seemed to have a permanent frown stuck on his face.

Nevertheless, Grimm had always liked the shorter man. He had shown the most promise of any of the recruits, and Grimm had even considered allowing the man to wield a sword instead of an axe or spear.

"What are your names?" Grimm asked menacingly as he eyed the two fighters.

"Paul, milord," the tall poacher answered meekly.

"He's not a fucking lord, you imbecile!" the other man shouted. "That's our commanding officer!"

Grimm smiled at the frowning man. "That's quite a long name. What can I call you instead?"

"Desmond, sir."

"So, what's the meaning behind this?"

"I was minding me own business, sharpenin' me blade, when this cunt tries to stab me with a knife!"

"Paul?" Grimm asked.

"That's true, but –"

"I've heard all I need to. Since you've already pled guilty, you are hereby sentenced to die for the crime of trying to kill your shield-brother."

"But sir!"

"I will hear no more of it. Men, take him away."

The poacher looked sullenly towards the ground as a group of soldiers escorted him out of the courtyard.

"Thank you, sir," Desmond replied smugly. "Can't have men like him in our lot."

"The rest of you: return to your quarters and get some rest," Grimm shouted as he ignored the man's remarks. "King Elbert will no doubt have another raid planned for us tonight. So best rest while you can."

He felt an incessant tugging at his arm, and looked down to see Sara staring at him with confused eyes. Grimm's eyes narrowed. "What?"

"You didn't even listen to the other man."

"Because I didn't have to," Grimm responded as he walked towards his quarters. "There is no good reason to kill your shield-brother. If you disagree, best to settle it with fists rather than blades."

The dwarf huffed and let go of the Islander's arm, but continued to follow him, wordlessly, back to his room.

Elbert had been kind enough to allow Grimm a bed inside Tjørholm's keep, but he had spent little time there. Between training his men and launching raids against his former brethren, he spent most of his nights sleeping beneath the stars.

Sara practiced her swordsmanship in the corner while the Islander sharpened his blade. Executions were never enjoyable. In his experience, very few men met their end with honour and dignity. Most were snivelling messes, who ended up kneeling in their own piss before the blade came down on their neck. And he had a feeling that the former poacher was a crier.

"Hiya!" Sara shouted as she stabbed a painting on the wall with the tip of her wooden sword.

From what Grimm could see, she was swinging her sword harder than usual. *Perhaps she is angry with me because of my choice.* He shook his head at the thought. *She needs to learn that there are rules in war, if she is to be a shieldmaiden.*

There was a sudden knock on the door. By the time he rose to his feet, Sara had already opened it. On the other side was a fuming Elbert.

"Evening, my lady," he greeted through a fake smile. "How are you?"

"Mad," Sara stated bluntly.

"As am I," Elbert confessed. "Mind if I speak to Grimm alone?"

The dwarf's body stiffened, and the Islander noticed her feet shifted into a defensive stance. "Are you going to yell at him?"

"No, just going to talk to him. I think there's been a misunderstanding."

Sara's body relaxed at the obvious lie. "Okay," she said cheerfully as she exited the room. Elbert rolled into the room, and one of his guards closed it behind him.

"Evening, Leg –"

"Who do you think you are?" Elbert shouted at him. "You do not get to pass death sentences on my subjects!"

Grimm stabbed his sword into the wooden floor of the room. "And what would you have me do? Allow him to continue to serve so that he can try to kill again? You gave me command of this company, and I'll be damned if I look weak in front of them."

Elbert threw his arms in the air. "I expect you to consult me on such matters and not pass judgement without my knowledge or blessing. But, obviously, the man has to die. We can't allow soldiers to kill each other."

"So you came in here to yell at me because I made the right decision?" Grimm said, a smirk appearing on his lips.

The king wheeled forward. "I came here to say never go above my head again. I will not have you undermine my authority. I am still your king."

"I have no king."

To his surprise, Elbert laughed at Grimm's verbal jab. "How so?" the king asked. "You serve in my army. You lead my men. How am I not your king?"

Grimm said nothing. He could tell by how red Elbert's face was that now was not the time to get under the crippled king's skin. He pulled his sword out of the oaken floorboards and sheathed it in its scabbard. "Will that be all?" he asked politely.

A smile appeared on Elbert's lips. "Yes. I'm glad we've come to an understanding."

Grimm nodded his head and walked past the king as he turned his chair around in the small room. Sara was waiting outside for him with a frown on her face. "He lied," she muttered.

"Kings often do," Grimm responded as he made his way out of the keep.

The chopping block was a gnarly looking stump of a pine tree that the army had cut down several days before. It was crooked, sloped, and had several branches sticking out of it. As this was the first execution of the campaign, nobody had thought to prepare a proper chopping block.

But it made no difference to Grimm. When he was Shield of the Isles, he had taken men's heads off on stumps, rocks, logs, and on one occasion, on the back of a horse. His men were gathered around the courtyard, and Paul was already kneeling, his head resting against the stump.

Surprising no one, the poacher was indeed crying. His sobs echoed off the stronghold's stone walls, and the smell of piss grew stronger, the closer Grimm came. He pulled his sword from its sheath and placed the edge of it on the poacher's neck. The cool touch of the steel made the man cry more.

Grimm turned his head and looked at each of his men in the eye. Everyone bore a sombre expression except for Desmond, who was wearing the same smug smile as before.

Grimm turned around and saw Sara standing tall behind him. He thought about telling her to look away, but eventually decided against it. The child was going to see her fair share of blood when Tjørholm came under siege, so she might as well get used to it now. He gripped the hilt of his sword tighter and raised the blade high above his head.

"Any last words?" he asked.

"He... said he was going to fuck her," Paul whispered, his voice barely audible.

"Fuck who?" Grimm asked.

"Sara."

Grimm felt the muscles in his arms tighten at the mention of the dwarf's name. Suddenly, his heart panged with regret for not hearing the poacher's side of the story. But there was nothing he could do now. He had already passed judgement. With a yell of frustration, he brought the blade down and severed Paul's head from his neck.

There was an audible gasp from behind him that he assumed came from Sara. Blood squirted from the stump and painted the snow of the courtyard red. The poacher's body convulsed and twitched wildly, while his eyes blinked uncontrollably in his severed head.

"Burn the body," Grimm ordered. "We have a raid tonight. Desmond, I'd like you to join me."

"As you wish, sir," the man replied curtly.

"Can I come?" Sara asked, her wooden sword already out of its scabbard.

Grimm smiled at the dwarven girl. He bent down and placed a hand on her shoulder. "No, you have to stay here. You'll be in command while I'm gone."

A smile lit up the dwarf's face before she ran off to bark orders at some of the bastards. He was proud of how the girl handled her first execution, but then remembered that she had probably seen worse than a beheading during her time as a slave. Most Islander slave owners burned their slaves alive when they were forced to kill them. That way, they would go to The Great Hall and serve Heimer for all eternity.

"Is it just me and you tonight?" Desmond asked, interrupting Grimm's thoughts.

"Yes, Lord Grelin's men said they saw a patrol of five men near Tjørholm. I figure we can handle that many." The lie tasted sweet on his lips. His heartbeat quickened at the thought of leading this twisted man to his doom. He was going to make sure Desmond suffered.

"When do we leave?"

"Now," Grimm replied, as he placed his sword in its scabbard.

The copse of pines offered scant protection from the whirling wind. They had been away for several hours, and the sun was setting.

Grimm watched the man with disgust as he blew on his hands for warmth. Desmond had spent the entire evening complaining about the cold. But the man's grievances fell on deaf ears. Grimm was too preoccupied about the man's supposed guilt.

Men often lied about things right before they were executed, usually in a desperate attempt to save their worthless lives. But something about the poacher's words stuck with him. There was a certain air of truth to them. But the man was a thief, and lying was second nature to men like that.

He contemplated what he was going to do with Desmond. On the one hand, if he let the man live and he harmed Sara, Grimm could never live with himself. But on the other hand, he knew that he'd need all the help he could get to repel Uthredd's forces.

Ultimately, Grimm decided to take the man's life. *Better to be safe than sorry,* he told himself. He thought about how he planned to kill him. He didn't want to give an innocent man a long and excruciating death; but then again, if what Paul said was true, Desmond deserved to have his last moments filled with agony.

Grimm silently pulled his sword from its scabbard while Desmond droned on about the cold. *Best to get it over with.* He raised the blade above his shoulder and with a sharp twist of his body, cleaved Desmond's head from his shoulders. He then sheathed his blade, mounted his horse, and leisurely rode back towards Tjørholm, eager to finally get a good night's sleep.

CHAPTER TWENTY-FIVE

ANNA

All the servants had gathered in front of the manor to wave their masters farewell. The ride to the Mallax estate took the better part of a day, and the tournament's festivities would surely carry on late into the night. But once they left, the Rawleys would have no reason to come back for at least several hours, which was just long enough for Anna and Randall to rob them blind.

While Odion tapped his foot impatiently beside the carriage, Alcina made a point of saying farewell to each servant individually. Although they were in her employ, she spoke to the servants as if they were long-lost friends. She asked about their families and interests, and about how they were holding up. It appeared that Alcina genuinely cared for everyone who worked in the house.

"Watch over the place for me while I'm gone," she whispered playfully in Anna's ear, before moving down the line of servants.

"By the Gods, Alcina, I'm going to die of old age by the time you're ready!" Odion said, exasperated. "I don't know why you insist on wasting your time on this filth."

Anna's body stiffened at the remark, and her eyes narrowed at the man. Her hands clenched into fists, and her knuckles popped from the pressure. Suddenly, she felt a soft, gentle hand on her shoulder.

"Remember to be pleasant," Cassius advised. "We don't want to be suspects in the robbery."

Anna nodded her head slightly and smiled at Odion, just as he made eye contact with her. The man's face contorted into a sneer of disgust.

After several more minutes of farewells, Alcina was finally ready to depart. She climbed into the carriage, and Odion followed. With a crack of the reins, they began to slowly roll down the cobblestone streets and towards the city gates.

Once the masters had disappeared from view, many of the servants talked cheerfully amongst themselves as they walked back into the manor. Anna noticed that even the guards seemed to relax, as several left their posts to socialize with some of the other guardsmen.

Randall walked over to her and Cassius and kept his voice to a low whisper. "Are you ready?" he asked, his eyes gleaming with excitement.

"Are you sure this will work?" Cassius asked skeptically. "Can your friends be trusted?"

Randall's lips curled into an ugly frown. "I've known Tig, A'Chula, and Chuckles for years. We're basically brothers. Just make sure to keep your end of the bargain."

"Let's go over the plan one more time," Anna suggested, hoping that one more explanation would catch any loose ends that they may have missed before.

Randall let out a frustrated sigh, but voiced no protests. "Tig, A'Chula, and Chuckles should have commandeered the wagon full of ale by now. Soon, they'll roll down this street, giving free drinks to anyone nearby. With their masters gone, the guardsmen will leave their posts to enjoy themselves."

"And if the guards don't leave their posts?" Anna asked.

"They will," Cassius assured them. "I've had many guardsmen ask me if I could sneak them a bottle of wine during their nightly patrols. I can attest to the fact that almost all of them are fond of a drink."

"You will lead Anna to the safe, and I will join you later. Then we simply take what is in the vault and walk out with the score of a lifetime. Everyone clear?" Cassius and Anna nodded their heads. "Good, let's get to work," Randall said mischievously.

The three thieves walked back into the house, took their places, and waited for the Maggots' distraction. Anna was dusting the dining room when Randall appeared in the doorway.

"What are you doing?" Anna hissed quietly. "We shouldn't be seen together."

"I know, but I wanted to give you this." Randall came close and pulled a small knife out of his pocket. The blade was curved, with a single edge, and had a wooden handle with brass accents. "In case things go awry," he explained.

Anna's heart sank. She did not want to consider the possibility of having to fight their way out of the estate, but she was also glad that Randall had thought of it. Better to have a knife and not need it, than need a knife and not have it. She quickly grabbed the knife from his hand and concealed it in her sock, before nodding her head in thanks.

It wasn't long until Anna heard the groaning of wooden wheels against uneven cobblestones outside the estate. She quickly rushed to the window, and her jaw dropped in amazement.

Outside the Rawleys' gate were Tig and Chuckles, with a mountain of ale casks on the back of a wagon. There was already a crowd of peasants clamouring around the cart to get free drinks. Tig was cracking open the barrels of ale and pouring it into the hands of the crowd, while Chuckles yelled boisterously to garner more "customers."

The ever-silent A'Chula drove the cart down the street. Anna swore she saw several guards lick their lips before abandoning their posts and beginning to chase the wagon down the road, far away from the manor.

Their plan relied on capitalizing on the guards' animalistic urges, which never sat well with her. She wanted something more concrete to base a heist on. She did not think people could be so easily manipulated, but to her surprise, here they were. The plan was going swimmingly. The majority of the guards had left the manor to go chasing after the Maggots and their free beer.

As Anna made her way towards the cellar, she was knocked to the floor by a man. She looked up, and realized that the man was not a servant, and that he was carrying a marble bust of the late King David in his hands.

"What are you doing?" she asked.

"What's it look like, love? Robbin' the place." The man smiled a gap-toothed grin. "The guards are all gone, and there's no one stopping us from ransacking the place. Now, be a dear and stay the fuck out me way!"

Anna quickly looked around, and noticed that many of the peasants outside the manor, and even some of the servants, had the same idea as the man. The mob of people had turned their attention from the free ale to the unguarded manor.

She quickly shot to her feet and hastily descended the steps to the wine cellar to find the sommelier standing there smiling at her, though his smile faded once he saw her face.

"What's wrong?"

"The peasants saw the guards abandoned the estate; and are now robbing the place."

Cassius frowned. "Most unexpected. But not to worry, they'll never find the safe."

"How can you be so sure?" Anna asked.

"Because I have the only key," Cassius explained. The eunuch reached into his pocket, pulled out a small iron key, and began walking toward the shelf of wine behind him.

He removed a bottle from the shelf, which revealed a small keyhole carved into the wall. Cassius slid the key into the hole and turned it. There was an audible click. He then placed both hands against the wall and pushed the hidden door open.

Odion Rawley's safe looked more like a dragon's hoard than the vault of a wealthy merchant. Mountains of gold coins filled the huge room, along with numerous priceless antiques. The longer she stared into the safe, the more Anna's eyes widened. Every time she blinked, it was as if another pile of coins appeared. She slowly shuffled towards the opening of the vault.

"Wha—wh - what," she stammered.

Before Cassius could respond, there was a crashing sound in the stairwell behind them. Anna and the eunuch turned around, to see the corpse of a bloody man tumbling down the wooden stairs into the wine cellar. Then, after a few seconds of suspense, a blood-soaked Randall appeared.

"We've got a prob—holy shit," he gasped. "How in the blazes are we going to move all of this?"

Anna shot a questioning glance towards Cassius, who simply smiled and laughed. "Follow me, children. You have much to learn."

"What if someone else comes down the stairs? There are only three of us, and there's a bloody mob upstairs ransacking the place!"

The sommelier ushered Randall inside the safe before he placed the bottle of wine back on the shelf and pushed the fake wall shut behind him. When the door locked, an audible click echoed around the cavernous vault.

"Why do you have the key?" Anna asked suspiciously.

Once again, the eunuch laughed playfully. "Do you really think that Odion Rawley accumulated all of this wealth legally? Sommelier is just my formal title. I'm also Master Rawley's bookkeeper for his more *discreet* business ventures."

"That still doesn't answer the question of how we are going to move all of this gold," Randall growled as he picked up a handful of coins from one of the piles.

Cassius sighed. "We aren't going to do anything with the gold. All we need to find is a small iron lockbox."

"What's in the box?" Randall asked.

"Find it, and I'll show you."

The three of them then began scouring the vault, hoping to find the lockbox, but that proved to be a harder task than Anna had expected. As she sifted through a pile of antiques, she thought to herself that she'd have a better chance of finding a needle in a haystack.

Behind the fake door, Anna could hear the mob of peasants smashing bottles of wine and shouting at one another as they tore the cellar apart. She must have had a worried expression on her face, because Cassius came over and placed a comforting hand on her shoulder.

"Fret not, child," he soothed. "That door is reinforced by the best dwarven metal that gold can buy. To get into here, they'd need a dragon."

Anna nodded her head in understanding when there was a shout from the other side of the vault. "I found it!" Randall came running through the sea of coins, carrying the small black iron box clutched tightly in his hands. He brought it to Cassius, who looked at the youths inquisitively.

"Either of you know how to pick a lock?"

Anna shook her head, and Randall swore under his breath. "A'Chula is the lock picker, and he's with Tig and Chuckles on the beer cart."

"Curses."

"I can meet with A'Chula later tonight. But you haven't answered my question, what's in the box?" Randall inquired again, this time with much more authority in his voice.

Cassius sighed exhaustedly, as if the very question sucked all the energy from his body. "It's the bill of sale for Rawley's estate. Everything, including the possessions inside the property, are listed under the estate."

"How will that help us?" Anna asked.

Randall's eyes suddenly lit up. "You want to take it to a forger, and give possession of the estate to someone else. Make it look like Rawley sold it."

A mischievous smile appeared on Cassius' lips. "Indeed. That's why I need you. My contacts are quite dated, and I'm afraid that anyone I knew who would be of use to us is either dead or legitimate now."

"So, one of us will be the estate's new owner?" Anna asked, not entirely sure she grasped the full extent of Cassius' plan.

"Indeed."

"Let me guess. You'll be the new owner?" Randall asked.

"Of course not!" Cassius giggled. "I suggest we transfer the rights to you."

"Me? Won't that raise questions?"

"This may come as a shock to you, but Odion Rawley is not a well-liked man. His ruthless business tactics have made him many enemies, and there are plenty in this city who dream of seeing him in ruin. And if the Master of Coin does indeed start asking questions, its nothing that a few well-placed bribes can't fix. We certainly have the coin for it."

A devious smile spread across Randall's lips. "Let's go and see Elmyr."

"How do we get out?" Anna asked as she stared at the solid metal backing to the false wall, realizing that there was no handle to release the lock.

"Follow me," Cassius replied, before escorting the two youths to the brick wall on the far side of the vault and pressing on a series of stones, which resulted in another loud, audible click. Once again, the sommelier pushed on the door and ushered Anna and Randall to the room behind the wall before closing it. On the other side of the vault sat a cramped, musky room, with several cots spread out along the floor.

"The servant's quarters, for the more permanent members of the help, such as myself," Cassius informed them.

"Looks like it hasn't been cleaned in years," Randall muttered.

"Well, if you spent every day of your life cleaning, you'd feel less inclined to clean during your leisure time."

There was a sharp, high-pitched scream from upstairs. Anna's head whirled around as she reached for the knife that was concealed in her sock. Randall tried to shout in protest, but it was too late. She had already bounded up the wooden steps to the main floor.

At the top of the stairs, Anna gasped at the appearance of the house. It looked as though a tornado had torn through the manor. Paintings were ripped from the wall, statues lay in smashed heaps at her feet, and windows were shattered. She turned and ran towards the entrance; then froze in place when she saw a wounded Alcina clutching her blood-soaked belly, while Odion fought off a group of peasants with a broken broomstick. *They were supposed to be gone the whole day,* Anna thought to herself. *Why did they come back?*

Alcina turned her head, and her eyes widened when she saw Anna's face. Her lips moved, as if she was trying to speak, but the only thing that came out was a soft, barely audible rasp.

Anna ran to her side and held her mistress' head. She looked down at the wound and noticed that it was deep, and more than likely fatal. She recalled the time when her father had shot a deer in the gut with an arrow.

She remembered it took her father almost two full days to track it down and bring it back to the hut. A puncture wound to the belly was a slow and agonizing death.

There was a sudden gurgling sound. Anna looked up from her mistress' fading eyes and saw a torrent of blood burst from Odion Rawley's throat as he collapsed to the floor.

"She's dead." Randall's voice caused her to jump and grip her knife tighter. She stared into the boy's eyes and saw that they held no sympathy for the dying Alcina. In fact, it looked as if he almost enjoyed the spectacle.

"He's right, Anna," Cassius said softly. "There's nothing we can do for her now. We should leave before anyone turns their focus on us."

Anna felt the tears swell in her eyes. Alcina deserved better than this. She was a good woman, who always treated her servants kindly. Anna dropped to her knees, held the blade of her knife to Alcina's pale throat, and with a swift flick of the wrist, put her out of her misery.

CHAPTER TWENTY-SIX

ELBERT

The smoke from the fire was overwhelmingly strong, as was the smell of burning flesh. All the other lords, and their officers, had gathered around the fallen commander's funeral pyre.

The only commander not present at the ceremony was Grimm, who was out on yet another raid. Elbert kept sending him on raids, hoping the Islander wouldn't return. But not only did Grimm return every time; he returned with all of his men. He had yet to lose a single soldier on a raid, and word was spreading throughout the fortress that the bastard company was looking like an elite force.

Elbert wiped the tears from his eyes, not out of mourning, but because he was standing downwind of the pyre, and the smoke was stinging his eyes. He hated cremations. The smell, the smoke, the arduous task of building a pyre... he much preferred a burial. *Just dig a hole and throw them in it,* he callously thought to himself.

As he watched the body of the young lord become engulfed in flames, he couldn't help but think of how the youth's father would react upon hearing of his son's demise. *Fat fuck will probably laugh himself into a coughing fit,* Elbert figured. *Hopefully, the bastard has already succumbed to the cough. Deny him this last pleasure in a life of clear over-indulgence.* A smile crept along the king's face as he pictured the plump lord hacking up blood and bile, when Thames discreetly elbowed him in the ribs. Elbert turned his head, realized his mistake, and quickly turned his smile into a faux frown. Thankfully, nobody seemed to noticed.

Surprisingly, the soldiers were of few words, as an awkward silence covered the entire funeral. Only two men spoke, both delivered meekly delivered and out of obligation rather than sincerity.

Perhaps it was because Lord Haustack's health had been rapidly declining over the last several days. First, the noble caught a fever, then his skin turned as white as snow.

Then came the stench. The smell of decay exuded from his wound, to the point where even the healer had to step outside the tent and grab some fresh air. Elbert had only made one visit since the lord had been wounded, and he was thankful that the man was unconscious when he arrived. He wouldn't have known what to say if he had found the wounded lord awake. Should he thank him? Comfort him? Promise him riches? What do you say to a dying man who died solely because of you?

The king shook the thought out of his head. He had more important things to worry about: such as the upcoming siege. His men had been working tirelessly to prepare the fortress' defences, and their exhaustion was beginning to show; the only company that showed no sign of tiring was the prisoner company, or the Bastards, as they were often referred to.

Elbert had to admit that the Islander had done a better job than he expected in whipping the men into shape for battle, and the fact that he had yet to report a single loss was outstanding. One man did go missing one night, but Thames credited it to desertion.

"It wouldn't be a real war if there weren't any deserters," Thames had remarked at the time.

The king turned his head, looked up at the scarred man, and felt the warmth of gratitude surge throughout his body. He appreciated Thames' candour and honesty. And Elbert was beginning to see that honest subjects were a rare commodity to a king. When the lords had brought him bad news, they often tried to undersell it, or cover it up by exaggerating the importance of some minor good news. The only commander who refused to sugarcoat anything was Grimm. Despite all his faults, the man was honest. *Perhaps if the Islander had been raised in civilized society, I would hold him in the same regard as Thames,* Elbert mused to himself.

"I think I've smelt enough burning flesh for one day," Elbert whispered to his guardsmen. The men sharply turned on their heels and began leading their king back to the keep.

The atmosphere in Tjørholm was tense. The soldiers' anxiety was visible in their bodies, and so was the fear. Nobody knew what to expect. The barbarians of the Isles had never massed such a force before. They had only mustered small raiding parties that were more of a nuisance than a problem; at least, that's how Elbert had always seen it.

But this time was different: he would be on the front line. The Islanders wouldn't be murdering and pillaging a far-off coastal town: they would be right in front of him. Blood-stained, and with a hunger for slaughter.

The keep was mainly empty. Most of the men stationed there had elected to attend the young noble's funeral. Elbert waved his hand to dismiss his guardsmen, and rolled into the mead hall, which had served as their briefing room for the last few days. He grabbed a flagon of ale and poured himself a generous glass.

Greedily, he slurped the bitter-tasting drink down his throat to soothe his nerves. He wiped the froth from his lips and thought about what he would give for some fine wine. Unfortunately, it appeared that the Islanders preferred stronger drinks than wine, and what little wine they had brought from the mainland had already been consumed.

The king's eyes scanned the crudely drawn map of the fortress, and his stomach churned. He saw hundreds of problems and hundreds of ways that he was going to die in the impending siege.

Nobody knew when Uthredd's army would arrive, although Grelin reported that it was getting closer. Elbert had already started rationing their provisions, and he hoped that the Islander king was not smart enough to simply wait them out.

There was also the problem of insubordination. Grimm was openly rude, and sometimes downright hostile, to other commander;, and his men had adopted the same attitude towards other companies. Fights between the Bastards and the other men had become commonplace, and were wearing on the king's nerves. He would flog the men involved, but knew it wouldn't make any difference. He had to punish Grimm, but without the Islander, he knew the prisoners-turned-soldiers would be leaderless; and at this point, they would never accept another. It was clear that the men respected their foreign commander, and it seemed like a perfect match.

"Your Majesty?" Thames said as he poked his head into the mead hall.

"Yes?"

"Some of the other commanders were wondering if you would like to join them in remembering Abram Haustack. I'll understand if you don't wish to attend. It isn't the most appropriate thing, fraternizing with your sub-"

"I'll join them for a few drinks, but only because I left the funeral so early," Elbert interrupted, although he wasn't sure why. Thames was right. Mingling with lords in such a manner was highly inappropriate. But he was the king, and who was going to tell the king what he could and couldn't do?

A look of surprise covered Thames' face, but he quickly regained his composure, nodded his head in understanding, and waved the other commanders into the mead hall. The lords shuffled into the room awkwardly, as they tried to avoid eye contact with the king. It was one thing to meet with the king over official business, it was entirely another to meet with him in such an informal setting.

"Gentlemen," Elbert began. "I wish we were meeting in better circumstances."

The lords looked around at one another, as if silently challenging each other to answer the king's greeting. Finally, Lord Grelin spoke. "It's a shame, what happened to the young Lord Haustack. I'm sure his family will be devastated."

Elbert barely contained his laughter. He knew damned well that his father wouldn't miss him. But then the thought of Abram's mother seeped into his mind. He hadn't thought about her before. Perhaps his death truly would be mourned back in the mainland. Elbert felt queasy when another lord chimed in.

"As much as I hate to say it, that boy dying was the best thing to ever happen to this army. That Islander has made those prisoners into a formidable force."

"Pah!" Lord Grelin spat. "Those men are cowards: the minute they see King Uthredd's army, they'll stab us in the back if they think it'll save their skin."

"I'm not sure about that," Thames confessed. "The men seem loyal to Grimm, but I'm not sure whether they are loyal out of respect or out of fear."

Most of the other lords had relaxed in their chairs by now and talked amongst themselves, ignoring the conversation between Thames, Grelin, and the other lord. Elbert watched intently as the subject quickly changed from Haustack's passing to the stronghold's defences; then to more trivial matters, as their state of inebriation grew.

"The men should be digging a damned trench!" one lord slurred drunkenly.

"Islanders don't ride horses, you old fool!" another called out. "They prefer to fight with their feet on the ground."

"The only thing horses are good for is for eating," called a voice from the end of the mead hall.

Everyone snapped their head towards the giant oaken doors of the hall, where they saw a blood-soaked Grimm holding a severed head in his right hand. The Islander smiled as the look of abject horror spread across each of the commanders' faces. Then he tossed the severed head onto the table. Blood splattered against the hard wooden surface, and several lords' mugs bounced off the table and onto the floor.

"Jarl Bulgruf sends his regards," Grimm laughed as he pulled up a chair at the end of the table.

The dead Islander's eyes stared deep into Elbert's. He felt his skin crawl under the lifeless gaze. He looked up to see Grimm smiling from ear to ear. "I take it the raid went well?" he asked, trying to mask his discomfort.

Grimm helped himself to a lord's mug of ale and finished it in two gulps. "Do you really have to ask?"

"We are in mourning, good sir!" Lord Grelin chastised the Islander. "If you insist on behaving like a boor, then I must insist you leave."

The smile on Grimm's face vanished in an instant. He rose to his feet and loomed over the lord, who immediately cowered in his seat. The warrior put a menacing hand on the noble's shoulder and squeezed. Grelin immediately winced and squeaked in pain.

"Enough!" Elbert shouted. "If you are going to terrorize us on such a solemn and hallowed occasion, I will have my guardsmen forcefully remove you."

Grimm stared at him in silent defiance, but released the cowering noble after a moment's delay, and returned to his seat. The Islander kicked both his legs up onto the table and poured himself another mug of ale. "So," he asked. "Who died?"

"Lord Haustack, the man whose company you were given control of," Thames responded through gritted teeth.

"Hmm," Grimm snorted.

The awkwardness in the air could be cut with a knife. Many of the lords looked at their king pleadingly, hoping that he would remove the Islander from the hall. But Elbert knew that he couldn't, not if he wanted to survive the upcoming siege.

"Leave us," he commanded. The nobles quickly rose to their feet and exited the mead hall with incredible haste. The only man who stayed behind was Thames.

"Didn't you hear your master, dog? He said to leave," Grimm jibed.

"I'm sworn to protect the king against all threats," Thames responded, effortlessly avoiding the barb. "And there is no bigger threat in this fortress than you."

"Tell me, did Uthredd put up with your insolence?" Elbert asked genuinely.

Grimm's face slackened, then tightened into a nasty frown. "Uthredd and I were like brothers. Inseparable since birth. We fought together, bled together, fucked together, and killed together. We are shield-brothers, and he will always have my respect."

"So you don't respect me: is that it?"

"Not only have you yet to see battle: you've yet to kill anyone."

"How do you know I haven't killed anyone?" Elbert asked, desperately wanting to confess to his brother's murder, to prove a point to the Ignorant islander.

"I can just tell. When you've been around as long as I have, you know a thing or two about reading men. Now this one," he said, while gesturing towards Captain Thames, "This one's a killer."

"I only do as I am commanded," Thames responded stoically.

"Horseshit, mainlander. You can't honestly tell me that you don't feel that spark of joy when you watch a man's life pour out from his eyes, and smile as he realizes that you were the one to beat him."

Elbert turned his head to Thames expectantly, but a wave of disgust washed over him when the captain hesitated. Rupert was a soldier, and killing was a necessary evil, but to get enjoyment out of it? That was another thing entirely.

"That's what I thought," Grimm stated smugly.

Just before Elbert could reply, a soldier burst into the mead hall, breathing raggedly.

"What is it?" Thames asked in an authoritative voice.

"Uthredd's army is approaching!"

Elbert felt the colour leave his face. His eyes darted between Grimm and Rupert. It took a moment to realize that they were waiting for him to give the orders. "Man the walls!" he shouted, coming out of his panicked, trance-like state.

The messenger nodded his head and hurried back out of the doorway. Both Thames and the Islander rose to their feet and exited the mead hall.

Elbert, on the other hand, sat frozen in place. This would be his first real battle as a king, but all he could do was think about how useless he'd be. A king, a true king, would be on the front line with his men. But what use would a cripple be? He couldn't shoot a bow or wield a sword. At best, he could sit on top of the ramparts and watch as the barbarian horde scaled the stronghold's walls.

There was a loud metallic thud in the room. Elbert lifted his head and saw that Grimm had returned, and had tossed a dagger onto the long dining table, in the middle of the room.

"In case you feel like a becoming a man today," he stated.

Elbert swallowed his nervousness, picked up the dagger, and cleared his throat. "How did you not see Uthredd's army?" he asked, a hint of anger in his voice.

"Uthredd must've come from the east, instead of the north as we expected. The last few camps we raided must've been diversions from the real force," Grimm concluded plainly.

Elbert dismissed the Islander with a wave of his hand, took a few deep breaths to regain his composure, and rolled out to see King Uthredd's army.

Tjørholm's grounds were in total chaos. Soldiers were scrambling to get ready, commanders were barking orders at their men, and the deafening sound of Islander war drums could be heard echoing ominously in the distance. Elbert flagged down some of his royal guardsmen and commanded them to carry him to the battlements, so that he could see the size of the enemy's army.

A trio of guardsmen hoisted the wheeled throne into the air and walked up the stairs to the ramparts. The king's eyes scanned the fortress, hoping to see some sort of reassurance that they would live to see tomorrow. He saw Lord Arlin's ballistas being prepared, he saw men organizing themselves into defensive formations, and he smelled the hot tar that was boiling in cauldrons above the portcullis.

Everything was ready.

He allowed himself to relax. But that relief soon vanished when he saw the size of Uthredd's army.

He had never seen ten thousand men gathered in one place before, but it certainly looked like the king of the Isles had a limitless supply of men. The sound of the war drums was like a curtain of thunder that was slowly signalling their impending doom. Ladders could be seen pointing up into the sky, and large, shadowy figures were looming above the Islander horde.

"Crazy fucker actually did it," Grimm remarked.

"What?" Thames asked.

"He got the giants of the Northern Isles to join his cause."

"How does one reason with such a beast?" Thames asked.

"Easily," Grimm replied. "Giants may be stubborn, but they are also thicker than an anvil. They will believe almost anything you tell them."

"Giants?" Elbert whispered audibly.

"You okay there, Legless? Or do you need to change your britches?"

The crippled king quickly regained his resolve and glared at the Islander. "You and your men will man the ramparts and defend against the ladders. Do you understand?" Grimm nodded his head.

Elbert turned his attention to the barbarian army once more, and felt an overwhelming sense of dread wash over his body. Coming here was a terrible mistake: one that was going to cost him his life.

CHAPTER TWENTY-SEVEN

ANNA

Stitch's hut stunk less this time, though the familiar smell of decay lingered in the air. The fireplace was gently crackling and popping on the far side of the main room. There was a large kitchen table that was stained with what Anna hoped was blood.

There were several unfinished meals on top of the table that had begun to mold. She swore that she saw something deep inside the potatoes move. A shiver ran down her spine.

"She's in the other room," the elderly healer stated. "Try not to make any loud noises."

Anna nodded her head in thanks and walked into the other room. It had been four days since the heist, and word was spreading throughout The Garden about the Maggots' deed. She had even heard murmurs of people talking about Randall as if he were a god. To steal an estate from someone as wealthy as Odion Rawley was unheard of. They had achieved the impossible.

Yet despite their achievement, Anna did not feel proud. Instead, she was sickened by the fact that Alcina had to lose her life during the process. Not knowing why the Rawleys had come back to the estate had slowly begun eating away at her.

The room behind the side door looked like it belonged in a butcher's shop, rather than a healer's. Buckets of blood and bile were sitting by the bedside. Every piece of cloth in the room was stained red with blood. The only source of light was a candle on the nightstand, which made the bedroom look even more ghastly.

"Hello?" Maeve croaked, her eyes barely open.

"It's me," Anna stated, before pulling up a chair beside the bed.

"How long?" Maeve asked. "How long was I out?"

"A week or so."

"My body feels stiff, like it's made of stone."

Anna let out a laugh. "You've missed a lot."

She helped Maeve into a sitting position, with the girl's back resting against the wall, and filled her in on everything she had missed. She told her about the deal they had made with Hammerfist, how they had scouted the Rawleys' estate, and how they enlisted Cassius' help to rob them.

When it came time to tell her about Alcina's fate, Anna hesitated. She could feel the words stick in her throat, and tears swell up behind her eyes. She shook her head and decided that the girl didn't need to know everything that happened.

"What about you and Randall?" Maeve asked.

The question took Anna by surprise. How could she know about her and Randall? She looked deep into the girl's eyes and saw a certain understanding behind them. *No.*

"Don't look so surprised. I saw the way he looked at you," Maeve replied with a slight smile on her face. "I figured something had to have happened while I was out." A sense of relief washed over Anna. "Besides," Maeve continued. "It wasn't so long ago that he used to look at me like that."

Anna's heart sank. How did she not see this coming? Of course, Randall had been intimate with the only other girl in the Maggots. How could she be so stupid? The room spun, and she felt her knees grow weak. She placed a steadying hand on the wall to keep herself from falling. Her eyes shifted towards Maeve, and she secretly began wishing that the girl hadn't survived.

"Do you remember what happened with the Blackguard?" she asked, eager to change the subject.

The mention of the mercenary-group-turned-city-guard caused what little colour there was in Maeve's face to leave. Her eyes darted wildly and sweat formed on the girl's brow. "I don't want to talk about it."

"Maeve –"

"You don't understand!" Maeve snapped. "I've never been more scared for my life. When that guard was beating me, I saw that look in his eyes... he was enjoying it. I told Greaver, and he won't do anything about it. I thought he was supposed to protect us from things like this. I thought we were safe."

Anna looked around the room to ensure that Stitch wasn't lurking in any corners, then lowered her voice to a whisper. "If everything goes according to Randall's plan, he won't be in power for much longer." A smile crept along Maeve's face. "That reminds me, I should probably head back to the estate and see how things are going, unless you want me to –"

"Go," Maeve interjected. "I'll catch up with you once I can move on my own."

Anna nodded her head and exited the room. In the main room, Stitch was staring absently into the crackling fire. She noticed that there were three lines of white powder on the wooden table beside him. She shook her head and left the hut, but collided with someone as soon as she stepped outside. She turned around, ready to lash out at the idiot who got in her way, until she saw that it was the King of Crooks himself.

"My apologies, Anna," Greaver stated. "I had just heard that Maeve had awakened and wanted to come by to see how she's doing."

"She's sore," Anna replied coldly. "That guard really did a number on her."

"Such a shame."

"Yes, if only there were someone with enough power to do something about it."

Greaver's lips curled into a frown before he let out a sigh. "Anna, you have to understand that the Blackguard are not to be taken lightly. I will not start a war with the crown simply because one of my children was stupid enough to get caught."

Anna let out a petulant scoff. At one point, she thought that the King of Crooks referring to his subjects as his children was a term of endearment, but now she saw it for what it really was: a degrading label meant to constantly remind them that he was their superior. Before the king could say another word, she spun on her heel and left The Garden.

"Careful with that, you fuckin' halfwit!" Regina Hammerfist shouted from atop a mountain of gold coins. One of the dwarves muttered something of an apology, before carrying a rather large oil painting past Anna.

The manor was in complete disarray. The once-pristine and neatly organized estate had transformed into a cluttered mess. It was evident that the dwarves held cleanliness in low regard.

Windows were shattered, there were holes in several of the walls, and even the Rawleys' dried blood still stained the floor. It seemed like all they cared about was their gold.

"Anna!" Randall beamed, as he pulled her into a tight embrace. "How's Maeve?"

"Sore," Anna replied as she side-eyed one dwarf, who had been leering at her from the moment she walked in. "How're things going here?"

Randall let out a sigh. "This entire ordeal should've taken a couple of hours, but these damned dwarves insist on counting every bloody coin. I'm starting to think that Greaver will die of old age by the time they're done."

Her lips parted to tell Randall that she ran into the King of Crooks outside Stitch's hut, but she thought better of it. She knew it would send him off on a tangent. For the last few days, Randall had been on edge. He was so close to dethroning Greaver that it was all that he could talk about, and it was grating on Anna's nerves.

"Where's Cassius?"

"No clue. That ball-less bastard fucked off the minute the forger finished the documents. You know, he's kind of like a blister."

"How so?"

"He only shows up after all the work is done."

Anna let out a laugh. Randall always knew how to make her smile, even in the most serious of times, which only strengthened her feelings for him. She wasn't sure if it was love, but what else could it be?

When she wasn't thinking about their plan to gift the kingdom to Regina, all she could do was fantasize about their life together. She imagined them growing up and stealing their way into nobility. Then they could retire to the countryside, where she could hunt and escape the smells of the city, and he could order their countless servants around.

Late at night, when she visualized this particular fantasy, she wanted to whisper it in Randall's ear, and confess everything to him. But she knew it would be a mistake, especially now that she knew about him and Maeve. *What if I tell him, and it drives him back into her arms?* The very thought of those two together made her stomach churn.

"Lovebirds!" Regina called out from her throne of gold. "Stop staring into each other's eyes and give us a hand here!"

Anna tore her gaze from Randall and started walking towards the dwarven queen, when the boy's hand reached out and stopped her. She noticed that he gave her breasts a subtle squeeze, and she felt her body grow hot with desire.

"That wasn't the deal, Hammerfist," Randall replied. "All you asked us to do was steal Odion's fortune, and we did that. You never mentioned us helping you count it."

Regina glared at the boy, but when it became obvious that he would not back down, she let out a laugh. "Can't blame a girl for tryin'. When we launch the assault on Greaver, can we count on yer Maggots' help? Or do me and my men have to do that all by ourselves, too?"

"I'm afraid that wouldn't be wise," a familiar voice said from behind them.

"What would you know, eunuch? You some ploughin' genius on deposin' kings?"

"No," Cassius confessed. "But I do know that Greaver still has a lot of men loyal to him. So it would be much better if we try to settle this diplomatically, rather than using violence."

Hammerfist snorted in amusement. "Why the fuck would I sit down with the gutless shit-heap?"

"Think about it," Randall chimed in. "If you go to war with Greaver, you'll be killing your future subjects, not to mention attracting attention from the Blackguard. But on the other hand, if you meet with him, show him the power you now hold, he'll realize that his goose is cooked, and concede. All without spilling a drop of blood."

Regina scratched her chin and groaned as she mulled over Randall's and Cassius' words. Then, after a lengthy pause, she finally spoke. "Fine, we'll try it your way. I can't wait to see the look on that bugger's face when he realizes he's fucked."

"Let's go tonight," Randall suggested. "Best to get it over with."

"Fuck that," the dwarven queen replied. "Let's go right now, unless you have somewhere else to be?" Although her voice was harsh and accusatory, nobody voiced any objections. "Men!" she called out. "Look after the place while I'm gone. Goin' to pay old man Greaver a visit."

"By yer command, my queen," one dwarf replied, while clumsily bowing low. Anna couldn't tell if the flourish was sincere or done sarcastically. In either case, Regina didn't seem to mind, as she walked straight out of the manor door and towards The Garden.

"Randall," Anna whispered, as she grabbed the boy's arm. "Are you sure that this is a good idea? What if Greaver attacks us? Cassius said it himself: many people are still loyal to him, and –"

"Do you trust me?" Randall interrupted in a soothing voice. He placed both hands on her shoulders and their eyes locked with each other.

"I do."

"Then do exactly as I say, and I promise it'll all work out."

Anna nodded her head. She wasn't sure why, but she felt a sense of security when she looked into Randall's eyes. She wished that she could be as confident in his decisions as he was, but that wasn't the way she was raised. Her father had always taught her to consider every outcome, every possibility, before committing to a plan. Because when you fought a werewolf or a corvan, you had to make the right decision.

Otherwise, you'd die.

The walk to The Garden seemed to take ages, rather than the several minutes that it actually was. Everywhere Anna looked, she imagined she saw Greaver's eyes lingering on the group of them walking down the streets. She knew that word would reach the King of Crooks long before their arrival.

Hammerfist's henchmen walked beside her at all times. These particular dwarves never seemed to leave her side: they were the same dwarves that she and Randall had encountered when they first walked through The Splints. It was as if these men were her royal guardsmen, sworn to protect her at all costs.

Anna knew the truth was probably less glamorous. She saw how Regina talked to each of them, and it was clear that she was sleeping with all of them.

"You're nervous," Cassius said as he slowed his stride to match Anna's.

"Is it that obvious?"

"Try not to worry. Randall's a smart boy. I'm sure he's thought of everything."

"You know he didn't trust you at first, right?"

Cassius let out a small laugh. "Very few men trust eunuchs. Perhaps it's our lack of balls that makes us so alien to them."

"What about women? We don't have balls, either?"

The former sommelier's lips curled into an ugly grimace, as if he was about to bear bad news. "Most of the men I've met view women as *things* rather than people. I'm afraid your kind is held in lower regard than mine."

"Oh."

"Fortunately for you, I think Randall has a progressive mindset when it comes to women and their role in the world."

"Why is that fortunate for me?"

"Oh come now, child. Don't play coy with me."

Anna's face turned red, and she shifted her gaze to the ground. She hated that everyone obviously knew about her and Randall. First Maeve, now Cassius, and if both of them knew, then she could practically guarantee that Greaver knew.

A shiver ran down her spine as a thought popped into her head. *Do I make Randall weak? What if Greaver tries to use our love as leverage against Hammerfist?* She shook her head to rid herself of the intrusive thoughts. She would never allow that to happen. Her hand instinctively reached down until she felt the bone handle of her dagger. *I'll kill Greaver before he ever gets the chance.*

When they reached the doorway to The Garden, Regina pulled the stone from the wall, revealing the menacing stare of the guardsman. Anna had never bothered to learn the man's name, but she knew that his hand would be on the sword that was always strapped to his belt.

"Password?"

"Putrid," Regina replied.

"Greaver's expecting you," the guard mumbled as he opened the door.

"Of course he is," Regina retorted smugly. "Word travels fast in this city, don't you know."

The guard grunted in response before closing the doorway to The Garden and resuming his post. The air inside was tense. Everyone in the central courtyard avoided eye contact with them, and quickly darted into the nearest building they could find.

"Smell that?" Hammerfist asked.

"No," Randall replied.

"That's the smell of change in the air."

"Regina!" a voice called out from across the courtyard. Anna turned her head and was surprised to see that the King of Crooks was approaching them, alone and unarmed. "How nice of you to come and visit me."

"Cut the crap, Greaver," Hammerfist barked. "We're here for your kingdom. You can either hand it over peacefully, or –"

"Please, join me in my dining room. We can talk about business there. You look absolutely famished."

Anna was confused. She wasn't sure what to expect when they entered The Garden, but a polite and welcoming King of Crooks surely wasn't it. She looked at Randall, noticed that his muscles weren't tense, and let out a breath of relief. *At least Randall isn't worried.*

With the blessing of Regina, they followed Greaver across the courtyard, into his throne room, and into the adjacent dining room. To Anna's surprise, the table was already set with several flagons of wine, a roasted pig, mashed potatoes, and a bowl of apples.

"Please, help yourself to whatever you like!" Greaver stated, as he reached for an apple out of the bowl and bit into it. Juice sprayed from between his teeth and onto the oak tabletop. Greaver and Regina sat at opposite ends of the table with the guardsmen, Anna, Randall, and Cassius filling the middle.

"Now: you say you're here to take over my kingdom?" Greaver asked as he poured himself a mug of wine.

"Indeed," Regina replied as she poured her own mug and quickly drank from it. "You know I won't just hand my kingdom over to you."

"And here I thought you had more common sense. Seems you've gone senile in your old age."

The King of Crooks smiled at the barb. "We have three options in front of us. The first is that I gift you my kingdom and abdicate my throne; which we both know I won't do. The second is that we begin an all-out war, costing hundreds of people their lives. Not to mention attracting the attention of Mortimer Black and his men."

"And the third option?" Hammerfist asked as she took another healthy swig from her mug.

"We divide my kingdom into two equal parts. I will rule the city's northern half, and have access to the market square and the nobles. While you control the southern half, giving you control over The Splints, the docks, and the main gatehouses."

Silence hung over the table. A few of Regina's guardsmen murmured amongst themselves, while the dwarven queen glared at the King of Crooks. Then, finally, a smile appeared on her lips.

"Maybe you're not as senile as I thought. We have a deal."

"Brilliant!" Greaver exclaimed. "Let us toast to a new era of peace and prosperity!"

Everyone filled their mugs with wine and held them up in the air. "Cheers!" they shouted in unison.

As Anna brought the cup to her lips, she felt a vice-like grip on her upper thigh. She looked down and saw Randall's hand squeezing her leg as hard as he could. She turned her head and saw him subtly shaking his head. Her eyes grew wide as she realized what he meant.

Poison.

She looked around the table and saw that Cassius, Randall, Greaver, and herself were the only ones who didn't drink to the toast. Her head snapped back to Hammerfist, whose skin had already turned pale.

"What's the matter, Regina? Not feeling so well?" the King of Crooks taunted as he poured his mug of wine out onto the floor.

The dwarven queen gurgled in reply, but no words came out.

"You see, the thing that you forgot is that I have eyes and ears everywhere. This is *my* city, and a rat doesn't shit in the streets without me knowing about it. You honestly thought you could come in here, demand my kingdom from me, and I'd willingly give it to you?"

The king's words echoed off the dining room walls as the dwarves began puking blood and bile profusely on the floor.

"Worst of all, you thought that the boy I raised like a son would betray me? That he'd just hand over my kingdom to a stranger? Your hubris killed you, just as much as that wine did. Let this be a lesson to you, Randall. If you're going to have ambition, you need at least half a brain to achieve it, unless you want to be like our dear friend Regina here."

"Thank you, sire. I'll remember that," Randall replied as he rose to his feet and moved to his king's side.

Anna locked eyes with the dwarven queen. Her eyes were bloodshot, and she was clawing at her throat as torrents of blood surged out of her mouth and onto the stone floor.

"And Cassius, excellent recommendation on the poison," Greaver complimented, as he picked up his cutlery and began slicing off a piece of pork.

"Thank you, sire," Cassius replied while customarily dipping his head.

"And Anna, I–" the King of Crooks began.

She turned her head back towards the head of the table and saw that a fountain of blood was gushing out of Greaver's throat. Her eyes quickly went to Randall's hands, which were tightly clutched around the king's steak knife.

"Long live the king," Randall said, as he pushed Greaver's dying body out of his chair and took Greaver's place at the head of the table.

ACT III

CHAPTER TWENTY-EIGHT

GRIMM

The thunderous pounding of the Islander's war drums echoed across the frozen plains. Men and giants alike bellowed in anger as they glared at the occupied Tjørholm. The cold winter wind blew snow across the empty field that lay between Uthredd's army and the stronghold's ramparts. The wind seemed to howl as ferociously as the army of Islanders.

Grimm stared out at his former countrymen and women with a slight sense of trepidation. Before Uthredd became High King of the Isles, the clans had always been at war with one another. Their petty squabbles often led to insignificant wars between two clans.

But this time, all the Islanders had unified under Uthredd's banner in common purpose, to take back what was taken from them, and to kill the invading army. An army Grimm was now a part of.

He had never felt this sense of uneasiness before a battle. In fact, he usually felt the opposite. Before a fight, there was a sense of excitement or giddiness that filled his body. Perhaps his time with the mainlanders was making him soft.

"By the gods," a soldier gasped beside him. Grimm could barely hear the man over the roar of the Islanders. He thought about not responding, but he also knew that the men needed encouragement. This would be the first actual battle many of the men had experienced.

"Don't pray to your gods now, boy," Grimm stated dryly. "The only thing that is going to save you from that horde is your skill with a sword."

The man smiled meekly in response. Grimm shook his head in disgust, and felt a tinge of pride that the soldier was not part of his company of men, which reminded him that his men were waiting below for his orders. He turned on his heel, cleared his throat, and shouted at the top of his lungs. "Bastards!"

"Yes, sir!" they shouted back in unison, their bodies snapping to attention.

"You are lucky. Your king has asked you to be the first line of defence. We will man the ramparts and claim all the glory!" His men cheered in unison and quickly began ascending the steps to the ramparts to relieve the soldiers already stationed there.

Grimm stared at the faces of his men as they marched past him, and he couldn't help but feel like a proud parent. He had beaten, broken, and rebuilt these men into warriors; and now, he offered them a glorious death in battle. His earlier uneasiness disappeared as he thought about fighting alongside the Bastards. Then, suddenly, he noticed Sara climbing the steps, sword in hand.

"What do you think you're doing?"

"Fighting, sir!" she shouted, in her fiercest voice. Grimm smiled in amusement, but when Sara saw this, her lips curled into a frown. "What's so funny?"

"You remind me of my son."

There was a sudden look of confusion on Sara's face, and her sword arm wavered slightly. "Where is he?"

Grimm swallowed his tears. He crouched down, so that he was eye to eye with the girl, and placed a hand on her shoulder. "This place is too dangerous for you; besides, I have a more important task for you."

The disappointment on Sara's face vanished quickly at the mention of a special mission. "What is it?"

"I need you to protect Legless. I've a feeling his guardsmen won't be half as brave as you when they meet a real warrior."

A smile cracked on the child's lips as she nodded her head and eagerly ran off to protect the king. Grimm turned his attention to the men who were preparing Arlin's ballistas. "You fuckers know how to work that?" The men offered a half-hearted muttering of assurance before resuming their duties. "Good, then make sure you aim for the big ones. If any of those cunts break through, we're fucked."

Suddenly, the war drums fell silent, and the only thing that could be heard was the howling wind as it bit ravenously at the men's cheeks. Grimm's body tightened with anticipation as he waited for Uthredd's signal to launch the attack.

Finally, after a few seconds of delay, the loud bass-heavy bellow of the Islander's war horns reverberated off the empty plains, followed by the screaming of ten thousand warriors as they began charging the fortress.

"Archers!" Grimm shouted, as he pulled his sword free from its scabbard and began walking along the ramparts. He watched the silhouettes of the Islanders become more and more defined as they drew closer to the stronghold's walls.

Once they were in range, he gave the signal for the archers to loose their arrows. The thrum of a hundred bowstrings started the symphony of bloodshed. Screams of men being struck by arrows filled the air, but did little to diminish the Islanders' numbers, or their animosity.

The ramparts shook violently as the ballista targeted one of the three giants that had joined the first waves of attackers. Grimm saw one of the ballista's bolts strike a giant in the shoulder and knock the goliath to the ground, crushing several Islanders underneath him.

But to his dismay, the giant rose to his feet, ripped the bolt out of his shoulder, and hurled it back at the walls. Grimm instinctively dived out of the way and watched as the bolt skewered four men and tore their bodies from the ramparts.

"Aim for their fucking heads!" he shouted to the men controlling the ballistas as he rose to his feet.

The audible thuds of wooden ladders smacking against the stone fortifications echoed along the battlements. Grimm quickly rushed over to the first ladder he saw and kicked it over, sending several Islanders back towards the ground. Many of his men had the same idea, but whenever they tipped one ladder over, two more appeared along the walls. This was a numbers game, one where they had a significant disadvantage.

"If any of those cocksuckers set foot on this wall, I'll throw you over the ramparts myself!" Grimm shouted, when suddenly he felt a hand grasp his shoulder. He spun around, sword raised above his head, only to find a worried Thames staring back at him.

"Command your men to protect the king!" the captain shouted. "If he falls, all is lost!"

"Fuck the king!" Grimm snapped back. "If this wall falls, then we're fucked." Thames' face curled into a sneer of disgust, but before he could utter any words, Grimm interrupted him. "Get him back to the keep if you're so worried about him. He has no place out here. You and I both know it."

"He won't heed my counsel!"

Grimm looked over his shoulder and saw a few of his men fighting off the ravenous Islanders on the ladders. His gaze then shifted to the crippled king, who was clutching Grimm's dagger close to his chest. Then, finally, his attention snapped back to Thames. "Watch my men. Make sure none of those fuckers set foot on this wall."

Thames nodded and pushed his way past the white-eyed warrior. As Grimm weaved his way through the chaos on top of the ramparts, he had a moment to look out on the field and the incoming assault. He saw several Islanders skewered by arrows, and a giant with a ballista bolt protruding from his eye. However, any joy he found in the sight was short-lived when he realized it didn't even make a dent in Uthredd's numbers.

Once he made it to the king, he grabbed him by the collar of his shirt and lifted him straight out of his chair. "What are you doing here?" he shouted.

"Standing alongside my men," Elbert replied valiantly.

"You'll be dying alongside them if you don't go back to the keep."

"I will not watch idly as my men are cut down by your –"

Grimm pulled the king close, so that he could whisper in his ear without being overheard by Elbert's guards. "Sara is with you, and if she dies because of your stupidity, I'll tear your flesh from your bones with my bare hands." He shoved the king back into his mobile throne, and was pleased to see that some of the colour in his royal complexion had disappeared. Elbert straightened his shirt and nodded his head before giving the order for his guardsmen to escort him back to the keep.

There was a sudden commotion back in the body of the ramparts. Grimm turned his head and saw that Thames was fighting off three Islanders who had somehow scaled the walls.

Along the battlements, he could see that the Bastards were faltering. He gripped his sword tight around the hilt and charged down the ramparts. He hacked and slashed at anything that wasn't wearing the mainlanders' colours.

The three Islanders attacking Thames easily fell to his sword. Grimm severed the hands of one warrior who was at the top of a ladder and sliced open the throat of another.

This was what he was made for. This is where he felt most at home. Even when he was with his family, back when they were alive, he yearned to be back in battle. The rush of adrenaline, the thrill of being seconds away from death at any given moment, and the pride he felt when he managed to best his enemy and claim their life made everything else in life seem dull.

Midway through his rage-induced frenzy, he heard a thud, and felt blunted steel bounce off the back of his skull. His knees instantly became weak, and Grimm fell to the ground.

Without checking his wound, he quickly rolled on to his back and stabbed his sword upward into the Islander's gut. The man's mouth opened wide as blood slowly oozed out.

Grimm twisted his blade and threw the warrior off the battlements. As the Islander's dying body fell, Grimm tried to pull his sword free but his grip slipped; and he watched in anger as his blade, and the body it was embedded in, disappeared beneath the horde of Islanders below.

Before he could rise to his feet, another warrior jumped on him, pinning him to the ground. His hands reacted purely by instinct, and he managed to grab the haft of the shieldmaiden's axe before the blade cut his throat.

The two Islanders growled and bared teeth at each other as they pushed against the axe's handle. The shieldmaiden was wisely putting all her weight on the weapon, and Grimm's arms were tiring.

Knowing that he would lose that battle, he stopped pushing against her and pulled the axe to the side, so that the blade bit into his meaty shoulder instead of his throat.

The shieldmaiden's eyes widened and hesitated. Grimm quickly seized the opportunity, wrapped a hand around the warrior's head, and pulled down so that their ears were almost touching.

He turned to face her and bit into her neck. Blood surged from the woman's throat and into Grimm's mouth, as his teeth tore skin and muscle from her body.

The shieldmaiden fell backwards, clutching her neck. Grimm spat the chunk of flesh hanging from his mouth onto the ramparts and pulled the axe from his shoulder with a grunt. He didn't feel it at the time, but he certainly knew that he would feel it in the morning, provided he lived that long.

The top of the ramparts had turned into a bloody melee. The Bastards were fighting bravely, but the Islanders outclassed them. With each passing second, more and more of his kinsmen were scaling the walls and joining the fray against the men under his command.

He took a deep breath in, mentally preparing for another charge, when he saw a giant on the field carrying a large ram heading towards the gate.

"The gate! Protect the gate!" he shouted over the sound of clashing steel, but either the men manning the ballistas did not hear him or they had other things on their minds.

His heartbeat quickened as he weaved his way through the fighting back towards the main gate. He swung the shieldmaiden's axe only when he needed to, making sure to conserve his energy for the fighting closer to the gate.

When he was halfway to the gatehouse, he heard the loud thud of the ram hitting the oaken doors in front of the portcullis. The force of the giant's attack shook the foundation of the battlements.

Then there was another thud.

And another.

The giant was setting a blistering pace, and if Grimm did not get to the gatehouse soon, all of his effort to this point would be for naught.

The adrenaline was wearing off, and the dull ache in his shoulder had grown into a burning sensation, as the cold winter air attacked the open wound. Suddenly, an idea popped into his head.

"The oil!" he shouted. "Dump the oil!" By some miracle, the soldiers at the gatehouse heard him, and began dumping the large cauldrons of oil on top of the giant. Grimm could hear the giant bellow in pain, and for a moment, he felt a tinge of hope.

But when the loud thudding of the ram started again, his heart sank. *How hard is it to kill this fucker?* he thought to himself, as he picked up his pace.

Just as he had reached the gatehouse, he heard the last thing he wanted to—the sound of the oak doors of Tjørholm shattering.

CHAPTER TWENTY-NINE

ELBERT

The oaken doors of the fortress burst open: on the other side were countless Islanders and a giant. Soldiers scrambled towards the front gate to prepare for the inevitable breach. Men stabbed their spears through the portcullis, trying to injure as many Islanders as they could.

The cacophony of battle rang in Elbert's ears as he watched in horror. For each savage that his men cut down, there seemed to be two more to take their place. They were simply outnumbered and outclassed.

"Your Majesty," Thames spoke, breaking the king out of his frozen state of terror. "Allow me to join the men at the gate. They need my expertise!"

"No!" Elbert blurted out, his voice full of fear. "I need you with me. Those are professional soldiers; they know what they're doing."

"Forgive me for being frank, Your Majesty, but no amount of training has prepared them for *that*," Thames rebuked, while pointing to the giant, who had begun lifting the portcullis with his bare hands.

Elbert froze again as he watched the horde of Islanders pour through the gates and swarm over his men. The giant roared as he held up the iron bars of the portcullis with ease. The king turned his attention to the battlements, hoping to see Grimm, but the white-eyed warrior was nowhere to be found. In fact, his men on the ramparts appeared to be routed, as more and more of the horde ascended the walls.

"We're doomed," he muttered absently. "It's all my fault."

"Take the king inside the keep and bar the door!" Thames ordered the remaining royal guardsmen. Then, without his king's approval, he charged into the fray.

Elbert clutched his dagger tightly as his guards ushered him inside the keep. His mind was racing. All he could do was picture his grisly end at the hand of Uthredd's warriors.

He wondered how they would do it. Decapitation? Drawn and quartered? Something so barbaric that he couldn't even imagine it? He had never been one to fear death, but now, when it was right in front of his face, it terrified him.

The guards began barring the door of the keep as Elbert started pushing himself to the mead hall, hoping to find a drink. His hands were shaking uncontrollably as the muffled sounds of fighting echoed off the keep's walls. Finally, after a quick search, he found a flagon of ale and greedily gulped it down.

"Look!" Sara shouted from across the mead hall.

Elbert had forgotten about the girl, and the sound of an unexpected voice nearly made him jump out of his chair. He turned his head, and saw that she was standing on a windowsill looking out into the courtyard, where the bloodbath was happening.

"Get away from the window!" Elbert shouted, as he hastily pushed his chair across the room to rescue the girl. The metal wheels of his throne glided across the smooth marble floor. His arms burned as he forced his chair to go faster and faster. After what seemed like a lifetime of pushing, he finally reached the window and threw the girl from the sill. After making sure she was okay, he mustered the courage to look into the courtyard.

Elbert's eyes widened at what he saw. There was Grimm, standing on the shoulder of the giant, axe in hand, hacking away at the beast's neck.

Blood surged from the giant's neck and covered the men fighting below in a thick coat of crimson. The monstrous goliath let out a guttural roar of pain before he finally collapsed to his knees, crushing a dozen men beneath his humongous frame.

That is a hero, Elbert thought to himself. *That's what I should be, not cowering in here like a child.* He turned to look at Sara, who had found another window to look out of, training sword held firmly in her diminutive hand. *Even the girl has more courage than me.*

"Your Majesty," a voice called out from behind him.

The king visibly jumped at the sudden noise. It felt like his heart was going to leap out of his chest. The sight of so much death and gore unnerved him. He wasn't sure which was worse, seeing the battle first hand, or witnessing the aftermath. He spun his chair around and saw Lord Arlin holding a small crossbow in his hand.

"What is it, Arlin?" Elbert asked, hoping the dwarf didn't see how frightened he was.

"How's it lookin'?" Arlin asked sheepishly.

A wave of relief crashed over the king as he realized the dwarf was just as scared as he was. Although it did not befit a king to show cowardice so openly, he had to admit that it felt nice to not feel so alone. "It's not looking good," Elbert replied solemnly. "I think we'll be lucky if we see the sunrise."

"Grimm will stop them," Sara whispered as she continued to stare out of the window.

"Care to join me for a drink?" Elbert asked as he motioned for the dwarf to sit down at the table. "Might as well enjoy it while we can."

Arlin nodded his head, set his crossbow down on the table, and sat across from Elbert, and poured the two of them a couple of mugs of ale. An awkward silence filled the air between them. Each man sipped his drink as they listened to the slaughter outside the keep's walls.

Finally, unable to bear the sounds of men dying any more, Elbert spoke. "I'm sorry for bringing you along with me, Arlin. You probably curse the day you made me this chair."

The artificer scoffed politely as he took a swig from his mug. "I'd do it again, Your Majesty."

"No, honestly. We are most likely going to die tonight, and for once, I'd like someone to be honest with me."

"In that case," Arlin began. "I hate this, and I hate what you've asked me to do. I became a craftsman to help people and to make life easier, not create weapons capable of death and destruction."

"Then why did you agree?"

"You're jokin', right? You're the king. I can't refuse your orders, even if you hadn't made me a lord. I am indebted to you."

"Well, if we make it out of this alive, consider your debt paid in full. When we get back to Artanzia, you will never have to make another instrument of war."

Arlin let out a small laugh. "The key word is *if* we make it out alive."

Elbert smiled as he took a drink from his mug. "My brother should've been king, not me. He would never've led our men into this mess. The people loved him, the nobility adored him, and he was always my father's favourite. He was the king Artanzia deserved."

"A shame that he fell from the ramparts," Arlin concluded.

Elbert's heart sank. The muscles in his chest tightened, and his throat became dry. He had never felt the need to confess to his brother's murder, except to prove Grimm wrong during their heated argument. But he figured that since he was going to die, he might as well unburden himself.

"Arlin, can I confess some–" Before he could finish his sentence, there was a sudden thud against the doors of the keep.

The three of them quickly exited the mead hall and found the retinue of royal guards standing ready, facing the door. Before Elbert could ask what was going on, there was another loud thud against the door. And another. And another.

Dust fell from the rafters with each successive ram. The sound of wood splintering filled the air. Elbert's heart quickened as he waited for Uthredd's forces to breach the keep's doors.

After a few agonizing minutes, the doors burst open, and a torrent of bloodthirsty Islanders descended on the royal guards. To Elbert's surprise, the guards held the line, but with each passing second, they lost ground. A small lake of blood stained the painting on the floor of the keep. Men were slipping as they conceded more and more ground to the horde of Islanders.

Elbert heard the thwack of Arlin's crossbow as he shot into the mass of bodies in the doorway. The bolt was a blur as it crossed his vision, but he saw that the dwarf had struck one of the savages in the chest.

His stomach sank at the sight of such wanton death. Although he was utterly terrified of the sight, he couldn't look away from the macabre scene. Limbs were being severed, innards were being spilt on to the ground, and the screams of death cut through the sounds of fighting.

He turned his head and noticed that Sara's training sword was lying on the ground, and the girl was nowhere to be found. A sudden wave of relief coursed through his body.

He clutched his dagger tightly, turned his attention back to the battle, and realized that some Islanders had broken through the royal guardsmen's ranks. What was worse was that he locked eyes with a blood-soaked shieldmaiden, who was eyeing him the same way a wolf eyes its prey.

Elbert threw his dagger at the woman, but she effortlessly swatted it out of the air with her axe. He grabbed the wheels of his throne and tried to make a hasty escape, but before he could turn around, she was upon him.

She slammed her shoulder into the side of his chair, knocking him to the floor. Elbert frantically began crawling back into the mead hall, desperately hoping he could find a weapon on the floor. He heard the nonchalant footsteps of the shieldmaiden as she stalked him.

"Where're ya going?" she asked mockingly.

The king looked over his shoulder and saw that the woman was smiling fiendishly as she embedded her axe in the long dining table. She took out a small paring knife from her belt and twirled it in her hands.

"King's blood will make a great sacrifice for the gods. Not to mention that Uthredd will probably make me a jarl for killing you."

Elbert's heart felt like it was going to burst through his chest. He tried to breathe, but he couldn't. All he could do was make a horrible wheezing sound as he gasped helplessly for breath. His vision blurred as the shieldmaiden closed the distance between them.

Just as he was about to pass out, he felt warm, sticky liquid cover his face. He opened his eyes and saw that the tip of a spear was protruding from the shieldmaiden's mouth.

Elbert let out a pained breath. He started shaking violently as he watched the woman's corpse fall to the ground. But standing behind her was not one of his men, but an Islander berserker. The man had malicious intent in his eyes.

"I've never fucked a king before," he said, as he unbuckled his trousers.

Suddenly, the panic that had left Elbert's body returned tenfold. He flopped back on to his stomach and crawled away again. Tears were streaming down his face as he realized how helpless he truly was. He felt the warrior's meaty hands grab his waist as he pulled the king's trousers down to his ankles.

"No! Please don't!" Elbert pleaded.

"I like it when they beg." The sound of the berserker's voice covered Elbert's body with goosebumps.

The warrior's hands pushed his body flat against the floor, and he felt the man's warm breath on the nape of his neck. When he felt the warmth of the berserker's body approach his bare ass, he wept and began to hyperventilate.

His ears were ringing, and the rest of the world faded away. The fighting, the war, even the coldness of the mead hall's floor. It was as if he was suspended in a blank void.

Suddenly, something brought him back to reality. He opened his eyes and saw the blood-stained face of Thames looking back at him. Elbert looked past the guard and saw the cockless, mutilated body of his assailant lying dead, next to the skewered shieldmaiden.

"I'm so sorry, Elbert. I've failed you," Thames said as he pulled the king into a tight embrace. His voice wavered with every word.

"What... what happened?" Elbert asked, not sure what was real and what wasn't.

"We won, but at a terrible cost."

CHAPTER THIRTY

ANNA

G reaver's death sent shock waves throughout the city. Everyone had heard about the King of Crooks' demise. They had also heard about the man responsible for the king's grisly end.

Randall had gained such notoriety that even the city guards no longer stopped him for questioning. Almost overnight, he earned an army of followers who immediately revered him as their new king.

But all this attention had a downside. There were whispers that the Blackguard knew his face and were actively looking for him. There were also those who openly defied his rule, but they never seemed to last long, with most of Randall's opposition mysteriously disappearing in the middle of the night.

Anna was perusing Winterhelm's market with Maeve, while Randall was busy back at the Garden. He had grown distant since he came to power, choosing to spend most of his time with Cassius rather than her. Her mind told her it was natural to pull back when he had an entire criminal empire to run, but her gut told her it was something more.

The fact that he enjoyed the eunuch's company over hers was the biggest warning sign. When they first met, Randall couldn't stand the sommelier and didn't trust him in the slightest, but now the two were inseparable. Cassius had become Randall's "royal advisor", and was dubbed a member of the Maggots, although nobody except Randall considered him as such.

"Isn't this lovely?" Maeve squealed, as she showed Anna a small silver brooch that she had lifted from a vendor.

Anna nodded her head politely and kept walking. Although Maeve was not healthy enough to pull jobs, it was nice to see that she could finally walk again. It seemed like she had been stuck in Stitch's bed for a lifetime.

"What's the matter?" Maeve asked, while placing a comforting hand on Anna's shoulder.

"It's Randall," Anna sighed. "I'm worried about him. I hardly get to see him any more. Ever since he took Greaver's crown, all he does is spend his days with Cassius in that damned throne room."

Maeve smiled. "Try not to worry. I'm sure being the new King of Crooks is a very taxing job."

"Hmph," Anna snorted as she scanned the marketplace for something valuable to steal.

"Besides, if he's the new king, that would make you the queen."

Anna stopped dead in her tracks. She hadn't thought about it like that before. The idea of ruling over Winterhelm's criminals terrified her. She saw how much power Greaver had, and she wanted no part of it.

From what she could tell, being in power had only one benefit and countless drawbacks. People constantly doubted you, you had to sleep with one eye open, unless you wanted to end up like Greaver, and you could never tell if your friends were truly your friends.

She wanted no part of that life. All she wanted was to live out the rest of her days with Randall in the wilderness. She could hunt and provide for them, and they would be far from the plotting and scheming that came with life in the city.

As the two girls continued to walk through the market, an entourage of black enamelled guards marched into the square. Anna quickly looked over towards Maeve, and saw the girl's face had gone pale. Her body was as stiff as a board, sweat covered her brow, and her eyes were as wide as saucers. The brooch that she had been admiring fell from her trembling hands.

The black armoured guards fanned out across the market. It looked like they were searching for someone. Suddenly, the ugliest man Anna had ever seen began approaching them, with a sinister sneer plastered across his face. He was seven feet tall and wore black plate armour, but without an accompanying helmet. He had a maul slung across his back. It looked like someone had skinned the right side of his face. There was a large hole in his right cheek where you could see the inside of the man's mouth. His head was devoid of any hair, save for his sweat-drenched brown moustache.

The man lumbered towards the two girls, then bent down to pick up the brooch. He gently placed the trinket in Maeve's shaking hands and folded her fingers over the top of it. Then he slowly rose to his feet, his sneer turning into a malicious smile, and looked directly into the girl's terrified eyes.

"You dropped this," he said in a gravelly baritone voice.

"T-t-th-tha–" Maeve stammered.

"What's the matter, girl? Cat got your tongue?" The man bent down once again, his face mere inches away from Maeve's. "What happened to your pretty little face?"

"She fell," Anna blurted out.

The man turned his head and examined Anna from head to toe. The longer his eyes lingered on her body, the more it made her skin crawl. *This must be the man that beat Maeve half to death,* Anna thought to herself, as she glared back at the man.

After a thorough examination, the man stood upright again and muttered, "Clumsy girl."

Suddenly, as if hearing something, his eyes snapped to his right, and he began scanning the crowd in the marketplace. After several seconds of searching, he wiped his sweaty moustache and turned his attention back towards the girls.

Anna noticed that the rest of the black armoured guardsmen began converging on their position. She instinctively reached for her knife, but stopped herself halfway. She took a moment to take a side-eyed glance at Maeve, who had not moved an inch since first seeing the guardsmen.

"We're looking for someone," the man explained. "Perhaps two fine ladies such as yourself have seen him."

"What's in it for us?" Anna interrupted, trying to throw off the scarred man's rhythm.

"Resourceful lil' tart," the man commented.

Before Anna could snap back another retort, two helmed guardsmen emerged from the crowd, dragging a flailing boy in their arms. Her heart sank when she realized that it was Chuckles, a pearl necklace clutched tightly in his hands.

"We found him, sir!" one guard reported.

The scarred man smiled, pulled out a small knife from his belt, and held it to Chuckles' throat. "Reginald Linus, it seems you've run out of hiding places."

"Fuck you," Chuckles responded.

"Any last words?"

"Go plough your mother!"

The scarred man sheathed his knife, grabbed Chuckles by the scruff of the neck, and dragged him towards the fountain in the centre of the marketplace. Then, with a violent shove, he forced the boy down on his hands and knees in front of the stone steps of the fountain.

"Bite down."

"Wha-what?"

Forcefully, he grabbed the back of Chuckles' head and pushed it down, setting his top row of teeth against the stone slab. Before anyone could react, the scarred man lifted his plate armour boot and stomped down on the boy's neck. A deafening crunch rang in Anna's ears, as she muffled the scream that escaped her lips with her hands.

A palpable silence hung in the air of the market as the crowd stared at the scarred man, who was grinning from ear to ear. The man in the black armour climbed the steps of the fountain and cleared his throat. "By the power of Her Royal Majesty, Queen Vivian, I, Mortimer Black, declare that all crimes, no matter the severity, are punishable by death."

There was a murmur of discontent amongst the crowd, but it quickly died down after a threatening stare from the man who stood atop the fountain.

Anna fought against the swelling tears behind her eyes, as she knew she couldn't reveal the fact that she knew Chuckles. Who knew what this man would do if he thought they were connected in some way? Her hand itched to grab the handle of her knife, and it took all of her willpower not to act out that impulse.

She counted the steps between her and the fountain, then measured the distance between Black's guards and him. She took a step forward, when she felt a soft hand grip her wrist. She turned around to see Maeve's bruised, tearful face staring back at her.

"Don't," Maeve mouthed.

Anna's head snapped back towards Mortimer Black and sneered in disgust. She would make him pay; both for beating Maeve, and for Chuckles' grisly murder.

Mortimer Black climbed down the steps of the fountain and walked back towards the girls. He did a slight bow before them, and the rest of the Blackguard exited the square.

Everyone in the market crowded around Chuckles' dead body and gaped at the sight that now plagued their marketplace. They began whispering amongst themselves, many people expressing anger and disgust at the Blackguards' impromptu execution.

Anna stepped forward, grabbed one of Chuckles' limp arms, lifted it over her shoulder, then began to drag his body out of the market, with a silent Maeve sulking slowly behind.

The walk back to the Garden was quiet and awkward. People stared at the two teenage girls carrying a corpse through the snow-covered streets. Anna's anger grew as she glared back at the people with shocked expressions glued to their faces.

She replayed the execution repeatedly, until her stomach no longer felt queasy, as the crunch of the boy's spine echoed in her mind. *I will kill him slowly for this. I'll gut him like a deer,* Anna vowed to herself as she continued to haul the corpse of Chuckles towards the Garden.

"He didn't even recognize me," Maeve said absentmindedly. "He almost killed me, and he didn't even recognize me."

"Probably for the best," Anna replied through gritted teeth. Chuckles was the one who had been horrifically murdered, and Maeve had the gall to make this about her? She caught herself wishing that it was Maeve had died instead of Chuckles, but she quickly shook the thought out of her head. *No. It's Mortimer Black that I'm angry with, not Maeve,* Anna reminded herself.

"This is going to devastate Randall," Maeve continued.

That made Anna stop in her tracks. She hadn't even thought about how Randall was going to take the news. He loved each of the Maggots like they were siblings, and now Anna would have to be the one to tell him that one of his brothers had been murdered. By the most fearsome mercenary, no less.

Dread slowly crept up into her throat as she thought about how Randall would react. Would he take his anger out on her? Would he collapse into a sobbing mess? Or would the death of someone close to him drive him back into her arms? She secretly hoped that it was the third. If there was going to be any silver lining from this, she prayed that it would bring the two of them closer together.

When they arrived at the Garden, they found the courtyard was mostly empty. Anna let out a breath that she didn't know she had been holding in. She was glad that it wasn't crowded. She couldn't stand the idea of more people gawking at Chuckles' remains. He deserved better than that.

The people who were in the courtyard paid little attention to the two girls and the corpse. There were some sideways glances, but nobody openly stared, as the commoners had on their journey from the market to the Garden.

Anna groaned as she set Chuckles down in front of Randall's empty throne. She turned her head and saw the red, puffy eyes of Maeve staring back at her. She clenched her fist in annoyance. Why did she have to think of everything?

"Fetch the undertaker," Anna instructed, trying to hide the irritation in her voice.

Maeve silently nodded her head and exited the throne room. Anna could hear muffled voices coming from the dining hall. The place where they took Greaver's life.

She hadn't set foot in there since it happened. She was far too busy to enjoy things like leisurely dining. Randall, on the other hand, presumably had all the time in the world, as he spent most of his time in the room where he had murdered two prominent figureheads of the criminal underworld.

Anna pushed open the door to the room, and saw Randall and Cassius hunched over the large table, pointing at things on a city map. She cleared her throat to get their attention. Cassius' head was the first to rise.

"Ah, Anna! How did things go in the market?" he asked in a playful voice.

"Chuckles is dead."

The eunuch's face sank, and his stare shifted towards Randall, whose gaze still had not lifted from the map. "How unfortunate," Cassius replied. "May I inquire how it happened?"

Anna marched over, grabbed Randall by the shoulder, and spun him around until he faced her. What she saw made her take an involuntary step backwards. His face was gaunt and was a sickly pale colour. He had deep purple bags under his eyes, and he stared off absently into the distance. Suddenly, life came back to his face, as his eyes locked on to Anna's.

"Anna, when did you get here?"

"Gods, Randall, what happened to you?"

"His Majesty works tirelessly to ensure the betterment of his people," Cassius interjected.

"When was the last time you ate something?" Anna asked, ignoring the eunuch's remark.

"I'm fine," Randall said, turning his attention back towards the map. "I just need to figure things out."

"Figure what out?" Randall didn't offer a response. Instead, he just stared blankly at the map that was sprawled out on the table. "Chuckles is dead, Randall! Don't you give a shit?"

Randall slammed his fist on the table and began massaging his temples, as he continued to stare at the map. Impulsively, Anna slapped the king across the face.

The reverberation of the audible smack filled the room, followed by a long, awkward silence. Randall slowly craned his head until his eyes met Anna's. She gulped nervously when she saw that behind his stare was the fiery glint of rage.

"Leave us," Randall ordered, his voice firm with regality.

"If I may, Your Majesty -" Cassius began.

"Leave!"

Meekly, the eunuch gave a flawless bow and shuffled out of the dining room, leaving the two lovers alone, glaring at one another.

"Have you lost your mind?" Randall started.

"Have you?" Anna retorted. "I tell you that Chuckles was murdered, and all you care about is that stupid fucking map!"

Randall took a step closer and extended his arm towards her, but she quickly took a step backwards, so that she was out of reach. The last thing she wanted was for him to touch her.

"What would you have me do? Track down Mortimer Black, bring him to the Garden, and execute him for all to see? Chuckles knew the risk of getting caught, as we all do."

Her lips curled into a sneer. She could hear Cassius' venom through his words. Right before she was about to snap another fiery retort, she stopped herself, as something dawned on her. She had never told him how Chuckles died, nor had she told him who did it.

"You knew."

"I was always amazed at how Greaver seemed to know everything the minute it happened, and thanks to his complex network of spies, now I do, too."

"Did you even shed a tear? Did you give a single shred of a fuck about him? He was like a brother to you!"

Randall slammed his fist on the table again. "Don't tell me how close I was to Chuckles: I loved him. But there will be time to mourn once I solve the current predicament we find ourselves in."

"What predicament?"

"The nobles," Randall hissed. "They poison this city the same way a carcass poisons a watering hole. They divide us and keep us fighting over the scraps, while they live in decadence and luxury. You saw how the Rawleys lived, and they weren't even nobles. It's time we end their reign of terror."

"You plan to go to war with the nobility? How do you plan to fight King Elbert's army, as well as the Blackguard? There are too many of them!"

"If I can unite the people, all the people, then we will have an advantage. When we are divided, we are weak; but together, we can claim this kingdom as our own."

Anna shook her head free of Randall's delusions. "Well, while you waste away in this shithole, I'm going to go and bury our friend!" Then, without waiting for a response, she stormed out of the dining hall and out of the Garden.

Brooding in her anger, she marched around the city, trying to blow off some steam. She couldn't believe Randall had been so callous about Chuckles' death. But she did only see him after he had already found out about it.

Perhaps he had crumbled when he first heard the news? Or maybe he was bottling it up, until he was by himself? After all, it's not very kingly to cry in front of one's subjects. Anna quickly shook the thought out of her head. *Don't forgive him. You saw him. He's too busy with his war against the nobles to even give a shit.*

She continued to walk through the streets until she came to a corner where a crowd of people had gathered around a man standing on a box. The man was old and wrinkled. He was wearing clean white robes that had red stitching along the seams. Anna recognized him as a clergyman, but to which god she could not say for certain.

"... and sinners beware!" the old man squawked. "For the time of reckoning has begun!"

She listened passively to the priest's sermon, but she was more focused on the mass of peasants who were clearly hanging on to the man's every word.

Suddenly, an idea came into her head. This was how Randall could get the populace on his side; by using the priests to sow discontent against the nobility, instead of peddling the gods-fearing hogwash they had spewed for centuries.

Anna waited until the sermon was over and approached the old man, once enough of the crowd had dispersed. "Lovely speech."

"Eh?" the old man said, his eyes widening once he saw Anna's body. "Well, aren't you a pretty young thing!"

"These people respect you, so I want you to tell them that the nobles are the source of all their misery, not the gods."

A devilish smile crept along the priest's face. "I could be persuaded to do such a thing, but first: let's talk about my reward."

The old man slowly extended his hand towards Anna's breast, but before he could reach it, she grabbed her dagger and held the blade to the clergyman's throat. In an instant, the man's smile disappeared.

"Your reward is keeping your miserable, shit-eating life. Imagine what the King of Crooks would say if he heard that you touched his queen?" Calling herself the queen of anything made her skin crawl, but she had a point to prove. "Do we have a deal?"

"Y... yes!" the old man stammered as he slowly backed away from the blade held to his throat. "Anything for the king!" he remarked, before quickly shuffling down a side alley.

Anna watched the priest scamper away, and smiled. If this is what it took for her to get the old Randall back, then she would do it: she would do anything for him. His war against the nobles had just begun.

CHAPTER THIRTY-ONE

ELBERT

Tjørholm's bailey looked like the floor of an abattoir. Blood, guts, and limbs covered the ground. Corpses of Artanzians and Islanders alike were strewn around the courtyard, tangled into a mess of mutilated bodies.

Severed arms and legs blocked Elbert's throne wheels from turning, which resulted in him having to be carried through the carnage. Elbert felt his stomach churn as he stared absently at the sea of bodies. When he looked at the cold, expressionless faces of his fallen countrymen, he couldn't help but feel responsible for their deaths. But when he stared at the faces of the fallen Islanders, all he could see was the smiling face of his assailant from the night before. He could still hear the joy in the Islander's voice as his pants were pulled down below his ankles.

Elbert lurched forward in his chair and vomited, covering two of the guards who were carrying him. He felt the bile burn his throat as it surged out of his stomach with every painful retch. The pressure behind his eyes made it feel like his head was going to explode. Tears formed at the corners of his eyes, and he shook uncontrollably as he tried to stop the heaving.

"Take His Majesty back to the keep. I'll assemble the remaining lords and bring them to him," Thames ordered.

"No!" Elbert shouted as he wiped the puke from his lips with the sleeve of his shirt. "I need to see my men."

Thames' brow furrowed with apprehension, but he ultimately nodded his head and continued to lead the royal guardsmen through the bailey.

The courtyard painted a tapestry of violence that told the story of the first battle. The further away from the keep that Elbert journeyed, the more dead Islanders he saw.

Thames had told him that the key to their victory was that the Islanders thinned themselves out too much, which allowed the Artanzians to encircle them and prevent them from retreating. However, even though the mainlanders held the strategic upper hand, they still lost countless soldiers to the barbarian horde.

Elbert's eyes continued to survey the macabre scene, trying to find a silver lining, a small glimmer of hope that would somehow justify the slaughter. He did not find one. All he could see were corpses, soon-to-be corpses, and men with mile-long stares.

Suddenly, he heard a blade piercing flesh, and a chill ran down his spine. He turned his head and saw that Grimm was walking around with a sword and dagger in his hands. Curious about what he was doing, Elbert watched intently.

Grimm roamed through the carnage until he found an almost dead Islander breathing his last breaths. He knelt down beside the dying barbarian, placed the dagger in his hands, and then slit his throat with the sword. He did this several times before Elbert finally realized what he was doing. *That bastard is making sure that these men die like warriors so that they can meet their savage god.*

Rage filled Elbert's body, and he slammed his fist on one of the armrests of his throne. "What the fuck do you think you're doing!" he shouted, as he pointed an accusatory finger at Grimm.

The white-eyed warrior paid the king no mind as he continued his search for near-dead Islanders. It wasn't until Thames grabbed him on the shoulder that he finally stopped. Grimm glared back angrily at Elbert. "These men fought well. They deserve to go to The Great Hall and dine with Heimer for eternity."

"They're nothing but barbaric savages who deserve nothing less than to rot beneath the sun."

Grimm pushed Thames aside and marched towards the king. The retinue of royal guards quickly drew their blades and blocked the Islander's path. Grimm stared at the men for several seconds before ultimately turning his attention back to Elbert. "Mind your tongue, Legless. If it wasn't for this barbaric savage, this courtyard would be filled with the flayed bodies of your men."

"Listen to me carefully, Islander," Elbert said, his voice shaking with anger. "You will not send any more of these goat-fucking barbarians to meet your backwards god. I forbid it."

"Fuck you," Grimm snarled.

"How dare you speak to your king in such a manner!" Thames shouted as he pulled his blade out of its scabbard. "Your Majesty, please allow me the honour of cutting out the knave's tongue."

Grimm twirled his sword in response and turned to face the scarred captain. "You're welcome to try."

"Enough!" Elbert shouted. "Grimm, I want a full report of how many men are left under your command, and I want it now."

Grimm shifted his attention once again and glared at the crippled king. Their eyes locked on each other. Stares full of anger and contempt. Grimm spat towards the king before walking off to gather his men.

Thames gave a pleading look towards his king. Elbert noticed that his hand was gripping his sword tightly. He shook his head, and Rupert begrudgingly sheathed his sword.

After a few more minutes of walking through the aftermath of the battle, Elbert found a blood-covered Lord Grelin, leaning up against one of the city's walls, tending to his wounds. The king was surprised to see that the man had survived the Islanders' onslaught.

However, he was pleased to be proven wrong. Once Grelin caught sight of the king and his entourage of guards, he quickly rose to his feet and saluted. Elbert smiled and gestured for him to relax once again.

"Lord Grelin, I'm glad to see that the Islanders didn't manage to cut you down."

"As am I, Your Majesty."

"How did your men fare today?"

Grelin's face paled slightly, and he scratched the back of his neck. "The Bastard Company took the brunt of the force, but once the gate was breached, we were forced to make our stand in the bailey. The Islanders quickly surrounded us and that... that *thing*." Grelin's voice shook as he pointed to the corpse of the giant lying in the middle of the courtyard. "It crushed my men as if they were bugs. Like we were nothing more than a swarm of ants."

"How many are left?" Elbert pressed.

"Just over half, Your Majesty," Lord Grelin replied meekly.

Elbert visibly winced at the news. This was not good. They had sustained too many casualties for their first encounter with the Islanders. If Uthredd launched two more attacks just like this one, then they would all be corpses. He just prayed that the High King of the Isles didn't know that.

"Yer Majesty!" a soldier called out from atop the battlements. Elbert turned his head and looked at the man. "Two riders approach!"

"To arms!" Captain Thames shouted. The remaining Artanzians lazily scrambled for their weapons, when Elbert raised a steadying hand.

"If it is just two riders, then I will meet them on the field."

"Your Majesty, you can't be serious," Thames warned. "What if this is some sort of ploy to get you out in the open?"

"It's not," Grimm interjected, as he descended from the battlements.

Elbert curled his hand into a fist. He had no idea how the man moved about the stronghold so quickly. It seemed like mere seconds before, he was standing in the courtyard, and now the Islander had somehow found his way atop the ramparts.

"I thought I ordered you to give me a full head count of your company," he growled.

"I'm no good with numbers, but fear not: I have my smartest man on it." Grimm's voice was rich with sarcasm.

Elbert was tempted to order his execution, but he knew that if the Bastards lost their commander they would surely revolt, which was something he couldn't afford.

"How are you so sure that this isn't a ruse?" Thames asked accusatorily.

"Because one of the riders is Uthredd himself, riding towards us."

"Why would he expose himself like that?" Thames asked.

"Because he knows he will not die. His seer must not have seen his death."

"What in the gods are you blabbering on about?" Elbert snapped.

"Uthredd has always revered the gods. Before every battle, he consults his seer to see if they favour him. I know this man. If he thought there was any chance of him dying dishonourably, he would not have shown himself like this."

"Your Majesty," Thames pleaded. "I beg of you, let us send this heathen to meet his god now. Without him, the islanders will crumble, and we can go back home victorious."

Elbert sat and weighed Rupert's words carefully. After some deliberation, he shook his head. "No."

"Sire –"

"I'll hear no more of this!" Elbert said with a wave of his hand. "If the islander king wants to meet, then he shall have his meeting. Men, we march!"

Elbert, Thames, Grimm, and an entire entourage of royal guards soon marched out of Tjørholm's broken gates, towards the Islander king standing in the middle of the snowy plains. The sun was just rising over the horizon, blanketing the sky in its orange glow, when they met in the middle of the field that separated the two armies.

"It seems I'm outnumbered," the islander king remarked jovially.

Despite being a king of barbarians, Elbert found that Uthredd's appearance was quite regal. He was well-groomed for an Islander, and his long red hair was neatly braided into a single plait, which ran down the middle of his back. His muscles bulged from beneath his furs, and his calloused hands rested on the pommel of a large greataxe.

When Elbert looked into the man's piercing blue eyes, he did not see malice or hate. Instead, he saw what looked like curiosity and respect. The man to the left of Uthredd was covered in tattoos. He had a greying beard, and a large battleaxe strapped across his back. While Uthredd's eyes bounced from person to person, this man's stare did not leave Grimm's face.

"So it's true what they say. I've been invaded by a king who can't stand on his own two feet," Uthredd continued.

Elbert swallowed his anger at the remark. He would not allow this islander to get under his skin as easily as Grimm did. Instead, he forced himself to smile politely. "High King Uthredd, it is a pleasure to finally make your acquaintance."

Uthredd smiled, which showcased his glimmering white teeth. "A funny way to acquaint yourself with someone, isn't it? By stealing from them."

"Like how you steal from my farmers?" Elbert retorted.

"Ha!" Uthredd guffawed. "A quick mind and a sharp tongue on you. Under different circumstances, I fear we might've been friends."

Elbert's gut churned at the mention of being friends with a bloodthirsty, pillaging savage. "What do you want?"

Uthredd's smile disappeared, and a grave expression soon covered his face. "I've come to ask for a favour. I would ask that you allow me to collect my fallen so that they can receive the proper funeral rites."

This time Elbert laughed. "Why would I allow such a thing?"

"Dead spread disease," Uthredd replied. "All me and my army have to do is wait till the dead rot and a plague ravages through Tjørholm. If you grant my request, then we will take our dead away from your walls and stop the sickness before it starts."

"And I'm supposed to just trust you?" Elbert asked skeptically.

"Even though your men don't believe in Heimer, they should not be denied entrance to The Great Hall because of that. I wish that all of your men die honourably, with a sword in hand, so that they can know true bliss in the afterlife. Perhaps I will have the honour to drink with them and hear their tales before this war is done."

"You always were a fanatic," Grimm interrupted.

"So, this is how you've eluded capture? By betraying your kin and allying yourself with the enemy?" the bald-headed man finally spoke. His voice was rough with anger.

"My kin betrayed me first, Bearn."

"What did you want me to do? He was my brother! I couldn't just execute him," Uthredd interjected.

"I was your brother!" Grimm shouted, his voice shaking as he stepped forward. "How many times did you dine with Freja and me? You were the one who taught Einar how to shoot a bow! They were as much your family as that miserable sack of shit –"

"Watch your tongue, White-Eyes," Uthredd snarled. "Don't you speak ill of my brother, lest you want this parlay to turn into a bloodbath."

"Don't hurt him!" a high-pitched voice called out.

Elbert turned to see a frightened Sara pushing her way through his retinue of guards, wooden sword in hand. "Don't you dare hurt Grimm!"

"And who is this little shieldmaiden?" Uthredd said, his smile returning to his face.

"I see ya still have that stray," Bearn commented.

Grimm's attention shifted away from the king and his former friend towards the dwarven girl. "Sara, what are you doing here?"

"I've come to help," Sara answered proudly.

"Go back to the keep."

Elbert silently waved his hand, and Thames stepped forward to gently usher the girl back towards the stronghold. Elbert grabbed hold of her wrist as she passed by. "Don't worry, I won't let anything happen to him," he whispered. Sara smiled as Thames continued to escort her back to Tjørholm.

"She reminds me of Freja when she was young," Uthredd remarked.

Grimm's head snapped back towards the king, and his blade quickly hissed out of its scabbard. "Don't you dare say her fucking name!"

"Grimm!" Elbert shouted. "I order you to leave."

"Legless, this might be hard for you to understand, but –"

"I said leave!"

A trio of royal guards stepped forward, and one even dared to set his hand on the islander's shoulder. Grimm glared at both kings before reluctantly sheathing his sword and walking back towards the fortress.

"A word of advice," Uthredd said, breaking the silence that had filled the air. "Watch that one closely. He'll stab you in the back, the minute he thinks he can make his escape."

"I appreciate that, and as for your request, I will allow your men to retrieve their dead, provided that they come unarmed."

"Excellent. I must say I am rather impressed you mainlanders held out as long as you did. But you must know it won't last much longer."

Fear began to set in as Elbert realized the truth in the islander king's words. He felt a bead of sweat trickle down his spine as he stared deeply into Uthredd's unmoving eyes.

His men had barely survived the first assault, and he didn't want to imagine what would happen if the islander horde broke through a second time. A lump formed in his throat as he began to vividly recall his encounter with the islander warrior in the hall.

"I have another fifty ships sailing from Artanzia as we speak," Elbert lied, trying to mask the fear he felt as best he could. "They will moor on your beaches in a week's time, and your army will be surrounded. So let me offer you some of my own kingly advice. If you want Tjørholm back, I wouldn't waste your time on the dead."

Uthredd nodded his head, mounted his horse, and rode back to his army without uttering another word. Elbert gestured for one of the guards to come forward. "If it looks like Tjørholm will fall, and that all is lost, I want you and your men to burn that fortress to the ground. Am I understood?"

"Yes, Your Majesty."

CHAPTER THIRTY-TWO

GRIMM

The walk back to the fortress was filled with silence and anger. Grimm bit his bottom lip in frustration as Uthredd's words echoed in his mind. *How dare he utter Freja's name,* he fumed to himself. *How dare he defend that cretin of a brother! I should've taken his head right there and then.* As he continued his long walk, his anger shifted from one king to the other. *That legless fuck. I never should have shown such weakness in front of them. I'm not just some dog he can order around. I am Grimm fucking White-Eyes!*

Once he reached Tjørholm's walls, he was greeted by a smiling Thames. The captain was sharpening his sword on a whetstone when the Islander crossed through the broken threshold. The sight of Thames' teeth made Grimm curl his fist in anger.

"I take it you didn't behave yourself?" the captain said mockingly.

"Fuck off," Grimm snapped back as he stormed past the scarred man.

"She's in the keep with Master Arlin, if you're looking for her," Thames replied, seemingly unperturbed by the Islander's insult.

Grimm said nothing in response, but continued marching towards the keep. He would have to check in on Sara and make sure that she never left the confines of the stronghold ever again. If she fell into Uthredd's grasp... He shook the idea out of his head. *That'll never happen,* he reassured himself as he quickened his pace.

The entryway of the keep looked like a lake of blood that was filled with corpses. The sight didn't bother Grimm in the slightest. He had certainly seen worse sights. But his mind drifted towards Sara. How would she react after seeing so much death and destruction? He knew it was likely that she saw her fair share of pain and suffering as a slave, but he would be shocked if she had seen anything of this magnitude.

He heard Sara's small, high-pitched voice coming from the mead hall. Grimm entered the room and was slightly relieved that there were no corpses in there, although the bloodstains still remained.

Arlin and Sara were sitting across from each other, each staring intently into the other's eyes. The craftsman would say a word in a deep, throaty language, and Sara would repeat it. Grimm cocked his head to the side, and he immediately grew suspicious. He cleared his throat loudly, and both of the dwarves' heads snapped to him.

"Grimm!" Sara squealed as she leapt out of her chair and hugged him tightly. For a moment, Grimm felt the tension and stress leave his body. But when Arlin rose to his feet, it surged through him once again.

"How go the negotiations?" Arlin asked meekly.

"About as well as our siege," Grimm replied.

"I was just teaching Sara the language of her ancestors."

"Did you know that there was once a whole city of dwarves?" Sara asked excitedly.

"No, I didn't," Grimm said, a slight smile coming to his lips. "Perhaps we can go and visit it sometime."

Sara's face slackened. "Lord Arlin says that nobody knows where it is and that it is lost to the canals of time."

"*Annals* of time," Arlin corrected.

Grimm shot a quick yet fiery glare at the craftsman before turning his attention to the girl. He bent down so that they were at eye level, and placed a hand on her shoulder. "I'm sure we can find it; we just have to leave the Isles first."

"Elbert says he'll sail us back to the mainland and that –"

"Don't listen to a word that comes out of that liar's mouth," Grimm growled, the grip of his hand tightening around Sara's shoulder. "Kings can't be trusted; they only look out for themselves."

"If I may, Master Grimm," Arlin interjected. "I believe His Majesty is cut from a different cloth than the rest. He had no reason to, but he made me a lord."

Grimm's eyes grew cold as they locked on to the dwarven craftsman. "He needed your loyalty, so he gave you a meaningless title and a bit of gold, and now you're a collared dog, like the rest of them."

Arlin's brow furrowed. "I would not say that so loudly, unless you want some of the more rabid dogs to hear."

Grimm rose to his feet. He stepped forward and loomed over the dwarf, who immediately cowered under the Islander's shadow. "Let them hear," he replied menacingly, before turning to grab Sara's hand and lead her out of the keep.

He led Sara hastily back towards the Bastards' camp, trying to avoid the more carnage-filled areas of the stronghold as best he could. However, it did not seem to matter, as Sara looked up at Grimm with a puzzled expression stuck to her face. As he felt the girl's stare burning a hole in the side of his head, he finally stopped and looked down at her.

"What?"

"Why don't you like anyone?"

The question's bluntness took Grimm aback, and the fact that it came from someone so young as Sara hit him that much harder. He turned his head forward and kept walking, dragging Sara behind him. "Because people let you down."

"You haven't."

"I'm not like most people."

"But –"

"Listen, Sara," Grimm started, eager to broach the subject that was eating away at the back of his mind. Seeing Sara at the negotiations made him feel a vulnerability that he would have preferred never to show Uthredd. Grimm remembered when Sara had managed to sneak up on him, back in the forest. He should have known there and then that the dwarf had a talent for going unnoticed. He cursed himself for not being diligent enough in his care of the child. But between the raids, the strategizing, leading the Bastards, and watching over Sara, it was all too much for him, and unfortunately he had allowed Sara to slip through the cracks. "You can't leave the stronghold any more. What you did today was unacceptable. You could've got hurt, or worse."

"Why?"

"Because those men out there," he said, pointing towards Tjørholm's walls. "want to see you hurt, and I won't let that happen. But I can't fight them and watch over you. So please, for the love of Heimer, stay inside the walls."

Sara let out a sigh and stomped her feet. "It's so boring in here!" she lamented.

"Do as you're told, and we'll be on the mainland searching for that dwarven city in no time."

A smile appeared on the girl's lips. "Do you mean that?"

"Of course," Grimm lied. He had no intention of going gallivanting through the countryside looking for some fabled city; but if it kept Sara safe, he would tell her anything he needed to.

The Bastards were sitting around a fire, many tending to their own or a comrade's wounds. Their numbers had dwindled considerably since the start of the siege, but that was to be expected. They were the first line of defence, and took on the brunt of Uthredd's forces. Once they saw their leader enter their camp, all the soldiers, no matter their condition, rose to their feet in a sharp salute.

A smile spread across Grimm's lips as he gestured for his men to stand easy. He then ushered Sara into his tent, so that he could speak to his men with some sort of privacy. Before he could sit down and join them, one of the more senior Bastards asked what was obviously on everyone's mind. "What did the Islander king want? Is he going to surrender?"

Grimm laughed at the man's juvenile notion. "Uthredd doesn't surrender. He's relentless, which is why he's High King of the Isles." He looked around the camp and saw that most of the men's faces were coloured with disappointment. They had finally had their first taste of real battle, and many were full. "But rest assured, he's never experienced a thrashing like that before. We did good."

"Did you see how many were out there?" one man asked. "We'll be dead in a week!"

"Then I suggest you die with honour," Grimm snarled as he rose to his feet. "I thought you lot were the meanest and toughest sons of bitches the mainland had to offer, but now, after you've tasted victory, you want to tuck tail and run?"

A wave of murmuring spread throughout the men. Finally, after a short delay, the soldier who spoke first cleared his throat. "What did Uthredd want?"

"He wants to collect his dead from the walls and give them a proper burial."

"That's where we'll get him, right?" the man replied, his voice brightening with hope. "When he comes to collect his dead, we'll ambush him and slaughter his people."

Grimm shook his head. "He'll be doing us a favour: the dead spread disease. Plus, there is no honour in that."

"Fuck honour!" one of the other men shouted. "We're the Bastards, remember? The worst of the worst! What else do they expect from us?"

"I don't know if King Elbert allowed him to retrieve his dead, anyway. I was banished from the meeting before I heard the final decision."

"Didn't play nice with the other Islanders?" one soldier mocked.

Grimm let out a small chuckle and looked at his men in the eyes. "Something like that."

The sound of armoured footsteps approached from behind them. Grimm turned his head and saw Thames walking towards the camp with a trio of royal guards accompanying him. "The king has returned from his meeting with High King Uthredd. He has requested your presence."

"Now he wants to speak with me," Grimm sighed. "If Legless wants to speak to me, he knows where to find me."

Thames shifted his stance and slowly inched his hand to the pommel of his sword. "This isn't a request," he said menacingly.

Grimm wanted to reach for his own sword, but knew that he couldn't make such a statement of open defiance in front of his men. They had to fight alongside the other lords' soldiers; and if they saw their commander refusing the king's orders, discipline might become an issue.

"Fine," he said. "Lead the way."

"You did what!?" Lord Grelin boomed.

The room of lords was in stunned silence, because the king had informed them of his decision to allow Uthredd to retrieve the dead Islanders. Even Grimm was surprised by Elbert's decision. When he first announced that he had agreed to Uthredd's terms, Grimm thought it was a sort of trick, but it seemed that the crippled king was deadly serious about allowing the Islander king to honour his dead.

"Your Majesty," Lord Grelin began again. "Do you think this is wise? This could be some sort of ruse!"

"It won't be," Grimm interjected. "I know Uthredd, and he would never use the dead to launch an assault. There is no honour in that."

"And we're supposed to take your word for it? The man who betrayed his own kin?" Grelin retorted.

Grimm's eyes narrowed on the oldest lord at the table. "Lordd Grelin, me and my men have shed enough blood to show you whose side we are on."

"They aren't your men: they're the king's men."

"Enough!" Elbert shouted. "I've made my decision. The Islanders have agreed to come unarmed, and our archers will be trained on them the entire time, so if there is some sort of duplicity, we'll be ready for it."

"What about our men?" Lord Penerack asked. "They will not like the idea of allowing the enemy to waltz into the fortress after fighting such a bloody battle. I fear that this could lead to a mutiny."

"Can you not control your men?" Elbert snarled. "You are their commander, and I suggest you squash any mutterings of mutiny, unless you want to be stripped of your title."

Lord Penerack's face paled. He pulled on the collar of his shirt and made an audible gulp as he wiped a bead of sweat from his forehead.

"We need to discuss a plan of action for the next assault because, rest assured, they will attack again," Thames chimed in from the back of the room.

"Agreed," Elbert concluded. "How many of our men are fit for battle?"

Lord Grelin coughed nervously before finally looking the crippled king in the eye. "We lost around a quarter of our forces from the first assault, with another quarter wounded."

Elbert let out a defeated sigh and pinched the bridge of his nose. The king shook his head and appeared to be holding back tears. Then, after a moment of awkward silence, Grimm stood up.

"Uthredd is going to be desperate. Tjørholm is sacred ground, and every day we occupy it is an affront to the gods. So his next attack will be an all-out assault."

"We barely survived the first wave. How are we supposed to survive another?" one lord asked.

"From what I've seen, they've lost all the giants they had under their command in the first assault. That's an advantage they no longer have," Thames interrupted once again.

"Agreed," concluded Grimm. "Our biggest concern is the gate. We need to repair that as quickly as possible. We need to force Uthredd's men to scale our walls."

"That's easier said than done," Lord Penerack scoffed.

"Lord Arlin, do you think you could devise a new gate for us? Preferably one that's a bit stronger," Elbert said, turning his attention to the dwarven craftsman.

"It shouldn't be a problem, Yer Majesty," Arlin replied, as he pulled on his beard. "But the issue is the material. I'd have to destroy our ships to craft something that sturdy."

"Lord Grelin, have your men demolish every building that holds no strategic importance. Lord Penerack, your men will assist Lord Arlin in the construction of a new gate. I want this stronghold to be re-fortified as soon as possible. Once Uthredd retrieves his dead, the siege will be back on, so is that doable?"

"Yes, Your Majesty," the lords responded in unison.

Grimm did not like the idea of ransacking a holy place in order to fortify their defences, but he knew that in times of war, sometimes you had to do the unthinkable. He was sure that Heimer would understand. He was only doing what he needed to do in order to survive.

Suddenly, the atmosphere in the room changed, and Grimm felt all eyes focus on him. He looked around the room and saw that his instincts had not betrayed him.

"Grimm," Elbert said solemnly. "I know that you and I have had our differences, but I just want you to know that I know where your loyalties lie. I'm grateful for your expertise and knowledge of the enemy, and as a result, I will make sure that you will sail back to the mainland with us."

A sly smile appeared on the Islander's face. He took a deep breath in and rose to his feet. "We're not out of this yet, Legless: let's get to work."

CHAPTER THIRTY-THREE

ANNA

The gold in the coin purse made an audible clink as it landed in the priest's hand. The old man let out a toothy smile, bowed politely, and shuffled off down the street, where he would deliver his next sermon, condemning the nobility and insinuating open rebellion as a solution.

When Anna had told Randall what she had done, he was ecstatic. For a moment, the boy she fell in love with came back into existence. He had shot out of the throne and pulled her into a tight embrace, then placed a soft kiss on her forehead.

A shiver ran down her body when she felt his stubble against her skin. But the moment was short-lived. As soon as their embrace was finished, he immediately turned back into the King of Crooks again and began plotting and scheming. He had insisted that they pay the clergymen, much to Anna's chagrin, explaining that it would make the priests deliver a more convincing performance.

Despite his inexperience, Randall refused to rule with an iron fist. He preferred to be loved rather than feared, which struck Anna as odd. When Greaver was the king, Randall openly ridiculed the man for being too passive, and yet it seemed that Randall had adopted the same strategy. *Probably Cassius' doing,* Anna hissed to herself.

Her hands curled into fists as she thought about the eunuch contemptuously. He was the reason for Randall's sudden change. He had to be, what other explanation was there? People didn't change overnight, unless they had a certain push.

"Isn't it a lovely day?" Randall asked aloud, jarring Anna from her thoughts.

The day was, in fact, miserable. The wind was gusting through the streets, kicking up snow into people's eyes, and it was unfathomably cold, even by Artanzian standards. "It's lovely, Randall," Anna responded, not wanting to put a damper on his mood.

Randall's moods were often volatile, and happiness or joy was quite rare. More often than not, he was brooding or sulking on his throne, as Cassius whispered venomous lies into his ears. To Anna, the crown seemed more of a burden than a privilege. She wished he could just give up his throne and things would go back to normal. *Maybe once all of this is over,* Anna told herself, trying to convince herself as she did so.

"What're your plans tonight?"

Anna's heart leapt up into her throat. Could Randall seriously be suggesting a date? Anna quickly tried to gather her resolve. "Nothing, why, what do you have in mind?" she lied. She had made plans with Maeve, but Randall took priority over everyone else.

"There's a tavern on the west side of town. I'd like you to accompany me there tonight."

"Why? Are we going to rent a room?" Anna asked seductively, as she gently began caressing Randall's arm.

The boy smiled politely before pulling away from Anna's touch. Her heart sank. It felt like a mule had kicked her in the chest. She cursed herself for believing that Randall would actually suggest a romantic evening with her. She was a damned fool.

"I'm hosting an event with some of the commoners, and I'd like my queen to join me."

The word "queen" made Anna's heart flutter once again. He wouldn't call her a queen unless she meant something to him. She reminded herself that Randall's coldness was simply due to him being preoccupied with the rebellion. He still loved her; he had to.

"What sort of event?" Anna asked.

"I plan to meet with all the angry commoners and march on the palace. Today is the day everything changes."

"In a tavern?" she questioned, her brow furrowing slightly.

"Nothing stokes the flames of rebellion quite like alcohol." Randall smiled.

Had Anna not known better, she would have thought Randall had done this before. He was so convincing when he spoke about the rebellion, and he seemingly had all the answers. Even his more questionable decisions were made with the utmost confidence.

"Fine, are the rest of the Maggots joining us?"

"No," Randall replied. "Tig and A'Chula will be elsewhere in case things go wrong. Cassius is charged with holding down The Garden while we're away, and gods know where Maeve is. I haven't seen her since she recovered."

The inclusion of the eunuch made Anna's blood boil. She was sure that everyone except Randall saw the man as she did, as an interloper. Cassius would often stay silent during their meetings, and when he ddid speak, it was usually only to Randall.

She wished with all her heart that the former sommelier would just disappear, never to be seen again, but she knew that was too much to ask. If the man was ever going to leave, it would have to be ordered by Randall.

"Randall, there's something I want to talk to you about," Anna began.

"There's no need," Randall interrupted. "I already know what you are going to say."

"You do?"

"Maeve told you about our past, didn't she?"

Anna's face turned red. This was the last thing she wanted to talk about. She had hoped that if she never brought it up, that she would simply forget about it and move on with her life. But now Randall was making it real, which was something she dreaded.

"How did you know?" she asked, trying to maintain her composure.

"You look at me differently now. It's as if you're watching me, the same way a wolf watches a deer from the bush. There's nothing going on between me and Maeve any more, it's ancient history." Randall then reached out, grabbed Anna gently by both shoulders, and pulled her in close. "I love you. That's all that matters."

As soon as she heard those three words, Anna's body melted. Her extremities tingled, and the world started to spin slightly. She leaned in to kiss Randall, and once their lips touched, she tightened her embrace. This felt right. Having Randall's arms wrapped around her not only made her feel safe, but like she belonged. Then, just as all of her doubts faded away, Randall pulled back.

"You should go back to The Garden and get everything you need. Tonight, we take the crown and for once, give it to someone who actually deserves it."

Anna smiled, nodded her head, and began walking across the city. On several occasions, she caught herself smiling gleefully as she made her way back to The Garden. Her muscles were relaxed, and she allowed herself to be enveloped by the bliss that came from Randall's affection.

Then, suddenly, two men in black armour stood in her way. Anna's joy quickly dissolved when she realized they were members of the Blackguard. She turned sharply to go down a side alley, but found that two more men were waiting for her there. She tried to turn around and leave the alley, but the first pair of guardsmen had blocked her exit.

Her heartbeat quickened. She felt like a rabbit caught in a snare. She reached for her knife but realized it would be no use. Realistically, she could kill one, maybe two, if she was lucky. But all four: that was impossible.

Her eyes darted to the surrounding walls and she noticed that some bricks in the buildings' sides were missing. When the Blackguard were about ten feet away from her, she leapt towards the wall and began scaling it.

Climbing buildings was easier than she expected. It was a lot like climbing trees. She leapt from one foothold to another, quickly ascending the wall. In a few seconds, she had scaled the fifteen-foot-high building and was looking down at the men, who continued to stare up at her. She smiled and gave the guardsmen a curt bow, before running along the rooftops towards The Garden.

She jumped from building to building, landing on the tiled or thatched roofs as gracefully as a cat. She wondered if the Blackguard would follow her, but from what she could see, the guardsmen had admitted defeat once she reached the rooftops.

As she drew closer to The Garden, Anna made her descent. First, she jumped onto a wooden balcony, and from there, shimmied down the wooden support beams until she could drop safely to the ground. Then, as she turned into the alley that contained The Garden's hidden door, she noticed that a large man in black armour was standing there.

"Resourceful lil' tart," the man complimented, as a smile appeared on his lips.

Anna's blood ran cold. How did he know she was coming here? And how did he know where here was? As she slowly reached for her knife, the man shook his head.

"I'd leave that little toothpick where it is if I were you, little girl." Mortimer Black's voice was as cold as the winter wind. "I never would've guessed you were the Queen of Crooks."

"I'm not," Anna blurted out reactively.

Black's face contorted into a disappointed frown. "Don't lie. It's unfit for a lady."

"I'm not a lady," Anna growled.

"Ha!" Mortimer laughed. "On that, we can agree. You're nothing more than scum."

"What do you want?"

"Me? Nothing, just thought I'd stop by and see your so-called kingdom."

The leader of the Blackguard approached, and Anna instinctively widened her stance. But instead of drawing his sword and challenging her, he merely walked past her, softly humming a catchy tune.

Anna quickly ran towards the door to The Garden and saw that it was slightly ajar. When she pushed it open, she noticed that the courtyard had been ransacked. The windows of the shops had been smashed, furniture was strewn across the ground, and blood stained the cobblestones.

She wasn't sure what compelled her, but she rushed to the throne room. When she arrived, she turned and vomited on the blood-stained ground. There, at the foot of Randall's throne, was a mountain of corpses. And sitting in his spot was the butchered and mutilated corpse of Maeve.

CHAPTER THIRTY-FOUR

ELBERT

Disgust covered Elbert's face as he watched a small horde of Islanders seep into the fortress. Through the stained-glass window of his temporary chambers, he could see that the savages had kept their word and left their weapons behind.

It wasn't long before the courtyard was teeming with the stinking, fur-covered barbarians. He could practically smell them from his room. While letting out an angry sigh, he turned himself away from the window.

"I never should have let these heathens through the gate."

"Agreed," Thames said softly, from the corner of the room. "But perhaps a gesture such as this will allow our negotiations with the Islanders to go more smoothly."

Elbert didn't hear the guard's response, and for good reason: he hadn't slept since his meeting with the Islander king. Uthredd was everything that Elbert wasn't. Able-bodied, handsome, beloved by his countrymen, and a fearsome warrior. He was the epitome of what a king should be. Elbert's nerves consumed him. He anxiously ground his teeth together as he imagined suffering a crushing defeat at the hands of such a man.

"Sire," Thames cut in. "There is something you should know."

These words broke through Elbert's frenzied thoughts; he looked up at his most trusted advisor, and for the first time since they had met, Elbert saw fear in the guardsman's eyes.

"Some of the lords have expressed their discontent about allowing Uthredd's soldiers into the fortress, an sentiment shared by many of the men. I fear they may mutiny against you."

Great, Elbert cursed to himself. *The last thing I need right now is to fight a war on two fronts. How can I possibly withstand the Islander's assaults while the loyalty of my own force is divided?* The king began tapping his finger restlessly on the armrest of his chair and ran his tongue across his dry, chapped lips. He felt a sharp pain in his chest, and his vision blurred. It wasn't until he felt Thames' steadying hand that his torrent of insecurities subsided.

"What would you have me do, Your Majesty?" Thames asked.

"Tell me," Elbert began. "Are the Bastards part of the malcontents?"

Rupert shook his head. "Surprisingly not. In fact, they seem to be the most loyal to you, apart from my men, of course."

Once again, Elbert was at the mercy of the white-eyed Islander, which made his heart sink. His brother never would've been so reliant on another man. He probably would have bested Grimm in single combat by now, and won the army's undying loyalty.

Elbert turned his head and looked at himself in a dirty mirror. The pit of sadness that had formed in his chest only grew once he saw his own reflection. Not only did he need another man's help to defeat an army, but he also needed their help to get dressed, ascend stairs, and wipe his own arse. He couldn't even defend himself when the Islander warrior attacked him. The thought of being so useless was emasculating.

"Thames," a teary-eyed Elbert started, planning to confess everything he was feeling to his closest friend, "can I tell you something?"

"Of course," Rupert replied.

Just as the words were about to exit his mouth, the sound of fighting came from the courtyard. Elbert quickly rolled himself to the window and saw that a skirmish had broken out between the Islanders and his own men. But perhaps skirmish was the wrong word, as the weaponless Islanders fought back in futility against the armed and armoured Artanzian soldiers.

A smile crept along the lips of the crippled king as he saw how easily the savages were cut down by his own men. But in an instant, his smile faded.

Grimm was charging into the courtyard, sword in hand, and he expertly began disarming the king's soldiers. Elbert's eyes widened, as he could see just how talented this man was with a sword. Every fluid motion the man made resulted in an Artanzian losing his weapon and, on one occasion, a hand.

Some soldiers backed away from the twirling warrior, while others dared to rush him, only to meet the same fate their comrades had.

It wasn't long before the rest of the Bastards rushed in and formed a defensive perimeter around the weaponless Islanders. Elbert slammed his fist into the armrest. "Thames!" he shouted. "Gather your men and take me to that courtyard!"

Rupert crisply saluted and whistled loudly, and shortly after, a trio of guardsmen came in and lifted the crippled king's throne down the spiral staircase that led from his chambers to the main foyer of the keep.

The white enamelled guardsmen burst through the shattered oaken doors and into Tjørholm's bailey. They surrounded the Bastards and the weaponless Islanders. In one swift motion, the royal guardsmen levelled their swords towards them. Elbert pushed his way through the wall of white armoured bodies, glaring at Grimm as he did so.

"What in the fuck is going on here?" he shouted at the top of his lungs. He could hear several soldiers take an involuntary step backwards.

"Your soldiers, Legless," Grimm started, "attacked these defenceless men and women, when they were only trying to honour their dead."

"Did it ever occur to you that your countrymen might have provoked such an attack? Perhaps one soldier saw them conceal a dagger or –"

"That would never happen. They gave their word."

"Do not interrupt me!" Elbert's voice reverberated off the stone buildings of the fortress. The veins in his neck and forehead bulged as he scanned the eyes of the weaponless Islanders. "This is war. Lies are told all the time."

"Like the lie you told Uthredd about not harming his men?" A palpable silence filled the air. "You don't understand, Legless. Uthredd will demand these men's heads. If you don't do the honourable thing, any hope you had of getting off this snow-covered rock will be lost."

"You can't seriously expect me to weaken my own forces purely for the sake of honour? We are at war, Grimm: these things happen."

"Spoken like a true warrior. Remind me, how did you lose your legs? Was it in battle?"

"Guards!" Elbert shouted. "Throw the Islanders in the dungeons, along with any Artanzian that stands in your way."

The royal guardsmen stepped forward, and this time, the Bastards lowered their weapons.

"You'll have a lot more dead men on your hands if you think you can throw us in a cell."

"Your Majesty," Thames said pleadingly. "Let me cut out this knave's tongue. I swear to you it'll –"

Elbert turned his head and saw that his entire army was watching him. A bead of sweat ran down his spine. The sound of his heart pumping echoed in his ears, and his mouth felt dry. Once again, the world started to blur and spin violently. Then everything went black.

The room was dark, cold, and covered in shadows. The soft furs of the bed gently caressed the king's waking body. Elbert shivered uncontrollably and looked around the room, unsure of where he was or how he got there.

After a couple of seconds of frantically searching the silhouettes of the room, he realized he was in his quarters. The curtains had been drawn closed, and the door was shut. Torchlight passed through the cracks of the oaken bedroom door, and he could make out two distinct shadows standing outside. The crippled king wiped his brow, which was still drenched in sweat. His lungs felt ragged, his chest was heavy, and his muscles were incredibly tight.

Suddenly, everything came back to him. He remembered how his men looked at him expectantly. His heart sank when he realized that they all saw him faint. *What kind of king passes out in front of his own men?* He felt his heartbeat quicken as the anxious thoughts quickly infected his mind. He tried to take a deep breath, but when he tried to exhale, the air got caught in his throat.

There was a knock on the door. The guards outside must have heard some sounds of life. Elbert tried to call out that he was fine, but the only thing that escaped his lips was a thin, raspy, wheezing sound. There was another knock, followed by a familiar voice.

"Your Majesty, are you all right?" Thames' muffled voice asked through the oak door.

"I'm fine," Elbert croaked, but he doubted the captain could hear his response. The muscles in his neck had tensed to the point where it was almost choking him, making speech next to impossible.

The door slowly creaked open, and Thames' scarred face peered inside. Elbert stared at him helplessly as he lay on the bed. The captain nodded his head at the other figure standing outside the door and entered the room, closing the door behind him.

"Sire," he began. "Permission to speak freely?"

Elbert nodded his head.

"I worry about you. The voyage, the siege, and that Islander have taken a lot out of you."

"I'm fine," Elbert lied, finally regaining his voice.

"You collapsed out of your throne in front of your army. There are whispers amongst the lords that you are unfit to lead. I have done my best to reassure them that you have merely caught some sort of sickness and that it will quickly pass, but I fear they are beyond persuading."

"What do you suggest?"

"I suggest that you show them you are still fit to be king, and prove beyond any doubt that you are the rightful heir to King David's legacy."

"How do I do that?" Elbert asked, his voice wavering. "The wolves are at our gates, we are stuck in this broken fortress, and my own men are turning against me."

Thames scratched his chin for a few minutes before he sat on the foot of the bed. "Perhaps it is time that we broker a peace with Uthredd."

"What?"

"You need rest, and this war is slowly killing you. We need to get out while we still can. We might not survive another assault."

Elbert threw his head back and stared at the ceiling. How in the world would he convince the Islander king to agree to peace? "Fine. Inform the lords that I plan to meet with Uthredd to broker a peace and ransom Tjørholm back to the Islanders."

"As you wish, Your Majesty," Thames replied as he rose to his feet. "What about Grimm?"

"Keep a close eye on him. If he continues to be insubordinate, have your men throw him into the dungeon."

"And the Bastards? They will not stand idly by while we throw their commander into chains."

"Tell them they have earned their freedom, and that if they continue to show undying loyalty to me, their king, they will receive half their weight in gold once we return to the mainland."

"As you wish, Your Majesty." Thames bowed, before exiting the room and leaving Elbert alone with his thoughts.

Perhaps peace wasn't the worst outcome. If Rupert didn't think they could withstand another attack, maybe now was the right time to ransom the fortress back to the Islander king and leave the Isles with most of his army intact.

However, the negotiations would have to be carefully navigated. Uthredd was a clever man, and if he smelt weakness, then the prospect of peace would be impossible.

Suddenly, a thought popped into Elbert's head, and a smile crept along his face. "Perhaps he can still prove himself to be useful."

CHAPTER THIRTY-FIVE

ANNA

The atmosphere in The Garden was tense. Corpses were being loaded on to a large wooden cart, then transported down the winding staircase into the throne room. Many of the people who were fortunate enough to be absent during the Blackguard's attack were either a sobbing mess or consumed by a fit of frenzied rage. Never in the city's history had there been an attack on The Garden, and it all happened under Randall's watch.

Anna turned her head to see how the King of Crooks dealt with the situation. She noticed that almost everyone rejected his advances of consolation. She also noticed that many of them looked at him with scowls of distaste plastered on their faces.

Randall was talking to the man who owned the cart that was now filled with the last of the dead bodies. He had long silver hair, and was missing as many fingers as he was teeth. His pointed ears stuck through his wispy hair and his arms were covered in scars. She watched as Randall placed a small purse of coin in the man's hand, then the elf began pulling his cart down the stone staircase to Randall's throne room.

"Who was that?" Anna asked, once Randall was within earshot, as they followed the man down the staircase.

"An elf named Logain. He's the most prolific smuggler in all of Winterhelm."

"Why do we need a smuggler?"

"The Garden is supposed to be a secret, and if we haul this many bodies out of the front door, everyone will know where it is. Which will leave us vulnerable to another attack like this. I can't allow this to happen again."

"Okay," Anna replied, not sure she completely understood Randall's reasoning. "But why take them to the throne room?"

"Logain has a barge at the end of the sewer way. He will load the bodies on the barge and send them down the river ablaze."

Anna bit her lip. She wasn't the most spiritual person, but it felt wrong to hold no kind of service for the dead, especially Maeve. She deserved to be remembered. Anna was about to voice her concern when a voice called out from behind them.

"This is all your fault, boy! If Greaver were still here, my Emily would still be alive!"

Logain, Anna, and Randall all stopped in unison. The King of Crooks took a deep breath and gestured for the elven smuggler to go on without them. Randall then turned around, ascended the staircase once again, and entered the courtyard full of distraught and angry people. Anna followed close behind.

"I feel your pain, brother. But now isn't the time to point fingers."

"Fuck you!" the man shouted. "I say we butcher this sack of shit the same way he butchered Greaver!" There were a few murmurs of agreement from the rest of the crowd.

"Listen to me!" Randall shouted. His voice boomed, making him seem older than he really was. "While it is true that The Garden has never been attacked before, we must look at this logically. There is a rat in our midst. I personally take the blame for not finding this rat and hanging him by his neck for all to see. And I promise all of you I will make this right. But we have to stay focused. It was not some lone perpetrator that caused so many of our loved ones to lose their lives so needlessly. It was the Blackguard and that bitch, Queen Vivian. As long as the nobles are in power, our streets will run red with the blood of the innocent. In a couple of hours, I'm meeting with other like-minded commoners who have had enough of this bullshit tyranny. I would like my subjects to join me, so that we can change Artanzia's history."

"Why should we trust you?" a woman shouted from the crowd.

"Think about it. We can finally seize our destiny and take control of our lives! No longer will we have to kiss the boots of the nobles as they walk by. No longer will our deaths go unrecognized. No longer will we starve in the streets while they live in decadence. Tonight, everything changes."

Anna was in disbelief as she watched the mob shift their resentment from Randall to the nobility. The way he weaved sentences together to get people to see his point of view left her in a state of awestruck admiration. Randall raised a silencing hand and cleared his throat.

"The life you've always wanted is within your grasp. All you have to do is take it! Who's with me?"

There was a roar of unanimous cheering from the mob, who began to disperse and leave The Garden.

"Head to the Puking Pixie, then wait for my signal!" Randall called out, as his newly gained supporters exited the courtyard.

"Well said, my liege," a familiar, venomous voice cooed.

Anna's head snapped, and she glared at the bald eunuch who was approaching them. His usual smug smile was stuck on his face.

"Where were you today? Randall told me you were supposed to be watching over The Garden?"

"It seems fate was kind to me today," Cassius replied. "Before the raid, I was going over who still owed us dues when I ran out of ink. So, I went into town to fetch some, but when I returned. Well, you can imagine my shock."

Anna turned to the king. "Randall, don't you see? He's the rat! You don't really believe him, do you?"

"Anna, are you accusing me of betraying Randall?" Cassius hissed. "Might I ask where you were when this attack was carried out?"

"She was with me," Randall interrupted, his eyes narrowing.

The smile on the eunuch's lips disappeared as one appeared on Anna's.

"Of course, but a tidbit of information that might interest you, sire, is that when I was making my way back from the market, I saw Anna standing in the alley, talking to none other than Mortimer Black. Curious, wouldn't you say?"

Randall's gaze snapped to Anna, and she felt her blood run cold. A shiver ran down her spine and sweat formed on her brow.

"Is he telling the truth?" the king inquired.

"Yes, but –"

"Ah-ha!" Cassius exclaimed. "Smells like a rat to me."

"It's not like that!" Anna cried out. "It was like he was waiting for me, and he said that he wanted to see my so-called kingdom."

"That sounds like quite the coincidence. Wouldn't you say, Randall?"

The King of Crooks' eyes darted between the sommelier and Anna. Her heart raced wildly as she clenched her fists in frustration. *Randall can't possibly think that I would betray him. I love him! This is all Cassius' fault.* Anna thought about taking out her dagger and slicing the eunuch's throat open, but knew that just tell Randall she was guilty. After a lengthy pause, the king let out an exasperated sigh.

"I'll deal with this later. Right now, we have a kingdom to overthrow."

Both Anna and Cassius nodded their heads as Randall exited The Garden. She went to follow, but a hand caught her arm. Before she could react, she was spun around and faced with Cassius' sneering visage.

"Next time you try to stab me in the back, make sure you finish the job," the eunuch said, before releasing her arm and following the king out of the Garden.

Anna stood there dumbfounded, ground her teeth together, and squeezed her fist until her knuckles popped. Turning on her heel, she glared at the back of Cassius' bald head. *I'm going to kill that bastard before all of this is over,* she promised herself as she left The Garden, not knowing that it would be the last time she would ever set foot within its walls.

Pints were flowing, and many of the would-be rioters were already drunk. Some had brought whatever they had as weapons, proving they were ready for a fight. There were pitchforks, broom handles sharpened to a point, sickles, hammers, and one person even brought a fence post with a couple of nails in it.

Everyone was eager to hear Randall's speech. A few of the patrons talked about how they would gut Mortimer Black themselves. Anna laughed to herself. She knew that if anyone was going to kill that monster of a man, it was going to be her. She may not be able to bring Maeve back from the dead, but she knew that avenging her murder would be the next best thing.

"Brothers and sisters!" Randall exclaimed, as he stood on a wooden tabletop. "Today is the day that history changes. Today, we will break the wheel of oppression that has ground us into the dirt for centuries. All I ask of you is to trust me. Trust in this vision we have built together, and trust that no matter the cost, we will see it to its fruition."

The crowd of drunken mobbers cheered and started stamping their feet on the wooden floorboards of the inn. Anna felt a chill run down her spine as she stared at the sea of angry peasants which was crammed into this small tavern.

"To the keep!" one man shouted, and people began funnelling out of the tavern door and marching down the streets.

Randall climbed down from the table, pulled Anna in for a tight hug, and kissed her cheek. "Are you ready? Do you have your knives?" Anna nodded her head. "Good. After tonight, you and I will be king and queen of Artanzia." A giddy smile appeared on the boy's lips.

Anna felt her heart flutter at the sight. She was willing to do anything to help see Randall's dream come to life. Once it was all over, things would go back to the way they were. Randall and her would go back to their thieving ways, without an inkling of concern in Artanzian politics.

The King of Crooks exited the tavern, with his queen following closely behind him. They joined the mob of angry peasants which had begun marching to the keep at the far end of town. Many rioters started chanting profanities and curses about the royal family as they marched.

Anna's skin was covered in gooseflesh, and her heart raced wildly. She hadn't felt like this since she was allowed to hunt for the first time back in the forest. The excitement and nervousness were palpable. Randall's words rang in her head. Every step she took was a step closer to claiming her destiny.

It wasn't long before a blockade of guardsmen met Randall's army, with the Blackguard at the front of the column. The two opposing forces stopped and stared at each other for several seconds before Mortimer Black stepped out of the guards' formation.

"Go back to your homes!" he shouted, his voice echoing off the stone buildings of Winterhelm. "Queen Vivian is merciful and will excuse this *obvious* treason if you disperse immediately!"

"Fuck you!" one woman in the mob shouted. "You're nothing but a rabid dog!"

"Stand your ground!" Randall shouted, as he worked his way up to the front of the mob. "Will you let these blind fools stand in the way of your destiny?"

"No!" the peasants shouted in unison.

"Gentlemen," Black called out. "Teach this rabble a lesson."

Like an arrow loosed from a bow, both armies rushed towards each other, and a bloody melee ensued. Anna quickly weaved her way through the sea of flailing bodies, stabbing anyone wearing armour along the way.

Her daggers hissed as they pierced air, steel, and flesh. Ribbons of blood flew through the air as she tore her knives free from the bodies of the guardsmen.

She had always wondered what battle would be like, but now that she found herself in the midst of one, she was disappointed to find that it was nothing like she imagined.

It was slower. Everyone seemed to move at half speed. Every time she came face-to-face with a guardsman, she could predict his attacks before he made them, which made skewering them that much easier.

After slicing her way through the mass of bodies, she saw the grinning face of Mortimer Black staring back at her. She gripped the handles of her knives tighter and rushed the man, while letting out a ferocious battle cry.

The man effortlessly pirouetted out of the way and swung his sword down hard. Anna quickly jumped to the side, Black's sword missing her by mere inches.

She spun around and threw a knife at Mortimer's face. The blade failed to skewer his eye, as she had intended it to, but it left the former mercenary with a deep gash right above his brow.

"Fucking little tart," Black growled, as he swung his sword wildly.

Anna danced out of the way of each swing. Mortimer was fast, but her father had been faster, and years of training with him in the forest had made her the perfect warrior.

A smile appeared on her face when she saw the frustration on Mortimer's. A fourteen-year-old girl was besting him, and he could do nothing to stop it.

Suddenly, Randall's voice pierced through the sound of battle. "Retreat! Retreat!" Anna's head turned, and her feet froze for a split second, but it was long enough for the mercenary's sword to cut her across the cheek.

She fell hard against the cobblestone street. Blood gushed from her face. She tried to push herself upright, but a heavy boot stepped on her back.

Randall's army was running back through the streets, and the guardsmen let out a cheer of victory. A mountain of bloody corpses was piled in the street.

Anna squirmed under the heavy plate boot, but a sickening voice whispered in her ear. "You're not going anywhere." Then, everything went black.

CHAPTER THIRTY-SIX

GRIMM

Dark clouds painted the sky a dismal grey. The air was thick, and the distant rumbling signalled the incoming storm. Grimm stood atop the battlements and watched the storm clouds slowly roll in.

He listened to the roar of Heimer's anvil in the sky as the god crafted new life. He fidgeted with his fingers nervously, as he tried to decipher the meaning of the storm. It wasn't unheard of for a thunderstorm and a blizzard to happen simultaneously on the Isles, but it usually signified great change when it did. However, the change in question always remained a mystery, even to the priests.

"Commander Grimm!" a voice called out from below.

The Islander warrior took one last look at the ominous clouds before making his descent from the ramparts. At the bottom of the stairs was one of his men, standing at attention. He never bothered to learn any of his men's names. He figured it would be easier when they all inevitably fell in battle. But the Bastards had surprised him with their resilience, which made him regret his decision.

"Hmm?" he grunted.

"Are the rumours true?" the soldier asked. "King Elbert is trying to secure peace with the Islanders?"

Grimm bit his lip. He had heard these rumours as well. He did not know whether or not they were true, but he knew that if they were, Elbert would be in for the toughest negotiations of his life. "I'm not sure," Grimm responded honestly. "But I know that we must keep our wits about us. Understand?"

The soldier nodded his head and took off back towards the rest of the Bastards. Grimm watched and stared, unable to stop the feeling that was overtaking his body.

The pride he felt when he stared at his men was the same pride he felt when he watched his son swing a sword properly for the first time. These men had come to the Isles as nothing more than petty thieves and criminals, but because of him, they had turned into fearsome warriors.

He decided to spend some time among the Bastards. Perhaps it wasn't too late to learn some of their names.

As he entered the camp, the soldiers stood up at attention, and a few even reached for their weapons. Grimm waved a dismissive hand, standing the company at ease.

He listened to some of the men's conversations, and smiled when he heard tales of bravery from the siege. After weaving his way through camp, he finally made it to his tent, where he opened the flap, expecting to find Sara playing with whatever she had found that day around the fortress. But to his surprise, she wasn't there. He quickly calmed the anxiety spreading throughout him and forced himself to think of where she could have gone. The training grounds?

Grimm exited the Bastards' section of the fortress and strolled towards the army's makeshift training grounds. He felt the fall of a snowflake on his head and looked up. The clouds that had seemed so far away had quickly moved in. He also noticed that the rumbling of the thunder had grown louder in the time since he had stood on the battlements.

Unknowingly, he quickened his pace. Once he reached the training grounds, the beat of his heart quickened. Sara wasn't there either. In fact, the training grounds were abandoned. Perhaps the rumours were true. Grimm shook his head in distaste. *They should still train. Uthredd won't bend to Elbert's will easily, especially after the mainlanders attacked his men while retrieving their dead.*

"Grimm!" a familiar voice called out, interrupting the Islander's thoughts.

"What is it, Arlin?"

"His Majesty has called a meeting of all the commanders," the dwarf reported dutifully.

"Have you seen Sara?"

The dwarven lord scratched his beard as he mulled over Grimm's question. "I... er... I think I saw her in the keep, practicin' her sword work."

A small sense of relief flowed through Grimm's body. At least someone had seen her. He followed Arlin back towards the keep and into the mead hall where Elbert held all his meetings. He was the last to arrive.

"Kind of you to join us, Grimm," Elbert said, passive-aggressively.

"Seems I'm the only one of your commanders who does any commanding, Legless," Grimm retorted.

"Now that we are all here," Elbert continued, ignoring the Islander's remark, "I wanted to inform you that I plan to broker a peace with King Uthredd."

There was a short period of murmuring amongst the lords, but eventually, they all quietened down to hear the king's reasoning.

"I'll be damned if I forsake my men, my *loyal* men, to die on this heathen-ridden rock. The chances that we withstand another assault, gentlemen, are slim at best. I say we try to get out while we are still in one piece."

"We will follow you, no matter what your decision is, Your Majesty," Lord Grelin replied.

"Uthredd won't concede easily," Grimm interjected. "He's a stubborn fucker, and will probably want lots in return."

"But we hold the upper hand; we hold the sacred fortress of Tjørholm, and I will burn this shithole to the ground before I let that man reclaim it."

"Uthredd is a pious man. There's no denying that. But I've known him for my whole life. He will want vengeance for what your men have done. So your best option is to offer them up as a sacrifice."

"We will not gift my men to that savage!" Elbert exclaimed, as he slammed his fist on the table.

"They're patriots!" another lord shouted.

"Perhaps we don't need to," Grelin interjected. "While Grimm is right, Uthredd will surely demand vengeance, he does not know which men carried out the assault."

"What are you saying?"

"Give him some of the Bastards. They're criminals, and surely we can sleep easily knowing that they actually served their kingdom in their miserable lives."

Grimm shot to his feet. "You can't be serious!"

"I agree with the Islander," Thames interjected. "Those men disobeyed the king's orders and deserve to reap the consequences of their actions."

"What about those criminals? Don't they deserve some form of punishment for their murdering, raping, and looting?" Lord Penerack shouted.

"Those men have served through their blood, sweat, and tears," Grimm snapped. "They served as your vanguard, as your fodder, taking the brunt of Uthredd's forces. They've earned their freedom."

Elbert began drumming his fingers against rhythmically on the table. Finally, after a few seconds of suspense, he cleared his throat. "If Uthredd *demands* it, I will give up the traitors. I will not condemn my army to die because of the treasonous actions of a few. However, I will also not openly offer them up to him on a silver platter. Am I understood?" Everyone nodded their heads in agreement. "Grimm, what else can I expect of Uthredd during negotiations?"

The Islander slowly lowered himself into his seat and thought back to all the times he and Uthredd went to a rival clan, to discuss them joining his crusade to unify the Isles. "He's crafty. He will not agree to a deal unless he thinks it will make him appear strong. Remember, he's not surrendering: we are. If he senses that we are desperate, he will deny all your requests and launch an all-out assault, taking back what is rightfully his."

Elbert nodded his head in agreement. "Last time we spoke, I told him we have a fleet of ships en route to aid us. Of course, this is a lie, but he must believe this. Hopefully, that little lie will mask our desperation. Lord Grelin, send a rider to the Islander camp carrying the message that I wish to parlay with Uthredd." The lord nodded his head and rose from his seat. "Then, if there is nothing else, this meeting is adjourned."

"Have you seen Sara?" Grimm asked suddenly.

"No, I haven't. I presumed she was with your men."

Grimm's eyes shot to Arlin. "I thought you said you saw her playing in the keep?"

"That - er - might've been yesterday. Unfortunately, my memory isn't what it used to be."

Grimm let out an exasperated snort, and stormed out of the mead hall and into the bailey. Snow was falling heavily, and soon the swirling winds that would accompany them would make it next to impossible to track Sara.

He sprinted across the courtyard and down the street, his eyes scanning for any tiny footprints in the snow. He checked the barracks, his tent, and the training grounds again, then the ramparts. She was nowhere to be found.

Finally, he found a small set of footprints leading out of the main gate towards the Islander's camp. Grimm's heart sank. He felt a hand on his shoulder. He turned his head and saw the scarred face of Thames staring back at him.

"She's gone out there, hasn't she?"

"Appears so," Grimm replied.

"Damn, she said something in passing about killing Uthredd, but I didn't think she would act on it."

Grimm clenched his fists in anger, and managed to stifle the angry retort that was forming in his throat. He looked at the captain and realized that the man's face was bright red, and his eyes were cast down to the ground.

"Do you plan to go after her?"

"Yes," Grimm stated harshly, unable to hide his frustration with the mainlander.

"I'll come too." Thames replied. This made Grimm's anger dissipate for several seconds. He could plainly see on the man's face that Thames felt regret, but he hadn't expected the soldier to actually do anything about it.

"Thank you."

"I'm not doing it for you. Sara's in trouble, and I should've stopped her when I had the chance."

Grimm grunted in approval. "Better get going: don't want to get caught in that storm."

CHAPTER THIRTY-SEVEN

ANNA

Frost covered the stone walls, and a blistering wind blew snow through the gated, south-facing window. Anna's body shivered atop the bed of piss-soaked hay strewn around the cell floor.

She watched the shadows silhouetted by the torchlight on the other side of the confining iron bars. Occasionally, she would hear an exchange of voices between two guards during their rotations, but otherwise, there was an excruciating silence.

The back of her head throbbed in pain, but that paled in comparison to the agonizing thoughts that were running through her mind. Was she going to end up like Maeve? Would Randall and his new-found army come to rescue her? Or was she doomed to spend the rest of her life confined to this tiny stone prison cell?

The sound of a door creaking open echoed in the corridor outside her cell. She heard two distinct sets of footsteps. One was heavily armoured and made a loud clanking sound, while the other sounded like someone wearing heeled shoes.

Anna rose to her feet, dusted the hay off her clothes, and stretched her aching back. Then, after a few moments of suspense, standing outside her cell was Mortimer Black, and a woman wearing an ornate crown, dressed in elegant robes.

"*This* is the usurper?" the woman asked in disbelief.

"Not quite," Black corrected. "I believe the true mastermind is the so-called King of Crooks, but she is his right-hand lady. The Queen of Crooks, if you will."

The woman took a step closer and grasped two of the iron bars. Her differently coloured eyes analyzed Anna's body with incredible scrutiny. "She's just so... young."

"Don't let her age fool you," Black responded. "She's as wily as the rest of those unwashed plebs."

"Fuck you," Anna snarled, as she took a step towards the edge of her cage.

The queen instinctively took a step back, and the corner of her lips twitched into a half-smile. "Such language doesn't befit a lady of your status."

"Fuck you too."

"Listen, you little shit," the mercenary captain growled. "You will speak to Her Majesty the Queen with the utmost respect. Unless you want me to come in there and teach you a lesson?"

"Like the lesson you taught me when we were fighting?" Anna retorted, a wry smile appearing on her lips.

Mortimer Black's face instantly turned a deep shade of crimson at the verbal jab. He started to reach for his sword when he paused, and chuckled maniacally. "Your friend had a mouth on her, too. But her sharp tongue only made me peel off her skin slower, and let me tell you, she had quite the set of lungs on her."

Anna lunged at the mercenary, her arm reaching through the iron bars, desperately hoping to grab the collar of his gambeson. But, unsurprisingly, Mortimer backpedalled out of reach and let out a loud guffaw.

"She's like a feral beast!" Vivian exclaimed.

Anna slowly slithered back into her cell after her failed attack, and looked out of the barred window, desperate to see any sign of rescue.

"What did I ever do to deserve such animosity? Have I not been a good ruler? Have I not been kind?"

The queen's words forced bile up into Anna's throat. The fact that Vivian didn't know why they were revolting spoke volumes about her ignorance of the problems of the common people. Anna clenched her fists in rage; her knuckles popping from the pressure.

"What are you going to do with me?" Anna asked, her voice shaking from a mixture of anger and fear.

"Well–" Black began, but was quickly cut off by Vivian.

"I wish to speak to you woman to woman, queen to queen. I'm sure two intelligent ladies like ourselves can resolve this conflict peacefully."

More lies, Anna thought to herself. *She'll have me butchered, just like she butchered Maeve and Chuckles.* "Fine," Anna said after a moment's hesitation, hoping that if she could get out of this cell, she might have a chance to escape and reunite with Randall.

Vivian clapped her hands together. "Excellent! Mortimer, have the guards bring her some new clothes. I'll not have her in my hall dressed in rags."

"Your Majesty, I don't think that is wise –"

"Please, she's just a little girl. What harm can she do? But if it makes you feel any better, she can wear restraints."

Mortimer bowed low and nodded his head. "As you wish, Your Majesty. Guards! Fetch some suitable clothes for the prisoner!"

Vivian gave a short curtsy and a smile towards Anna, before making her way back down the long hallway. The sound of her dainty, heeled footsteps faded until the closing door silenced any reverberation. Once again, Anna was in deafening silence, only this time she was accompanied by Mortimer Black.

"Listen, girl," he began. "The queen is a generous woman, so if you try anything, I'll have your head on a pike so fast –"

"What makes you think you can catch me?" Anna scoffed arrogantly.

"Who taught you to fight like that?" Black responded with a hint of annoyance and admiration staining his voice.

"My father."

"Where is he now, this legendary fighter?"

"Dead."

"And do you think this is how he wanted his little girl to be remembered? As a brigand?"

Anna whirled around and glared at the mercenary through the iron bars. "You know nothing about him, so shut your mouth! Besides, he's dead: it doesn't matter what he thinks."

"What about your mother? Surely, she would want a better life for you than being a criminal."

"I never knew her. She died when I was young."

Mortimer Black let out a sigh, as if Anna's comments explained everything, then pulled up a stool and plopped down on it. "I like you, girl. I truly do. Not only are you a fighter, but you're a survivor. Perhaps in another life, you could've been my ward."

"I'd slit your throat," Anna snapped.

A slight chuckle escaped the mercenary's lips. "I'm sure you would. But it's all irrelevant now. Soon you will be executed, and made an example of in the streets, for everyone to see what happens to traitors."

"That's not what the queen said."

Black leaned forward on his stool. "You and I both know that you're not the brains behind this coup. You have as much authority to organize a truce as I do. First, you'll talk with the queen, then you'll return to this cell and wait, until I drag you out to the gallows."

Anna turned away and faced the window once again. This man wasn't as clever as he thought he was. He underestimated her, and he was going to pay dearly for it. Once she was alone with the queen, she was going to drive a knife through her heart and end this once and for all.

The sound of the door at the end of the corridor opening echoed once again, and shortly after, a set of heavy footsteps approached her cell. She turned around and saw one of the royal guards holding an exquisite turquoise gown with golden seams. Anna's heart sank at the sight of the dress; it looked so uncomfortable. Surely the queen wouldn't expect her to wear that, would she?

"Here you go, Your Majesty," the guard said sarcastically, as he tossed the dress into the cell.

Anna picked up the gown, and was amazed at how soft it was. It felt like she was holding a bundle of clouds in the palms of her hands. She looked up at the two men. "A little privacy?"

"Sorry, milady, got to do my due diligence," the guard replied, with a sickening smile stuck on his face.

Surprisingly, Black elbowed the guard hard in the ribs and glared at him. "If you want to see some tits, go to a fucking whorehouse."

Without uttering another word, the guard hung his head and walked back down the corridor. Mortimer Black nodded and turned around to give Anna the privacy she deserved.

She quickly shook off her disbelief at the mercenary's actions, shed her soiled clothes, and slipped into the dress. Although the gown fitted her body well, she still preferred her own clothes. She looked down at her body, and while the dress was pristine, her arms and hands were bruised and caked with dirt and dried blood. Once she had finished checking herself over, she cleared her throat, and Black turned around and smiled.

"Well, don't you look like a proper lady?" His voice was rich with sarcasm and condescension. The keys jangled as he took them off his belt and unlocked the cell door. "Hold out your hands, and no funny business."

Anna complied, and considered reaching for his sword or knife, but thought better of it. Surely, he would expect her to make a move, and besides, she wanted to hear what the queen had to say to her.

Perhaps if she could broker a peace on Randall's behalf, things would go back to how they were. The steel manacles locked around her wrists with a loud click. Mortimer placed a hand on her back and ushered her out of the cell and down the corridor.

Beyond the door at the end of the corridor was a spiral staircase that ascended into a garish throne room. The room was divided into thirds by two columns of stone pillars. The marble floor was so highly polished, Anna could almost see her reflection in it.

Black led her across the throne room and through a pair of oaken doors. On the other side was another large room, illuminated by several gargantuan windows. A long dining table sat in the middle of the room appeared to hold enough food to feed the population of Winterhelm for a week.

Black quietly gestured for Anna to take a seat at the far end of the table. As soon as she lowered herself into the chair, another set of doors opened, and Queen Vivian entered, accompanied by a retinue of royal guards.

The queen sat at the head of the table, then dismissed the guards with a graceful wave of her hand. The guardsmen hesitated for a second, then exited the room. Vivian then turned her head toward the mercenary captain, with a disapproving frown on her face.

"You can leave as well, Mortimer," she said, with an air of authority colouring her voice.

"Your Majesty, I'd feel more comfortable if you weren't left alone with her."

"That wasn't a request." The queen's voice was as cold as ice. Anna looked over, and saw that Black was at a loss for words. Finally, he bowed and exited through the same doors he escorted Anna through moments before.

Vivian turned her attention back to Anna; a warm, friendly smile appearing on her lips. "Dig in," she said, as she reached for a bunch of grapes. "Would you care for some wine?" Anna had heard tales of nobles poisoning the wine they served their guests. She wasn't entirely convinced that the food wasn't poisoned as well. But her expression must have betrayed her thoughts, because the queen let out a small laugh and clapped her hands together. "If I wanted to kill you, dear, I wouldn't waste this much decadence on you."

Anna nodded her head politely. "I'd love some."

"Perfect!" Vivian exclaimed. "I have the best sommelier that gold can buy." The queen raised her hands over her head and clapped loudly before shouting. "Cassius!"

Anna's heart sank. Her body tensed at the mention of the eunuch's name. Had she misheard? Was she just imagining things? Then, in a few moments, her fears were confirmed when the bald sommelier entered the room with a bottle of wine in his hands and a smug smile on his face.

"You called, Your Majesty?" Cassius cooed.

"My guest and I would like to have some wine."

Cassius held out the bottle so that the queen could inspect it. "I expected as much. This is a lovely vintage with an absolutely marvellous finish."

"You haven't led me astray yet, Cassius," the queen chuckled, as she helped herself to a glass of the red drink.

Once Vivian had poured her glass, Cassius carried the bottle over to Anna. She stared at him the entire time; she could feel the rage boiling up inside her. She gripped her cutlery with white knuckles as he approached. She hoped that he would break his character, but it seemed he was committed to his facade.

"Would you like a glass, milady?" he asked as he held out the bottle, ready to pour for Anna.

"Yes," she replied through gritted teeth. While he poured the liquor into her cup, she couldn't help but stare at the eunuch's exposed neck. He was so close, and it would be so easy to kill him. The fact that he was the royal sommelier confirmed that he had betrayed Randall. But she also knew that if she acted on her impulses, it would most likely condemn her to death. *Would it be worth it?* she thought to herself. *To sacrifice myself for the good of the rebellion?*

Before she could decide whether or not to end Cassius' life, her glass was full, and he began to walk away. "Will there be anything else, Your Majesty?"

"No, that'll be all, but why don't you join us?" Vivian asked.

Cassius gasped. "I'm afraid I'm severely underdressed to dine with two women of your stature."

"Nonsense!" Vivian squealed. "Please join us. We'd love to have you!"

Cassius tossed a questioning glance towards Anna, who refused to meet his gaze. Instead, she just stabbed the food on her plate, imagining that it was the eunuch's throat. Seeing no objection from the Queen of Crooks, the sommelier placed the bottle of wine on the table and sat down in an empty chair.

"So," the queen began. "What do you people want?"

"You people?" Anna asked.

"Yes, the rabble that thinks they can overthrow an entire kingdom in a night." The warmth in Vivian's voice had disappeared as she sipped from her glass of wine.

"We are tired of being treated like dogs. We deserve to have a say in how we are governed. We deserve to be ruled by the people, not by some pompous blowhards that happened to be born into the right family!"

The room fell silent. Cassius' expression was one of shock, which Anna knew was a clever facade that he put on for the queen's benefit. But Vivian's expression was different. Her eyes narrowed slightly, and her face twitched uncontrollably. However, her expression didn't last long, as she quickly donned a smile again and sipped from her wineglass.

The queen cleared her throat. "My dear, you must understand, you people simply aren't fit to rule. If we left the kingdom in your dirty hands, we'd be at war with every other kingdom on the continent. We'd be broke in a fortnight, every act of debauchery would be legalized, and chivalry would come to a grinding halt. Is that what you want for your kingdom?"

"Do you truly think that little of us?" Anna snarled.

"I believe Her Majesty is just looking at this logically," Cassius interjected. "Us commoners are victims to our vices, whereas the prestigious blood of the nobles is free of any such shortcomings. Not to mention that the gods have ordained their families to rule over us."

"Fuck you, you ball-less fucker!" Anna shouted as she shot out of her chair. "How can you sit there and betray Randall? He trusts you! But you're nothing more than a lapdog for this pampered cunt."

"Hysteria is a plague that ravages today's youth, Your Majesty. I fear that this *thing* is not capable of having a civilized conversation," Cassius replied matter of factly.

"Guards!" Vivian exclaimed. The pair of oak doors opened instantly, and the retinue of guardsmen, including Mortimer Black, rushed in. "Take her back to the dungeons."

Anna quickly grabbed a knife from the table and hurled it at Cassius. The blade twirled through the air, the sunlight from the windows making it glimmer like a diamond during its flight.

Unfortunately, it was lighter than she thought, so she missed her mark. Instead of puncturing the eunuch's throat, she had merely stabbed him in the shoulder.

Cassius screamed dramatically in pain as he fell out of his chair like a sack of potatoes. Mortimer Black quickly tackled Anna to the ground and dragged her back to her cell.

She writhed and shouted curses at the eunuch until she was tossed into the pile of piss-soaked hay, and the barred door of her cell was slammed shut.

"That was foolish, girl," Black commented, before walking away from the door.

"I'll kill you, I'll kill you all," Anna whispered, as she curled up in the fetal position.

CHAPTER THIRTY-EIGHT

GRIMM

Lightning illuminated the sky with a bright, brilliant white light, while the powerful gusts of wind blew the falling snow into the two men's eyes. The deafening crack of thunder echoed across the frozen plains.

They had marched their way into the eye of the storm. Grimm turned his head, and saw Thames shielding his eyes from the onslaught of the blizzard with his arm. Although he and the guard had certainly had their differences, he appreciated that Thames had joined him to rescue Sara: two swords were always better than one.

"Do you see any sign of her?" Thames hollered, through a mouthful of snow.

"No," Grimm responded. "But she has to be close. We're getting near Uthredd's lines."

"If we haven't crossed them already," Thames muttered audibly.

Grimm had been worried about the same thing. A storm like this would make it next to impossible for scouts to see them, unless they stumbled directly into them, which was highly likely. The nagging thought that Sara had got herself captured by the Islanders gnawed at the back of his mind. "If any of them have laid a hand on her, I'll butcher Uthredd's entire army," he whispered silently to himself.

"Get down!" Thames said, somewhere between a shout and a whisper. Grimm immediately dropped to his knees.

"What is it?"

"Movement up ahead."

The Islander squinted his eyes, but all he could see was a torrent of snow cascading into his line of sight. "I don't see–"

Suddenly, another flash of lightning lit up the sky, outlining the silhouettes of three Islander warriors. As the light faded, Grimm could make out the barely audible thrum of a bowstring.

Instinctively, he fell prone. Seconds before another crack of thunder, he heard the loud thump of an arrow hitting its mark. Grimm's head snapped to the side, and he saw Thames' body hit the ground, an arrow protruding from his gut.

"Bearn said you'd come for the girl!" one voice shouted through the blizzard.

Grimm bared his teeth, unsheathed his sword, and charged at where he last saw the warriors standing. As he rushed forward, he heard crunching footsteps approaching from either side of him.

He quickly leapt backward and swung his sword in a downward arc, hoping to catch one of his would-be assailants. He felt the blade bite into someone's flesh.

He tore the sword free, spun sharply on his toes, and dropped to his knees in one fluid motion. The hiss of an arrow in flight rang in his ears as he felt it miss the nape of his neck by inches. Only one man on the Isles could shoot that accurately in such a storm.

Bodin the Bowman.

The other warrior was stumbling aimlessly in front of him, seemingly unsure where Grimm had disappeared to. The white-eyed warrior lunged forward, drove his sword through the man's chest, and tackled him to the ground.

Grimm then quickly rolled to his side, using the fresh Islander corpse as a shield from the archer's arrows. Unsurprisingly, an arrow burst through the dead warrior's neck, stopping a hair's breadth from Grimm's.

"Bodin, is that you?" Grimm shouted, as he tossed the bloody corpse aside.

"I wish we could've met under different circumstances, White-Eyes," Bodin replied.

"'Tis Heimer's will."

Just as he was about to rush the archer, he heard a muffled scream coming from that general direction. Cautiously, Grimm approached the area where the sound came from, and he was soon standing over Bodin's corpse, blood gushing from the Islander's slit throat.

He turned his eyes upward and saw a wounded Thames standing over the archer's dead body.

"They know we're here," Thames coughed, blood escaping his lips as he spoke.

"Go back to Tjørholm. I'll finish this," Grimm stated coldly.

"And let you have all the fun? Not a chance!"

Grimm smiled. "I knew you were a killer, just like me."

The two men crept further into the storm, not sure when the next ambush would appear. They tried to use the brief flashes of lightning to examine the landscape as they trudged forward.

Then, after several moments of scurrying through the knee-high powder, another flash of lightning illuminated two warriors walking through the snow. Grimm leaned forward on the balls of his feet, ready to pounce, when something heavy collided with him.

His backside sank into the deep powder, and a cold, stabbing sensation pierced his skin, just under the shoulder. He felt the weight of a man on top of him, the stench of his breath assaulting Grimm's nose as the man twisted his dagger in the fresh wound.

Grimm tried to reach for his sword, but it had fallen out of reach. When the man finally pulled the blade free, Grimm caught his arm and twisted it violently, breaking it at the elbow.

The warrior screamed in pain for a moment, before his throat was slit with his own dagger.

The sound of two blades clashing pricked Grimm's ears. Thames had to have found his own warrior to fight. He tried to rise to his feet, but was quickly tackled again by another person.

The attacker drove his meaty fists into Grimm's face. His head bounced off the frozen ground with each blow. Grimm plunged the first attacker's dagger deep into the belly of this new assailant, but it didn't slow him down.

So he did it again, and again, and again, and again. Grimm stabbed until entrails were falling out of the man's body. Finally, the flurry of punches stopped, and Grimm tossed the bloody corpse off him.

He lay there, face battered, eyes swelling shut, as he tried to catch his breath.

The fact that he could still hear the sound of swords clanging against one another was a good sign. At least Thames was holding his own.

Grimm pushed himself to his feet, retrieved his sword, spat out a mouthful of blood, and walked towards the fighting. For the third time, someone rushed him, but he was ready for it this time.

He quickly sidestepped out of the way and brought his sword down, cleaving the head free from the attacker's shoulders. He continued to push towards the sound of fighting.

In a few moments, he came across several dead bodies, each one was more mutilated than the last. A smile appeared on his bruised lips. *Not bad, mainlander, not bad.* The sound of steel splitting bone rang in Grimm's ears, as he finally reached the melee.

"Come on, you bastards!" Thames shouted, as he whirled around.

"It's me, mainlander."

Thames let out an exhausted sigh, dropped his sword, and collapsed to his knees. "Bloody hell," he spat.

Grimm examined the guardsman and saw that he was bleeding profusely. Thames' hands were shaking violently, and blood was dripping steadily from his mouth. "You all right?" Grimm asked, already knowing the answer.

"Fucking brilliant."

Grimm knelt beside the wounded man, and he gently placed Thames' sword back into his hand, closing his armoured gauntlet around the hilt. "You stay here and rest. I'll find Sara and come back for you."

"I told you–" Thames replied, before being interrupted by a coughing fit.

"Rest," Grimm commanded, as he rose to his feet.

Thames offered no response. Instead, the guardsman let out a long breath, and his body stilled. Nodding his head in gratitude, Grimm continued to march into the storm.

The cold winter wind aggravated the open cuts on his face. He could feel blood trickling down his chest from the stab wound in his shoulder.

"Sara!" he shouted, hoping that he would hear her high-pitched voice over the sound of the gusting wind and the bellowing thunder. There was no response. "Sara!" he shouted louder.

"She's not here," a voice replied.

Grimm froze in place, readied his sword, and listened to the sounds around him. His swelling eyes limited his vision, but he thought he saw four shadowy figures surround him. Each figure had a weapon. "Where is she?" he growled.

"Oh, you'll be seeing her soon, just not in this world," the voice responded.

Grimm leapt towards the voice, sword slicing through the air. The figure leapt out of the way and cut Grimm deep along the ribs. He fell to his knees and clutched his wounded side.

He heard footsteps to his right, so he spun to his left, only to find a spear tip waiting for him. The head of the spear sank into his flesh, just below the armpit.

He quickly twisted his hips and broke the haft, then thrust his sword into the gut of the warrior. A plume of blood splashed his face, letting him know that he had hit his mark. He ripped the blade free and rose to his feet, eyeing the three remaining figures.

"Not bad, White-Eyes," the voice commented. "Seems Bearn was telling the truth about you,"

Grimm leapt towards the voice again, anticipating that the man would sidestep again, but the warrior backpedalled out of range.

Then, hearing footsteps behind him, Grimm quickly spun around and sliced his sword level with the attacker's hips. Unfortunately, the sword hit nothing but air.

He let out a grunt of pain as a sword pierced through his leg. As he fell to the ground, he grabbed a handful of snow and tossed it into the warrior's eyes.

A confused voice escaped the shieldmaiden's lips before Grimm stabbed his sword into the Islander's mouth and out of the back of her skull.

Pulling the sword from his leg, Grimm stood up, wavering slightly as he did so. He gripped the hilt of a sword in each hand and eyed up his remaining two foes. This time, he would wait for them to make the first move.

After several heartbeats, the Islander on the left rushed towards him; the one on the right following soon after. Grimm limped backwards as he parried blows from both warriors simultaneously.

In a desperate move, he extended his wounded leg, hoping that the warrior on the left would trip over it. The Islander fell face-first into the snow, while shock waves of pain surged up Grimm's spine.

He let out a frustrated yell as he brought both swords across his body at the same time, slicing through the standing warrior.

Grimm's momentum spun him completely around as he fell into the snow. He lay there staring up at the sky, watching the flashes of lightning ripple through the dark storm clouds. With a laboured breath, he rose to his feet and retrieved both his swords.

The other warrior was on her knees, wiping the snow out of her face, when Grimm drove a blade deep into her skull, staking it to the frozen earth.

"Sara!" Grimm shouted again as he limped forward. He forced himself to trudge forward, despite a face full of broken bones and multiple sword wounds. He surprised himself at the fact that he was still standing.

"Grimm!" a high-pitched squeal replied.

His heart leapt up into his throat. His eyes narrowed, and he saw the small dwarven girl standing beside a hulking warrior with a knife held to her throat. "Let her go, Bearn."

"You cut your way through my finest bannermen. I'm –"

"Let her go!"

Bearn let out a long sigh. "You know I can't do that, old friend. She's a slave. No better than a dog or the sword in your hand. You've grown weak, Grimm, risking your life over property."

"Are you not a man?" Grimm shouted. "Do you seriously intend to use a little girl as a shield? You are craven, a coward."

After a moment of hesitation, Bearn let out a long breath, tossed his dagger into the snow, and pushed Sara away, before unsheathing his battle axe.

Grimm let out a ferocious battle cry as he rushed towards Bearn.

The blades of both weapons met with a deafening clang. The two Islanders grimaced at each other as they separated themselves, only to come together once again.

Each time the sword and axe met, sparks flew into the air, briefly illuminating their two faces. Desperately, Grimm threw a haymaker at Bearn's jaw.

His old friend effortlessly countered the attack and followed up with a knee to Grimm's sternum.

The air surged out of Grimm's lungs. He knelt, coughing, gasping for air, when he saw the looming shadow of Bearn standing over him. "I'm sorry it has to end like this, friend," the hulking Islander said apologetically.

Gathering all his remaining strength, Grimm lunged forward, wrapping his arms around Bearn's ankles and tackling the man to the ground. He then climbed on top of the jarl and unleashed a torrent of blows.

Punches, elbows, headbutts, every and any strike he could throw that would inflict damage. He felt the bones in Bearn's face shatter beneath his fists, and he felt the warm blood stick to his face as it splattered upward after every blow.

"Grimm, stop!" Sara shouted, her voice shaking.

"Argh!" Grimm screamed as he continued to beat the life out of his former friend. Finally, he felt a pair of diminutive hands on his shoulder, nudging him to stop.

He gently pushed her away and slowly rose to his feet. He limped towards his sword and picked it up, twirling it in the air.

"My axe... give me my axe," Bearn begged, as he choked on his own blood, his arms outstretched, reaching for his weathered battle axe.

Grimm kicked the axe away with his wounded leg and spat on the jarl's body. "You'll never see The Great Hall."

"No!" Bearn shouted, but it was too late. Before he had fully articulated his protest, Grimm's sword cleaved his head in half.

Exhausted, Grimm fell lifelessly to the ground. He had lost too much blood. He would never make it back to Tjørholm, and he was all right with that. His hands tightly gripped the hilt of his sword.

"Grimm, get up! Get up!" Sara pleaded, as she tried to shake some sense into the old warrior.

"Let me die," Grimm whispered as he stared into the heavens. For a moment, he swore he saw the faces of his wife and son in the clouds between the flashes of lightning.

"No!" she screamed, tears rolling down her face. "No, you can't!"

Then a thought popped into Grimm's head. He couldn't rest until he knew she was safe. Otherwise, his death and Thames' death would be for nothing, and she'd perish, just like Freja and Einar.

So, with the final remnants of strength left, he rose to his feet and stared at the dwarven girl. "Can you lead us back to Tjørholm?"

"Mhmm!" Sara nodded her head emphatically.

"Lead the way," Grimm said, praying that they didn't meet any more of Bearn's men on the way.

The walk back seemed to take ten times longer than the walk into Uthredd's camp. Each step was agony for Grimm, yet somehow, perhaps by the grace of Heimer, he persevered.

As the first rays of light broke through the storm's clouds, they reached the gate. The soldiers on the wall aimed their bows at them, before recognizing Sara and opening the gate.

A smile broke on to his face. He did it.

He had saved her.

CHAPTER THIRTY-NINE

ELBERT

After the previous night's storm, a fresh layer of snow had blanketed Tjørholm's grounds. Elbert looked out of the window into the fortress' bailey and saw his men training sluggishly in the deep powder.

Rumours about a peace had spread through the camp like wildfire, and the crippled king attributed that to the soldiers' lethargy. He tore a stale bun apart with his hands and plopped half of it into his mouth. His eyes drifted across the mead hall, but there was no sign of Thames anywhere.

It was not like him to miss the king's morning briefing, but Elbert knew that Rupert would be busy doing something important. A royal guardsman, clad in white armour, entered the room and bowed deeply to him as he chewed the other half of the bun.

"Your Majesty," the guard began. "The Islander has returned."

"He left?" Elbert raised a questioning brow.

The guardsman fidgeted uncomfortably and sweat formed on his forehead. "He and Captain Thames left the fortress last night during the storm."

Elbert swallowed. His heart sank in his chest, and his anxiety ate away at his composure. Why hadn't Rupert reported to him? And why didn't he attend the morning briefing? This wasn't like him at all. "Take me to him," Elbert ordered as he rolled his chair out of the mead hall.

The healer's tent was uncomfortably warm. Grimm sat on the examination table as the healer was busy working on him. Elbert was mesmerized by the Islander's body.

Even though he had seen it before, he couldn't get over how the seasoned warrior's torso appeared almost entirely composed of scars. Some of the scars looked to be decades old. They had weathered and cracked along with his skin as the man had aged. Grimm winced as the healer stitched the gash on the side of his body closed.

"What do you want, Legless?" the Islander asked, his voice rasping.

"Where is Thames?" Elbert demanded, his voice shaking from both anger and fear.

"Dead, but he died well."

"Leave us."

The healer looked up from the Islander's body. "But Your Majesty, I need to seal this wound or else it may fester and –"

"Leave us!" the king shouted.

Quickly, the healer packed up his tools and exited the tent with his head hung low and his eyes cast to the ground. Once they were alone, Elbert rolled his chair closer to Grimm. He took a few seconds to control the rage that was boiling inside him. He knew getting angry with the Islander would be no use. He had to remain calm.

"What happened?" Elbert hissed through clenched teeth.

"We went to rescue Sara. She left and ended up on the outskirts of Uthredd's camp. Thames didn't make it, but as I said, he died honourably."

"Fuck honour!" Elbert blurted out. "My friend is dead, all because you couldn't keep that girl in Tjørholm!"

Grimm's eyes narrowed violently. "I'd suggest you watch your tongue, Legless. I may be on death's doorstep, but I still have enough fight in me to kill a cripple."

"How dare you speak to me in such a manner! I should've cut out your tongue and fed it to the dogs long ago. Your hubris was tolerable, but now you've mounted an expedition without my consent and cost me the life of my best man? I shall have you hanged for this!"

Grimm straightened his back and hopped off the table, but as soon as his feet hit the ground, his legs crumbled under the weight of his body. There was an exhale of relief from Elbert as the Islander's chiselled body lay motionless on the ground.

"I'll have the healer see to your wounds. Wouldn't want you to die on us," the king mentioned callously as he rolled out of the tent.

Although the talk with Grimm had not gone as planned, Elbert found himself lighter in the chest. Perhaps he needed to shout at someone, and no-one was more deserving of it than the Islander. A retinue of royal guardsmen waited outside the tent, standing at attention. Elbert raised an eyebrow.

"Your Majesty," one man began. "The messenger you sent yesterday has returned, and High King Uthredd has agreed to meet."

A nervous breath escaped Elbert's lips. He had been dreading this moment for days now. If there were any hope for his men to escape this snow-ridden rock alive, he would have to channel all of his charisma and hope that he could work something out with the Islander king.

"Take me to him."

"There is one catch, Your Majesty," the guardsman added. "He will only do it if you two meet alone in good faith."

"Is he mad? Does he seriously believe that I'll expose myself like that?"

The guardsman had no response. Elbert rested his head on the heel of his hand and thought hard about Uthredd's request. On the one hand, he would be putting himself in danger, as the Islander king could undoubtedly kill him with ease, but on the other hand, what choice did he have?

He was all out of options. *I wish Thames were here,* he thought to himself. *He would know exactly what to do.* Reluctantly, he let out a long sigh and nodded his head. "I'll meet him in the field again. Alone."

The guardsmen shared a look of surprise on their faces, but quickly gathered their resolve and nodded their heads in understanding. The men parted out of the king's way, and Elbert exited Tjørholm's broken gates, and towards the Islander camp.

The two men stared at each other for quite some time. Neither king dared to speak the first word. Uthredd stood there, holding a bloody burlap sack in one hand and a long bastard sword in the other.

Elbert sat in his chair, trying to hide the anxiety that was slowly eroding his confidence. His hands fidgeted nervously as he waited for the Islander king to make the first move. Finally, after what seemed like a decade of staring, Uthredd cleared his throat.

"I thought I told you to come alone."

Elbert turned his head and looked at the unarmed man who had pushed him through the snow, standing fifteen paces away. Elbert ensured the man was far enough away that Uthredd didn't feel threatened. "You can't honestly expect me to push myself through all of this snow? I'm just a cripple."

After a brief pause, a smile spread on Uthredd's lips. "You know, when I heard that you wanted to parlay, I was surprised. But when your soldiers attacked my men during the storm last night, I must admit I didn't see that coming. I thought you'd have more honour than that."

"Those men acted without my blessing," Elbert corrected.

Uthredd gave the crippled king a questioning glance. "So you say this man betrayed you?" The Islander king reached deep into the burlap sack and tossed the severed head of Rupert Thames at Elbert's feet.

Bile surged up into the crippled king's throat as he stared at the grey, lifeless eyes of his friend. The skin had already paled considerably, and if it weren't for the cold weather, the stench of decay would have assaulted his nostrils. Elbert clenched his fists together and glared at the Islander king, but quickly calmed himself down and reminded himself that he had to keep his wits about him.

"I knew nothing about the raid last night, and those responsible are being punished accordingly," Elbert reassured.

"You mainlanders are always so diplomatic. Never accepting fault, and never living with any honour. If I were –"

"Did you only agree to this meeting so that you could insult me? If so, I'll gladly return behind my walls, and happily slaughter your men if they try to breach the gates."

Uthredd's lips contorted into a frown. "Your man mentioned peace. I have some conditions."

"As do I."

"My men that you are holding hostage: I want them returned to me. If any are harmed, then I also want the men responsible, so that I can deal out a fair and honourable punishment."

"Agreed."

"And what are your terms?"

Elbert cleared his throat. "My men and I are not to be harmed. As a result, we will willingly abandon Tjørholm without burning it to the ground. Islander raids against Artanzia will come to a halt, and –"

"You don't seriously expect us to give up our way of life, do you? We're a nation of raiders; it's what we do."

"If you let me finish," Elbert snarled. "And as a result of this, we will grant your warriors free passage through our lands to the neighbouring kingdom of Keten. They are a rich kingdom, and have been accumulating wealth for centuries. So, not only would your people continue their way of life, but you would also be weakening our biggest enemy on the continent."

A smile appeared on the Islander king's lips. "Go on."

"Those are my terms. Agree to those, and we will leave your Isles without further incident."

"I must admit, that seems to be a fair deal, but I'm afraid that it's not enough. My men will not accept a fair trade. I need them to think that we came out on top of these negotiations."

A smile appeared on Elbert's lips. "I believe I have something else that you want."

"And what would that be?"

"A man, by the name of Grimm White-Eyes; the man that murdered your brother. As a token of my gratitude, I will hand him over to you."

"Grimm will not go quietly."

"He led the raid against your camp last night, and is badly hurt. He can't even stand on his own two feet. Since I met him, he has been nothing but a thorn in my side. It's time for that arrogant arse to get what he deserves. Do we have an agreement?"

Uthredd furrowed his brow and extended his hand outward after a few seconds of deliberation. "We have a deal."

Relief surged through Elbert's body as he reached out and shook the Islander king's hand. Finally, it was time to go home.

The war was over.

CHAPTER FORTY

ANNA

The dungeons were empty for the most part, and if anyone *was* inhabiting the other cells, they never said a word. This gave Anna a lot of time to be alone with her thoughts.

She knew the queen would probably order her execution for her outburst in the dining hall. She also knew that Mortimer Black would probably be the executioner.

A plan formulated in the back of her mind. It was desperate and crazy, certainly, but it was the only chance she could think of. With every passing second, the likelihood of Randall coming to rescue her was diminishing. The only person she could rely upon was herself.

The first step of her plan involved her cutting herself, and making it look like she had committed suicide, which would draw the guards to her cell. From there, she would kill any man that was foolish enough to enter her cell.

Then, she would hunt down and kill Mortimer Black, the queen, and Cassius. In her heart, she knew the plan was riddled with flaws, but she knew she couldn't just sit and wallow in her own filth, waiting for them to drag her out of the cell to the chopping block.

The only reason she hadn't carried out her plan yet was a lack of anything sharp to cut herself with. She had pulled a loose, jagged stone out of the foundation, and had been slowly sharpening it against the walls, but she wasn't making much progress.

She touched the tip of her finger to the edge of the stone. It was sharp enough to make a superficial wound, but not enough to draw a convincing amount of blood. Suddenly, a familiar set of boots clunked down the dungeon hallway. Anna quickly hid the stone under some straw and stood up straight. She knew that guards probably wouldn't see the rock as a weapon, but she felt compelled to hide it anyway.

"Milady," a guardsman croaked, a smile appearing on his lips. This particular guard always came to visit her during his shift, but she wasn't sure why. He was young, no more than sixteen summers, with wavy brown hair and an ugly moustache.

"What do you want?" Anna snapped.

"Just thought you could use some company. I reckoned you might as well talk to someone before the big day."

Anna's heart sank. Was it today? She had run out of time. Panic gripped her body. Her hands went clammy, and her throat dry. The room started to spin slightly.

The guardsman unexpectedly tossed the water skin off his belt, and into the cell at her feet. She quickly picked it up and greedily guzzled down the refreshing water. It felt like it had been months since her last drink, but in reality it was only a day or two.

"Thank you," she said, the harshness in her voice no longer there.

"Looked like you needed it," the guard smiled politely, as he leaned against the bars.

"Why do you visit me?" Anna asked bluntly.

The youth's face turned a bright shade of red. He scratched the back of his neck. That's when it dawned on Anna. *He likes me.* Two emotions surged through her body. First was disgust: how could someone who served the nobles think they could be anything but enemies? But after her initial wave of revulsion subsided, she felt flattered.

It had been a long time since anyone had shown any genuine interest in her. Randall would only show her affection out of necessity; the passion they once shared hadn't been there for a while. As Anna mulled over her emotions, she raised a questioning brow, hoping that it would make the guard spit out an answer.

"I just wondered… you might be lonely?" his voice cracked at the end of his question.

Anna looked over at the straw that concealed the jagged stone. Could this be her chance? If what the guard said was true, this would probably be the only opportunity she would get. She quickly donned a smile, and tried to approach the steel bars of her cell as seductively as possible.

"Tell me," she began, speaking in her softest, most sensual voice. "Have you ever been with a woman?"

The guard immediately began coughing, and his face was a bright shade of crimson. He tugged on the collar of his gambeson and cleared his throat. "Plenty! I've been with scores of women!"

"Good," Anna replied. "I want to be fucked properly before I die. Thankfully, you're experienced." The words tasted like acid in her mouth as they left her lips. She could see herself saying something similar to Randall, but that was Randall. She loved him. This guard was just a means to an end. Her bluntness was born of desperation. She needed to get out of this cage.

The young guard's smile widened, and he reached for the keys dangling from his belt. "We don't have much time," he said. "Master Black will be here soon, to escort you to the city square."

As the guard turned the key in the lock, Anna felt a lump of guilt in her throat. Was she really going to kill this boy? He had never harmed her; she didn't even know him. She quickly reminded herself that he served the nobles, not the people. If she was ever to reunite with Randall, this had to be done.

She took the guard by the hand and led him to the straw. He reached to take off the dress that she wore to the dining hall, but she swatted his hand away. "Not yet. Let's take it slow."

The guard nodded his head as she gently forced him to lie on his back. Anna then hopped on top, straddling his legs, and hesitantly began kissing his neck.

She felt disgusted with herself. The fact that she was kissing someone other than Randall made her stomach churn. She forced herself to lower her right hand towards the boy's crotch.

Her mind raced wildly as her nerves took over. What if he was different from Randall? What if things weren't where they were supposed to be? A soft moan escaped the boy's lips. Anna swallowed her anxiety and continued to lower her right hand, while her left searched the straw for the stone. Her heartbeat quickened when she couldn't find it.

The guard placed both of his hands on her breasts. A hiss of disgust escaped her lips, and she had to fight the impulse to swat the boy's hands away. She remembered she was supposed to appear to be enjoying it, and begrudgingly forced herself to let out a breath of fake pleasure.

Her eyes widened when she felt it: the stone! She sat up and raised the rock high above her head, knowing that she would need all the momentum she could muster for this to work.

Suddenly, the bells of every tower in Winterhelm began chiming frantically. The guard opened his eyes and stared up fearfully at Anna, who was holding the stone high above her head.

In an instant, she drove the rock deep into the fleshy part of the boy's neck. Blood spurted from the wound. She grabbed the stone with both hands and stabbed him again.

The guard twitched violently as he choked on his blood. Anna rolled off him, pulled the dagger from his sheath, and shortened her dress to make it easier to fight in.

She stood up, wiping the blood off her face. She looked down at the corpse of the boy with a pang of regret in her heart. Even though he supported the wrong side, he deserved a better death than this.

Anna shook the guilt from her mind and walked to the barred window that looked out on to the city. Her jaw dropped when she saw the columns of smoke in the air and an orange glow reflecting off the buildings. When she listened closely, she could also hear the sounds of battle. Randall: he was coming for her.

Turning on her heels, she saw that in his excitement, the guard had forgotten to close the cell door. This made Anna's stomach twist. If she had noticed it earlier, she could have just slipped out and closed the door behind her, leaving the guard alone in the cell.

She let out a frustrated groan. *What's done is done,* she told herself. She quickly exited the cell and began creeping down the long corridor of the dungeon.

She remembered the path to the throne room and the dining hall, but that was the only part of the castle she had seen. She also didn't know where the guards would be. Would they be out fighting Randall and the other rebels? Or would they be protecting the queen? Anna presumed it would be the latter.

So, preparing for a fight, she surged out of the dungeons and into the spiral staircase leading to the throne room. She shot up the stairs like an arrow, and barged through the door on the other side.

Inside, the throne room was in complete turmoil. Servants, diplomats, dignitaries, and nobles were panicking and running around, screaming. The guards tried to keep order, but there were far too few of them.

Anna used the chaos and confusion to her advantage. She kept to the side walls, slinking her way through the castle. First, she was going to kill the queen. Then, she was going to kill Black. Then, if he was still here, she was going to kill that snake of a eunuch.

A firm hand grabbed her shoulder as she tried to exit the throne room and enter the dining hall. "Excuse me, miss?" a voice said from behind her.

Anna quickly spun around and drove the point of her newly gained dagger upward. The blade slid into his neck, effortlessly splitting the column of the man's throat. She ripped the dagger free and sprinted the rest of the way towards the doors. Screams of horror filled the throne room, as the rest of the people saw what had happened to the guard.

"Halt!" a guard shouted, but Anna didn't listen. Instead, she burst through the doors leading to the dining hall, then sprinted towards the doors Vivian had arrived from.

The heavy clanking of the guardsmen's plate boots told her they were chasing her, but she knew they would never catch her, not while their clunky armour was weighing them down. The only problem was: she didn't know where she was going.

On the other side of the doors at the far side of the dining hall was a large kitchen. Anna stared at the surprised servants cowering in the corner of the room for several seconds before she continued to run through the room.

Hurdling over tables, she grabbed as many knives as she could find. The door behind her burst open and the heavy plate footsteps drew closer. She jumped in the air, grabbed one of the stolen knives by the blade, and flung it across the room.

When she landed, she heard a scream of pain, followed by the loud thud of a body hitting the floor. She couldn't help but smile at the sound.

At the end of the kitchen was a small hallway with a door at each end. Anna hesitated for a couple of seconds, unsure which way to go.

Then, hearing the other guards closing the distance, she darted left and opened the door at the end of the hallway. Unfortunately, instead of a room, she had found a broom closet. Anna turned on her heels, only to find the guards blocking the way to the other door.

"Come here, you little bitch!" a guard shouted, as he drew his sword.

Anna sprinted towards him. She gripped the handles of her dagger and her knife tightly as she closed the gap between them. The hallway was too narrow for the guardsmen to fight side by side, so thankfully, she could kill them one at a time.

The guardsman with the sword shifted his right leg back and pivoted the foot outwards, which told Anna he was preparing to thrust, not slash.

Regardless, she continued to charge towards him, and when he pushed his sword towards her, she turned her body parallel to the blade and stabbed the knife directly into the man's eye.

Without uttering a sound, the guardsman fell to the floor, blood oozing out of his eye socket.

The next guard wasn't ready for Anna's attack. She spun around and stabbed her knife into his chest. Unfortunately, the blade snapped on the white enamelled breastplate.

After the initial wave of shock faded, the man delivered a crisp, back-handed slap that staggered Anna. Her head bounced off the hard wall of the hallway.

She opened her eyes, and saw that the guard was swinging his sword at her head. She dropped to her knees, dodging the edge of the sword by a hair's breadth, and plunged her dagger into the side of the guard, slipping it between two plates of armour.

The man let out a hiss, and delivered a hard elbow to her back. Anna instantly hit the floor.

She felt the man grab her by the hair and lift her into the air. Instinctively, she delivered a swift kick to his groin and plunged her last kitchen knife into the man's ear.

He let out a pained scream. Anna reached down, retrieved her dagger from his ribs, and slit his throat with it.

Blood painted the walls of the hallway. Seeing no more guards, Anna let out an exhausted breath and touched the bruise forming on the side of her head. After regaining her composure, she marched down the hallway and through the other door.

As she left the hallway, she collided with something hard. The surprise knocked Anna off her feet. Then, in a daze, she looked up: and saw the shocked face of Mortimer Black and his guardsmen staring back at her.

"Go! Secure the queen!" Black commanded. "I'll handle this."

Without a word, the rest of the Blackguard departed. Mortimer Black smiled as he drew his blade. "Resourceful lil' tart," he said, a smile appearing on his lips.

Anna quickly rolled backwards and on to her feet, then tightened her grip on her dagger, only to find it wasn't there. Her eyes frantically searched the floor for it, and saw it was lying at the mercenary captain's feet.

Black let out a sigh and kicked the dagger over to Anna. Confused, she looked up and saw that he had lowered himself into a fighting stance. "Let's see how good you really are."

Anna picked up the dagger and lunged at him. They danced around each other, each parrying and countering the other's attacks.

Her head was ringing, and her vision was slightly blurred; but even in this state, the mercenary was slow. She had trained to fight beasts much faster than the average swordsman.

Black caught her with a left hook and stabbed his blade forward. She spun out of the way, but the edge of the sword kissed her midsection, leaving a superficial mark across her stomach.

Anna immediately countered with a stab to the mercenary's neck, but Black must have expected that, as he effortlessly parried the blow with his sword and backpedalled out of range.

"And who did you say your dad was?" Black asked, breathing heavily.

"I didn't," Anna retorted, as she tried to mask her own laboured breathing. "But don't worry, you'll meet him soon."

Before Black could counter with a verbal jab, Anna darted forward in a serpentine pattern. She used every trick that her father had taught her. Head fakes, misleading with the eyes, planting a foot and spinning in the opposite direction. Everything.

But Black had seen them all before. Although he was slower than her, he wasn't taking as many risks as he did during their previous encounter.

That's when Anna saw her opportunity.

She feinted a stab with the dagger with her right hand, and when Black moved his sword to parry it, she tossed the blade to her left hand and plunged it deep into the artery below his collar bone. Black fell to the ground with Anna on top of him, blood leaking out of the corners of his mouth.

Exhausted, she rolled off him and lay beside him, trying to catch her breath.

"Not bad," Black coughed. He slowly moved himself into a sitting position, his back against the wall. He looked down at the dagger and flicked the pommel. "Excellent spot. If I take it out, I'm a dead man."

Anna rose to her feet, walked over to him, and ripped the blade out without making a sound. Blood surged from the wound and painted her legs a deep coat of crimson.

As the mercenary captain bled out on the floor, she heard the bells coming from down the hallway. She ran towards the sound, hoping it would lead her to a staircase to the ramparts. Which is precisely where the corridor *did* lead her.

From the ramparts, Anna gasped in awe. Winterhelm was in flames. The smell of ash filled her nose. The bells were ringing relentlessly. Her eyes scanned frantically, hoping to find a clue as to where Randall was.

She saw a horde of commoners breach the castle gates. *Must be inside somewhere.* Just as she was about to turn on her heels and go back inside, she heard a voice from behind her.

"Anna?"

She whirled around and saw a blood and soot-stained Randall standing in the doorway to the stairs. She ran towards him and wrapped her arms around him. She rested her head against his muscular chest. It felt like home.

"I knew you'd come for me. I knew it," she said aloud.

"I'm so happy you're alive," Randall responded, his voice having a tinge of sorrow in it.

"Where are the others?" Anna asked.

"Taking care of the remaining guards. Tig and A'Chula went to the queen's chambers to capture her, so we could make a public example of her. Cassius is back at the Garden and –"

"Cassius!" Anna exclaimed. "Randall, I have to tell you about Cassius. He's –"

"I know. He told me everything."

"You know?"

"Anna, I'm the one who told him to use his connections to get a job in the castle, so that we could spy on the queen and her guards. I ordered him to be there."

Anna's heart sank. Was it possible that she had been wrong about Cassius this entire time? Had she misjudged the eunuch?

"What I did not order, however, was you to broker a peace with the queen on my behalf."

"I thought it would help! I thought I could end this, and –"

"You thought peace was what I wanted?" Randall shouted, veins protruding from his neck. "This! This is what I wanted!" he said, as he gestured at the burning city around him. "I'd sooner die than make peace with that filth. Cassius was right about you."

"Randall, please. Let me explain," Anna begged, as she reached out towards the King of Crooks.

He grabbed her by the shoulders and planted a kiss on her lips. "And to think I loved you," he whispered, before shoving Anna off the top of the ramparts.

CHAPTER FORTY-ONE

GRIMM

"The king returns!" a soldier shouted in the distance.

Grimm sat on his cot in the healer's tent and stared up at the white canvas roof. It was cold, but not completely unpleasant, at least not for an Islander. He looked down at the stitched wounds in his body, and a laugh escaped his chapped lips.

It was only now that he realized how close he had come to death. Then he thought of Sara, and although there was a touch of resentment towards the girl for keeping him from reuniting with his family, he realized she had become his new family. She was the daughter that he never had. A smile appeared on his face as he stared back up towards the ceiling.

"Get back to your posts, knaves!" a gruff voice shouted from outside the tent.

Curious, Grimm forced himself into a sitting position. He wanted to walk out and investigate, but the wound in his leg was too serious. The healer had said he had done the best he could, but was quite sure that Grimm was going to walk with a limp for the rest of his life.

He fingered the stitches in his legs as he waited impatiently for more sounds outside the tent. There was a long silence before the flaps of the healer's tent flew open and a handful of royal guardsmen entered, followed by a maliciously smiling Elbert.

"I am pleased to announce that King Uthredd and I have struck an accord."

"I'm glad to hear it, Legless. I'm eager to start my new life on the mainland."

Elbert sucked air through his teeth before making a motion with his hand. The guards immediately grabbed Grimm by both arms and lifted him forcefully off the bed and on to his knees.

One guard handed Elbert a pair of iron shackles. The Islander's heart sank. "Here's the thing, Grimm," the crippled king began. "As part of our deal, I am to surrender you back into Uthredd's custody. I tried to persuade him into letting you go, but the man was adamant. So, I reasoned, what's one life instead of thousands?"

"You crippled whoreson!" Grimm snarled. "We had a deal!"

"Yes, and now I have a new one. I wish I could say that I'll miss your company, but ever since you joined our ranks, you've been a serious pain in my ass. And after you cost Thames his life, I must say that whatever punishment Uthredd gives you is well deserved."

"I'll kill you!" Grimm hollered as he tried to surge to his feet, only to painfully collapse back on to his knees.

"No, you won't." Elbert smiled wider. "The only good thing to come from your little rescue mission is that you are completely and utterly helpless. I mean, look at you! The mighty Grimm White-Eyes can't even stand on his own two feet!"

The Islander let out a defeated sigh. "What about Sara? You can't condemn her to a life of slavery."

The king's smile vanished. "She will be taken care of. She will know a life of luxury. Try to take some solace in that, when you face the hangman's noose, or however you barbarians execute one another."

Before Grimm could utter another word, the royal guardsmen dragged him from the tent and out into Tjørholm's bailey. He looked around the fortress, and saw that the entire army had gathered to see the spectacle.

By the gate, he saw the group of Islanders held prisoner in chains, along with what remained of the Bastards. Grimm turned his head so that he could call back to Elbert over his shoulder. "What are you doing to my men? They have nothing to do with this!"

Elbert gestured for the guards that were dragging him to stop, and the king slowly wheeled his chair until he was side by side with the islander. "Those are the men who attacked the company of Islanders Uthredd sent to retrieve his dead. An unruly lot, but that's how convicts are." The crippled king winked, before the guards continued to drag Grimm out towards Tjørholm's gates.

"You fucking bastard! I'll kill you for this!" Grimm howled, as he squirmed in the guardsmen's arms.

Just when he thought he was about to get free, he felt something hard hit his head, and everything went black.

There was a dull ache in his head when he awoke. His vision blurred slightly, and the room that he was in was spinning. A small fire illuminated the tent walls, and a small hoard of animal hides covered the floor.

Grimm went to massage his temples, but his hands were stopped by a chain. He looked down and realized that he was still shackled. Even with the haze in his mind, he quickly deduced where he was. He shifted himself into a sitting position, crossed his legs, and waited.

"You're awake," a voice said from behind him, after several moments of silence.

Grimm offered no response. If Uthredd was going to execute him, he'd rather that the Islander king just got on with it. No point speaking to a man who's already decided.

"My men found Bearn's body this morning. I'm surprised you were able to defeat him. I'm even more surprised that you gave him a dishonourable death."

"He stood in my way," Grimm blurted out, not taking the time to think about his answer.

"And my brother?" Uthredd responded. "Did he stand in your way as well?" There was a certain harshness to the king's voice. Understandable, given the circumstances, but still, Grimm resented his old friend's tone.

"You should thank me. I cleansed the Isles of weak blood."

Instead of bursting with rage at the verbal barb, as Grimm had intended, Uthredd let out a small laugh. "You always know how to goad people. I always admired that about you."

"Are you going to kill me or not?" Grimm snarled.

Again, the Islander king laughed. "See, Grimm, you've always been an unlikeable bastard, but we put up with you, because you were useful. I always thought of you as a tool, like a sword or an axe, but now I see that you're more like a rabid dog. Give it too much freedom, and it'll bite the hand that feeds it."

"What're you trying to say?"

"My brother's death is as much my fault as it is yours. I gave you too much power, and it cost me the only family I had left."

"I was your family," Grimm muttered under his breath.

"Yes, you were," Uthredd snapped. "Out of all the men and women that I bled with on the battlefield, you were the one that I thought could never betray me."

"What was I supposed to do? He butchered my family."

"And instead of coming to me, your *king*, you committed treason and butchered mine."

Grimm chewed on his bottom lip and stared deeply into the Islander king's eyes. If he was being honest with himself, he did feel a bit of guilt for his actions. Not for killing the king's brother – he deserved it – but because he saw how much pain it caused Uthredd.

He had known this man since they were children, and knew all of his emotions. Grimm could hear the wavering in his voice, see the slight furrow in his brow, and the tiniest glimmer of tears in the corner of his eyes. "How'd you get the giants on your side?" Grimm asked, hoping to have one last good memory before his shield-brother sentenced him to death.

Uthredd let out a laugh and lowered himself down, so that he was sitting across from Grimm. "You wouldn't believe me, even if I told you."

"I just finished serving a king who can't walk. Try me."

"I had to win a trial by combat."

"No shit?"

"I challenged their chieftain. If I won, they had to be my vassals. If he won, then they could feast on me and my men's corpses."

"High stakes."

"You should've seen me, Grimm," Uthredd said boisterously, a smile appearing on his lips. "I rolled between the big fucker's legs and sliced the tendons in his heels with a single swing of my sword. Then, when he dropped to his knees, I climbed onto his back and stabbed my sword through his spine. It was glorious."

"I'm surprised they kept their word."

The smile disappeared from the Islander king's face. "I'm sorry for what I have to do, Grimm."

"As am I."

Rising to his feet, Uthredd called for some of his warriors, who dragged Grimm out into the middle of the Islander camp. The warriors shouted insults and hurled moldy food at Grimm's head as he was led to a giant wooden platform.

He visibly winced when he saw the tortured and mutilated bodies of the Bastards lying next to it. The warriors helped him up the stairs and set him down in the middle of the platform. Both men held their swords to his throat, mainly as a deterrent to doing anything stupid. He heard Uthredd clear his throat from behind him.

"Brothers and sisters!" The king's voice was loud and regal. "As you may have heard, King Elbert of Artanzia and I have brokered a peace!" There was a murmur of dissatisfaction, but it was quickly stifled. "In exchange for his safe passage from our Isles, he has given us the man that murdered my brother. Grimm White-Eyes!" The crowd erupted in angry jeers and began throwing curses at Grimm once again. After a few seconds, Uthredd raised a silencing hand. "For the crimes of murder, rape, and treason, I hereby sentence Grimm White-Eyes, former Shield of the Isles, to die a dishonourable death!"

Grimm's heart sank. He had half-hoped that his old friend would show him some last form of kindness, but apparently that was too much to ask for. He let out a controlled breath from his nose, and tried to stifle the tears that were forming in his eyes.

"Grimm," Uthredd said. "You will live out the remainder of your days chained to the mast of a ship. You will receive no food or water. Your body will rot under the sun, and the gulls will feast on your flesh. Once you are nothing more than a pile of bones, you will be tossed into the sea and left behind. Do you accept this punishment?"

The question was a formality. Nobody had ever said no to a king's punishment before, mostly because it would not change anything. Grimm took a moment to clear his throat, but when the words wouldn't leave his lips, he nodded his head in response.

"Chain him outside my tent: we will find him a ship when we return to Skotheim," Uthredd commanded.

The warriors sheathed their swords and helped Grimm to his feet once again. With a single tear rolling down his face, he accepted his fate.

CHAPTER FORTY-TWO

ELBERT

A soft knocking on the door stirred the king from his sleep. Unlike the voyage to the Isles, the seas seemed to be much smoother on the journey home.

The gentle rocking of the ship was exactly what Elbert needed to be lulled into a deep, dreamless sleep. The blankets hugged him tightly, begging him not to leave the warmth of their confines. He begrudgingly wiped the crust out of his eyes and looked around his cabin.

The soft orange light from the candles cast large, ominous shadows on the walls. On the far side of the room was Sara, curled up into a ball on the luxurious couch that Elbert had brought from Winterhelm when they first set sail, all those weeks ago.

The dwarven girl refused to say a word, ever since she learned Grimm had been arrested. Elbert felt a smidgen of guilt at the child's wails, but he was sure that she would get over the betrayal.

However, they were almost back to the mainland, and Sara still refused to acknowledge their presence unless they brought food. He had tried to assure her that Arlin would take good care of her at his estate, but if the idea of living on a lord's estate intrigued Sara, she didn't let it show. Elbert thought it was only fitting that the girl stayed with one of her own kind.

Another knock on the door. Elbert let out a small sigh before rolling himself off the bed and dragging himself into his chair. He had spent most of the voyage in his bed, as rolling around the deck of a moving ship was an unpredictable hazard. One moment, the ship was still; but one wayward wave could tilt the vessel in any direction, sending the king speeding towards the railing.

Elbert rolled across the room, opened the door, and saw that the deck of the ship was eerily still. Everyone who was awake had stopped work, and was staring over the port side of the ship.

Lord Arlin stood in the doorway; his face was turned away from the king's cabin. Elbert thought he caught the distinct smell of smoke and ash in the air – before he heard it: the distant chiming of Winterhelm's bells. He rolled past the dwarven craftsman and looked deep into the distance. He saw a beacon of orange glowing in the night sky.

His city was burning.

CHAPTER FORTY-THREE

RANDALL

A lake of blood blanketed the once-polished floor of Winterhelm's throne room. Mutilated corpses lay motionless in the pool of red, their limbs and heads crudely hacked off.

Randall sat atop the throne and drummed his fingers impatiently on the gilded armrest. The screams of Queen Vivian, as the commoners took out their frustration on her, echoed around the throne room. Under different circumstances, he would have smiled at the sound, but now, all he could think about was Anna.

The stunned look of surprise on her face before he pushed her off the ramparts haunted him. Although he would never admit it out loud to anyone else, he *did* love her. In fact, the only person who he had ever loved more than Anna was his sister.

But he also knew that Cassius' idea to kill her was the right one. Anna's presence complicated things. With her alive, he could not marry a noblewoman, which would legitimize him as a king in the eyes of the other kingdoms. Cassius had also advised him that violent coups had failed in the past; so if Randall wanted his reign to last, he would need a martyr, and who better than the Queen of Crooks?

Even though the eunuch was right, it did nothing to ease the pain that Randall felt in his heart. He tried to further justify Anna's death further by reminding himself that she had betrayed him. *She tried to broker a peace behind my back. She couldn't be trusted,* he told himself, even though he had a hard time believing the words.

"Your Majesty?" Cassius' voice broke through Randall's thoughts. The king looked up, and saw that the eunuch was standing in the pool of blood.

"What is it?"

"A fleet of ships is approaching from the north. It appears King Elbert's campaign in the Northern Isles was a success."

Fear gripped Randall's throat. It was one thing to take a city when most of the army was away, but to defend it? He was ill-prepared for a siege so soon after his conquest. "What do we do?"

"Well, that is the other thing," Cassius mused. "There's a man here to see you, who says he can help with that sort of thing."

"Send him in."

The doors to the throne room opened, and an old, dishevelled man approached the throne, wading through the lake of blood as he did so. Despite the man's age, he walked without a limp. The man gave a toothless smile once he locked eyes with Randall. The king's skin crawled as the man approached him.

"I hear I can be of service to you, Your Majesty," the man said in a gravelly voice as he bowed low, his nose almost touching the pool of blood by his feet.

"The former king, Elbert, has returned at the most inopportune time. I don't have the men, nor the resources, to withstand a siege against his army. So tell me, how can you help me?"

"Your Majesty, I'm a magus. I can achieve feats that others think are impossible. Tell me what you want, and I will make it come true."

"And what would you want in exchange? I know things like these are never free."

The magus' smile widened. "I only ask for the thing that you have, but do not value."

Randall raised a questioning brow. After a few moments of deliberation, he responded, "No."

A look of shock and confusion appeared on the magus' face. "What do you mean, no?"

"Unlike most of the nobles that you undoubtedly dupe with your vague promises, I have lived most of my life on the streets. And the one thing I learned while being a thief on this city's streets was that if something sounds too good to be true, it is."

The man's face contorted from a look of confusion to one of pure fury, but before he could say anything, Cassius interjected, "Are you sure that this is wise, sire? We don't have a lot of options in front of us."

"I'm sure. The people banded together once under my banner, and they'll band together once more. Now leave us, old man. Go and spread your filth elsewhere."

The magus sneered, before ultimately bowing low and exiting the throne room. Randall watched as the old man walked out of the room, then immediately began strategizing for the imminent siege.

If Elbert wants a war, he'll have one.

Afterword

If you've made it this far, I want to personally thank you for seeing this book through. This story took a lot for me to write, it was emotional and stressful at times but I wouldn't change it for a second. If you enjoyed it, please consider leaving a review on Amazon or Goodreads, it truly means the world to us authors. Once again, thank you for giving my book a chance, and I sincerely hope that you were able to lose yourself in my world.

About Author

A.J. Rettger lives on a farm near the small town of Aberdeen Saskatchewan with his dog, Zeke. He has a bachelor's of education degree, as well as a certificate from a private vocational college. His hobbies include playing Dungeons and Dragons, listening to heavy metal, and reading and writing fantasy books.